"NOW YOU WILL KEEP YOUR PART OF OUR BARGAIN, DIANA. . . .

"Three years is a long time for a man to go without his wife, and I don't intend to go another night—another hour, I vow—without mine."

"I'll not share a bed with you!" she declared angrily. "You're not truly Lad Walker. You're nothing at all like the man who left here three years past."

"No," he agreed. "I'm not. I'm the man you wished me to become. The Earl of Kerlain."

"A stranger," she whispered. "I prayed for Lad to come back to me."

"He's gone, Diana." He took a step nearer. "Now you must make do with me. Come."

Mute, she shook her head.

"Then I will fetch you," he said, and gave the promise life.

DARK WAGER

Mary Spencer

Devil's Wager

A Dell Book

Published by
Dell Publishing
a division of
Random House, Inc.
1540 Broadway
New York, New York 10036

ISBN: 0-440-22493-4

Printed in the United States of America

Published simultaneously in Canada

January 2000

!0 9 8 7 6 5 4 3 2 1

OPM

*To the wonderful readers who flooded me
with e-mails and letters asking for Lad's story,
this book is fondly dedicated.*

Prologue

England, June 1818

How easily a dream could turn into a nightmare, even a dream that already held no claim to pleasure.

Diana.

She heard him saying her name and chided herself for a fool. Three years he'd been gone, and still he haunted her. But she was done with being foolish, just as she was at last done with him.

Was she sleeping? With an effort, Diana moved, feeling the deep ache in the muscles of her shoulders and lower back. She must have fallen asleep in the chair, she realized dimly, groaning with stuporous dismay. She'd been so determined to remain awake, to spend each precious moment during her last night at Kerlain with full awareness, and to see the sun dawning on the day that would bring an end of all that she'd known and loved, of her very freedom.

"Diana."

That voice. That tone. She felt a bleary aggravation that he should sound so irate. He didn't have the right to be angry over *anything* after all he'd done.

With a great effort, she opened her eyes and blinked into the darkness of the room. She felt drugged, exhausted, so heavy and weary that she couldn't possibly make her limbs move. Parting her lips, she drew in a long, easing breath, exhaled it slowly, and let her eyelids drift shut once more.

"Sleeping Beauty, is it?" He sounded amused now. She heard footsteps nearing the chair and struggled to open her eyes again. Cold fingertips brushed lightly against her cheek. "Then I suppose I must be your Prince Charming." His voice was nearer, as if he were bending closer. "Shall I wake you with a kiss?" he asked more softly.

"No," she murmured, turning her face away from his touch. It couldn't be him. Not now, when it was too late. For three years she had waited for his return, prayed for it. Hours she'd waited and looked for him. Days. Months. Gazing out the highest window at Kerlain just to see his approach, convincing herself that he'd come riding into view any moment if she only kept looking.

"No?" he repeated, still amused.

She groaned again, lifting a numb, leadened hand to rub her eyes. Drawing in another breath, she forcibly pushed the last dregs of slumber aside and made herself come fully awake. Several moments of silence passed as she collected her wandering thoughts and made her vision focus. She wasn't dreaming. She'd heard Lad's voice.

The room was dark, but not so dark that she couldn't see the tall figure standing beside her. Diana straightened in the chair, lifting her head to gaze up at him—and was instantly filled with alarm. The voice had somehow tricked her into thinking that the earl had returned, but everything else about the man was completely unfamiliar. His stance, his manner of dress—everything. This wasn't Lad. Did she even know who he was? she wondered, straining to make out his features in the darkness. But no, she realized with a shiver of fear. He was a stranger.

"Who are you?" she asked, her voice unsteady. She lifted her hand again to push the hair back from her face. "How do you dare to come here, to my chamber?"

"I dare very easily," he replied calmly. "Stay where you are." He moved away from the chair.

Diana leapt out of it, every nerve fully alive and tingling now. One good scream would have servants running from every quarter, but she'd rather he leave without creating a scene that would overset one and all, especially tonight of all nights. She pulled her robe more tightly about herself and demanded, "How did you manage to get into the castle?" Neither Swithin nor any of the footman would have allowed a stranger to cross the threshold at this time of night. "What have you come here for?"

He was turned away from her, striking a flint on a tinder-box to light a candle. The candle caught flame, and the light glowed about his broad shoulders and shapely head, revealing hair the color of gold—a gold such as Diana had seen only once before in her life, on only one person. Her eyes widened at the sight, and she murmured, in disbelief, *"Lad?"*

Holding the candle aloft, he turned to face her.

"Do you know me now, Diana?"

She stared at him for a long, still moment, then slowly began to shake her head.

"No," she whispered.

His green eyes were solemn, searching her face.

"I've changed a great deal since last we met, Lady Kerlain," he said, his tone cultured and polite, just as if he'd been born and raised in England, rather than his native Tennessee, "but I believe this will be welcome to you. I have fully claimed that name and title that you so insistently pressed upon me. You do not deny that you know who I am?"

She had used up so many tears over him that she'd thought she had none left, but she was wrong. Grief, which had been her constant companion for the past three years, was as nothing compared to what she felt now. Tears pricked at her eyes, but Diana made no effort to check them. Even his voice had changed. That voice, which had once poured over her as slowly and sweetly as warm honey, now sounded as clipped and perfect and cold as that of any other English aristocrat. For that alone, she might have wept, but so much else of him had been lost as well.

"Yes," she murmured. "I know who you are."

She took him in from the top of his perfectly groomed head, down the length of his elegantly fashionable clothes, to the toes of his brilliantly polished Hessians, which gleamed even in the candlelight. He was every inch a nobleman, in his stance, in his demeanor, in the slightly bored expression on his utterly handsome face. She had read a great deal about the Earl of Kerlain in the papers that came from London and knew that he was considered to be one of that city's most accomplished and admired gentlemen. Women threw themselves at him, men strove to copy his manner of dress, and the *ton* vied mightily to claim his presence at their parties and balls.

He was looking at her in much the same way, assessing her with narrowed eyes.

"You appear to be well, my lady. My absence has clearly been of no account. I imagine Viscount Carden is the one to thank." He looked pointedly at the cases that were packed and waiting near the door. "You were very certain that I wouldn't return, it seems. Or, perhaps, you were merely eager to join your lover at his estate. But, no," he said before she could remonstrate, "that isn't likely, is it, Diana? You'd never leave Kerlain of your own free will, would you? Kerlain is all to you, and no man could ever compare. Not even your dear viscount."

"There was hardly any word," she told him, still staring at him with amazement. "Only two or three notes in three years, and nothing more. I thought that you had . . . that you wouldn't return."

"Did you?" he repeated. "Indeed, there was little word—from you, though I hoped in vain. But the matter is too far beyond us to be remedied now. I have met the requirements you set for me, Diana, to make amends for my many sins. Now I have returned—to claim what is rightfully mine."

He stepped forward, slipping one elegantly manicured hand inside the coat he wore, pulling out from somewhere within a folded document.

"Three years I spent, gaining this for you," he said softly, moving forward to lay the document upon a nearby table. "It's a bank draft, made out to Viscount Carden, dear wife, in the amount you commanded of me. Down to the last farthing."

Diana remembered the sum she'd named on that night of anger and pain three years past. It had been an impossible amount of money, more than a man might dream of making in a lifetime, much less three years. She had known he'd never be able to fulfill her requirements, and yet there had been no other way. He was the one who had thrown their lives into the fire; she had done what was necessary to snatch them out again.

"You've had many wealthy lovers," she murmured, surprised to hear the words coming from her lips. He would know that she'd kept track of him, that she'd read the London papers to discover where he was, what he was doing, and who he was doing it with. The highly popular Earl of Kerlain had spent the past three years living a life of ease and pleasure, while his people had struggled to get by. "This is the manner in which you meet the demand laid upon you? This is what you bring to me—an insult for your own sins?" Anger flowed through Diana, steeling her. Three years he had dallied and played, while she had died a thousand times over for the lack of him.

"I bring what you demanded of me," he said in an even

tone. "Three years of my life I gave for it. Now you will keep your part of our bargain, Diana."

"My part? . . ." She wasn't sure she understood him. He couldn't mean . . . not *now,* when he had returned to her so completely a stranger.

He nodded and reached up to untie the cravat about his neck.

"Three years is a long time for a man to go without his wife, and I don't intend to go another night—another hour, I vow—without mine."

She looked at him as if he were crazed.

"I'll not share a bed with you this night!" she declared angrily. "Not after all you've done . . . all your faithlessness!"

He uttered a low, dark laugh and shrugged out of his coat, tossing it aside.

"My faithlessness, or what you may perceive as such, has certainly been far less dire than your own, Lady Kerlain. I wouldn't allow your sensibilities to worry overmuch on what's in the past, for I assure you I'll not let myself think of your dalliance with Viscount Carden—which is now at an end." With slow, measured steps, he neared Diana. She backed away. "I shall make certain that you've no cause to turn to other men for your needs. *Any* of your needs."

Stumbling back, Diana said, "I've done nothing to be ashamed of, certainly not with Eoghan Patterson."

"It matters not, just as I've said. It's all in the past. Come, Diana." He fell still and held out a hand to her. "I mean to have you, one way or another, as is my right. Come to me of your own free will. I don't wish to force you to lie with me."

"I should think not," she said tightly. "Raping your own wife will be remarkably dull after all you've experienced in London. I'm amazed you returned to Kerlain at all, my lord."

"I am the Earl of Kerlain," he replied simply. "And your husband."

She glared at him with open disdain. "You may be able to claim both titles, but you're not truly Lad Walker. You're nothing at all like the man who left here three years past."

"No," he agreed, his hand yet held out. "I'm not. I'm the man you wished me to become. The Earl of Kerlain."

"A stranger," she whispered. "I prayed for Lad to come back to me."

"He's gone, Diana." He took a step nearer. "Now you must make do with me. Come."

Mute, she shook her head.

He sighed and dropped his hand.

"Then I will fetch you," he said, and gave the promise life.

Chapter One

England, October 1814

The wind was what she would forever remember of this endless night, Diana thought as she wearily climbed the long upward path of stairs. The wind, so fierce and untamed, shrieking through every crack in Castle Kerlain's decaying walls and bringing the dark, ancient dwelling to life with whistles and moans and the creaking of lumber too old to do anything but sag and sway against the mightier force of God's elements. Aye, the wind was what she would remember. 'Twas a cold wind, bitterly so, icily knifing through the thin clothes she wore as she traversed the stairway, making a very mockery of her efforts to draw her tattered shawl more tightly about herself.

She was weary—God above, so weary. Her body ached with it and her mind was numbed by it, yet she knew she could not rest. Not until the earl had made his passage into the next life. She had promised him that she'd not abandon him until the last, and she would not, no matter how many hours he might cling to his earthly self. She had kept her vigil since yesterday afternoon, when the change had come upon him and the doctor had told her there was nothing else to be done save to make him comfortable. Diana had not slept a moment since then, just as the servants had not, or even the people of Kerlain, all of whom were gathered below in the great hall, for none would allow the last Earl of Kerlain to die while they slumbered. But it would not be long now before Kerlain was made bereft, for he was rapidly weakening and would soon die. Then they could sleep and wake to a day that would pass, for the first time in hundreds of years, without an heir to claim the lands and titles of the proud estate of Kerlain.

Maudie met her outside the earl's chamber door, a fluttering candle in her hand and urgency in her manner and expression.

"He's been calling out for you, miss. 'Twon't be long, I fear. Sir Anthony's been looking for you to come back all the while. Most anxious, he is, what with Doctor Rushford fussing and shaking his head so dismal and dire. 'Tis enough to make a sane body crazed, i'faith, going on like that. He gives me the shudders. Even Swithin's overset, and you know there's little on God's earth could do that."

"I'm sorry I was so long, Maudie," Diana said soothingly. "Lord Kerlain's seal wasn't where he said it would be, and I was obliged to search the desk for it. Has Stuart brought more coal?"

Maudie nodded. "Aye, miss. 'Tis warm as Samhain's own fire, but still he's shaking with cold. Oh, miss, what will we do when he's gone? What will become of Kerlain?"

"None of that now," Diana said more sternly. "I can't have you falling to pieces on me, Maudie. I need you too much." Reaching out, she took the older woman's arm in a reassuring grip, feeling with a pang of distress how thin and bony it was. God above, but they were all too close to starving. The remembered knowledge—added to all that had so lately occurred with the earl's sudden illness—was like a heavy stone set upon her shoulders. "All will be well," she insisted as convincingly as she could, "even if we must leave Kerlain. I promise you, I'll find a way to—"

"Leave Kerlain!" Maudie cried, trembling beneath Diana's touch. "Oh, miss! Never say it. 'Tisn't to be thought of. Oh, nay, never. God help us!"

Diana understood how frightened the aging maid must feel. Maudie had been born at Kerlain, as had generations of her family. It was all she had known during the sixty years she had lived, and the same could be said of most of the people of Kerlain. Diana was among the few who had not been born on this land, but she had been brought to the estate at so young an age that it was all she could remember, and all that she knew of home and love.

"Come, now." Diana straightened and pushed her own fears aside. "We must return to my godfather and show him no tears. I'll not have him overset. We must make his passing as easy as possible. We owe him that."

Maudie wiped her cheeks with the edge of her apron and nodded. When she spoke, her voice was its old self—stern and chiding. "Aye, and that we must. 'Tis his due, and 'tis how it will be. You've no need to fear that old Maudie will do aught but what she must, miss."

Diana smiled at her warmly. "You always have, dear Maudie. I should not have made it through this night without you."

Sir Anthony, a neighboring squire who also served as the sheriff of Herefordshire, stood from the comfortable chair near the fire when they entered the room. Relief was plain on his face at the sight of Diana, but she had no time to spare him yet. She moved toward the great, curtained bed upon which George Charles Nathaniel Walker, the last Earl of Kerlain, lay, his face white, his breathing slow and labored. His body, beneath the covers, seemed thin as a child's, and he shivered as if the chill that permeated the rest of Castle Kerlain also reached this chamber—but that was not so, for the fire had been kept burning continuously this past week, during his illness, and the room was almost uncomfortably warm.

Doctor Rushford looked up from where he sat next to the bed, his expression grim. Swithin, who had been the earl's manservant for over fifty years, was beside the doctor, stoically aiding him in whatever manner he could. His expression was as it had ever been, as if emotion of any kind was utterly foreign to him, but the rigid line of his mouth gave away what turmoil was hidden within. Diana offered him an encouraging smile as she neared the bed, then gave her full attention to her godfather.

The earl's eyelids lifted very slightly as she sat beside him on the bed.

"Diana?" His voice was a strained whisper, and his thin, bony hand moved to find her.

She set her fingers lightly over his own to still his movements.

"I'm here, my dear," she assured him softly.

"Did you find—"

"Yes. I have everything, just as you wished."

He stiffened, his hand fisting briefly beneath her own as he strove to push speech past his lips, though the effort was great.

"The document?"

"It's here in my hand, dear. Shall I give it to Sir Anthony?"

"No, you . . . open it." He closed his eyes and drew in a long, shaking breath. "Read it."

She did as he asked, first setting aside the paper and ink and other items that her godfather had requested before unfolding the thick, waxy parchment.

"It's a certificate of"—she looked at the earl in disbelief—"of marriage?"

"What? Marriage?" Sir Anthony moved to peer over Diana's shoulder. "By gad! So it is."

"My son, Charles," the earl said faintly. "Charles's marriage."

Diana saw the proof of it before her eyes and heard the earl saying the words, but the shock of it left her feeling faint. She shook her head and murmured, "But, sir, you always told me—everyone—that he and the American woman weren't truly wed. She wrote so many letters—"

"Lied," the earl said. "I did. Couldn't bear . . . thought of it . . . Charles and that . . . woman. God forgive me."

Memories assailed Diana on all sides. Memories of the earl railing against Charles, the son he had disowned and who had thereafter left England for America. He had taken a wife, Elena, in Tennessee, though the earl had insisted the marriage was invalid and refused to recognize either of the two sons who'd come of the union as being true Walkers. Elena had written the earl innumerable letters, begging him to accept her children as his grandsons, but he'd been unmoved. Diana was his sole heir, a fact that he'd made legal almost as soon as she'd been born. Kerlain would be hers one day, and the title would pass through her to her firstborn son. Or so the earl had always told her, and so she had always believed. The document she held in her hands changed everything.

"The sons," she murmured. "Charles's sons . . . the eldest will be the Earl of Kerlain."

"The earl," Maudie repeated from the foot of the bed, her voice a reverent whisper. "God save us."

"You should have told us sooner," Diana said. "If only you'd told us—I might have written to him already."

A tremor shook the earl's body, and he groped again for her hand. "Write . . . now," he said, squeezing her hand with little strength. His fingers were as cold as ice, and Diana's curled about them. "Sir Anthony . . . witness. Make certain all is right."

"I will, George," Sir Anthony promised. "You have my word of honor upon it."

"Sibbley has . . . my instructions. You'll have . . . Kerlain, Diana. Just as I promised you. Lad . . . my grandson . . . will have the title. He'll be the earl. Tell Farrell and Colvaney . . . they're to . . . respect him. Respect the Earl of . . . Kerlain." He gasped for breath as if he were suffocating.

"I'll tell them," Diana promised quickly, leaning over to stroke his icy brow in an effort to calm him. "You must worry for nothing, my dear."

A moment passed and he began to breath more evenly, opening his eyes again.

"The letter, Diana. I'll tell you . . . what to write."

"You mustn't weary yourself."

"I'd be glad to write for you, George," Sir Anthony offered. "You've not the strength for it now."

A glimmer of old defiance glittered in the earl's eyes. "I'll do it. After all these . . . years . . . it's the only thing I can do for . . . my grandson. Write it now, Diana."

She obediently did as he said and moved to the table near the bed, upon which she had set the paper and ink. The earl closed his eyes and began to speak, slowly, haltingly, not stopping save to draw breath and ignoring the faint murmurs of surprise that his words wrought from those in the room. Diana, the most surprised among them, strove to keep at bay the mingled sense of outrage and shock that filled her as she wrote. He should have told her what he had planned long before now. To spring it on her like this, at so late and dire a moment, was the cruelest blow he could possibly have dealt her.

She folded the missive when she was done and addressed it as he instructed, then melted a small amount of wax and dripped it upon the closure. With Doctor Rushford's aid, the Earl of Kerlain sat up long enough to fix his seal to the still-hot wax.

"You are my witnesses," he said, groaning with the effort he made to push the ring against the paper. "The deed is done."

He seemed to faint after that, and Diana nearly tossed the missive onto the floor in her rush to attend him, but he came to himself after a moment and, laying again upon his pillows, smiled up at her in a manner she'd never before seen on his face. He looked pleased, relieved almost, by what had passed, and whatever anger and resentment she'd felt at the same event melted away.

"You must rest now, dear," she murmured, smoothing strands of thin white hair from his face.

"In time," he said. "Don't be angered with me, my child. I could not leave you so alone, in all this ruin."

"I'm not angry," she told him softly. "I'll let no harm come to Kerlain."

"I know you will not." His smile grew weary. "You've always loved it so. Promise me . . ."

"What?"

"Keep away from Carden."

"From Eoghan?" She was surprised. Her godfather had always seemed to like Viscount Carden so well. There had even been a time when the earl had spoken of Diana wedding the lord of Lising Park so that their neighboring estates might be joined together, but she had always laughed at the idea. Eoghan had grown into a handsome, charming man, but she would never be able to look at him as anything but the crafty, rather troublesome boy who had been her closest—her only—childhood playmate. "He's but a friend, as you very well know. There's nothing to be feared from him. Certainly not now, when he's been traveling abroad for so many months."

"He'll return once I've gone," the earl said. "He wants you. And Kerlain. He . . . told me . . . threatened . . . before he left England. Swore he'd have you."

His long illness had affected her godfather's mind, Diana thought. This wasn't the first time he'd spoken of dangers that weren't real.

"You misunderstood him, dear," she said. "Eoghan's flirted with me in the past, but nothing more. You know that. And every man in the county wants Kerlain, including Sir Anthony." She gave that man a smile. "But I'll let none of them have it."

"Promise you'll . . . keep away from Carden," he said more insistently, words once more becoming difficult for him to speak. "Don't let him . . . have Kerlain. Or you."

"Never," she promised, striving to ease his mind. "I give you my solemn vow, Eoghan Patterson will never have me or Kerlain. I will hold it for you, and for the future earl."

"Good girl," he said with a sigh, closing his eyes. "Such a good girl you are, Diana. Such joy you've brought me. I thank God for . . . the day that brought you here . . . to me."

She kissed his cheek with tender affection. "Rest now," she murmured. "All will be well." She stroked his forehead with a gentle, soothing touch. "Only be at peace, and rest."

An hour later Diana descended the stairs with Sir Anthony behind her. The murmuring in the great hall below grew silent as she neared the crowd gathered there. One hundred and fifty-four faces gazed up at her, weary, anxious, waiting. Another twenty-two—young children and babies mainly—lay wrapped in their mother's shawls, sleeping near one of the four remaining hearths that, out of the dozens in the hall, were still capable of putting some small amount of warmth out into the cavernous chamber.

They were all here, each of the twenty-five families that comprised the citizenry of Kerlain. More than half of them were Colvaneys, and the rest, save a family or two, were Farrells. The two clans had farmed the lands of Kerlain for generations, and in that same time had carried on a friendly rivalry. In the midst of danger or trouble, however, they came together with a fierceness such as Diana had never yet seen matched, bound by their love of this land and their lord.

Two men headed the Farrell and Colvaney clans and were called—odd as Diana had ever found it, for they were Welsh and not Scottish—The Farrell and The Colvaney. Now, as Diana neared the bottom of the stairs, the two patriarchs detached themselves from the front of the small crowd and approached her.

"He's passed over," she told them directly, too weary now to feel the grief and pain that would come on the morrow.

A rush of whispering filled the chamber, echoing against the high ceiling. Men pulled the hats from their heads and lowered their gazes, women began weeping softly, and whatever children were still awake pressed close to their parents, their eyes wide and afraid.

"That's final, then," The Colvaney said in a morbid tone. "The end of Kerlain. He was the best of them all, I vow."

"He was a grand lord," The Farrell agreed, nodding. "We'll not forget him. Is that not so, Farrells?"

The Farrell clan murmured, variously but firmly, "Aye."

"And for the Colvaneys," The Colvaney said, to which the Colvaneys replied with even louder affirmation.

Diana would have smiled if she'd not been so weary, for even in this dark time, the gentle feuding continued.

She cast her gaze about those assembled before her, at the sorrow and fear mingled in their expressions. They had loved the earl, stern lord though he'd been, but he was gone and with him their proud history, finished now, as well as all their hopes for the future. Or so they believed.

"He went peacefully?" The Colvaney asked.

"Yes," she said. "He passed in his sleep. Very peacefully. But more than that, he left us with peace as well. There is a new Earl of Kerlain."

"What?" The Farrell said, while The Colvaney demanded, "A new earl?" Gasps and exclamations rose up on all sides.

"She speaks the truth," Sir Anthony told them. "I stand as witness to the fact. Lord Kerlain himself told us of it before he fell into slumber."

"There is a grandson—a legal grandson," she amended quickly, for they'd all heard of Charles Walker's supposed American marriage and the two sons who'd come from it—bastards both, as they'd always thought. "It seems that Lord Charles's marriage was true. I have a copy of the certificate to prove it." She lifted the document for all to see. "The eldest son is now the rightful Earl of Kerlain."

"But he's an American, miss," The Farrell stated in dire tones. "We cannot have such an earl as that. We're at *war* with the United States, by God. He's our enemy."

"I know, but he's all that's left to us," Diana replied. "We'll have him, just as the earl wished it, or we'll have none of Kerlain at all. There's a letter here to be sent to him in America, in the wilderness called Tennessee." She thrust the sealed missive high into the air so there could be no doubt of what she said. "Written by my own hand, it is, but spoken by the earl, each and every word of it," she said tautly, her voice rising as they began to mutter in dissent. "Sir Anthony will bear me witness, as will Doctor Rushford and Swithin. *And* Maudie Farrell. You'll not call one of your own a liar, will you, Farrells?"

The Farrells grew silent.

"Nor will you, Colvaneys?" Diana charged. "Maudie

Farrell's word has ever been held true as gold in Kerlain. Will you name her false before her own clan?''

The Colvaney shook his head. "We'll not. Maudie Farrell's name stands rightly with the Colvaneys, and ever will.''

"And ever has done with the Farrells,'' The Farrell added tartly, shooting the other man an angry glare.

"Then there can be no dispute,'' Diana said as the two sides in the crowd began to grumble at each other. "The earl might have chosen to stay silent, leaving us fully alone, but he deemed it the better road to give us a new earl, and him a true Walker.''

"What's his name, then?'' The Farrell demanded. "This new lordling of ours.''

"P. Lad Walker.'' Diana repeated the name with a measure of discomfort. It seemed an odd name for a grown man, let alone the new Earl of Kerlain.

"P. Lad Walker?'' The Colvaney repeated. "What kind of name is that for a man? P. Lad?'' Soft laughter rippled through the assembled, and more murmuring. "And what will the P be standing for, miss? Peter? Paul?'' He laughed aloud. "A good disciple our new lordling will be.''

Weariness robbed Diana of her usual humor, though she managed to smile and shake her head.

"Nay,'' she said when the laughter had died away. "His name is Proof. Proof Lad Walker. I do not know why, but it matters not. His name might be anything, and he would yet be our lord. We must give him all due respect when he comes. It was one of the last commands the earl gave me, to tell The Farrell and The Colvaney that they must give respect to the Earl of Kerlain.''

"And we would rightly do so,'' The Farrell retorted with indignation, "if he came. Though I cannot think he will. What would any American want with Kerlain? There are no riches to be had, nor profits to be made from this poor land. He'll not come."

"He *will,*" Diana said. "He is the Earl of Kerlain. His place is here. He must renounce his ties to the United States and become a British subject, but I'm sure he'll gladly do so to gain the title of Kerlain."

"Nay, The Farrell has the right of it," The Colvaney said. "We'll never set sight upon the scoundrel, unless he comes to take what little is left to us."

The crowd in the great hall agreed with this heartily, making clear their displeasure at the idea of a heathen American being set as lord over them.

Fury seeped through the edges of her exhaustion and made Diana's tone harsh.

"I'll not listen to such as this!" she shouted above the din, gaining their full attention. "Not after my godfather made his wishes so perfectly known. You *will* give respect to the new earl or shame the last, even as he lies being readied for his grave! I'll have the words for his sake alone. *Now.*"

The Farrell and Colvaney exchanged looks; all those assembled were silent. Diana stubbornly stood her ground, ready to wait the rest of the night if she must to have her godfather's desire fulfilled.

The Colvaney said it first, the words grudging. "God bless P. Lad Walker, sixth Earl of Kerlain."

"Aye," said The Farrell.

Diana looked at him sharply. *"What?"*

The Farrell sighed. "God bless P. Lad Walker, sixth Earl of Kerlain." Then he turned to his people, repeating the words until they said it too. "God bless P. Lad Walker, sixth Earl of Kerlain."

The Colvaney clan said it too, only louder, which prompted the Farrells to not only match but outdo them.

"God bless P. Lad Walker, sixth Earl of Kerlain!"

The words grew louder and louder, until the hall was ringing with them. Diana sat down on the steps, closing her eyes with relief.

He would come, this new earl of theirs. P. Lad Walker, an American with an utterly foolish name. He would come to Kerlain and love it as she did, as they all did. He would make everything right again—surely he would—for if he did not, they, and Kerlain, would be lost completely.

Chapter Two

Tennessee, January 1815

He wouldn't go. Never. Not in a million years. Not for all the riches on earth. Absolutely, without a doubt, *never*.

The sixth Earl of Kerlain. *Bah!*

The words made him want to retch. After all these years . . . when it was too late . . . he was suddenly the Earl of Kerlain. How ironic that it should happen when the only people who would have cared about it were dead. His father, his mother . . . even Joshua.

Lad himself didn't give one good damn. Not about the estate or the title, certainly not about the old man who'd labeled both Joshua and him bastards, ignoring their mother's pleas for the recognition that might have reconciled them to their English relatives. Family had meant so much to her, and she had known, though he'd never spoken of it, that her husband had longed to at least achieve some measure of peace with the ties that had been broken in his life. Especially with his father, the Earl of Kerlain. He'd not spoken of the old earl much, but Lad had heard the longing in his father's voice whenever he'd recalled Kerlain. And that had been often. Lad couldn't count the number of times during his childhood when he'd been lulled to sleep by tales of Kerlain. It had seemed to him, then, that it must be the most wonderful, magical place on God's earth, for so his father had ever made it sound. How violently his image of it had altered over the years, until the very word—*Kerlain*—had become the most profane in his vocabulary. It had brought nothing but pain and grief to his family. Now he'd rather take up residence in a sod house, his own master, than as lord there.

Not that he'd ever come to such dire straits. Fair Maiden was one of the most prosperous farms in Tennessee, and the manor house that his father had built had rightly gained a reputation as being among the finest in the county—in the entire state, for that matter. His mother had made an invitation to Fair Maiden one of the most enviable in Tennessee, being as renowned for her gatherings as she was for her beauty, and even with her gone, something of her grace and warmth remained. Lad could still smell her perfume everywhere, just as he could yet see his father in his study, reading one of his beloved horticultural tomes, or Joshua out on the long front porch after a day's work in one of the orchards or fields, laughing with the servants or some of the farm workers who'd come up with him to the house to refresh themselves with the food and drink that Mother always made certain was there.

The long porch had been the gathering place for everyone who lived at Fair Maiden, and Lad had always loved sitting out there with his family and friends on a warm Tennessee evening. But not now. In fact, there was hardly a spot within Fair Maiden's boundaries where he didn't feel the pain and loss that had haunted him so deeply these past months. He had discovered an important truth in the weeks that had followed both his mother's and brother's sudden deaths—coming only months after his father's equally untimely death. It wasn't the house itself that made a home a good and pleasant place to be, it was the people who lived with you there. Fair Maiden was the place where he'd been born and raised, where he'd expected to live all his life with his own wife and children, and which he'd thought to pass down through generations of Walkers. But it no longer felt like home. It was a beautiful, empty dwelling, and the memories that might have once filled him with contentment now only left him aching.

He was alone, and Fair Maiden, which he loved so well, was the most lonely place of all.

With a sigh he stood and tossed the letters aside, moving restlessly toward the picture window that looked out over the wide lawn separating the home estate from the actual farm. It was still snowing, as it had been doing for what seemed like days now, and everything was blanketed in white. How his mother would have loved to see it like this, Lad thought with a smile, and how his father would have worried over his precious crops—and rightly so, for Fair Maiden had a reputation to maintain as a source of the highest quality seeds and seedlings to be had in the Southern states. Joshua would have been out in the weather, uncaring of the cold, and Lad probably would have been out alongside him. They'd often spent winter afternoons hunting, or on the pond fishing, or entertaining the guests Mother had so often invited to Fair Maiden for the holidays by taking them skating or sledding.

He hadn't had much interest in going outdoors since he'd been home. He'd had enough of the cold during the war, enough of sleeping on the hard, icy ground on freezing nights, of tracking the British on the equally cold mornings that followed. Joshua had died on one of those mornings, just outside New Orleans. Lad had found him in the arms of a weeping comrade, dead only minutes but his body already half frozen. He didn't believe he would ever stop thinking of what it had felt like to lift Joshua's slight body into his own arms to carry him back to camp. The cold—God. He woke up nights in a panic, still feeling it, seeing Joshua again and his mother's face when he'd brought Joshua home.

"God." He rubbed a hand over his eyes, trying to force the memories away.

"I'd better not be hearin' what I think I'm hearin', Lad Walker," a chiding voice said from behind him. "Takin' the Lord's name in vain? I'll tan your hide but good if that's what I'm hearin'."

With a sigh, Lad dropped his hand, still staring out the window.

"I apologize, Uncle Hadley. I didn't know you were there."

"Makes no difference," Uncle Hadley said gruffly. The sound of a cane thumping along the hardwood floor told Lad that his great-uncle was moving into the parlor. "You'll not be takin' the Lord's name in vain whether anyone's about to hear it or not! Your mother would turn in her very grave to know you'd taken to such talk. Come and help me sit, nephew."

Lad dutifully moved to help his uncle into his favorite chair near the fire. Uncle Hadley made a slight growling noise as he sat, both looking and sounding like the bear of a man that he was, then gave a long sigh and said, "Now pour me a glass of whiskey, boy. The good whiskey, mind you."

What Uncle Hadley meant was his own whiskey, which he distilled every year at Fair Maiden. Lad poured him a large tumbler full and set it near his hand.

"There's a good boy," Uncle Hadley said, lifting the glass and sipping appreciatively. "Ah. Now, that's as good as it'll ever get in Tennessee. Ted Harrowfield can try all he likes, but he'll never match the like." He set the glass aside again. "Now. Sit down, boy, and tell me about these letters you've had."

"I don't know why I should," Lad said, filling a glass for himself with his uncle's brew. "You read them before I had a chance to see what they were."

"You weren't home to read them when they came, were

you?'' Uncle Hadley charged in a fully disgruntled manner.
''Poor things, sittin' there, waitin' to be read after such a
long journey. What I want to know is what you're goin' to
do. That little gal in England is all set to wed you, after all,
and the old earl took you back as is right and proper. Your
mother would have cried her eyes out with pure joy to know
you'd been welcomed into the fold after all these years.
You'll remember what it meant to her to have things made
right.''

''Yes, I remember very well,'' Lad replied curtly, returning to stare out the window. ''A shame she didn't live
long enough to know the old bastard finally gave way. On
his deathbed, yet. What a miracle of irony that is. He knew
the truth all these years, but gave in only when it was too
late. Well, Kerlain will have to do without an earl for once.
And as for Miss Diana Whitleby—what kind of a female
would agree to marry a complete stranger just because her
godfather told her to?'' He cast an aggravated glance in his
uncle's direction. ''She's either ugly and desperate or crazy
out of her mind.''

Uncle Hadley stamped his cane on the ground. ''Lad
Walker!'' he remonstrated. ''You'll mind your tongue when
you speak about a lady. Any lady, English, American, or
otherwise, or I'll come over there and teach you better.''
The cane was waved threateningly in the air. ''Your mother
didn't raise you to behave like a God-cursed heathen.''

''Yes, sir,'' Lad said, his features set and stony. He
should have remembered, before speaking as he had, how
much Uncle Hadley loved women. All women. Young, old,
and everything in between. He'd been through three wives
in his lifetime and would soon be married to number four if
Widow Nehls ever gave way beneath his constant courting.

''Miss Whitleby wrote you a real nice letter too. Very
proper, it was, considerin' how she must feel about the way
her hand has fallen. Poor thing. I'm right sorry for her.''

Lad very nearly suggested that if his uncle felt that way, then perhaps he should go to England to marry the girl, but wisely refrained. Instead, he murmured, "I suppose you're right. But, nice as it was, she can't really want to marry someone she doesn't even know—especially an American. The war's only been over a few weeks, and it'll be a long while before I stop thinking of Englishmen as the enemy. She won't be feeling any different, I'd wager. Nor anyone else at Kerlain." He shook his head. "No, they won't be wanting an American for a lord, no matter what the bloodlines may be. They'd just as soon shoot me on sight, I reckon, as welcome me. God knows that's what I'd want to do to any Brit who tried to set foot on Fair Maiden land. I'd get out my hunting gun but fast."

"Why, that's a shameful thing to say!" Uncle Hadley returned. "And your own father as British as any man who ever walked the earth."

"He was an *American*," Lad retorted. "And as much a Tennessean as if he'd been born here. He gave up every claim to England after he married my mother, and you know it."

"But that couldn't change what he *was*, Lad. He was a British nobleman until the day he died, and he longed for that place he'd loved so well. Grieved for it, he did, and nothin' so sad did I ever see as that man when he spoke of his homeland." He sighed aloud, and Lad heard him pick up his glass to drink from it. When it had been set down, Uncle Hadley went on, his tone more thoughtful. "Didn't you ever want to see Kerlain, Lad? The way he described it?" His voice grew wistful. "I wanted to see it, more times than I can recall, for he did make it sound so pleasant a place. Only England ever interested me, mind you."

Lad made no reply, only took a long sip of whiskey and told himself that it was as true for himself as for his uncle— he *had* dreamed of seeing Kerlain, just as his father had described it. The green fields, the beautiful lake, the ancient castle where knights of old had fought great battles. Both he and Joshua had spent countless hours talking of it, how they'd one day journey to England to see their ancestral home, which their father had made so alive for them.

"I'll write her—the girl, Diana Whitleby—and tell her I can't come, that they should find someone else to be the earl. Then she can marry whomever she wants and the people there can choose a proper Englishman to be their lord. I'll let the whole lot of them off the hook that my dear, departed grandfather baited on his deathbed."

"Oh, Lad," Uncle Hadley said with great sadness. "It won't do any good, boy. There's no one else to take the title on—that's what the letter said. And that poor Miss Diana will be left all alone with the burdens of the estate, and no man to take care of her. And you—it won't be any better for you if you stay here at Fair Maiden. You'll be alone with your misery and memories. That's the worst of it."

Lad turned to look at his elderly uncle. "Fair Maiden is my home," he said slowly. "And my inheritance. It's where I was born and where I'll spend the rest of my life, where my children will be born and raised. I'm not going to abandon it now for some"—he cast about for the right word—"old, dead dream."

"Old it may be," his uncle admitted, "but it's not quite dead, is it? You're the Earl of Kerlain, boy, as your father should've been. And if he *had* been, Kerlain is where you'd've been born and raised. To be the earl. If he was still alive, you know what he'd be tellin' you to do, don't you? And your mother, and probably Joshua too. And even if you don't agree with that, you can't argue with knowin' that they'd never want you to stay here alone at Fair Maiden, hidin' away—"

"I'm not hiding!"

"Never even goin' out of doors—"

"It's been snowing! Only a damned fool would go out in this weather!"

"Far be it from me to tell you what's right," Uncle Hadley said, putting up a staying hand. "But you'd best be thinkin' on what your folks would want you to do. That's all I'm sayin'."

Lad made a sound of exasperation. "All right. You have a point." More than a point, he had to admit, as Lad knew very well that his mother, and more certainly his father, would have wanted him to go. His father had left Kerlain only because he'd been banished and disowned; nothing less could have made him leave the place he'd loved so well and that he had been raised, from his cradle, to believe would be his own. "But I can't just leave Fair Maiden. Father built it up from nothing, and it's as much a part of him as Kerlain once was. I can't abandon it."

"Abandon it?" Uncle Hadley's thick, shaggy eyebrows rose. "Your cousin Archie's been runnin' the place since you went off to the war and has kept it up with not a word from you since you came back. You don't think we'd yet have our heads above water with you mopin' about like you've been?"

Lad scowled, unable to dispute the truth of this but not wanting to hear it regardless.

"That's going to change, in time," he muttered.

"Think so?" Uncle Hadley asked. "I don't mind sayin' that I have my doubts, but that's neither here nor there. What I think doesn't matter at all in the end, does it? It's what you think that counts, and maybe what you should be thinkin' about is going over to England to have a little looksee."

"A little *looksee?*" Lad repeated with disbelief. "Uncle Hadley—"

"Just for a few months," Uncle Hadley went on, waving his hand. "Get away from all the sadness here at Fair

Maiden and let me and Archie take care of things. You go on over there to Kerlain and see what's to be done, see how the situation stands, and then come back home if you don't like what you find. Fair Maiden will always be here, after all.''

"Uncle Hadley—"

"Just somethin' to think on, that's all," Uncle Hadley assured him quickly. "No need to decide this very hour. Come and help me out of this chair, nephew. I'll go and make myself presentable for dinner."

Lad did as he was asked and, with a measure of relief, watched his elderly uncle make his way out of the parlor. Uncle Hadley was eighty-five years old but as sharp as any man Lad had ever known. Still, he could hardly believe that his uncle actually wanted Lad to travel all the way to England for a little "looksee." England was their enemy—or had been, until very recently. Only a complete fool would put his life in his enemy's hands after such a bitterly fought war.

With a sigh, he poured himself another glass of whiskey and sat down to look at the letters again. The one from his grandfather was stiff and to the point, which might be due, he admitted fairly, to the dire circumstances under which it had been written. But the one from the girl was a whole other matter. He took it up, looked it over. Her handwriting was neat and delicate, wholly female and very unlike his own ragged scrawl.

What was she like, this Diana Whitleby, who so willingly went along with what her godfather had decreed? Her words gave little clue, though they were far kinder and more honest than the ones the earl had written.

Dear Sir,
    It is with deep sorrow that I inform you of the death of your grandfather, George Charles Nathaniel Walker,

fifth Earl of Kerlain. Lord Kerlain died yesterday, the tenth of October. His passing was peaceful and expected, as he had been bedridden with illness for several days beforehand. Please convey my deepest sympathies, and those of the people of Kerlain, to your family.

Accompanying this letter you will find another missive, which was dictated to me by your grandfather, only hours before his death, concerning your inheritance of the title and lands of Kerlain, which I'm sure you will greet with some measure of surprise, as well as the matter of a proposed marriage . . .

Chapter Three

England, late March 1815

As a beginning, Lad decided, standing in front of the Walborough Inn, his first few days in England were less than promising. He had underestimated just how greatly an American would be disliked by the people here, and since his arrival in Portsmouth a week earlier he'd been roundly cursed, spit at, had dogs set upon him, been refused food, drink, and lodgings, been threatened—on more than one occasion—with bodily harm, and been treated, overall, to the sort of enthusiasm that might greet the return of the Black Plague to England's fair shores. And now Lad stood in the falling snow, staring at where the coachman had tossed his leather traveling bag into the wettest, muddiest spot in front of the inn, shouting a "good riddance" as he'd done so.

Lad supposed he should be glad that he'd been able to secure passage on the coach in the first place, as both the coachman and his tiger, along with the other male passengers, had been in favor of tossing him off altogether. If it hadn't been for the women passengers—God bless their sweet souls—he'd have found himself walking the rest of the way to his destination.

With a sigh, he stooped to lift the bag from the ground, shaking it off before carrying it to the inn. The coachman and his fellow passengers had already gone in to refresh themselves while the horses were changed. Lad was the only one who wasn't traveling on, which, considering how small and unremarkable the village of Walborough was, didn't surprise him in the least. Kerlain, it seemed, was in the middle of nowhere, a little fact that his father, during his grand storytelling, had neglected to mention.

The Walborough Inn looked a warm and inviting place, but Lad could see, as he approached the tavern door, that those who had gone before him had told their tale. A great burly man with a distinctly unpleasant expression on his bearded face was standing at the entrance to bar Lad's way.

"You the American?"

"Sir," Lad began wearily, "I only want a tankard of ale and a few minutes by your fire to warm myself. I won't cause any trouble, and, yes, I have money to pay. Now, if you please, it's snowing."

The man shifted to stand in his way when Lad attempted to move past him.

"My cousin lost a leg during the war," the man said. "And no American will be enjoying the comfort of my inn."

Snow dusted Lad's face beneath the short brim of his hat, wetting his cold-reddened skin as he gazed full into the other man's face. He'd had just about enough.

"My brother died during the war," he said in a slow, deliberate tone. "Now move aside. I won't be kept out in this weather like some damned dog."

"You will," the innkeeper said threateningly. "For that's just what I think you are—a damned American dog."

Lad dropped his bag and grabbed the other man by the collar, dragging him out into the snow with the happy intention of relieving his entire fury toward the British nation on the fellow.

"Hold a moment, gentlemen!"

A solid, darkly clad body pushed between them, shoving Lad and the innkeeper apart with some difficulty.

"Calm yourselves. Harry! Come, now. What manner of greeting is this to give your guests?"

The innkeeper made a low growling sound, glowering at Lad before replying, "I won't have the likes of him at my inn! A filthy, God-cursed American, he is!"

Lad easily thrust away the restraining hand the other gentleman held upon him. "I'll teach him about God-cursed Americans—"

"Sir, please!" The newcomer stepped physically between the two, raising gloved hands, laughing as if the whole thing were a farce. "Please, there's no need for this. Scuffling out of doors like animals? In the snow, yet? Come, now." His tone was reasonable, friendly—probably the only friendly tone Lad had yet heard from an Englishman. The man's face was equally open and affable, smiling at Lad with a charm that was clearly well-practiced, but seemed sincere enough.

Lad stepped away, lowering his fisted hands to his side. "I only want a drink and to get out of this weather for a bit before I continue on my way. The same as any sane man would want."

"Of course. It's perfectly reasonable. I've stopped for the same reason myself and to allow my horses to rest until this snow stops. You'll be my guest, will you? Harry won't mind that, will you, Harry?"

Harry was still grumbling. The charming Englishman turned to him with the full force of his smile, the capes of his elegant greatcoat dancing at the movement.

"We'll have the private parlor with the fire nice and hot, and a bowl of your special punch." He glanced reassuringly at Lad. "It sounds tame, but you've never had the like, I vow. Harry has a magic touch with mixing his special brew. Is that not so, Harry?"

The innkeeper was still glowering at Lad but gave a slight nod. "It's always a pleasure to make it for you, Lord Carden."

"That's fine, then," Lord Carden said happily. "Then we're all agreed. Now, let's get out of this dreadful weather before any of us takes ill. Janet will be quite put out with me if I should let that happen to you, Harry, old boy." He began to herd the still-reluctant innkeeper toward the door. Lad, wholly bemused, took up his bag and followed, only to be stopped again when the innkeeper's thin, bedraggled wife appeared.

"Just a moment there, sir!" she said sharply, pointing at the bag. "I'll not have such filth as that dragged in, after I've spent the whole day washing these floors from all the mud and wet that's been tramped in. Leave it out here by the door."

Lad thought that the influential Lord Carden might step in again, but he didn't require that man's aid in this instance. He knew how to manage women and had been as successful in England—perhaps even a bit more so—as he'd been in Tennessee.

"You're just as right as you can be, ma'am," he said slowly, letting his Tennessean drawl linger and lifting his gaze to give her a helpless, sorrowful look. "I do apologize for the state of my bag. Brought it all the way across the Atlantic, I did. Sure wish I knew how to make it more acceptable, as my English father would be sorely unhappy to know how offensive I was to the fine people of his home county. He raised me to have better manners than that, and I hope you'll not set the lack at his door, ma'am," he finished, looking at her with all the innocence he could muster.

She stared at him for a few silent seconds, as women usually did, before her stern, unrelenting face softened.

"Well, of course you won't be knowing how to care for

it,'' she said chidingly. "You're a man, after all, aren't you? Here, now, you just give it to me.''

She reached out even as he protested. "Ma'am, I couldn't ask a lady for such as that—and it's quite heavy— my mother would—''

"Your mother wouldn't want her boy going about with his baggage in such a state. God above knows that none of *my* boys would go out in such a manner. Now, hand it here, and no argument. In by the fire with you. Go on!'' She waved the men into the tavern with an authoritative hand. "I'll have the maid bring this back to you, sir, when it's been wiped up.''

The private parlor at the Walborough Inn was everything that Lad might have hoped for. It was clean, warm, and comfortable, and with a sigh of relief he sank into a chair near the fire.

"Thank you,'' he said to his companion, who was removing his greatcoat. "I was just about ready to commit murder to get in by a fire.''

Lord Carden smiled. "I could see that, and, as I'm terribly fond of Harry, I'm relieved that you managed to constrain yourself. You'd best get out of your overcoat if you don't want Janet pulling your ears from your head for getting one of her chairs wet. You managed to charm her well enough about the bag, but I can promise you from experience that she's not so charitable when it comes to her chairs.''

With a grimace, Lad did as he was advised, standing and pulling off his outerwear—hat, scarf, overcoat—and hanging them on a hook near the door beside the far-grander garments that Lord Carden had removed. The fellow was clearly wealthy, as well as being a nobleman, and Lad cast a regretful glance at the state of the clothes he'd been traveling in for well over a month now. They were good, serviceable clothes but definitely well-worn and, at present, dirty.

"Harry will be here in a moment with the punch," Lord Carden said as he took the seat opposite the one Lad had returned to, stretching out his booted feet toward the warmth of the drying flames, "and Janet will send in some of her famous beef pasties, if I know her. You're hungry?"

He was a handsome man, Lad thought, surveying him more closely now. Blond, blue-eyed, slender and aristocratic. He looked a great deal like many of the British soldiers Lad had killed during the war, a memory that made him look away.

"Yes," he replied tonelessly. "Though some of the women on the coach were kind enough to feed me earlier, or I'd be in a pretty sorry state."

Lord Carden laughed. "Yes, I imagine they did feed you, and probably quite well if the skill you displayed with Janet is anything to go by. You've clearly a talent for charming women."

"You're not too bad at charming folks yourself," Lad replied. "Even if ol' Harry didn't particularly want to be charmed."

Lord Carden nodded graciously. "You're quite right, and I gladly accept the compliment from a fellow master at the art of having one's way. My name is Eoghan, by the way. Eoghan Patterson. My estate is quite near here, though I don't expect you to know that. I've only just returned to it a few days past, having been traveling on the Continent for the better part of a year."

They would be neighbors, then, of a sort, Lad thought, even as he gave him a curious look. "I thought the innkeeper called you Lord Carden?"

"Carden is my title—Viscount Carden, of Lising Park— though I hope you'll address me by my Christian name. All my friends and close acquaintances do, and I believe it's what you're used to in the United States. Or am I mistaken?"

Lad very nearly said that they weren't friends or close acquaintances but was too tired to argue fine points at the moment. And the fellow had been remarkably kind to him.

"You're not mistaken," he said. "We're not quite so formal in the States as you folks are here. Glad to know you, Eoghan Patterson. I'm Lad."

Lord Carden stared at him.

"Lad? Just . . . Lad?"

He nodded. "Just Lad. I'm afraid if you knew my last name you might decide to join with Harry and toss me out into the snow again."

"Never!" Lord Carden promised, then leaned forward to ask, "Why should I want to do such a thing? You're not a known criminal, are you? Come all the way from America to terrify us here?"

"No." Lad laughed. "But I've had a few strange reactions to my full name since arriving in England, and I'd just as soon keep it to myself until I've gotten to where I'm going."

"I see. And where might that be?"

Lad sighed. "I'd just as soon keep that to myself too." Carden would find out soon enough what the truth was, if his estate was truly nearby, for Kerlain wasn't but another five miles away, but Lad couldn't seem to find the energy to face the questions that such a declaration would create at the moment. "Sorry to be disobliging, but you probably wouldn't believe me, even if I told you, considering the way I look."

"Please don't apologize," Lord Carden said reassuringly, though Lad both saw and heard a slight tightening in the man. "I shouldn't be bothering you with such tiresome questions, in any event." He sat back in his chair more comfortably, remarking, "You did tell Janet that your father was English, though? And that Herefordshire was his home county?"

Fortunately for Lad, a scratching at the door indicated the arrival of Harry and a serving girl carrying in the punch, or, rather, the ingredients for the punch, which Harry, with great ceremony, proceeded to mix. The smell of rum and apples and spices filled the air, reminding Lad of holidays at Fair Maiden, when his mother had served hot punches.

"The missus sent some of her pasties, m'lord," the girl said, offering the tray to Lord Carden with a shy, blushing look. When he'd made his careful selection she gave her attention to Lad, her blue eyes promptly widening at the sight of him. He gave her a smile and she responded with the same slightly stunned stare that the innkeeper's wife had earlier given him.

Women liked the way he looked, which was a fact Lad had learned early on in life. Joshua and his parents had used to tease him about the way females reacted to him, but it had proven to be as much a curse as a blessing. Certain women seemed almost afraid to speak to him, while others nearly threw themselves at his feet, and though he'd be the last to deny that he'd used his particular powers for his own advantage, he often wondered what it might be like to meet a female who didn't react to his outward appearance. Just to talk to a woman who wasn't blushing and flirting with him every moment would be a strange and wonderful thing.

"Your . . . your bag is cleaned and ready for you . . . sir," she said, stammering. "I've just now finished with it." The tray of pasties she was holding out nearly slid into his lap while she yet gaped, and Lad reached out to steady it.

"Thank you. You're very good, miss . . ."

"This is Martha," Lord Carden said with amusement heavy in his tone. "And, indeed, she is very good," he added, his meaning, much different from Lad's, perfectly clear.

Martha blushed the more and curtsied, murmuring to Lad, "Sir."

"Thank you, Miss Martha," Lad said gently. "If you'll be so good as to bring the bag to me when you have a spare moment, I'd be most grateful. Let me take this, will you?" He grasped the tray firmly as it began to dip toward him again. "I'll just set it on this table, if that's all right?"

"Oh, yes, sir," she assured him in a fluttering voice, as if he'd just committed the most chivalrous act she'd ever beheld. "Thank you, sir." She curtsied again. "I'll bring your bag right away. Right away."

"Get on with you, girl!" Harry, the innkeeper, growled at her as he filled two cups with the hot, steaming punch. Martha hurriedly quit the parlor and so did the innkeeper, just as soon as Lad and Lord Carden had taken their cups from his hands. He'd cast a thoroughly unpleasant look at Lad as he'd given him his drink, making it clear that he still didn't want the American in his establishment and was counting the minutes until he was gone.

"Do you make a conquest of every female you meet?" Lord Carden asked wryly when they were alone again. "But it's a foolish question, for you surely must."

"No," Lad replied with feeling. Women might like him, but he liked them as well—far too much to make such light sport of them.

"Well, I've never seen Janet behave as she did earlier, and you nearly had Martha licking your boots. You can have her, you know, if you like. A few coins is all it takes, and she's well worth it. To be perfectly honest, it's what I really stopped here for, though the snow made the prospect even more pleasurable. Martha's chamber is a cozy little nest, and she's a warm and biddable companion, even if a bit dim-witted. I believe I even thought of her a time or two while I was abroad. This has been my first opportunity since returning to Herefordshire to become reacquainted with her charms, which I assure you are many. Though perhaps you wish to discover them for yourself.'' He chuckled before lifting his steaming cup to his lips.

Heat started in Lad's brain and made its way to his hands, one of which he reflexively fisted. He kept his features perfectly calm, but inside he was seething with fury. To speak of a young woman that way, as if she were a dog or a whore . . . well, it was a damned good thing Uncle Hadley wasn't there, or Viscount Carden would have found himself whacked soundly on the noggin by a cane. Lad was sorely tempted to perform the same duty on the viscount's face, using his fists, but forcibly pushed his angry feelings down. He'd met hundreds of men like this in his lifetime, in the United States and now in England, and had no doubt he'd meet hundreds more, who viewed the greater portion of the female population as existing solely for their good and pleasure. This man had been kind to him and perhaps could not help his baser nature, especially if his parents hadn't raised him to know better, as Lad's had done from his very cradle.

"Miss Martha certainly looks to be a fine young lady,'' he said with care, still flexing his hands, though more slowly. "But I fear I'm not looking for such company just now. It's possible that I may be getting married shortly.''

Viscount Carden stared at him as if waiting for something more, until he finally said, with a spurt of laughter, "You mean to say . . . I'm sorry, for I'm sure I misunderstand . . . but you can't mean that an upcoming marriage would keep you from—''

"Yes,'' Lad said, shifting uncomfortably in his chair. "That's what I mean. Are you married?'' He hoped to change the subject.

"No, but as it happens,'' Lord Carden said, still clearly amused, "I'm also soon to be wed. It's what brought me home from the Continent before I had finished my intended travels. My betrothed's guardian died rather suddenly, and it has become possible for us to embrace our wedding vows sooner than he would have allowed. His passing is a sorrow, of course, but something of a blessing in disguise. I've been quite eager to wed my dearest these many years past. I suppose we should wish each other happy, Lad.'' He lifted his glass in salute. ''To you and your possible future bride. May you both be fully content in every way, if you do indeed marry, and even if you do not.''

''Thank you.'' Lad lifted his glass in turn, feeling awkward in the face of the other man's smooth manner and eloquently spoken words. His own Tennessean drawl seemed uncouth in comparison. ''I wish the same to you and yours.''

Eoghan graciously nodded his thanks.

''Is she an Englishwoman, this possible bride of yours?'' he asked.

''Yes,'' Lad replied simply.

''And I don't suppose you'll be any more forthcoming with her name or place than you've been with your own?''

Lad smiled. ''No, I'm afraid not. But you can tell me about your bride, if you like.''

The viscount's expression softened, and he smiled as if to himself, gazing down at the cup in his hands. ''Words can hardly do her justice. You'd have to see my sweet lady to understand what I mean. I can only say that she's been the dearest friend of my heart since we were both children and that I love her as I could never love another. I missed her dreadfully while I was gone from England, but that's at an end now. We shall never be parted again.''

The fellow certainly seemed to be sincere, Lad thought, though his happy infidelity made this love he spoke of somewhat suspect. Still, it was none of his business what another man did or didn't do, and he merely nodded and smiled and said, ''You're lucky to have a woman like that.''

The conversation grew less personal, and they drank

their punch while it was yet warm and ate the pasties Janet had sent in. Martha soon delivered Lad's bag, cleaned and brushed and looking better than it had in a long time. He dug into a pocket to give her a coin, and she giggled and blushed and asked if he'd be spending the night at the inn.

The bold invitation had Viscount Carden laughing. "Leave him be, Martha, sweet," he told the girl in a mockingly chiding voice. "He may be getting married soon and cannot be swayed from the admirable path of virtue that the hopeful event has inspired in him." The girl's face fell until Lord Carden added, with a wink, "You'll simply have to make do with my poor company, I fear. Can you possibly accept me, my sweet?"

"Oh, yes, my lord," she said with another giggle. "I'd be pleased." Bobbing a curtsy, Martha hurriedly quit the room, her spirits clearly restored.

"I'm sorry," Viscount Carden apologized when they were alone again. "I should have asked if you meant to spend the night here at the inn, rather than assuming otherwise. I can arrange a room for you, if you like, as I think Harry will be more willing to oblige me than yourself."

Lad knew that he should press on to Kerlain, but one glance out the window showed that the snow was yet falling fast, and truth to tell, he was fairly worn out from his travels. A night of rest in a warm, if inhospitable, inn would do him good. In the morning, if the snow had stopped, he'd make his way to Kerlain and greet whatever awaited him there with at least enough vigor to keep from making a complete fool of himself—which was what he'd envisioned happening since before he'd even left the States.

"I'd be grateful," he told the viscount, thinking that he owed this man, whom he couldn't even say he liked, a great deal. "But I don't know that I should ask it of you. I don't want to get you on Harry's blacklist."

"Not at all," Lord Carden said reassuringly, setting his

cup aside and standing. "I'll go and have a word with him now, shall I, and have the matter fully settled for you? I'm rather anxious to be on my way now that I'm warmed, and my horses should be ready to continue on. And there is Martha to see to as well."

"I'm in your debt, sir," Lad said, standing and extending his hand, which Viscount Carden looked at with a moment of amusement before taking and shaking it. "Thank you for everything. Hope I can return the favor someday."

"It's been my pleasure, Lad," Lord Carden said, bowing in a very formal manner, though he yet smiled as if they were enacting a great farce. "I can't tell you how much. Good luck to you in all your future plans, and Godspeed."

Lad was almost relieved when the other man left, and he sat down again with the strange, undefined feeling that Lord Carden, despite his friendly manners and politeness, had somehow been making sport of him.

With a sigh, he leaned back in his chair and contemplated the dancing flames in the hearth. How strange everything had seemed since he'd left Fair Maiden. Even the warmth of a simple fire could not be taken for granted when a man was a stranger in a foreign land.

He wondered, as he had wondered perhaps thousands of times since having her letter, what Miss Diana Whitleby looked like. What she sounded like. Moved like. Her letter hadn't given him the answers to any of those questions, and yet it had held the power to draw him all the way from his home, across the ocean, to this unfriendly place. He pulled the letter now from the inner pocket in his jacket where he always kept it ready at hand. It had nearly fallen to pieces from being opened and read so many times, and he unfolded it with care to look once more at the neat, elegant writing upon the page.

You will find within the earl's letter more details pertaining to the marriage that he desired, namely that you and I should wed in the interests of Kerlain itself. I realize that this determination upon the part of your grandfather will come as an unexpected, perhaps an unwelcome, condition for your claiming of the title, but I would allay whatever concerns you may have toward my own feelings. I am fully willing in the matter, and, if you should be equally desirous, will wed with you as soon as it may be arranged upon your arrival at Kerlain. If, however, it is not what you should wish, we may yet find another and equally desirous course upon which we may agree and be satisfied. There is no need for you to fear, sir, that you must be married to me in order to gain the title, and I will take no offense whatever you may decide.

Please, sir, make haste and journey to Kerlain as soon as you may. We are in desperate need, and I am particularly pressed on all sides. I will look for you each day come February and will pray Godspeed for your journey.

Respectfully, Diana Whitleby

Lad stared at the page another moment longer, then carefully folded and replaced it in his pocket. Tomorrow, Diana Whitleby would have what she'd pleaded for—his arrival at Kerlain. He couldn't begin to know what their meeting would mean for either of them, but it would happen, against his every deep misgiving, against what common sense dictated, against his own desire to never step foot in his father's ancestral home. Tomorrow he would be there, and Diana Whitleby would see what manner of man had come to be the lord of Kerlain.

Chapter Four

"I tell you, Diana, never have I seen such a complete bumpkin. I was obliged to exert myself a dozen times or more to keep from laughing outright at his ridiculous speech and manner. And his dress! God's mercy!" Eoghan laughed and gave a shake of his head. "He looked as if he'd just crawled out of one of his American wildernesses, having been lost within for a six-month period. I think Harry wanted to keep him out of the tavern at least partly for that, though more so because he was an American."

Diana looked up from the repairs she was making to a torn bed-curtain, the needle she'd been speedily plying momentarily still as she said, "You're cruel, Eoghan, to make sport of a man who is clearly suffering misfortune."

Eoghan made a scoffing noise. "I made Harry take him into the inn, didn't I? And allowed him to share the private parlor *and* bought him both food and drink. I don't call that cruel."

A great sadness filled Diana for both Eoghan and those upon whom he played his wretched games. He'd once used her as a source of his amusement, when they'd been children, until she'd threatened to stop playing with him. He'd been her sole friend in those days, as he'd been the only child among the neighboring estates whom her godfather would allow her to play with, and despite his horrid cruelty, she had been afraid of losing him. Indeed, if he hadn't given way first and pleaded with her not to cut their friendship, she might very well have been the one to fold. But she was very glad she had not, for she'd learned two important things about Eoghan Patterson: He was far more terrified of being friendless than she was, despite all his airs of superiority, and those who wanted to win a contest with him must hold perfectly fast to their determinations. Eoghan always put up a ferocious fight, but he didn't have the strength of character to prevail against anyone more steadfast.

"You only lent him aid in order to amuse yourself," she said. "He had no idea that you were making such sport of him, poor fellow. Where was he going to?"

"I have no idea." Eoghan crossed one leg elegantly over the other. "He wouldn't tell me anything about himself, though I did what I could to persuade him."

"Truly?" Diana bent more closely over her work. "That seems rather strange. But if you couldn't charm him into betraying confidences, no one could. You've the devil's own tongue, Eoghan."

"He did let a few hints fly, at my urging. His name is Lad, and he's going to be wed soon—perhaps." He laughed again. "He wasn't even certain about that. And his father is English, or was, rather. It's a pity about the marriage, really. He had the most frightful effect on every woman who set sight upon him."

"Frightful?" Diana repeated, her voice a faint whisper. "How so?"

Eoghan grinned at her. "He was handsome. Didn't I tell you that? The sort of fellow who makes women behave like greater idiots than they usually are." His expression sharpened, grew more cunning. "I wish now that I'd accompanied him to his destination, just to know where he might be found. What fun it would have been to have dressed him up, taught him some manners, and taken him to London. Can you imagine the entertainment I might have had, introducing him to the *ton?*''

Diana felt faint. Stunned. He had come, at last. Lad Walker was in England, only a few miles away, and surely tomorrow he would . . .

She stood, her needlework falling to the ground.

''Oh, dear God.''

''Diana? What's the matter?'' Eoghan stood as well.

Everything, she thought. Kerlain, which she had striven to make fit these past months, was far from ready to receive its new lord. The curtains . . . the furniture . . . the people . . . and *her,* most of all.

''Diana?'' Eoghan reached out to take one of her icy hands. ''I'm sorry, darling. My thoughtless tongue . . . I know how it upsets you when I rattle on that way.''

She pulled her hand free and bent to retrieve her fallen needlework. ''It's not that. And you *always* rattle on that way.'' She tried to infuse a note of teasing into her voice, though her head was spinning with a hundred distressing thoughts and her hands were trembling. Lad Walker was coming. And she would—perhaps—very shortly be his wife. ''You always have, and you always will.''

He knelt beside her and began gathering the heavy curtain up, taking the weight of it out of her arms and standing to place it on the chair she'd risen from. ''Not always,'' he said with all seriousness. ''For you, Diana, I'll be better. Once we're married, you'll never have cause to be angered with me. I swear it. I shall be the model husband, little though you may credit the idea.''

''We're never going to be married,'' Diana replied without emotion. Eoghan had only returned to England four days ago, and already she was weary with turning him away. He'd ridden to Kerlain on each of the four days and made the most foolish, exhausting pest of himself, speaking nonsense about them being able to marry now that her godfather had died. She didn't know where he got such mad ideas from—they had only ever been friends, and the idea of anything more made Diana's stomach turn. She was convinced it was only more of Eoghan's cruelty. He probably assumed she'd gladly fall for his avowals of love now that Kerlain had no earl to guide them; and if she did fall, Eoghan would laugh and call her a little idiot and tell her that he'd only been playing a game to see how quickly she'd jump. But he was far, far wrong if he thought that she would *ever* be so desperate as to leap at the chance to marry him. She would have the last laugh. Soon, within but a few days, Eoghan would no longer have cause to bother her with his nonsensical talk of marriage, for she would be wed—to the very man he'd called a bumpkin.

How strange that he should not know who Lad Walker was, but, then, Eoghan had never been much interested in what had occurred between the previous earl of Kerlain and his son, Charles. Indeed, he'd never been much interested in anything about Kerlain. Or so it had seemed to Diana. And he'd been away from England for too many months to know that the new earl had been sent for. Within another week or two, once he'd become more settled following his return to Herefordshire and had the leisure to mingle with more of the common folk, he would have begun to hear the rumors that had been spoken regarding Lad Walker, though it was widely held that the American would never come, and talk of him had died down a great deal since the late earl's passing.

As to the marriage that the earl had proposed between herself and Lad Walker, Diana had said nothing of it to anyone and had sworn those few people who'd witnessed the earl's final hours to secrecy. She'd been too ashamed at the thought of how humiliated she would be before all the people of Kerlain if the new earl never arrived. The Farrells and the Colvaneys would never cease rattling on about such an insult as an American had dared to give their lady, and Eoghan would never cease laughing and teasing her over it.

Now that Lad Walker had come, that particular fear was gone, but Diana yet hesitated to speak aloud of her coming marriage. The news might silence Eoghan, but more likely than not he would be angry at having his jest spoiled.

"Of course we'll be married," he replied confidently. "And very soon too. I've already written to arrange for the license."

"No, we will not," she said, beginning to grow angry with him. She turned away and began rolling up her needle and thread. "And I wish you'd stop teasing me in such a ridiculous manner."

He set his hand on her arm. "Diana—"

"Please, Eoghan." She shrugged free of his touch, moving away. "If you're going to persist in this foolishness, I must ask you to go."

"I love you," he said insistently, grabbing her arm to swing her back to face him. "I have always loved you, and you *will* be my wife."

"Eoghan!" She struggled against his strong grip, but he only held her the faster and bent his head to find her mouth with his own. Diana turned her face to the side, well-used to fending off Eoghan's sudden, violent expressions of affection. As a boy he'd stolen kisses, but he'd learned, even then, the price he would pay for such effrontery. With every ounce of strength she possessed, Diana shoved him forcibly away, and as he fell back she followed to strike him across the face with her open palm.

He shouted out, stumbling and coming to rest, half bending, against the chair that had been behind him.

"When will you ever learn?" Diana demanded furiously, her body shaking with her anger. "I'll not have you touching me!"

He set a hand against the place where her stinging slap

had landed, and slowly straightened to look at her. His blond hair was in disarray, and his handsome face was contorted in both pain and anger.

"And when will you learn," he said slowly, breathing harshly, "that I mean what I say? I *will* have you for my wife, Diana. No other man will have you as such."

He was *serious,* she realized with shocked disbelief. All these years, since they'd been children, he had teased and flirted and played at being in love with her while at the same time behaving so outrageously that she couldn't possibly believe that he meant what he said.

"Is it Kerlain you want?" she asked, staring at him. But that couldn't be right, though her godfather had made that claim. She knew Eoghan better than anyone, and he had always despised Kerlain, both the lands and the castle, which he'd ever pronounced as too poor and decrepit for any fool to desire.

"It's you I want, Diana," he said, "and you I'm going to have. With or without Kerlain, though I don't suppose I'd turn it aside once we're wed. You love the place, even if I've never understood why, and for that alone—for you—I'll keep it. And care for it too," he added somewhat sourly. "I know you too well to think you'd give me peace otherwise. Your beloved Kerlain." The last three words were hard and bitter.

"Yes, mine," she said firmly, "and never yours, or any other man's, so long as I live." She drew in a calming breath before continuing. "We're friends, Eoghan, and that is what we will ever be. Never husband and wife. I can't think how you've come to believe otherwise, for I've certainly not given you cause to think it." She shook her head, then gave a slight smile, attempting to lighten the angry mood between them. "Such foolish ideas you take into your head, just as you did when you were a boy. But you must put a stop to it now, Eoghan. If you cannot, then I'll no longer see you or receive you here at Kerlain. We're too old for such nonsense."

He dropped his hand and took a step toward her.

"Oh, no, Diana. You'll not send me away as you once did so long ago. I'll not let you."

Her eyes narrowed. "Stop it, Eoghan. If you value our friendship at all, you must put an end to this . . ." She cast about for the right word, finding none.

Eoghan finished it for her. "Madness?" he suggested. "Aye, and that's just what it is, Diana. A madness. It's what you are for me, and what you've ever been. I don't know how to tell you any more plainly what I feel."

"It's not love," she told him flatly. "You aren't capable of it. God alone knows how you've ever scorned it."

"If it's not love, then it's a damned good impression of it," he replied with an empty laugh, running his fingers through his hair to straighten it. The cheek she'd struck yet glowed red. "I only know that I can't lose you, as I nearly lost you when we were children. If it was a terrible thought then, it's far worse now. I must have you, Diana, love or not. And I don't know why you should be so stubborn in the matter. You're alone here at Kerlain, now that the earl has died." He swept a hand about the chilly, sparsely furnished parlor they were in. "You need a husband, and you'll never find another man to wed you who has the funds to take on this decrepit pile. Even despite your many charms." He smiled at her in an unpleasant manner, baring his teeth. "You know I speak the truth, Diana. Would you rather live here alone, growing old in this freezing tomb, than be my viscountess?"

"I won't be alone," she said, then suddenly wished she hadn't. Now she'd aroused his curiosity. The simple words she'd just uttered were enough to fill his eyes with a cunning that she recognized only too well. He looked like a hound that had just caught the scent of its quarry.

"Will you not?" he asked in careful, quiet tones. "Are you expecting that someone will indeed come forward to accept the earldom and all that it entails? Including this . . . wonderful estate?" he said with a smirk. "The earl had no living blood relatives who could claim the title. At least," he amended, giving her a considering look, "not legitimately. But, no. That would be quite impossible. We both know that the old man would never bend in that direction, not even on his deathbed." Setting a finger to his chin, he regarded Diana more closely. "Who would it be then? Some cousin from a distant branch in the family tree? Or perhaps it's not that at all. Perhaps you've had an offer of marriage from some other quarter? Could that be it, Diana, my sweet?"

Years of dealing with Eoghan had taught Diana how to keep her features perfectly blank in such moments as this. He was far too quick to notice even the slightest blush or change of expression.

"It's no concern of yours, Eoghan Patterson. Think what you please, but do so elsewhere. I've a great deal to do today and must ask you to leave. Now." She moved to the bellpull and tugged.

Eoghan stayed where he was, giving a single, slow shake of his head. "You're wrong, Diana. Far wrong. It is my concern, whether you wish it to be or not. No other man will have you, just as I've said. It's a promise I make. On my honor."

The parlor door opened, and Maudie entered, wiping her hands on her apron.

"Yes, miss?"

"Viscount Carden is leaving, Maudie. Have Stuart make his lordship's horse ready."

"Never mind, Maudie," Eoghan said, stopping the older woman. "I'll see to it myself. I shouldn't wish to take one of Kerlain's few servants away from his many tasks. God alone knows how you manage this ancient heap with only the three of you to tend it." To Diana he said, "Remember what I told you, Diana. I meant every word."

"And so did I," she replied.

He nodded. "Very well. I bid you good day." He strode across the room, stopping at the door and turning back to look at her. "I'll come to visit in a few days. Perhaps you'll have thought better on what we've discussed, and we can speak more calmly. And reasonably."

"Perhaps," she said without emotion, as if she weren't rigid with fury. "Good day to you, my lord."

She sank into the nearest chair when he'd gone, setting a trembling hand over her face and striving to collect her roiling thoughts. She couldn't decide which was more unsettling—Eoghan's horrid behavior or his unknowing pronouncement that Lad Walker was even now less than an hour's ride from Kerlain.

Diana had nearly given up hope that he would come, but he was here at last, or would be on the morrow. God above, how she prayed he would make it to the castle without further deterrent. She had thought they might have some time to come to know each other before marrying, but that was impossible now. Eoghan had made it so. They must marry as soon as it might be arranged—perhaps, even, within a day or two.

Until then, she must take no chance that Eoghan might discover the truth. She could tell no one—not the servants in the castle or the people of Kerlain—that their new lord was at Kerlain until the marriage had been agreed upon and set into motion. There would be nothing Eoghan could do after that, save make himself as unpleasant as he likely would, and there was nothing she could do about that save weather the storm.

Dropping her hand, Diana leaned back in the chair and gave a long, weary sigh. Soon, so very soon, many of her burdens would be lifted away. Or at least they would be shared and thus the lighter. She would have a husband to help her save Kerlain and make the estate profitable once more, to return the castle to its former glory. And the people of Kerlain would have a new lord to guide and keep them. They would resist him at first, she knew, but if Lad Walker truly desired to be accepted, he would find the way to win them over. She would be beside him to help, and once they'd had a child, a properly born heir, the people would forgive their lord his unfortunate American heritage. He was a Walker, after all, a true and proper Walker, and his place was here, at Kerlain.

She tried to imagine what he must feel, how glad he must be to be so near to the place that was his natural home. Perhaps Kerlain's present shabbiness would not seem so dire to him as it did to her, for, though she loved it, he would love it that much more.

For Lad Walker, Kerlain would truly be the place of his heart's every desire.

Chapter Five

This was Kerlain?

God help him.

Lad drew his mount to a halt in the middle of the partly snow-covered, partly muddy road and gazed with a measure of distress at the view before him. A half mile or so away stood a dwelling that Lad believed, with a deep, sinking feeling, was to be his new home.

His father had been an artist of no small skill and had left behind, upon his death, several sketchbooks filled with studies of the various plants and trees that he'd propagated at Fair Maiden. He'd sketched Kerlain too, at the insistence of his young and curious sons, but either Lad had landed in the wrong spot in Herefordshire or his father's memory had grown decidedly fanciful after leaving England. This looked nothing at all like the grand and beautiful place his father had created, both on paper and in the minds of his sons.

Kerlain.

The reality of it was such a disappointment that he felt it physically, as a loss, as a deep, sharp pain that only time might heal. *This* was what his father had been talking of all these years? A run-down, crumbling relic? A brown and gray landscape, which even the snow couldn't hide with its passing beauty, and which was as unappealing as any he'd ever before seen? Diana Whitleby had said that the people of Kerlain were in desperate need, but he'd never dreamed that things would be like this. Even the fields he'd passed on his way were poor and uncared for. Lad's trained eye had seen at once that any attempt to produce crops in them would be difficult at best and useless at worst. His father had spoken of the English countryside where he had been born and raised as being the most beautiful, unparalleled place on earth, and perhaps it had been—once. If his father were alive to see it now, his heart would probably break into a hundred bitter pieces.

He was stopped at a slight rise in the road from which he could see the castle and its surrounding walls—or, rather, what was left of the surrounding walls. At this distance, Castle Kerlain seemed to be comprised of a strange jumble of buildings, ranging from what appeared to be a partly decomposed medieval fortress to a more modern, manorlike addition that, though thankfully intact, was clearly in need of much repair.

Lad stared at the dwelling for a long while, mindless of the cold, striving to reconcile it with the drawings his father had made. His thoughts drifted to Diana Whitleby, who was probably somewhere inside that crumbling heap, assuming she wasn't foolish enough to venture out in such cold weather. He wondered what she would think of him, and what he would think of her, and if she would still be so willing to wed him once they'd met, or if she'd want to pursue the *equally desirous* course she'd mentioned in her letter. He was just vain enough to think she'd prefer the marriage, and just worried enough too. He didn't know which of them was the crazier—her, for agreeing to marry a complete stranger at the bidding of her godfather, or him, for journeying halfway around the world just to take a look at a woman who'd do something like that.

At least he was more presentable today than he'd been the day before. He'd awakened in his room at the Walborough Inn to find his clothes neatly laid out by the fire, brushed clean, and his worn boots looking almost new again. Martha, giggling and curtsying, had delivered hot water shortly after that, and Lad had shaved and washed and later made his way down to the taproom with the knowledge that he was at least as presentable as any respectable country gentleman might be. Even Harry, the innkeeper, had looked at him with a small—very small—measure of approval as Lad sat down to break his fast with the delightful feast Janet brought out to him. He'd paid well for his room and meal, had generously tipped Martha, and had been gratified to see that he'd taken them by surprise—especially Harry, who had clearly decided that Lad was a penniless rogue no doubt intending to weasel his way out of paying his debts. The coins Lad readily produced didn't precisely endear him to the burly innkeeper, but they were enough to sufficiently unbend the fellow to let him hire a horse for the ride out to Kerlain.

He'd brought plenty of money with him on his journey from the States, not knowing how long he'd stay in England or what he might require in the way of clothing to make himself presentable as the Earl of Kerlain. Things were different here, he knew, especially in the manner of dress, and he'd been ready to wear what he must so as not to be offensive to his new status—no matter how he disliked the idea of being decked out in such fancy duds as he'd seen on a number of men in Portsmouth and Bristol.

Along with the funds Lad brought for his own personal needs, he'd also had a large sum of money transferred to a bank in London to meet whatever *desperate need* Diana Whitleby had spoken of in her letter. Now, seeing for himself just how things stood, he knew full well that it wasn't going to be enough. He was a wealthy man—Fair Maiden alone was worth a sizable fortune—but he'd have to be rich as a nabob to fix the troubles at Kerlain.

Two men appeared suddenly, coming over the rise in the

road, their tall, hatted figures bobbing up and down as they walked at a brisk pace. Their heads were bent in conversation, and they didn't see Lad at first, then, looking up, their loud, laughing talk came to an abrupt halt and their footsteps slowed. Lad stayed where he was, aching with a cold that he felt to his very bones, and waited for them to near him. The taller of the two was a young man, perhaps near Lad's own age, dark-haired and broad-shouldered. The other man was older and somewhat less powerfully built, though he yet appeared to be as strong and fit as his companion. They had the look of that peculiar breed with which Lad was so familiar: rough, hearty men who had farmed the land all their lives, fighting it mightily one moment and tending it with loving care the next.

"Good day," he said civilly when they'd come close enough to hear. "Can you tell me, if you please, whether this is Kerlain?"

They lifted well-formed, sun-bitten faces to him, eyes filled with suspicion. In their features Lad saw anew the ancient, noble lineage that so many of the English possessed—Roman, Saxon, and Norman melded together in the creation of a wholly distinct civilization. It was part of him too, this melding of blood and features, a realization that unsettled him no small measure. He had always identified himself first as a Tennessean, a proud son of the best and proudest state in the Union, and then as an American . . . but *never* as an Englishman, despite his father's heritage. But he was English, at least partly. The fact struck him as baldly as knowing that he'd killed these people during the war—people with whom he would have fought, side by side, if his grandfather hadn't disowned his father. God above, what a strange twist of fate that was. And even stranger was that he was here now, come to England for a purpose he didn't even quite understand.

"Aye, 'tis Kerlain," the eldest man said, his tone wary. "And who will you be, then? Eh?"

Lad blinked at the man, momentarily stunned at the sound of his voice. It had been two years since he had heard it, this unique manner of speech that was as familiar to him as his own. The accent was heavy with the influence of Wales, the border of which lay but a few miles away, and with the roughness of the country itself. It was his father's speech, though far less refined, which Lad had never heard in another man before now and had not expected to hear again.

"My name is Lad Walker." He wondered if they'd been expecting him and, if so, what manner of welcome he'd receive. "I've come from Tennessee to . . . well, I had a letter from a Miss Diana Whitleby, regarding the death of the Earl of Kerlain, and I—"

"Oh, Gawd," the elder said. "You're him, are you? Gawd's toes. You came after all. Damn me." He turned his head and spat on the ground, then muttered again, "Damn me."

The younger man's reaction was less severe. He gazed at Lad in a frank, assessing manner and said, "You're the American who's come to be the new earl, then?"

"I'm afraid so," Lad said, and with an easy motion dismounted. The best way to start, he decided, was to be perfectly up front about things. "At least, I'm an American, and I've come to see Kerlain. I don't know about taking on the earldom." He stepped nearer the other men, equal in height and breadth to the younger. "You live here? At Kerlain?"

"Aye," the elder answered, looking Lad over with a pained expression. "Born and bred, the both of us. I'm Conyn Colvaney. *The* Colvaney. And this is m'son, Braen. The Colvaneys hark back to Kerlain's earliest days, to before the first earl. Did your father, Lord Charles, never speak of us?''

"Indeed, he did,'' Lad replied truthfully. "And of the Farrell clan as well.'' Lad removed his glove and extended his bare hand in the American fashion of greeting, though he was perfectly aware that the British weren't given to shaking hands as casually as their former colonials were. "I'm pleased to know you both, Conyn and Braen Colvaney.''

They stared at his hand, then exchanged glances, their expressions as distrustful and questioning as if they'd found themselves faced with a madman and were wondering what to do. At last, slowly, Conyn Colvaney removed his tattered working glove and lifted a heavily callused hand to meet Lad's. He gave Lad a long, hard squeeze of a shake, saying, "Well, I suppose if you're t'be the new earl, we must at least give you a try. You do have something of the look of your father, and that's better than naught. Now we must see what you have of your grandfather in you. Until then, welcome to Kerlain . . . m'lord.'' The last word was one that he clearly had difficulty forcing past his lips, but Lad understood why. He wasn't what a proper lord would look like to these men. His manner of dress alone was far more suited to a commoner than a member of the aristocracy.

Braen Colvaney was friendlier. He pulled his hat from his head with one hand and shook Lad's hand with the other, giving a slight smile and a nod. "Welcome to Kerlain, m'lord. We've been looking for you to come this past month and more. Miss Diana will be that glad to have you at Kerlain, safe and sound.''

"Will she?'' Lad gazed beyond him to the castle. "She said in her letter that she was in need, but I had not expected this. Does she really live there? It's hard to believe anyone does—any human creature, I mean. It looks like it would be more suitable for animals.''

"What, the castle?" The Colvaney asked, his voice rising with anger. "Of course Miss Diana lives there, and no one loves it better. 'Tis as grand a place as God ever allowed on His earth, is Castle Kerlain. Generations of your family were born and died there, m'boy," he said, addressing Lad as if he *were* a commoner rather than his new lord, "and you'll not be forgetting it, for all that you've been born and raised on the wrong side of the ocean. 'Twas a terrible misunderstanding that sent your da away, for it is *here* he should have lived and *here* he should have died." He pointed a long finger at Lad. "And if you're a true Walker, Castle Kerlain is where *you'll* live and die too."

"Da," Braen said uncomfortably, "he's only just come. We must give him a chance. The earl told us—"

"I know what the earl said!" The Colvaney declared angrily. "But we'll have none of this strange talking here at Kerlain. 'Tis unnatural for a Walker to speak of his own birthright so! The earl would be turning in his very grave to hear it, by God. And your father with him," The Colvaney said to Lad, "for he was as true a Walker as ever graced the earth, and I can but imagine what he suffered, being sent away from Kerlain, with the love of it flowing in his veins like his own life's blood. Ah, ye cannot deny that, then, can ye, Lad Walker? I see it by the look on your face that you understand me full well. Lord Charles grieved for it, did he not? For Kerlain, every day he was away from it, I vow."

He had, Lad thought, turning his face away. Toward the end of his life he'd not spoken of it so much, but Lad had known what was ever in his father's thoughts—this land, these people. Kerlain.

It was a truth that he wasn't about to admit to anyone, certainly not to these men.

"My father," he said slowly, deliberately, "was a Tennessean—an *American*—and glad to be both." He lifted his face to gaze with defiance at the men before him. "He built an estate, Fair Maiden, in Tennessee that was the pride of his life, and *that* was where his heart lay. Not here. Now, if you'll excuse me, I'll be on my way." He turned away to mount his horse.

Conyn Colvaney followed.

"Aye," the older man said angrily, so close that Lad could feel the heat of his breath on the back of his neck before he swung up into his saddle, "and that's just what you should be, if that's how you're feeling about Kerlain— on your way back to America! You're no Walker, by God, nor any kind of proper lord!"

"Da, come away," his son pleaded, pulling at his father's arm to move him out of Lad's path.

The Colvaney refused to move. "Go back to your heathenish ways and your heathenish country!" he shouted up at Lad. "We've no use for you here!"

"There's nothing I'd like better, I assure you," Lad replied stiffly from his greater height, easily moving his horse past the older man. "Good day to you both." He spurred away at a fast clip.

But Lad couldn't ride fast enough to avoid hearing Conyn Colvaney shouting loudly after him, though he was grateful that he couldn't decipher the words. His back and neck were rigid with his anger, and the cold air that he breathed in with such furious vigor knifed at his nose and lungs.

God, but he hated England and everything in it, Kerlain most of all. What a *fool* he'd been to come here, to listen to Uncle Hadley's sentimental hogwash, to let his own heart trick him into thinking any good might come from such a fruitless journey. There'd been nothing he'd come upon since leaving Tennessee that had made the expedition worthwhile—not a blessed thing.

Fine. Very fine.

He'd go to the crumbling castle that his father and The

Colvaney seemed to think so perfect, find out what he could do for Miss Diana Whitleby, do it, and then get the hell off this wretched island. For good.

Damn!

He drew in a long breath and pulled the horse to a slower pace. His heart was racing after his encounter with the Colvaney men, from his fury at the older man's accusations. He'd done nothing wrong. He'd tried to be polite and—damn it!—he'd been downright friendly and proper. A man couldn't do more than that, and nothing else could be expected, at least not in a civilized land like Tennessee. These English folks were beyond comprehension with their ideas of right and wrong. If anything could make him know that he'd never fit in here, Conyn Colvaney's behavior was it.

Any sane man looking at that antiquated heap of a castle would have made the same comments he'd made, despite the fact that they'd been . . . well, a bit rude. The part about the animals especially. His mother would have wrung the ears off his head to hear him talking like that about anyone's home. But that was beside the point. What kind of a person would actually take pride in something like that wreck? he wondered, glaring at the castle in the ever-closing distance. It didn't even begin to approach what Fair Maiden was in beauty and elegance. If Lad ever did decide to take on the earldom, the first thing he would do was tear Castle Kerlain down and build in its place a *real* home—something that'd make the people of Kerlain appreciate the difference between a stuffy English lord who was stuck in the past and an American man who had his thoughts firmly in the future. *Then* they'd realize what was what and be damned glad he'd come across the sea to set them straight. And Conyn Colvaney would take back what he'd said about Lad not being a Walker.

The thought spurred Lad on and steeled his resolve. That was what he'd see before he left England to return to Tennessee: Conyn Colvaney—and everyone else at Kerlain—hailing him as the son of Charles Walker, the grandson of George Walker, the rightful heir to everything that the first Earl of Kerlain had set into motion so long ago. He was a *true* Walker, and he'd prove it, by God, and have Conyn Colvaney eating his words.

Chapter Six

Lad stood before the enormous wood and iron doors and wondered just how a body went about making himself known. He could knock, he supposed, but sincerely doubted that anyone would hear it, or he could pound loudly and shout—which didn't strike him as a particularly impressive way for the man who might be the new Earl of Kerlain to announce himself.

Stepping back, he stared up at the massive structure and felt a sense of awe. Despite its poor condition, there was no denying that the sheer size of the castle had the ability to take a man's breath away. They didn't have anything like this in Tennessee—or anywhere in the United States, that he knew of. He couldn't imagine anyone even attempting to build it, with its huge stone blocks and great height.

He walked down the wide steps to the large courtyard where he'd left his horse, looking all about. The road he'd been on had led directly here, through an ornate arch and gates set in the midst of a tumbling wall that enclosed the area. In his mind's eye, Lad had envisioned knights of old riding through those same gates, ready to fight to defend the castle—or to overtake it. The courtyard itself had been a pleasant surprise, much in contrast with its surroundings, for even dusted with snow it was neat and well-maintained and had clearly been the object of someone's devoted labor. It appeared to wrap around the castle on one end, while at the other it gave way to another gated wall, much lower than the first, beyond which Lad could see a thriving garden. Though it was winter-white now, enough green showed through to make it clear that whoever had cared for the courtyard had also cared for the garden.

The horse stamped impatiently as Lad set his hand upon the reins. He murmured to it soothingly and stroked the animal's nose, wondering if there was a decent barn or stable to keep the beast in for the night, until it might be sent back to Walborough. He hoped against all hope that Kerlain possessed horses of its own, as he had assumed it would. Otherwise, he'd be doing a great deal of walking on his way back to the States.

He contemplated the large doors again and, higher above, the dark and empty windows. It all seemed so lifeless and austere, but he had seen smoke coming from at least two of the chimneys and knew that someone was within. But perhaps this wasn't the entry to the dwelling. Perhaps he should go around to the more modern wing, which looked like a small manor house, and see if that was the way.

He'd make one try here at least, he thought, patting the horse's neck before striding back up the steps with determination. He knocked on the door first, waited a few seconds, then gave three fisted pounds. Nothing.

"Fine," he muttered, tugging at his gloves to pull them on more tightly. "Just dandy. Can't even get into my own castle." He glared at the mighty and immovable doors, and, suddenly, they swung open.

The man who stood there gazed at Lad with a perfectly calm, level expression. He was tall and angular, with a great, bony nose that seemed to take up most of his thin face and clothes that, though spotless and perfectly pressed, were aged and dull. His eyes, betraying no surprise at Lad's presence, moved slowly from the top of Lad's hat—which Lad promptly removed—to the soles of his wet and muddy boots. Then he looked Lad full in the face again and said, "My lord. Welcome to Kerlain."

Lad stared at him, shock tingling from every pore. It was a strange sensation, so unutterably strange, to see this man—this almost mythic figure from his imagination—come suddenly to life. He felt a compelling urge to step forward and hug him, to hail him as a longlost friend, but knew that the gesture would be greeted as both bewildering and unwanted. Lad's voice, when he at last made his mouth open, came out sounding just as stunned as he felt.

"Swithin?"

The tiniest smile curled the elderly servant's lips. He gave a brief nod.

"My lord." His manner was stately and refined, as was his voice. Lad had heard his father's imitation of it a hundred times and more. "You are much like your father, Lord Charles."

"I know," Lad said, feeling stupidly unable to say anything more suitable. "He told us—me and my brother, Joshua—about you. He spoke of you often. And always with great affection."

Again the minute smile pressed upon the man's lips, and a faint stain of pink spread over the papery-white skin of his cheeks. Otherwise, he appeared completely unmoved by the words.

"It was one of the saddest days Kerlain has seen," he said in that same proper tone, "when Lord Charles left us. I was very sorry for it. Shall I send the footman to tend your horse, my lord? Miss Diana will desire that you be brought to her right away."

So much for the sentiment of days gone by, Lad thought with an inward sigh. Aside from that, wasn't *he* supposed to be the earl around here? Wasn't Miss Diana supposed to wait on *his* pleasure?

"Yes," he said, casting a glance back at the horse, which

had wandered a short distance away in search of something to nibble beneath the snow. "He's to be returned to the Walborough Inn tomorrow morning. Kerlain has horses of its own?"

"Yes, my lord," was Swithin's rather frosty reply. "I'm sure you'll find the earl's—the former earl's—mounts to be of the finest stock and temperament. He was a renowned horseman, as was—"

"My father," Lad finished for him. "Yes, I know."

"One more thing, my lord?"

"What is it?"

Swithin stepped stiffly out to the landing and turned to his right.

"The castle isn't properly staffed to keep someone always on watch for your arrival and to make certain the door is opened for you in a timely manner. However, in future, should you wish to make your presence known, you need only tug at the bellpull and I'll come at once. The rope there, do you see?"

"You mean this?" Lad moved to take hold of the rope that appeared from beneath a low stone ledge, and he tugged. Bells sounded from within the castle, deep and loud.

Swithin's expression was patient. "Yes, my lord. Now, if you will be pleased to follow me? Miss Diana will have realized that you've arrived. I'll send Stuart to tend the horse," he said, giving a concentrated look to the lone bag attached to the horse's saddle, "and bring in your . . . things . . . just as soon as I've taken you to her." With that, he turned and walked back into the castle. Lad followed.

It was dark in the entryway, and almost as cold as outdoors, but Lad felt at once as if he'd walked into another world, another . . . time. The size of it, the massive blocks of stone, felt even larger within than without. He was a big man, taller than most other men of his acquaintance, but Castle Kerlain made him know just how small and insignificant he really was. How feeble it had appeared a mile away, but standing now inside it, he felt the strength and secureness of the place, just as his ancestors must have done, along with the difficulties of maintaining such a place. How on earth did one *heat* a dwelling this size, anyhow?

But he hadn't realized the half of it, he discovered a moment later as he followed Swithin through a short hallway, around a corner, and into the biggest single room he'd ever beheld.

"This," said Swithin, pausing as if he understood the awe that kept Lad frozen in place, "is the great hall. Castle Kerlain is rather famous for its grandeur, most specially the great hall. Kings, queens, and the noblest families in Europe have graced this hall with their presence. To receive an invitation to Kerlain," he said, giving Lad a look heavy with meaning, "was to receive a great boon. Many dreamed of being so honored, with good reason."

It was *huge*. Beyond anything Lad could have ever imagined without being forewarned. His gaze moved slowly upward to the ceiling, which loomed high overhead like those of the great European cathedrals he'd heard tell of. The manor at Fair Maiden was big, but four of them could have fit inside this hall.

"It's . . ." He shook his head, unable to say exactly what he meant.

Swithin nodded his understanding and turned his gaze to share the view.

"In my youth," he said, "it was ever kept with banners hanging from the high ceiling and the fires lit at all seasons with a footman stationed on the side of each, ready to serve. Powdered and gloved they were, my lord, and properly dressed. 'Twas always proper here then, my lord, and every man and woman in the castle proud to serve Kerlain and its master.''

Things had clearly changed, Lad thought, as he cast his gaze about the cold, aged, and austere hall. The high walls were unadorned, blackened by centuries of smoke that had been put out by the twelve large fireplaces set at intervals along their length. Indeed, the entire hall was empty of decoration and nearly of furnishings, but Lad could almost envision it the way it had once been, many years ago, as his father had described it to him, lined with tapestries and fine carpets, filled with dark, beautiful furniture. He could imagine great lords and ladies feasting here, and knights of the realm clattering about in full armor—and centuries of Walkers living and dying here, just as The Colvaney had said.

''Pretty cold,'' Lad said, rubbing a hand against one arm in a vain effort to stay warmer. ''Anybody actually live in this part of the castle?''

''No, my lord,'' Swithin said sadly. ''Not for many years, since Lord Charles left Kerlain. A great many things changed after that. The earl remained in his chamber above until his death, of course, but Miss Diana and the servants have lived in the West Wing of the castle since she came to live at Kerlain.''

''In the manor house, you mean?''

Swithin turned his head to give Lad a rather steely look.

''The West Wing of the castle,'' he repeated. ''There is no *manor house* at Kerlain, my lord.'' It was as if the very idea were a grave insult. ''Follow me, please. I'll take you to Miss Diana.''

They walked the length of the great hall, coming midway to an arched doorway that led to a short passageway and from there into what Lad recognized at once as the ''modern wing.'' The room they walked into looked like a large parlor, though it clearly was some sort of greeting area. It was very plain, with a fireplace in one wall and a series of hooks along another, near a set of double doors. Like the rest of what Lad had seen thus far, it was scrupulously clean, though the stained carpets on the floor had seen their share of mud and wet.

"This is the entryway to the West Wing, which is more commonly used," Swithin said, turning to Lad with outstretched hands. "If you please, my lord?"

Lad readily handed the elderly servant his hat and gloves, then shrugged out of his heavy overcoat and passed that over too. Swithin placed them on a nearby table, saying, "Maud will wish to brush them out. This way, please, my lord."

Lad had grown used to the fact that homes in England, like many homes in the Northeastern United States, went upward rather than spread out. At Fair Maiden his mother had greeted visitors in a parlor that was on the same floor as the entryway, and only the bedrooms and sitting rooms had been upstairs, but here people did everything upstairs, except, it seemed, eat.

He followed Swithin up the long, narrow stairway at the end of the room to reach the "living" portion of the wing, to be greeted by the strong, fresh odor of beeswax. Evidence of the polish was everywhere in the hallway into which they stepped, for everything, from the floor to the ceiling to the furniture in between, was immaculately clean and in perfect order. And yet, like the rest of the castle, an aged dullness pervaded the furnishings, carpets, and drapes, giving the dwelling a look of faded elegance, like a once beautiful and vibrant woman grown old and weary.

Swithin walked with his stiff, upright gait to a set of double doors midway down the hall and opened them with a brief movement that was clearly both long-practiced and correct. The odd thought passed through Lad's mind, as he strove to tamp down the sudden fit of nerves that possessed him, that Swithin and Lad's mother—another advocate of perfect protocol—would have gotten along very well.

Swithin looked into the room, straightened full height, and announced, in what sounded to Lad like excessively dire tones, "The Earl of Kerlain has arrived, Miss Diana." He stepped away from the doors and looked at Lad. "My lord?"

Lad drew in a breath, adjusted his neckcloth, and walked forward.

The moment was one of impressions, most of them fleeting save for her. The parlor was large, filled with blues and yellows, very clean and correct, somewhat faded, as the rest of Kerlain was, and very inviting. There was a fire in the hearth, though the room itself was only passingly warm. She was standing near the fire, her hands pressed flat against her skirt.

He didn't know how long he stood there, letting his brain wander in a thousand different shattered directions, unable to collect himself to form some kind of coherent speech.

She was beautiful. God above. *Beautiful.* Raven haired, with enormous dark eyes and skin as white and pure as a china doll—which was very much what she looked like. Her rosebud mouth had opened slightly at the sight of him, showing equally white and perfect teeth, and Lad found himself helplessly staring.

She was tall for a woman—he wouldn't have to bend far at all to kiss her—and possessed of the kind of figure that set his masculine mind to envisioning all sorts of things that might follow such a kiss. The plain gray gown she wore was supposed to show that she was in mourning but only served to make her look utterly dignified and lovely. Her black hair was pulled up from her perfect face, but soft, inky curls escaped at the sides to frame the luminous glow of her skin.

"My lord," she said, and all he could think was that

even her voice sounded beautiful. "Welcome to Kerlain. I'm Diana Whitleby."

She was moving toward him with one hand held out, giving him a smile that made his heart kick from one end of his chest to the other. He took her hand as she drew near and held it, gazing into her face in wonder, not quite sure what to do or say. It occurred to him, dimly, that she wasn't staring back at him in the same way—in the way that women almost always stared at him—or falling over herself because of his looks. In fact, she seemed to be in perfect possession of both her senses and balance.

"I hope your journey was pleasant," she said after a moment, "though I regret that it was made under such unhappy circumstances. Please accept again my sincerest condolences regarding the recent passing of your grandfather, the earl."

She was going to be his wife, Lad thought to himself. This beautiful creature was *his* for the taking—and for a lifetime. What a sensation she was going to cause back in Tennessee, when he took her home to Fair Maiden! Every man in the county was going to fall madly in love with her.

"Ahem." Her smile thinned a bit, and she made a brief attempt to reclaim her hand. Lad's fingers tightened the more, holding her. "I'm so very grateful that you've come to Kerlain in response to my missive," she said, "though I'm certain you'll wish to discuss the details of it in full before assuming any of your responsibilities here." She tugged at her hand again. "Won't you . . . won't you please be seated near the fire and make yourself comfortable? My lord?"

Her growing discomfort finally registered beyond Lad's whirling senses, and he made himself release her. She took an immediate step back, and he held himself in place only by great force of will. Why was she looking at him like that? As if he were some kind of strange animal rather than the man who'd come across half the earth just to wed her? Women *never* looked at him like that. He had to make certain that she didn't have cause to do so again—starting now.

Gathering his frayed wits firmly in hand, or at least as best he could, he said, "Yes. Thank you, Miss Whitleby. It'd be nice to sit for a spell and warm up. It was a cold ride out from Walborough."

The moment he walked past her, Diana let her rigid composure fly and gave way to her complete shock, gaping at Lad Walker's turned back with disbelief. Eoghan had warned her that he was handsome, but he'd not told her the half of it. He was a stunning man. *Stunning.* It was impossible *not* to stare at someone who was so utterly beautiful, who looked as if he'd been fashioned by a Michelangelo. Indeed, a body could only gape at Lad Walker and believe that God had been in a particularly good mood on the day that he was fashioned.

His eyes were the loveliest shade of emerald she'd yet beheld, his thickly waving hair was the color of sweet, ripening wheat, his nose was straight and classically proportioned, his cheekbones were high, but not too prominent, and his mouth—merciful heavens, his mouth was purely sinful. Perhaps he'd been fashioned by the devil rather than by God. Diana wouldn't have been surprised. She'd always found it easy to resist the temptations men sent her way but had an unsettling feeling that she'd not be able to resist *him* at all.

Drawing in a steadying breath, she followed him to the chairs near the fire and fixed her composure upon her face once more before sitting down. Lad Walker waited until she had settled, then took his own seat, stretching his long legs out in a relaxed pose.

"Swithin will have tea sent up directly," she told him. "Though perhaps you may desire something stronger? My godfather—the earl, I mean—kept a supply of brandy in his study, and I should be glad to send for it, if you like." Though she sincerely hoped he'd not, for there wasn't much left, and the earl's tastes had been dreadfully expensive. Diana wanted to make every drop of the few remaining bottles last as long as possible.

"Tea's fine," he said cheerfully. "My mother didn't allow anyone at Fair Maiden to drink hard spirits before four in the afternoon, so we drank plenty of tea and cider during the day. I'm mighty fond of tea."

His words, spoken in his slow, deep Southern accent, flowed one on top of the other like honey pouring out of a jar.

Sin, Diana thought. The man was a walking invitation for a tumble straight into wickedness. It could hardly be wondered that women fell at his feet when he spoke in a manner that could only be termed . . . well, sensual. The thought made Diana hot with embarrassment, and she prayed that she wasn't as flushed as she felt. Sitting across from her, Lad Walker gave a slow, knowing smile that matched his voice, and she hurriedly looked away.

"This portrait above the hearth," she said, turning her thoughts to the first thing she set sight on, "is of the late earl, your grandfather." Her voice, to her dismay, sounded slightly breathless.

Lad Walker, in turn, sounded amused. And pleased. "Is it?" From the corner of her eye Diana saw that he continued to look at her rather than at the painting.

"Yes," she said nervously, wondering at how strangely he behaved. Surely he wasn't a lunatic? Her godfather had always spoken disparagingly of Americans, saying that they were ungodly heathens, contemptuous of every manner of civility, but surely he'd not have asked her to marry one of them if it was really true. "It's considered one of the best likenesses done of him." She rigidly kept her face turned toward it.

Lad Walker gave a slight sigh, then turned his face to look upward at the painting. Diana had always loved it, though it depicted the earl from a time long before she'd known him, as a handsome young man dressed in his most stately attire. Lad Walker apparently didn't share her admiration; a very brief moment passed before she heard him giving a low chuckle.

"Well, well, so that's my granddaddy, the great tyrant. He was a mighty fancy fellow, wasn't he? You couldn't wear clothes like that at Fair Maiden and get a day's work done, most assuredly not. Though I don't suppose he ever lifted his hand to a field tool in his life, so I doubt he worried over such things." His tone grew more thoughtful. "Don't see much of my father in him. Not anything, really. My father had the most gentle nature I ever knew, but this fellow looks about as gentle as a rattlesnake. It's no wonder that they didn't get on. Was he as stern as he seems here?" He was looking at her again.

Diana hardly knew how to reply. The earl had always been held in such great reverence that no one, save perhaps Eoghan, would have dared to speak of him thus. But Lad Walker had a right to an honest answer, and she gave him one.

"There were those who might say that he was a strict master, perhaps even harsh, but he was always very good to me and claimed many loyal friends. He was held in the greatest esteem in this county—most especially by all those at Kerlain. You'll find no one here who'll speak badly of him."

"I gathered that," he replied, tenting his fingers together and setting them just beneath his chin. "I came across Conyn Colvaney and his son as I rode to the castle and was read something of a sermon by The Colvaney on my lack of proper feeling.''

"Oh, dear," said Diana, wishing very much that such a meeting hadn't occurred. The Colvaney would have by now spread word of the new earl's arrival throughout Kerlain's citizenry. She could only pray that Eoghan wouldn't hear tell of it.

Lad Walker gave a brief nod. "It didn't surprise me overmuch. I hope you'll understand, Diana—Miss Whitleby—that my feelings for my late grandfather, and for Kerlain, aren't what you may expect. My home is in the United States, at Fair Maiden, where I was born and raised. I want to do what's right by both you and the people here, but, though he missed this land until his last living day, my father never meant for me to take up the title. He didn't prepare either my brother or me for such a thing. I think we might do better to talk about this marriage you proposed and about whether you'd like to leave this drafty old relic and come back to the States to live at Fair Maiden." He sat forward, warming to the subject in what Diana perceived to be a flatteringly eager manner. "It's just about the finest piece of property in all of Tennessee, and far and away the most beautiful. You'd think you'd died and gone to heaven the minute you set sight on it—both the house and the land. The house isn't near as big as this old place, of course, but hardly anything is, for that matter." He smiled in a way that made Diana's heart thump loudly in her ears. "But it's one of the best homes in Tennessee, and people just about fall over themselves to get an invitation to visit. You'd be one of the most envied hostesses in the state, just as my mother was."

Tennessee? Diana thought with confusion. Surely he couldn't be thinking of Tennessee now that he'd seen Kerlain. Kerlain was one of the noblest, certainly one of the oldest, estates in England. Nothing could compare to it, as anyone must see. But perhaps he was overwhelmed at realizing the boon that had come to him in such an unexpected manner. He'd not been raised to know that he'd be the Earl of Kerlain and would be awed by the thought of what it meant for him—who had only ever thought to be a mere commoner—to be elevated to such unimagined heights.

"It's perfectly understandable that your father, Lord Charles, would have had no expectation that either he or his sons would inherit the title," Diana said, striving to reassure him on the matter, "certainly not after the manner in which he and the late earl parted. It was due to the great kindness of my godfather that any hope of reconciliation was realized, and if Lord Charles were still alive, I believe—truly, sir—that he would have been exceedingly glad to know that one of his sons could return to England to take his rightful place at Kerlain. Do you not agree that this is so?"

He looked a little taken aback. "I suppose so, but you have to understand about Fair Maiden, what it meant to him, and to everyone in my family—"

A soft scratch came at the door, and he fell silent. The next moment Swithin opened the parlor doors and Maudie, head held perfectly high as if she were a maid in the king's household, entered bearing the tea tray. Her gaze was kept on Diana, who knew perfectly well that the older woman was tremblingly aware of their strange, new American master, just as they all were.

Maudie carried the tray to a low table near Diana, set it down, then gave a formal curtsy to her mistress before turning to curtsy to Lad Walker.

"My lord," Diana said, as formal as Maudie, "this is Maudie Farrell, of the Farrell clan. She has served at Castle Kerlain for forty-five years, since she was but fifteen years of age."

To her great surprise—and no little distress—Lad

Walker rose from his chair, standing to take Maudie by the hand.

"I'm glad to meet you, Maudie," he said warmly, seemingly unaware of the manner in which Maudie shrank from his touch. "My father spoke of you to me often. You were his nursemaid?"

Maudie shook her head and pulled her hands free. Diana both heard and saw with a sinking heart just how unsettled she was by Lad Walker's rude informality. "No, my lord," she said, stepping back and striving to regain her dignity. "I only helped the nursemaid as I could, when she required it. Though 'twas ever a joy to tend to Lord Charles, and I was pleased to be of service." She curtsied again. "Welcome to Kerlain, m'lord."

She left the parlor as quickly as she could, and Swithin, giving Diana his chilliest look, closed the doors behind her.

Lad Walker stood where he was, gazing at the closed doors, until Diana said, "Please, sit and be comfortable, my lord. I'll pour the tea."

He stayed where he was, shaking his head. "I don't understand you people. You're so . . . different."

He thought *they* were different? Diana thought with disbelief. *He* was the one who was so strange, who didn't know how to behave in a proper manner. Hadn't he realized how greatly he had overset Maudie with his forward behavior? She'd come to give him honor, to greet him with all the respect and properness due the Earl of Kerlain, and he'd turned the moment away from its solemnity to something casual and offhanded.

"Much will be different here from what you've known in your country," she said softly, "but in time you will learn. Your heritage will surely show itself—the strength of it— now that you've returned to your proper home."

He uttered a humorless laugh. "Because I'm a Walker,

Diana? I don't think that counts for much. I'm still half American, you know.''

She was flustered at his easy use of her Christian name but made no comment against it, as they were soon to be wed and she supposed he could be allowed such a familiarity.

''This may be so, but that part of you can't compare to the half that's English. The Walkers are descended through hundreds of years in a line of great nobility and of the finest, most honorable blood England might claim. It flows strongly in your veins and ties you to Kerlain and the earldom as no mere human desire might. I love Kerlain greatly—more than I can put into words, I vow—but for all that I can't claim the same ties to it that you can. No matter how desperately I wish I might. My prayer now is that my children will be able to do so, because—if we marry—they will have that blood running through them, and it will tie them to Kerlain as I cannot. You will pass such a precious heritage to them because of that English part of you—not the American part.''

He muttered something that she couldn't hear and gave a shake of his head. Diana sat where she was, waiting, and at last he turned to face her, his gaze searching.

''You're to inherit the castle, and I'm to have the land and title, isn't that right? I had a letter from some lawyer in London, Sybble or some such . . .''

''Mr. Sibbley,'' Diana corrected. ''Yes, he was my godfather's solicitor and has all the papers regarding our coming union.'' She flushed, and turned her attention to pouring him a cup of tea. ''If it comes, that is. You needn't feel forced to wed me, despite your grandfather's wishes. I should never make any man wed me against his will, even for Kerlain.''

''But you're willing if I'm willing,'' he stated flatly. ''Why is that?'' He moved to accept the cup she offered.

"How is it that you even came to be at Kerlain and my grandfather's ward? We're not related, are we?"

"Only distantly," she said, "else a marriage between us could never have been considered. In truth, the connection is so thin it might as well be water rather than blood. As to my being here . . ." She hesitated, gazing up at him with a measure of uncertainty. "Did your father tell you why he and the late earl had such a falling out?"

"Some of it," he replied. "There was a woman involved. Someone the earl had picked out for my father to marry."

"Yes. That was my mother. The woman your father was betrothed to wed."

Lad Walker set the teacup down on the tea tray with a rattle, then straightened and stared down at her.

"Your *mother?*"

Diana didn't know whether to be insulted or amused. "Do you find it so difficult to believe?"

"God almighty," he said, pacing away from her and running a hand through his hair. "That does make things a bit peculiar, doesn't it? What was the old man trying to do?" He turned back to look at her. "Fix you and me up in place of them?"

The same thought had occurred to Diana, but she hadn't been able to believe her godfather capable of such duplicity.

"I don't think so. I believe, truly, that he merely thought of the good of Kerlain when he revealed the fact of your birth, that it was legal and that you were therefore the new earl. As to our marriage, I think he simply wished to make certain I should remain here and be cared for. You might have very well thrown me out of Kerlain otherwise."

The heated, blatantly appreciative look he set upon her made Diana's toes curl in her slippers.

"I'd never have done that, honey," he replied slowly, his

tone full of meaning. "That'd be the last thing any fool would do, and I hope and pray I'm not that kind of fool."

"Oh," Diana said stupidly, blinking at him. What on earth could she say in reply to *that?*

"So, your mother was the one with the money?" He began to saunter back toward her. "My father told me about that. He was supposed to marry her and then use her money to fix up Kerlain. My grandfather had it all arranged, but when Daddy refused to go along he was disinherited and thrown out. Seems like a pretty harsh punishment for a fellow who's just following his heart."

"Your father was banished, that's true," Diana admitted, "but the fault was his own. He and my mother had been betrothed since childhood, and the earl had every expectation that her money would come into Kerlain upon their marriage. That may sound mercenary to you, but in our parents' day it was commonly done in England and is still perfectly acceptable even now. My mother knew why she'd been chosen as Lord Charles's bride, and her expectation was that, in exchange for the money she would bring to the union, she would become the Countess of Kerlain. It is a title any young woman would covet, and she was more than willing to honor the bargain made between the earl and her father."

"That's fine for her end of things," Lad Walker conceded, "but there's no reason why my father should have gone along with it if he didn't want to. When he married my mother he married for love, and because of her he was the happiest man on God's earth until the day he died."

"How nice for him," Diana said tightly, anger surging through her. She set her teacup aside and stood, wishing she were taller so that she might meet Lad Walker eye to eye. "His selfish act of abandoning my mother insured his own happiness but brought shame and ruin to hundreds of others—most especially the people of Kerlain, who might have expected a greater measure of loyalty from the man who was to one day be their lord!''

Lad Walker's eyes widened with surprise at her vehemence, and he stepped back, away from her. ''I didn't mean—''

''No, I daresay you didn't,'' Diana said hotly, moving to stand directly in front of him. ''But men seldom do, as I've learned to my regret. You think only of yourselves, your own comforts and pleasures, and the rest of your fellow men may just as well rot for all that you'll do to lend them aid. Every evil that's befallen Kerlain has come from men. The late earl, living as if the land were in its past glory, turned a blind eye to the condition of the crops and the castle until it was nearly too late to find a remedy, and when he *did* find a remedy''—she poked Lad in the chest with a stiff finger— ''*your* father refused to go along with it. And my mother's father! He was the worst of all. When she did marry, it was to a man he didn't approve of, and he disinherited her completely!'' She was shouting now, still poking him in the chest to punctuate her words, and she didn't particularly care. ''We were so poor that my parents didn't even have the money to buy a doctor's services when my father fell ill, and my mother after him. After they died I'd have been sent to a workhouse, though I was but a babe and useless to one and all, if your grandfather hadn't felt some remnant sense of responsibility for what had befallen me because of his son's selfish behavior.''

''Diana, I'm sorry,'' Lad Walker said soothingly, reaching out at last to grab her hand and stop her from poking him. ''I didn't know. I never knew, or realized—''

''Of course you didn't, but it's the truth all the same. If your father had only stayed, none of it would have happened, none of the misery that the people of Kerlain have suffered since the day he left.''

Now he was starting to look angry.

"That's not fair. You can't lay the blame entirely at his door."

"Oh, yes, I can! And all I want to know from you, Lad Walker, is what your intentions are toward Kerlain. Are you going to stay and face your responsibilities or run like your father did?"

His face darkened with tight fury and he grabbed Diana up by the arms, pulling her against himself.

"You look sweet as a little china doll," he muttered, "but you've got the temper of a shrew."

He bent and pressed his mouth against hers in a hot, hard kiss, holding her even more tightly when she struggled. His mouth was demanding, seeking, but—surprisingly—not painful. After a moment the pressure against her lips softened, as did the grip on her arms, and he lifted his mouth slightly, only to press it down again, kissing her as gently as a lover might do. When he lifted his head, he was smiling.

"I'm going to stay and marry you, Diana Whitleby, that's what I'm going to do, and God help any man who tries to stop me. After that I guess I'll become the Earl of Kerlain, and you'll be the countess, and we'll see what happens from there. That sound all right with you?"

"Yes," she whispered, breathless and trembling. "P-perfectly all right."

"Good," he said, and lowered his mouth to hers again. "Now that we're engaged we can get to know each other better. How do you do, Miss Diana?" he said, and kissed her without waiting for a reply.

Chapter Seven

So many rules. So many "proper" ways of doing things. Lad was just about ready to make a run for the hills.

Nothing about him seemed to be right, but everything that was wrong had to be fixed within the span of one day, because Diana insisted that they be married as quickly as possible, preferably on the following morning. The idea had amazed Lad, for he would have thought it impossible to make arrangements so quickly, but she had assured him that a special license for their marriage had already been procured by the local sheriff, who would also officiate at their union, and that the strictures of mourning could be overlooked due to the circumstances in which they found themselves. Lad hadn't argued, even though he'd wondered what circumstances could possibly be so dire that they couldn't spend a few days getting to know each other better. But that didn't matter. He'd known he was going to marry Diana Whitleby from the very moment he'd set sight on her, and whether it happened tomorrow or the day after or the following week, she *would* be his wife.

His person was the first objectionable matter. His hair was too long, his hands too rough, and the recent bath and shave he'd had at the Walborough Inn not worthy of the Earl of Kerlain. He'd barely been escorted to the chamber that was to be his before both Swithin and Maudie descended upon him with all the vigor of a well-trained battalion. He was amazed at how thorough they were, especially Swithin, who had an amazing amount of energy for a man his age. He scrubbed Lad's skin until it was raw, burning, and free of dirt. Working in the fields at Fair Maiden and carrying a gun during the war had left his hands with thick, dirty calluses that Lad would have sworn he'd carry to his grave, but when he emerged from the bathtub at Kerlain those same calluses had somehow disappeared, along with every speck of mud and grease beneath his fingernails. He was as fresh and clean as a newborn babe.

His clothes were the next object of disapproval. Diana was aghast that Lad hadn't been wearing mourning for his grandfather, the late earl, and was more distressed to discover that he hadn't brought clothing suitable for anything more than the hard journey he'd just completed. He explained that he had every intention of having himself correctly outfitted just as soon as he could, but that wasn't soon enough for Diana. The Earl of Kerlain must be properly attired—in mourning—for his marriage, and that was that. Anything less would be a grave insult to the title, as well as to the people of Kerlain. Lad didn't like the idea of wearing mourning for a man who'd branded him as a bastard even before his birth, but in the end he and Diana came to a compromise. She would find suitable mourning clothes for him to wear, and he'd wear them—but *only* in memory of his mother and brother.

While Lad was having his transforming bath, Diana was rummaging through the late earl's clothes, unearthing several complete outfits that dated from the earl's younger years. They were, in Lad's opinion, the most laughable and absurd costumes he'd ever seen. There were white leggings and black knee breeches made of the finest silk, pure linen shirts covered in frills and lace, black silk waistcoats ornately stitched with so much gold and silver thread that they were blinding, and matching jackets that looked so small and tight that he figured he'd be fortunate to move his arms without splitting all the seams. With Swithin's aid, however, Lad managed to squeeze into the ancient garments, grateful, at least, that his grandfather had been a big, tall fellow in his youth.

He stared at himself in a mirror for a full half minute, then burst into a fit of laughter that had Swithin frowning.

"These things must be sixty years old!" Lad declared, grinning at the sight of himself looking as if he'd just stepped out an era long past. "All I need now is a powdered wig and I'll be ready for court." He made the elderly servant a mockingly elegant bow. "At your service, m'lord," he said, and laughed.

Swithin was clearly unamused.

"The late earl, in his day, was one of the most admirably dressed men in the country," he informed Lad stiffly.

Lad lifted his arms to more closely inspect the ridiculously long fountains of lace at his wrists.

"I'll just bet he was, but in Tennessee he'd have been the laughingstock of the whole state. Not that we didn't ever see the like, you understand. There were a few British dandies dressed up just so during the war—some of the officers and such. Never could understand why anyone fighting a war would dress like he was about to attend a fancy ball, but they did."

Swithin looked at him with mild reproof. "Officers in His Majesty's army are gentlemen and noblemen, my lord. It is quite right that they should be accordingly attired. Just as you shall be from this day forward."

Lad was amused. "Will I?"

"Oh, yes, my lord," Swithin assured him dryly. "I shall serve as your valet, and you may certainly believe that I will perform my duties with diligence, no matter how challenging they may be."

When Lad rejoined Diana in the parlor an hour later,

having been combed and brushed and polished to perfection, she circled him, a smile on her face, and then gazed up at him with glowing approval.

"Now you are the Earl of Kerlain," she said happily, "or will be as soon as we're wed on the morrow. You are truly a nobleman of the highest order, my lord."

He took her hand, bowed over it in as courtly a gesture as he could manage, then lifted it to his lips and kissed it. He'd never felt such enchantment with a woman before. The way she looked at him—smiled at him—did things to him inside that he couldn't begin to understand. Perhaps he'd fallen in love with her at first sight, though he'd never believed anything like that was possible. Or perhaps he'd simply been overwhelmed by her beauty, though he'd known many beautiful women before and never felt the like with any of them. All he knew was that he couldn't leave her: beyond that he couldn't discern what would happen, though he envisioned his own preference. They'd be married, and he'd do what he could for Kerlain. In time, he'd talk her into going back home with him to Tennessee, and then they'd truly begin a new life together.

"I'm glad you approve," he told her now. "I just hope you'll let me get a tailor in here sooner than later to fix me up in something more comfortable. Sure isn't much I could do in these things. Like ride a horse. Or sit. Or walk." He grinned to let her know he was only teasing.

"They are rather ancient, I know," she said with gentle commiseration. "There's a tailor at Woebley who can come within a few days if we send a missive to him now. My godfather's tailor is in London, and he'd go twice a year to have his wardrobe updated."

"He had the money for that?" Lad asked. "Seems like there's better things around here to spend money on than fancy clothes twice a year."

She flushed and moved away, and he was sorry for having embarrassed her by speaking of Kerlain's financial troubles.

"He was the Earl of Kerlain," she said quietly. "It was right that he be properly dressed, and his people would have been terribly distressed were it otherwise. Indeed, they would have gone hungry before seeing their lord dressed in a manner beneath his station."

Lad made a scoffing sound. "That's crazy."

"I realize it sounds strange," she admitted, "but you must understand how commoners view the aristocracy—and how they expect them to live and behave." She turned to face him. "It's what they'll expect of you too."

"What," he asked with growing suspicion, "will they expect? Exactly?"

Her hands fluttered in a nervous gesture. "The people of Kerlain will only truly accept you as their lord if you behave in a certain manner, as a proper lord would do. Your birth decrees that you've been touched by grace"—she ignored the laugh he gave—"as they have not been, and they expect you to be different in almost every way. In your speech, your dress, your home"—she indicated their surroundings—"and in what you eat and drink. You're a nobleman, and your life must be far above theirs."

"But I'm not a nobleman," he said calmly, evenly. "I was raised a commoner, though there's no denying that we were better off than most folks or that my mother taught my brother and me to have good manners and to behave ourselves. I've worked in the fields at Fair Maiden alongside my brother and my father's hired laborers, and I've mucked out the barns and taken care of the livestock. I was a captain during the war, and although I rode a horse while my men walked, I carried a gun and fought alongside them in every battle. *Beside* them, Diana, and not at the rear of the lines where some of your noble British officers remained. That's what I am, Diana, and it can't be changed."

"Not your essential self, of course," she said, "though I yet believe the noble blood within you will prove itself more strongly as time goes on. If you had been raised properly at Kerlain, as was your birthright, you'd never have worked in the fields or served so closely beside your men during the war. You would have known that such behaviors were far beneath your due as a nobleman. Indeed, such things would have gravely offended both the people of Kerlain and any common British soldiers you might have commanded. I've told you already that English noblemen are considered to be touched by grace, but perhaps you don't fully understand. We have none of your American equality here," she said earnestly, "and want none."

"I know what you people think, but it's plain foolish," Lad told her, striving to control his growing anger. "All men are created equal. That's what I grew up knowing, and that's what I'll believe all the way to my grave."

Diana knitted the fingers of her hands together and looked at him pleadingly. "I don't ask you to stop believing it. I only want you to understand what the people of Kerlain believe and to consider their sensibilities. These people *want* the nobility to be different from them and to live differently. You'd not wish to offend them, would you, Lad?" Her expression was intently hopeful. "You're the Earl of Kerlain—the lord to whom they owe allegiance. Can you not attempt, even a little, to meet their expectations?"

"I can't be anything but what I am," he replied grumpily.

"Certainly not. But there are lesser aspects of your person that you might bring a change to." She seemed to have a hard time meeting him eye to eye any longer and lowered her gaze to stare at her folded hands. "Your appearance has already been made acceptable, in but a few short hours, and will improve even more greatly when the tailor from Woebley has done his work. But, now, I think"—she cleared her throat—"we might address your manner of speech."

He stared at her. "My speech? Is there something wrong with it?"

"Oh, no," she said hastily. "At least, I'm sure it's perfectly acceptable in a place such as Tennessee. But in England, a member of the aristocracy is expected to speak with a certain measure of distinction. And polish. I don't believe anything can be done about your accent, though you might strive to lessen it somewhat. But a nobleman is also a man of education and should speak with great authority and ease."

"I see," he said, wondering where that bottle of brandy was that she'd mentioned earlier. A drink right about now would be welcome. He turned to look about the room, wishing that he could get out of the clothes he was in. They felt more confining every moment.

"It shouldn't be a very difficult thing to do," Diana said, and he could hear the anxiety in her voice. "You need only think a moment before you speak, and attempt to make yourself sound like—"

"I know what you want me to sound like," he bit out tightly. "I met a fellow at the inn in Walborough the other day who would have suited your notions of a proper earl to the letter. He was a viscount—Viscount Carden." He cast a glance at her, saw the pained expression on her face, then turned away again. "He would have suited you perfectly. Very well-spoken, he was. I could parrot him, I suppose. If it means that much to you."

He couldn't believe what he was saying. He'd fallen head over ears for the girl, and she clearly didn't give a damn about him beyond making him over in the image of the late earl. He was furious at her, and hurt, and equally furious at himself for being so ready to give in just to make her happy.

"Lad."

A soft touch fell on his arm. He glanced down to see her hand on his sleeve, her impossibly perfect hand. Turning, he looked into her face and saw a measure of sorrow and remorse that tore at his heart.

"I don't want you to speak like Viscount Carden," she said softly. "I don't want you to speak like anyone but yourself." There were tears in her eyes, but she smiled. "Forgive me, please? It was very wrong of me to ask such a thing of you."

"No, I'm the one who's sorry." He covered her hand with his own, thinking that he would do anything, perform any feat, to keep this woman from knowing tears—especially tears he'd so stupidly wrought. "I'm rather stubborn, which I suppose is something you'll learn about me pretty soon. I mean," he amended, striving to speak more properly, "something you'll learn about me in time." He smiled too. "I'll do my best to give the people of Kerlain the kind of man they want in an earl." He bent and kissed her swiftly. "But when it's just you and me, I get to relax. Is it a deal?"

She gave a watery laugh, nodding. "Yes, my lord, we have an understanding. Thank you. I shall consider it my wedding present—the best gift you could have given me."

"Wedding present, is it?" he repeated thoughtfully. "I didn't think about that, but it's a good idea. Maybe we should spend a few minutes thinking about what you can give me." He grinned at the way she blushed, and ran two fingers across one of her cheeks in a gentle sweep. "Yes, indeed, my lady, I have a few definite thoughts that we might discuss."

She surprised him by rising up suddenly on her toes, setting her arms about his neck, and placing her mouth against his in a sweet, melting kiss that left Lad feeling dizzy.

Tears yet shone in her eyes as she gazed up at him. "By

God above, I vow that I'll do everything in my power to make you happy, Lad Walker. You've come to save Kerlain, and me, and I shall spend all of my life being grateful. But come.'' Stepping back, she took one of his hands with both of hers. ''Let me show you something of Kerlain before the day grows too dark. You'll wish to know something of your new land, and there is much I wish to tell you about it before we wed on the morrow.''

Chapter Eight

Diana had dreamed of the day when she would wed. She'd envisioned the moment hundreds of times, imagined every detail in full—and now, finally, it had all come to pass. Oh, it wasn't exactly what she'd hoped it might be. The once grand church at Kerlain was now as ancient and crumbling as the rest of the castle; in more than one place the pale winter sun filtered in tiny streams through cracks in the high ceiling, the faded tapestries hanging on the walls were tattered with both age and lack of care, and the few remaining pews were so fragile that no one but the children dared sit on them. After the wedding was over, the assembled would move to the great hall in the castle proper, where Diana and Maudie had laid out a very modest repast by raiding Kerlain's even more modest larder, and where beer would be drunk in place of wine. People would dance to stay warm as much as to celebrate, though it would certainly be more comfortable in the hall than in the church. It was so cold in the huge structure that Diana felt the chill straight through to her bones and knew that everyone else present was suffering too.

No, it wasn't quite the grand wedding of her dreams, but that didn't matter. None of it mattered, not even the wedding gown she was wearing, old and unfashionable as it was. What mattered was that she was at Kerlain, surrounded by all the people of Kerlain, and marrying a man who exceeded beyond measure all that she had hoped and dreamed for. There had been a few moments since Lad Walker had arrived at Kerlain when Diana had thought he might prove to be a figment of her imagination, that he might suddenly disappear and leave her wretched and lonely for the remainder of her life. But he was real, and he was here, standing right beside her, holding her hands in his and repeating the vows as Sir Anthony, accompanied by Parson Moore, spoke them.

Everything had been provided for beforehand by her godfather—the license, the proper papers, even a beautiful ruby wedding ring for Diana, which she recognized at once as a family heirloom that had descended throughout the years from the very first Countess of Kerlain. Tears filled her eyes as Lad slid the ring gently on her finger, and she gazed up at him, blinking, only just realizing the great import of what they were doing. She was not only becoming his wife, and he her husband, but they were becoming the lord and lady of Kerlain, carrying on a great and noble heritage and taking on the grave responsibility of both the title and the estate. How fitting it was that the people of Kerlain should stand as witnesses to the union—as unwilling as they'd been to do so. She'd spent the better part of the previous evening arguing, in private, where Lad couldn't hear them, with both The Farrell and The Colvaney. They'd been adamantly opposed to accepting Lad Walker as their lord and had insisted that they'd never recognize him as such, even if he did marry her and claim the title. Diana had been forced to use every wile she possessed in bringing them to the point of simply agreeing to attend the service and bless the union—for, having no father to give her away, she had dearly hoped that she might receive the blessing of these two men whom she held in the greatest esteem. They'd seemed little mollified by this, but once the idea of standing up for her had taken root, the two men had puffed out with pride and decided that they must put aside their animosity toward their new lord in order to fully support Diana. It was enough for a start, she had decided. First the wedding, and then she would face each day as it came in her attempts to win the people over to Lad's side.

Almost before she knew it, Lad was kissing her and the ceremony was over. All those surrounding them, who had stood in such silence beforehand, burst out into a sudden, raucous cheer, breaking the spell of solemnity. Lad flushed, grinning down into Diana's face, then gave a loud whoop to match the cheering and picked her up by the waist, lifting her from the ground and swinging her about in a circle before bringing her back down to meet his ardent kiss.

"And now, my lord," said Sir Anthony, laughing and clapping Lad soundly on the shoulder, "let us, I pray you, get into the castle and out of this cold!"

"Yes," Diana agreed happily, addressing all the assembled. "The fires have been lit in the hall and food and drink laid out. We'll dance and make a merry day!"

The cheers that greeted this pronouncement were louder than the first, and Lad and Diana pushed through to lead their guests out of the chapel.

Just as they neared them, the doors were thrust open, and Diana came to an abrupt stop, gripping Lad's arm to keep him with her.

Eoghan stood at the opening, breathing harshly. Behind him in the courtyard was a horse that had been hard driven, flanked by two of Eoghan's footmen, also on mount.

"Eoghan," Diana murmured, frightened by the expression he held upon her. It was beyond fury, beyond hate—he looked as if he would gladly commit murder in that moment.

Lad's hand slid comfortingly about Diana's waist, holding her closer as if he understood her agitation.

"Viscount Carden," he said, his voice filled with pleasant surprise. "You must be a closer neighbor than I'd thought. Have you come for the wedding?" He glanced at Diana with a questioning smile. "I mentioned Viscount Carden to you yesterday, but you didn't tell me that you know him."

"She knows me well," Eoghan replied, still breathing harshly, still holding his intent gaze on Diana. "Exceedingly so. How strange it is to see you here, Lad. Or perhaps I must now call you Lord Kerlain, for that is who you are, is it not?" At last he looked at Lad. "You may imagine my surprise to find that the gentleman I lent aid to was a nobleman in disguise. What a clever fellow you are, Lad Walker."

Diana felt tension stiffening Lad's body, close as he stood beside her, and she sent up a silent prayer that he'd not let Eoghan goad him into a temper. His tone, when he spoke, was calm and friendly.

"I'm sorry about not telling you straight out who I was when we met at the inn, but I told you why that was."

"Oh, yes, indeed," Eoghan said. "You thought I'd help Harry toss you out of the inn if I knew the truth." With a bitter laugh he took a step nearer the newlywed pair. "How ironic to think back upon it now, my lord. And to think of how you spoke of your possible marriage to the same woman I meant to make my own wife. God, yes," he murmured with simmering rage, "I would have helped Harry. I would have gladly tossed you out into the snow with the prayer that you'd freeze to death, you thieving bastard!"

"Lad!" Diana held him back with difficulty. "Please. Don't."

"*Diana* was the woman you meant to take as your wife?" Lad said with disbelief.

"Aye, and she would have been mine if you'd not come to force her to the altar!" Eoghan shouted furiously. "And for naught but the sake of a title that a man such as you should never be allowed to claim.''

"Stop this, Eoghan!" Diana cried. "It's not true. Not a word of it.''

"Is it not?" he charged, facing her. "Everyone in Kerlain knows the truth of what I say. You would have been my wife, and I their lord—the lord they would have chosen for themselves before ever letting a filthy American lay claim to Kerlain. Is that not so, people of Kerlain?" he shouted aloud, addressing the assembled.

A loud murmuring started up, pushing Diana beyond civility. She pushed out of Lad's protective grasp and rounded on Eoghan.

"No." Diana said the single word with such authority that the room fell silent almost at once. Circling Eoghan slowly, making him turn at her own measure to hold her gaze, Diana shook her head. "The choice was not theirs, Eoghan Patterson, but *mine,* and mine alone. This castle is mine,'' she said, flinging out a hand and daring anyone present to contradict her, "and the land and title come through me.'' With slow care she neared him, and her voice grew soft in the rapt silence that surrounded them. "I told you that I would never wed you, Eoghan. Even if Lad Walker had not come, I would *never* have wed you. Say what you will,'' she said even more softly, her hard, narrow gaze held fast on his own, "but that is God's own truth, and it cannot be changed.''

"It can, Diana,'' he said with equal quiet, in so hushed a tone that she knew she alone could hear his words. "Only stand back, my girl; watch me do it.''

He straightened all of a sudden and turned to face Lad.

"I find myself rebuked,'' he said, gruff and unfriendly, but apparently vanquished. "And perhaps rightly so. I had word of your marriage only hours ago, and was deeply . . . well, I can only say that I was deeply distressed. My hopes

. . . all my hopes for the future . . ." He ran a hand through his hair in a gesture of despair and turned away. "But that can in no way excuse my reprehensible behavior, as Lady Kerlain has so rightly reproved me." His face darkened at the words, his countenance filled with remorse, and no one watching him—save Diana—could have been unmoved by the sight of such blatant contrition.

As for Diana, she had never seen such a performance and knew full well that his sudden turnabout was entirely false and to his own purpose. She could scarce believe that everyone else present was so easily taken in by the act, but that had ever been Eoghan's greatest gift—gulling one and all to his benefit. She certainly wasn't going to be taken in. He'd ruined her wedding day, and for that she'd never forgive him.

She felt a hand close on her arm, pulling her away from where Eoghan stood. It was Lad, looking as if he'd had enough.

"I think you'd better apologize to my wife before you make any more speeches to the rest of us," he told Eoghan. "And then you'd best leave."

"Of course," Eoghan began, but Diana cut him off.

"I don't desire Lord Carden's apologies," she said, setting her hand on Lad's muscular arm. "I only wish to celebrate our marriage." Smiling up at her husband in a manner that she knew would infuriate Eoghan, she added, "Can we not proceed to the hall, as we meant to do before we were interrupted? I'm certain Lord Carden would wish to let us pretend that he had never come at all." She gave Eoghan a brief, pointed look, which he returned with emotionless silence.

Lad covered Diana's hand warmly with his own.

"Of course. If you'll excuse us, my lord?"

Eoghan was forced to stand aside to let them walk past him and out of the church.

Lad escorted her out into the courtyard as grandly as if they were the king and queen of England, a gesture for which Diana was exceedingly grateful. He must have understood that the people of Kerlain might not follow them if they'd displayed any less grandeur and assurance, and yet she still suffered a moment of fear as she and Lad walked toward the entrance to the great hall, waiting for the sound of other footsteps to trail their own. When it came, many long, agonizing seconds later, it came all at once, a rush of footfall exiting the church and filling the courtyard with the sound of snow being trampled underfoot.

Diana released the breath she'd been holding and was surprised to hear Lad doing the same. They looked at each other, exchanging first wide-eyed amazement and then, after a self-conscious moment, laughter. It was the first moment of true intimacy that Diana had known with Lad, going beyond the few brief kisses they'd shared. It was a sharing of selves, and, even more, she thought, as they neared the doors to Kerlain that had been thrown open for them, it was a good beginning.

''Are you certain you'll be all right, then?'' Maudie asked, standing beside the hearth, where she'd been poking at and rearranging the coals. '''Tis awful cold, miss. I mean,'' she amended quickly, ''m'lady. I must come used to giving you your proper name, now, mustn't I? And it's true that you're the lady of Kerlain, not that you haven't been all along, since the very day you came here, though you were but a babe at the time, of course.'' She rubbed one hand along her arm and gave a shake of her head. ''But for all that, I can't understand why you should insist upon staying here tonight. It's so very cold.''

Diana sipped the hot cup of tea that she held cradled in both hands, striving to make herself warmer. Of the three fireplaces that were meant to heat the large chamber, only one worked well enough—and that only just—to make use of.

"This is the chamber belonging to the Countess of Kerlain," she told her maid, "and this is where I've ever sworn I would spend my wedding night, just as every other countess has done before me. The fire will warm the room presently," she said, striving mightily to keep her teeth from chattering. "And there are plenty of blankets on the bed to keep my lord and me warm." She looked longingly at the tall, grand bed in the middle of the room, counting the seconds now until Maudie left her so that she could dive beneath those same covers.

"Let me just run this beneath the covers, miss," Maudie said, approaching the bed with the long-handled warming pan, "and you'll get right in and be even warmer. Now, is there anything else you'll be needing, miss . . . m'lady?" With a deft movement she flicked the covers up and pushed the heated pan beneath, running it along the length of the sheets to warm them. "Do you feel ready for what's to come? As your dear mother's no longer alive to advise you on such matters, I'd be glad to tell you what I can, if you like. Old Maudie's not been widowed so long that she's forgotten what there is to know about men. Not that there was much to forget in the first place, mind you," she added with a glancing wink.

Diana laughed and said reprovingly, "Maudie Farrell!"

"Ah, my Samuel was a good man, no mistaking it, and took the Farrell name without a fuss, as some of those who marry into our good family are given to do. But he was a man all the same, my lady, which you'll soon come to know is a difficult thing to overcome, no matter how good a fellow may be. Though my Sam was better than most, and that's God's own truth."

"Samuel was indeed a wonderful man," Diana said, setting her teacup aside. "If Lad Walker is half so good to me, I'll be a fortunate wife."

Maudie nodded. "He may not know all he should about being a proper earl, and he may be a heathen American, but for all that he's a fine figure of a man—God's my witness I've never seen the like—and he looks at you just the way a husband should. And you," she said matter-of-factly, pulling the warming pan out from the sheets, "look at him in much the same manner."

Diana was too embarrassed to meet the other woman's eye. "I'm sure I do no such thing," she protested without much force.

"Oh, indeed and you do, my good Lady Kerlain, and there's no shame in such as that between a wife and her lawful husband, nor in anything else that's between them alone. Now, you just bear that in mind this night, my lady, and you'll be fine." Maudie moved to set the warming pan near the fire once more. "Come along now, and we'll get you warm under the covers."

Diana hugged her long and hard. "Oh, Maudie. Thank you. For everything, especially for today. It wouldn't have been half so wonderful if I'd not had you to help me."

Maudie patted her back with loving hands. "Now, now, none of that. There's no need to be thanking old Maudie for anything at all. Get you into bed before the sheets grow cold again, and let me send Lord Kerlain in before he begins to freeze to death too. Poor man will be shaking in his bones, I vow, without any fire to keep him warm in the earl's chamber. Now that he's come, I hope we'll soon be able to keep all the fires burning on such cold nights, just as we used to do before the hard times came."

"I'm sure we will," Diana said. "Now that he's come to his true home, I'm certain that the earl will do everything he can to bring things about. He knows a great deal about crops and new ways of planting. He told me all about it, when he spoke of the estate that Lord Charles began in America.''

Maudie pulled away and looked at Diana with concern. ''Oh, but The Farrell and The Colvaney won't be liking that, miss—my lady. That the earl should have any say in the crops and such . . . no, they won't like it at all. And you know they'll have none of those American ways here at Kerlain.''

''The earl is the earl,'' Diana told her, ''and Farrell and Colvaney will have to accept that, no matter how stubborn they may be. But I'll speak to Lord Kerlain about it. Perhaps he can hire a steward, such as Mr. Blaythen used to be before the old earl had to let him go. The Farrell and The Colvaney never used to mind what Mr. Blaythen said.''

''They never minded because they never did what he asked,'' Maudie said bluntly. ''Just as they'll do none of what the new earl says, and you know I speak the truth. But we've no time to worry over that now. Into bed with you, my lady.'' She scooted Diana along with both hands. ''Into bed with you. I'll go and let Swithin know that you're ready for his lordship to attend you here.''

But was she ready? Diana wondered a few minutes later as she sat in the midst of the bed, the covers pulled tightly up about her neck. She had worn the only pretty nightdress she possessed but was certain he would find it lacking, just as he would probably find *everything* about her lacking. He was most certainly experienced with women. It was infeasible that any man could look as Lad Walker did and *not* be perfectly expert in every possible way. Diana, on the other hand, knew very little about men, and most of what she did know was because of Eoghan. She ardently hoped that Lad was more skilled than her childhood friend and was comforted by the fact that he certainly knew how to kiss far better.

Sooner than she expected, the door that adjoined the

earl's chamber to her own opened, and in the dim candle-light and firelight she saw Lad stride in, shutting the door behind him. He was wearing a thin silk dressing gown that she recognized as having belonged to her godfather—and that she imagined Swithin must have insisted upon. He looked about the vast chamber for a moment, saw her sitting in the high bed with its tall posts that nearly reached the ceiling, and immediately began moving about the room, blowing out the few candles that were yet lit.

"It's damned well freezing in this damned castle," he muttered, shoving his hands deep into the robe's pockets. "Worse than the spring house back at Fair Maiden, I swear. This room alone is bigger than most houses I could name. How on God's earth is it supposed to be warmed by one fire?" he demanded grumpily. "And what in the name of all that's holy was someone thinking when they built this . . . this . . ."

"Castle?" Diana supplied meekly from the covers, glad to be beneath them. The air, where it touched her cheeks and forehead, was like ice.

"This great, *damned* castle," Lad agreed, stomping about the chamber with a fury until the last candle was out. "You know, I'd just about walk over live coals for you, sweetheart, but after tonight I hope you'll let us sleep in the manor house. Or the West Wing. Whatever it is that Swithin calls it."

"Yes, of course," she murmured, her mind whirling from what he'd just said about walking over live coals for her. He surely hadn't meant it for a romantic statement, yet she thought it the most wonderful thing any man had ever said to her.

"Good." He moved in a straight course for the bed. "Because this is nothing short of crazy, sleeping in this freezing relic, with no proper heat. My God, how did all those centuries of Walkers survive in such a place? It's

hardly a wonder that so many of them died young.'' He began to pull his robe off, tossing it onto the mattress and bending to pull off the matching slippers. ''We'd do just as well to sleep outside in the stables. Better, probably. At least we'd have the horses for warmth. Here, let me get in there beside you, sweetheart, before I freeze to death.''

The mattress dipped with his weight, and the covers that Diana clutched were briefly pulled up as he slipped under them. She instinctively began to scoot over as he moved close, but an arm came about her waist, pulling her right down against his hard—and cold—body.

''Oh!'' she said foolishly, stiff with nerves and fear. What a strange sensation it was to lie next to a man in bed. She wasn't certain that she liked it at all.

''I know we've only been married a few hours, Diana,'' he said comfortingly, as if understanding her thoughts, ''but if you don't let me cuddle up with you for a few minutes I think I might freeze solid, and that isn't exactly the sort of wedding night I had in mind.''

''Oh,'' she repeated foolishly, turning toward him tentatively. ''Of course, Lad. Can I help? What shall I do?''

He snuggled closer, burrowing his head against her neck. ''Just hold me a little bit. Put your arms around me, will you, sweetheart? Yes, just like that. Mmmm . . . feels good already. Tighter, yes. I'm already starting to warm up.''

She slid her hands over the nightshirt he wore, rubbing his back and shoulders as hard as she dared.

''Yes, sweetheart, that feels so good. Here, let me rub you too, and we'll get even warmer.'' He began to suit action to word. ''Do you like that?''

His big hands moving over her back felt heavenly, and Diana said, ''Oh, yes.''

''Am I doing it too hard?''

''No . . . it's wonderful.'' And it was. She was beginning to feel a lovely warmth now, from her toes all the way up her spine, where his hands gently massaged. "I'm sorry if you found it very unpleasant in the earl's chambers. We couldn't afford to light both fires, and I thought, as we were to sleep in here, that this would be the better room to warm. It must have been dreadfully cold while you waited."

"It was pretty chilly," he admitted, "though Swithin seemed to think I was a poor character for not bearing up better than I did. Kind of embarrassing to stand there shivering like a baby while an old man like that didn't twitch a muscle."

Diana giggled, a combination of mirth and nerves.

"Back at Fair Maiden," Lad went on, "all the fireplaces work just fine, and we've got plenty of fuel to keep them burning. The manor is always nice and warm during the cold months."

"Is it?" Diana asked, thinking that Kerlain had once been rich enough to make the same claim and praying that Lad would find a way to make it so again.

"Yes, it is," he said, the words pelting warm breath against her neck, where she could feel his mouth moving against her skin as he spoke. "You know, Diana, if we'd met in Tennessee, I could have courted you proper, done all the things a man should do when he's sparking after a woman." He lifted his head slowly, until they were face to face and his lips were near her own. One of his hands moved up to softly rub the back of her neck in a manner that Diana found both appealing and unnerving. "I would have danced with you at local gatherings and then asked if I could maybe take you to church some Sunday. And after that," he murmured as his other hand traveled down her back to bring her more closely up against him, "if we were getting along all right, you'd invite me to have supper with your folks one evening."

"I didn't have any folks," she said breathlessly. His

hands, moving so slowly in their caressing motions, were making her light-headed with sensation. "Only the earl."

"Well, that's all right," he whispered. "In Tennessee, he would have been like your granddaddy, I suppose, and you'd have invited me over to meet him, and after supper me and you would go out to sit on the porch and enjoy the evening and the sun setting. It'd be spring, or summer, and the night would be warm. If we were all alone out there, I'd probably try to steal a kiss."

"Would you?" She closed her eyes as his lips moved nearer to her own.

"Yes. Like this." His mouth pressed on hers lightly, tenderly, but far too briefly. "And then I'd go home thinking myself the luckiest man in Tennessee, and I'd dream about you all night long and try to figure when I could see you again. So I could steal another kiss."

He kissed her again, longer this time, and the hand on her back slid lower, stopping only when Diana murmured a feeble protest at the strangeness of being touched so intimately.

"Shhh." He made the soothing sound even as his hand slid lower. "No, sweetheart, don't be afraid. We're married. Husband and wife. I know it's been too fast for you, but it's all right."

"I'm sorry," she whispered, distressed and embarrassed. His hand was cupping her bottom, pulling her up against himself in a terribly intimate manner. "I'm not quite certain what to expect. Couldn't you just get it over with, please? I'll be less foolish after."

"You're not foolish. Never that." He slid the hand at her neck up to cup her chin, to bring her mouth to his again, kissing her fervently. His breathing was harsh when he pulled away. "If we were back in Tennessee, Miss Diana Whitleby, I'd court you 'til my dying day, I swear, until you were my wife. I'd never give up."

She moved against him, filled with a strange agitation that she knew must be fear.

"Make me your wife, Lad. Please. Before I lose my courage."

"I'm going to, darling," he promised. "Try to relax, and let me make you ready." His hand slid downward to caress her breast, but it was too strange, and she shook her head and squirmed at the unfamiliar touch.

"No, please." She was beginning to feel desperately afraid. "Do it now."

He fell still for a silent moment, then said, "All right, Diana. Do you know what you're supposed to do?"

"No," she said sorrowfully. "Except Maudie once told me that the wife just lies still and lets the husband do as he pleases. Is that what I should do?"

"I'm afraid Maudie's got it all wrong, love. You'll have to do your fair share in the matter if we're to get it done."

Diana groaned. "But I don't know what I should do."

"It's all right, sweetheart," he soothed. "Just stay calm. I know everything there is to know, and I'll tell you what we're to do." He pushed up slightly on one elbow, gazing down at her. "First, we have to take off all our clothes."

Diana stiffened. "Take off . . . all our clothes? My gown? And your nightshirt . . . I don't . . . Maudie never said anything . . . *anything* . . . about that."

"That's how it's done, love," he told her. "I'm sorry, but there's no other way. Maudie clearly never had a decent instructor in the matter. Here, let me help you take your gown off."

"But, Lad . . ."

He was already tugging the garment over her head, talking all the while.

"Relax, Diana. Every married couple has to face this moment. It's perfectly natural. There, it's off. Doesn't that feel better? Have you ever slept in the raw? No? I do, all the time. Well," he amended, rising up to pull his nightshirt off and toss it out of the covers, which he pulled completely over the both of them as he lay back down, enveloping them in a warm, intimate darkness, "only at home. At Fair Maiden. It'd be risky doing it anywhere else. There." His hands rested gently on her bare waist. "We'll be much warmer now. Trust me."

"I do, Lad," she whispered, resigned to becoming as obedient a wife as she might possibly manage. And, really, this wasn't as bad as she'd thought. It was embarrassing to lie naked beside him, but his touch was careful and pleasant, and she began to think she might tolerate this odd new intimacy. "What shall I do now?"

"Now we must be very brave and touch each other," he said. "All over."

Diana swallowed heavily.

"All over?"

"Yes, love," he murmured. "Everywhere, to give each other pleasure. Like this." His fingertips brushed lightly over her breast, caressing. "Very gently." The soft touch came again, and again, and Diana's mouth fell open at the way it felt. "You see? Just to give pleasure. That's all."

"Oh."

The caress grew bolder, until the palm of his hand cupped her breast completely.

"You're so beautiful," he whispered, finding her mouth with his. "I wish I could see you."

Diana murmured unintelligibly beneath the pressure of his ardent kiss. She felt as if she had somehow lost all her strength and gave no resistance when he pulled her flush against his naked body, despite the shock of the sensation. She felt his manhood pressing on her leg, hard and long, and made a sound of protest and fear.

Lad took no notice; indeed, he seemed to know what the trouble was and, rather than politely move away, he pressed

Diana into the mattress and half rolled atop her, giving his member leave to thrust up against her even more intimately. She felt as if she were under siege, reeling from the rapid, and thoroughly sensual, attack on her senses. His hands were in constant motion, smoothing over her now-heated flesh, caressing, massaging, encouraging her to give way and let them do as they pleased. His mouth opened over her own by small degrees while his clever tongue licked and teased and begged for entrance. Diana knew that she shouldn't give way, for the idea of it—a man's tongue in her mouth!—was thoroughly repulsive, but . . . it didn't *feel* repulsive. It felt sinful, and utterly wonderful, just as his caressing hands on her felt.

He gave a low moan when she timidly parted her lips and gently—oh, so very gently—took what she offered. Then it was Diana's turn to moan. God help her, it was beyond sinful. It was beyond anything she'd ever known. By the time he lifted his mouth away she felt dizzy, suffused with weakness from head to toe.

"Lad," she murmured, wanting him to kiss her again, but his head—and mouth—had moved downward, kissing her neck, nipping at her shoulders, and then she felt the wet heat of his tongue on her breast, licking, and then his lips closing over her nipple and suckling on her.

Diana just about flew off the bed, but he held her down and continued the pleasurable torture first to one breast, then to the next, until Diana was writhing uncontrollably beneath him.

Finally he released her and moved back up to find her mouth and kiss her, as hard and fast as he was breathing.

"Touch me," he pleaded. "Please, Diana . . . just put your hands on me. Anywhere."

She lifted her hands to his face, setting her palms tentatively against his cheeks, and he pressed needily against them, turning his head so that she began to run her fingers through his hair, down the nape of his neck, stroking the hard muscles of his shoulders.

"It feels so good," he said, half groaning, lowering his forehead to rest against her neck. "Your hands on me."

She grew bolder then, caressing his chest, pushing him to his back and rolling atop him as he'd earlier done to her, leaning to kiss his face and neck while her hands moved over his nipples and lower, to his belly. She delighted in the way he groaned and twisted, and knew a heady sense of power to be able to make him as weak and helpless against her caresses as he'd made her.

"Diana," he said at last, grasping her hands and lifting them high, rolling with her until he lay fully on top. "You're making me crazy. I want to love you."

"Yes," she whispered, kissing him, pulling her hands free to stroke them over his back, loving the feel of him, his hardness and strength. "Love me."

His hand moved down between them, pushed her legs to open so that he could lie between them, and then she felt something else—his manhood, she knew it must be—pushing inside her. It was happening, just as she'd known it must, and yet it seemed impossible.

Fear began to rise up in her again, and she stiffened.

"Lad . . ."

"Shhh." He kissed her gently. "It may hurt a little bit this first time, love, but we'll fit together just fine, and the next time there won't be any pain at all. Put your arms around me, tight, and hold me as hard as you can."

She did as he instructed and squeezed him with all her might, shutting her eyes and pressing her face against his warm, damp neck. Above her, she felt Lad's body clenching as he pushed himself farther inside. It stung badly, but Lad sounded as if he was in far more pain than she. He lifted up a bit, and she opened her eyes to see that he was breathing through bared teeth and had an expression on his face that was nothing short of tormented.

"Am I hurting you?" she asked fearfully.

"No, love." He shook his head, keeping his eyes yet closed, still pushing into her. "I think you're killing me. Oh, God!"

He broke through whatever barrier had been keeping him at bay and slid suddenly all the way inside her. Diana gave a gasp and twisted beneath him, but Lad brought his heavy weight down on top of her again, holding her still.

"There," he said, breathing harshly, taking her face between his palms and setting their foreheads together, though Diana yet struggled. "We're one now. Man and wife. Is it very bad, darling?"

"It hurts!" she accused, shoving at him. He didn't budge.

"I'm sorry," he said, and groaned as she moved her hips. "No, love, don't—give me a moment or I'll—" He finished the frantic sentence by pressing his mouth over hers and kissing her hard.

Diana made a protest of "mmmm!" but to no avail. He kept kissing her, and then, after a long moment, he began to move. She fell still, waiting for the pain to grow worse, wondering at how he could torment her so, but what happened was just the opposite. He was moving, his manhood sliding gently up and down inside her passage, and what should have hurt was instead soothing, causing what pain there had been to fade away.

He lifted his mouth and murmured, "I love you, Diana," and then kissed her again before she could make a reply. His movements came more quickly, thrusting harder, until she began to feel something altogether different from pain and closed her eyes against the tide of sensation. Lad stiffened and groaned against her neck, and Diana felt his heat flooding her deep within. She smiled and let out the breath she'd unwittingly been holding, and when he collapsed on top of her, still groaning, she set her arms about his shoulder and held him tightly.

"I'm sorry," he muttered against her neck. "I couldn't help myself. You drove me crazy."

Diana nuzzled the side of his face, still smiling. It had felt strangely good at the end, and she was far from displeased at the thought of doing it again. He'd said it wouldn't hurt the next time. "I'm glad," she whispered, and kissed his ear. "I'm your wife now, in full."

He gave out a sigh and lifted up onto his arms to look down at her in the darkness. The covers had slid down far enough so that their heads were exposed, and he reached to pull them back up over them again, nesting them in warmth and darkness.

"Yes, you're my wife now, in full," he murmured, kissing her. "And I'm your husband. The Earl and Countess of Kerlain." With an indrawn breath he pulled his body free of hers and lay down beside her, sliding an arm beneath Diana's shoulders to draw her near. She nestled into his warmth, comfortable and happy, remembering that he'd said he loved her. She wondered if he had meant it or if it was what a man said to a woman in such a moment. She was so ignorant of such things that she couldn't be sure, but it had been nice to hear the words, anyway.

"I'm sorry it hurt, Diana," he said, stroking her hair with a lazy hand.

"It wasn't so bad," she told him truthfully. "I think not knowing what would happen was the worst part. I was so foolish."

He chuckled. "I meant to give you the same pleasure that you gave me, but I lost control. That's never happened to me before. But I never felt this way about another woman before. I want you to know something."

"What?"

"I mean to be a faithful husband. You won't ever need to worry that I'll stray or do this with anyone else. I swear that to you."

"Oh, Lad." Diana thought she might weep at the sweetly spoken words. They were more precious to her than he could ever know. "Thank you. I shall always be faithful too."

She felt him smile against the top of her head. "I know that, love." His hand smoothed down the length of her back. "It's nice in here with you. Warm and cozy. Come here, sweetheart." He turned on his side and pulled her until they were spooned together, so that Diana lay with her back against his belly. His body enveloped her own in a cocoon of protection and warmth. "Comfortable now?" he asked, yawning and looping a heavy arm about her waist.

"Yes," she murmured, so weary and replete that she could barely keep her eyes open.

"Let's get some sleep, then. Newlyweds need their strength, and tomorrow morning I'm going to see what I can do about making love to you more properly."

Diana smiled and said, in a mock-chiding tone, "Lad." He gave no reply, just another sigh, contented and sleepy, and Diana closed her eyes, yet smiling, and followed him into slumber.

Chapter Nine

"Look, all I'm saying is that you might want to consider the idea. There are no guarantees, of course, but I have seen it work before."

"Bah!" The Farrell stood from where he'd been kneeling, tossing a handful of dirt aside with disgust. "American ways. They'll do us no good. The land is old, that's all it is. There's naught to be done but let it rest."

Lad stood as well, brushing his trousers free of mud and dirt. The snow had melted a week earlier into a frozen slush, which in turn had slowly melted the fields of Kerlain into huge patches of icy mud. "Resting the fields is a fine method when there's enough good land left to plant, but that's impossible at Kerlain."

"Aye," The Colvaney agreed dourly. "There's not an inch of it that hasn't been overworked these many years, i'faith."

"But that doesn't mean that it has to be left unproductive for three years," Lad countered. "Not just to let the land rest."

"And not unless we want to starve," Braen Colvaney agreed with a laugh. "Though we nearly managed to do that with last year's crops, poor as they were. Even the apple trees were feeble, and the cider that came from them."

"Hush, Braen," his father chided, clearly displeased with his son's friendly familiarity with the new lord of

Kerlain. To Lad, he said, "Your ways won't work here. It's always been barley, wheat, and the apple trees at Kerlain, for hundreds of years, by God. That and naught else, save what the folk plant in their own plots."

"Aye," said The Farrell. "We've never had beans or corn. " 'Twould be strange and unnatural to grow such things now in this soil, which has never harbored the like. Nay, and no proper lord has ever asked it of us. Or of the land."

"*Kerlain* land," The Colvaney stated firmly. "Barley, wheat, and apples."

"I don't like it." The Farrell shook his head, frowning at the plot of land on which they stood. "'Tisn't right. The Farrells will have none of it, sir." He at last lifted his gaze to meet Lad's. "None of it, I say."

"Nor the Colvaneys," The Colvaney declared.

"Da," Stuart Farrell murmured in a soft, pleading tone, speaking for the first time that morning since accompanying Lad to the field. He was The Farrell's oldest son, of an age with Braen Colvaney, and a quiet, peaceful young man. Lad knew him better than the rest, for he lived and worked at Castle Kerlain alongside Swithin and Maudie and had, in his shy and fumbling way, done his best to make the new earl feel at home. It was a feat, Lad thought, that was just about undoable.

He let out a sigh and wearily rubbed a gloved hand across the bridge of his eyes. It had been two weeks since the wedding. Two weeks of unspeakable bliss with his wife, and two weeks of sheer frustration with the people of Kerlain. He was beginning to think they didn't *want* things to get better on the estate; every attempt he'd made to suggest a plan for the future had been met with open contempt or, even worse, a stony silence that exceeded contempt. If it hadn't been for Diana's love of the place, Lad would have packed her up and headed back to the States already. At this point, he was only praying that she'd soon get as fed up as he was and agree to leave without a fuss. Once he got her back home to Fair Maiden, she'd probably be sorry only that she'd waited so long to abandon the rapidly sinking ship that was Kerlain.

"All right. Listen." He dropped his hand and looked at the other men. "I've already ordered enough lime to cover these fields for the rest of the winter and spring. At the start of summer if they're tilled and another layer of lime spread out, they shouldn't need more than a year's rest to be ready for planting. But the crops will have to be rotated, and even then—" He stopped and shook his head, knowing full well that more wheat and barley would exhaust the soil so rapidly that their efforts would be as nothing. "But we'll see about that. In the meantime, the older sections of the orchards can be tended and replanted with new seedlings."

" 'Twill never taste the same as what's always been grown at Kerlain," The Farrell predicted gloomily. "Kerlain trees always put out the finest cider in Herefordshire."

"For hundreds of years," The Colvaney added with a nod.

"Fine." Lad was beginning to feel the edges of his temper fraying. "We'll propagate seedlings from Kerlain apple seeds"—which was at least something he knew how to do, for he'd begun helping his father cultivate seedlings when he was but a boy—"but it'll take ten or even fifteen years before any profit comes of it."

That damning silence followed this, though the men seemed thoughtful. Drawing in a steadying breath, Lad decided it was time to put forth his latest consideration, though Diana had earlier warned him it would be greeted with scorn.

"Part of the land can be used for cattle. This field right

here, for instance, could be rested and fertilized all at once, and Kerlain would still be profitable.''

The silence changed from damning to shocked as the four men stared at him, wide-eyed.

''I realize you've never done any herding at Kerlain. I'm not particularly well-versed in it myself. But Herefordshire grows some of the best cattle in the world, and there's no reason why Kerlain shouldn't use part of its land for the same purpose. Heaven alone knows there's plenty of acreage going unused, and it'd bring in a good, steady profit year to year, if everything went all right.''

''Cattle,'' Stuart repeated slowly, as if he couldn't believe what he'd heard, ''at Kerlain?''

''Never, in all my days—'' The Farrell blurted out, his face tight and red with anger. ''By all that's holy, can you be standing there, right there''—he pointed with a callused finger to Lad's feet—''on this very land, suggesting such a—such a''—he cast about for the right word—''*evil* thing?''

''Evil, aye, and that's just what it is!'' said The Colvaney. ''Never have we had cattle here, save what the earl kept for his own table and what the folk had their uses for. But to *herd* it!'' He spat on the ground. ''Bah!''

''We're farmers, my lord,'' Braen said more respectfully. ''Generations of farmers, always working the land.''

''*This* land,'' his father added.

Braen nodded. ''Aye, just so. It's all we know, my lord, and all we've ever known. What would we be doing with cows and the like?''

''Keeping your families from starving?'' Lad suggested curtly. He'd known prideful men in his life, but the people of Kerlain went beyond anything he might ever have imagined. Change was inevitable, and if these people refused to budge, they'd not only bring destruction to themselves and their families but drag the whole of Kerlain down with them.

"The old earl never would have lowered himself—or us—to such as that," The Farrell told him. "Cattle! At Kerlain?" He gave Lad a look as if to say he was utterly mad. "It's wheat, barley, and the apples we've got here, and have ever done, and that's as it is."

The other men nodded in agreement, and Lad threw his hands up into the air.

"Fine!" he said. "Starve, then. Watch your families starve. You want none of my suggestions? None of my help?" He looked from one man to the next. "Then I'll give you no more of them. Good day to you, gentlemen." He turned to see where his horse had wandered off to, only to find himself staring at Eoghan Patterson instead, mounted upon a fine steed on the road that ran beside the field. Behind him, on another horse, sat a servant, and being led by the servant was yet another horse, a beautiful roan mare.

"Good day to you, my lord Kerlain," Viscount Carden called out across the space between them. "May I beg the favor of a word with you?"

Grand, Lad thought dismally. This was just what he needed. He hardly wished to be reminded of Viscount Carden's behavior on his wedding day or of the other man's greater polish in manner, dress, and speech. He could almost feel the eyes of the Farrell and Colvaney men as they stood behind him, making the comparison between Lad's stained work clothes and the elegant apparel worn by the viscount. The viscount's words, spoken during his untimely appearance on the wedding day, yet rang in Lad's ears. *You would have been my wife, and I their lord—the lord they would have chosen for themselves before ever letting a filthy American lay claim to Kerlain.* How very true that had been, and was, Lad thought bitterly.

The other man swung down from his horse as Lad neared

him and met him at the edge of the field, careful, Lad noted, not to actually step into the muddy ground and dirty his shining boots any more than he already had.

"My lord," the viscount began, "I've come to make my apologies to both you and Lady Kerlain for my inexcusable behavior on your wedding day, two weeks past. I can only say that I deeply regret whatever pain and insult I visited upon you and hope that my foolishness and thoughtlessness were incapable of ruining a moment that should only ever be a joyous one. Please, I pray, forgive me, if you can find it in your heart to do so, and accept this token of my sincerity." He indicated the mare, which at this closer view Lad could see was an exceptional animal. "Her name is Maeva, and she is the finest of my stable. I realize she can hardly compare to those the late earl kept, but I hope you may be able to find a use for her."

The late earl had, indeed, kept a fine stable of horses— much at the expense of his people, Lad thought silently, gazing at the mare—but none of them could begin to compare with an animal such as this one. And Eoghan Patterson probably knew that all too well. So much for sincerity. But Lad was growing used to playing this manner of word games that the British seemed to love so well. Trying to decipher what Swithin meant whenever he deigned to speak to his new lord had given Lad good practice.

"I should probably pick you up by the scruff of the neck and toss you off my land," Lad said, "which is what we do with scoundrels back home in the States. But seeing as we're bound to be neighbors and figuring that you were fairly well thrown for a loop by my marrying the woman you'd decided on for yourself, I'll accept your apology and your gift, and here's my hand on it."

He drew off his scruffy, dirty glove and extended his hand, and was surprised to see Eoghan draw off his perfectly elegant, spotless glove and offer his own. He gave Lad a firm handshake, staring him full in the face as if to convince him of his good faith.

"Thank you, Lord Kerlain," he said as they drew their gloves back on in deference to the coldness of the day. "You are kinder than I deserve. I have spent the past two weeks wallowing in self-condemnation, striving to find the humility and the courage to make a proper apology. I cannot think Lady Kerlain will be as readily forgiving, nor can I blame her for such."

"That's probably true enough," Lad agreed. "I'd give her a wide berth for a month or two before trying to soften her up, if I were you."

Eoghan's gaze sharpened. "Has she spoken of me to you? Of our past friendship? I had hoped she might reassure you that the desire for a more permanent union was on my side alone. Diana never felt as I did. To her, we were only friends. I didn't wish you to think otherwise, for she would never have married you if her heart had been given to another."

Lad hoped that the smile on his face didn't give away what he was thinking, of how sweetly and tenderly his wife had reassured him on that count. Diana hadn't yet told him in so many words that she loved him, but she'd shown him in other ways what she was feeling. Her inexperience in lovemaking had given proof to the fact that she'd had almost no physical contact with other men, but her eagerness to learn how to please him had told Lad that she cared for him. Just thinking of it made his body harden with desire, but Eoghan was watching him closely, and Lad forced himself to concentrate on matters at hand.

"She's reassured me," he replied truthfully. "More than once."

Viscount Carden's mouth tightened slightly at the words, but his expression remained steadfastly pleasant.

"I'm relieved," he said. "It would have been vastly unfair if my behavior had given you any cause to distrust Diana. She's been my dearest friend these many years, and it would grieve me deeply to know that I'd caused her any lasting pain because of my foolish hopes.'' Looking past Lad, he saw the four men standing in the field. "Forgive me for interrupting you at such a poorly chosen moment. I had intended to take the animal to the castle and make a more formal appearance, but we came upon you as we made our way and I took my chance. You were in the midst of discussing some matter of import with The Farrell and The Colvaney?''

Lad glanced back at the men who were still in the spot where he'd left them. It was clear that they were yet grumbling over his words. The Colvaney met Lad's eye and purposefully turned away, an act of complete insult for a tenant to give his lord.

"If you can call it that,'' Lad muttered. "More of a disagreement, is what it was. We're having a little trouble seeing eye to eye on things.''

"You give them too much free rein, if you will pardon me for making so bold a remark, my lord.''

Lad turned back to him. "Look, why don't you just call me Lad, like we agreed at the inn in Walborough, and I'll call you Eoghan, and we can forget about 'my lording' each other to death. Fair enough?''

Eoghan smiled a smile of such beguiling charm that Lad had to grin and shake his head. The fellow was smooth, no doubt about it.

"I should be pleased, Lad, though before your people I will address you in the proper manner. They'll never recognize you as their lord if your fellow noblemen don't accord you the same recognition. Our dealings with each other will go a long way toward reconciling them in your favor.''

"Gad, I'm starting to think I don't want them reconciled either for or against me,'' Lad told him. "I've never met such a stubborn breed in all my born days and hope to high heaven never to meet the like again.''

Eoghan looked thoughtful for a moment, considering the words, then said, ''I don't mean to offer insult, Lad, but would you allow me to guide you in this matter? I believe I may be of some help, at least insofar as your understanding of the nature of these people. Perhaps in this way I might make greater amends for the insult I've given?''

If anyone could teach him about such things, Lad thought with a twinge of amusement, it would have to be Eoghan Patterson. He'd never heard a man speak so eloquently as Viscount Carden. He was a nobleman to perfection.

''It'd be fine by me,'' Lad said, ''though I doubt there's much you can do. They don't like me much because I'm an American, and, truth to tell''—he leaned forward and lowered his voice—''I don't particularly like them either.''

''Because they're English,'' Eoghan said knowingly. ''I understand perfectly. But we could speak more easily elsewhere, I think.'' He nodded off to the side of the road. ''Is that your mount there? The gelding? I seem to recognize it as one of the late earl's favorites.''

The horse stood nearby, sedately nuzzling the muddy earth in search of grass.

''If you've the time, perhaps you might like to give Maeva a run?'' Eoghan suggested. ''I've a flask of my best brandy hidden away''—he patted the elegant, multicaped greatcoat he was wearing to indicate an inner pocket—''and we can discuss the matter at hand more fully. I'll have my servant remove the saddle from the gelding and make her ready for you. He can then return the gelding to the stables at Kerlain.''

It seemed a good plan, and though Lad was eager to return to Castle Kerlain, and Diana, he was curious to see what Viscount Carden had to say.

"Don't make your servant dismount," Lad said. "I can saddle the horse." He moved to do just that, but the viscount stopped him.

"No, Lad. Be pleased to allow my man to do it." With a wave of one hand, he set the servant into motion, dismounting from his horse and heading for the gelding. When Lad turned back to look at him, Eoghan gave him a speaking look. "The first and most important lesson you must learn is that a nobleman never does what a servant can do for him. That's what they exist for, and it is your right to expect such service from them. I realize that in your country all men are created equal, but things are different here. At this very moment, Englishmen are fighting—and dying—to keep the evils of *liberté, égalité, démocratie* from touching Britain's fair shores."

"Is that what they're fighting for?" Lad asked, cocking an eyebrow. "I thought maybe it was Napoleon they were trying to keep at bay."

Eoghan laughed with pure amusement. "If that's what you think, then it's hardly a wonder you don't understand the English. Here's Maeva, ready for you. Come. We'll have a word with The Farrell and The Colvaney before we make our way, and I'll show you the proper manner in which to address them."

The viscount moved to mount his steed and, with an easy motion that bespoke his obvious strength, swung up onto the back of his horse. He waited for Lad to mount as well before spurring his horse in the direction of the four men who yet stood in the field. Lad, unused to the mare, followed with far less certainty. By the time he reached the group he saw that the men on the ground had removed their hats for Viscount Carden—a measure of respect they hadn't shown Lad for more than a week now.

"Alwan," the viscount greeted The Farrell, surprising

Lad by his informal use of the man's Christian name. "Conyn, Stuart, and Braen. How does the day find you?"

"Well, m'lord," The Farrell replied. "May the same be with you."

"It is," the viscount replied. "Although one might wish it were less cold, but I needn't tell that to any of you. Keeping yourselves and your families warm enough, are you?"

The men all nodded and murmured "aye," though Lad could have sworn that he'd earlier heard them complaining about a lack of fuel to keep their fires burning.

"Come to see our poor fields, have you, m'lord?" The Colvaney asked. His manner was friendly but respectful.

"No, no, Conyn. I've come to visit with Lord Kerlain. And to bring him a wedding gift, which you see. We're on our way now to give her a bit of a run, but I wished to stop first and offer my regards."

"Thank you, m'lord," The Farrell said. "Always a pleasure to see you, it is, sir."

"Aye," The Colvaney agreed. "Always a pleasure, m'lord."

Viscount Carden gave a gracious nod. "Stuart," he said, "will you be so good as to escort my man back to the castle with Lord Kerlain's mount." Lad noted that the words were a command, not a question. "I shall collect him there before I make my return to Lising Park."

"Yes, m'lord," Stuart replied with what seemed, to Lad, almost eager agreement. "I should be happy to."

"Very good." Viscount Carden gave a curt nod. "A pleasant day to you all."

Turning their horses about, they made their way back to the road.

"I'll admit, I'm impressed," Lad said. "But even if I could look and speak like you, they'd still treat me as an outsider. They'll never get past what I am—an American."

"No, not so long as you are one," Eoghan agreed. "You'll have to become an Englishman if you wish to win them over completely. How do you like Maeva?"

"She's a rare animal," Lad said, feeling the grace and strength of the horse beneath him. "A beauty, right and true."

"You know how to handle the animal," Eoghan noted, glancing at him. "That's a good start. The English admire a man who rides well."

"A man who rides well," Lad said with a laugh. "A man who dresses well and speaks well and treats others as if they're not his equal. Nobody here seems to care about what a man really is. Those fellows"—he jerked his head back to the field where they'd left the men—"would probably be as happy to have a murderer for a lord than an honest man, if he looked and sounded as you do."

Eoghan gave a low chuckle. "Don't let the Farrell and Colvaney clans bother you overmuch, Lad. They're long descended from the Welsh and very prideful about their ancestry. The women retain their lineage when they marry, making the men they wed take their names rather than the other way around, and the older folk still speak Gaelic among themselves. They're set in their own ways, and you'll not be changing them."

"Stubborn is what they are," Lad muttered.

"Yes, that too. Do you like fishing, Lad?" Eoghan asked, abruptly changing the subject. "Hunting?"

The questions made Lad think of how much he missed Tennessee, the green, rolling hills where he and Joshua had spent many an early morning hunting.

"Both," he replied.

"The river Wye is nearby. Wonderful fishing. Some of the best salmon in England. We'll have to go one day, when the weather has warmed a bit."

The idea appealed to Lad. Spending a day fishing with a

friendly fellow like Eoghan Patterson certainly sounded better than spending more time trying to overcome the thickheadedness of the occupants of Kerlain.

"I'd like that," he said. "And it'd be nice to bring some salmon home, just for a change. I imagine Diana would like that."

"My thoughts exactly," Viscount Carden murmured. "Diana would be more than pleased, I'm certain. Look, the road is straight and clear ahead, and not too muddy. I'll race you to the turn."

But Lad had already guessed his purpose. He set Maeva into motion just as Lord Carden spurred his own horse on and within a few seconds passed his companion, leaving him easily behind.

Chapter Ten

"You were with *Eoghan?*"

Shocked beyond measure, Diana repeated what Lad had just told her, striving to keep the dismay she felt out of her tone. It was, she feared, a lost battle.

Lad relaxed the embrace he'd held her in while kissing her and looked into her face with concern. They stood in the middle of their bedchamber in the West Wing, where he had surprised her as she'd been working on the monthly ledgers with his sudden appearance and ardent kiss. Diana had been waiting all afternoon for him to return to the castle and make love to her, just as he had done every day since they'd married, but his explanation for what had delayed him so long pushed every thought of his sweet lovemaking out of her head.

"He came to apologize for what he did on our wedding day," he said, "and he was sincere about it. I suppose I should have tossed him out of Kerlain without a word, but you told me that he was your closest childhood friend and, even though you're angry with him now, I figured you'd eventually want to heal the breach."

"Of course," she replied softly, "but I didn't think it would happen so soon. It's only been two weeks."

"He apologized," Lad said once more. "I couldn't throw that back in his face. One of the first things my father taught me was to ask forgiveness when I was in the wrong and to accept an apology when it was offered. After everything he went through with the old earl, I reckon my father knew a thing or two about being sorry for something.''

''I'm sure he did,'' Diana agreed, laying a hand gently against his cheek. He turned his mouth into her palm and kissed it. ''But you don't know Eoghan as well as I do, Lad. He's not the kind of man who can be readily trusted, no matter how sincere he may seem to be. He can become . . . unpleasant when he doesn't get his way.''

Lad searched her eyes intently. ''What do you mean, love? Has he threatened you in some way? Before I came to Kerlain? I know he meant to marry you, but if he ever dared to lay a finger on you or gave insult—''

''Oh, no,'' she said quickly. ''It's nothing like that, I promise you. I'm certainly not afraid of Eoghan.''

The lie stuck in her throat, but the last thing she desired was to see Lad haring off to Lising Park to throttle Viscount Carden. By the light in his eye and the tension in his body, she could tell that it was exactly what he was ready to do if she but gave him cause for it. The knowledge made her heart sing, knowing that he cared for her so much, but she wouldn't use it to create trouble with Eoghan. Trouble was just what Eoghan wanted, and she'd not give him the satisfaction of having it. But she was furious with him for using his wiles on Lad, who was as open and honest as Eoghan was crafty and dishonest. It would be too easy for Lad to be taken advantage of, trusting as he was, and Eoghan, unfortunately, knew it; worse, he clearly meant to make use of the knowledge. But if she could just keep them away from each other and at the same time maintain peace, Eoghan would eventually grow tired of the game and give way.

''It's just that he was dreadfully spoiled all of his life,'' Diana said with care, ''and isn't used to being denied his will. He can be difficult when crossed, and, until things are more settled at Kerlain, I can't think it wise to become too friendly with him.''

Lad frowned. ''Perhaps I should have the horse returned to him, then. It doesn't seem right to keep Maeva if we're not going to be on friendly terms.''

Diana blinked at him.

''Maeva?''

''That's the peace offering he brought to us. The most beautiful roan mare you ever set sight on, and just about the finest mount I've ever ridden.''

''I know,'' Diana said sharply, then clamped her lips together and regretted that she'd said anything.

Lad looked at her with surprise. ''You know?''

Oh, yes, she thought furiously. She knew very well. Maeva had been her horse, or almost as good as hers, from the day that Diana had turned thirteen. Eoghan had given the beautiful mare to Diana as a supposed gift, and she had loved her so dearly, but true to his nature, Eoghan had included certain conditions with his present. He had insisted upon keeping Maeva at Lising Park, saying that he wished to spare the Earl of Kerlain the expense of the horse's care and feed. Diana had understood what it really meant—that she would be forced to visit Eoghan if she wished to ride the mare. Over the years, and true to his nature, Eoghan used Maeva as a means of having his own way, threatening to sell or even shoot the horse if Diana wouldn't do as he commanded, until Diana, in a fit of anger, finally told him to do as he pleased. That had been the end of such taunts, but now he was using Maeva yet again, and just as cunningly as he had done before. He knew full well that the mare was the only thing he possessed, the only gift he could have given, that Diana wouldn't throw back in his face. It would be the greatest kind of cruelty to send the poor creature back into his conniving power, and she would never do so. But her acceptance would seem odd to Lad now, after all she'd just said. Worse, Eoghan would ever be able to say that as Diana had taken his gift, she must also have taken his apology.

"I used to see her at Lising Park, when I visited Lord Carden in my youth," she told Lad.

"You've ridden her?"

Diana nodded. "Yes. Not for many years now, but when Eoghan and I were younger, she was the mount I always rode when I visited his estate." Which was nothing but the truth, she told herself, striving to push away a feeling of guilt. "I agree that she's truly a fine mare, and a . . . a very fine gift."

His expression softened. "Then you must see that he was sincere in his apology. A man wouldn't part with a horse like that if he didn't truly wish to make amends." He lifted a hand and gently pushed the curls from her shoulder, curving his fingers about her neck as he did so. "But I'd be pleased to give her back if it'd make you feel better." He smiled at her, his fingers grazing softly over the sensitive skin at the top of her gown's neckline. "We don't have to have Viscount Carden here at Kerlain, love. It's not the kind of hospitality we'd practice in Tennessee, unless there was some kind of family feud going on, but I know things are different here."

"Oh, Lad," she said sorrowfully. "I don't want you to think me inhospitable. Please, don't. It's just Eoghan, that I know him so well—"

He kissed her to silence, gently, tenderly.

"Hush, Diana," he murmured afterward. "I don't think any such thing. I'm only trying to let you know that I'll never choose anyone else's side over yours, no matter what I think of him, even if he is a friend. You're my wife, and I'll always stand with you. So if you want the horse to go back"—he kissed the tip of her nose—"then back she goes. With nary a word from me."

Diana gazed up into the face of her husband, so impossibly handsome, and wondered how she could have been so fortunate to be blessed with such a man. He was so different from every other man she'd known, so gentle and giving and pleasing. He spoke kindly to everyone he met and greeted commoners, and even servants, as if he were one of them and not a nobleman. To Diana he was freely affectionate, surprising her moment to moment with his readiness to kiss and touch and say such astonishing things. If this was the way that mothers in the United States raised their sons, then the old earl had been far, far wrong—it wasn't in the least a heathenish, uncivilized country.

"No, I want you to keep Maeva, Lad," she murmured. "As a wedding gift, and not as an apology, though we'll accept that from Lord Carden too."

He smiled. "She'll be your mount, then, as you used to ride her. I'd like to see you on her someday soon. Perhaps tomorrow? Will you go riding with me?"

"Yes," she whispered, and lifted up on her toes to close the distance between them and kiss him on the mouth. She loved him. With all her heart and being she loved this man, and with her kiss she tried to tell him now what she was too timid to speak aloud. He responded with a low groan, pulling her tightly against himself and opening his mouth to the shy caress of her tongue.

She rubbed her hands over the hard muscles in his shoulders and arms and chest, both feeling and hearing his response. He had taught her how to touch him, how to please him, and she delighted in the confidence she had—the power she held in her very hands—to make him weak with sensation.

"Lad," she murmured against his lips, "make love to me."

His breathing was harsh as he pulled back. "Yes, ma'am." His fingers were already unfastening her gown. "With pleasure."

Moments later, their clothing cast all about the chamber, he laid her on the bed and put his mouth to her breast.

"Don't," she pleaded, tugging at his hair to make him stop. "That makes me crazy."

"Mmmm" was his only reply.

He was merciless, licking her nipples with his tongue, teasing and tormenting until she writhed helplessly beneath him, half begging, half groaning. When he pulled one nipple into his mouth and sucked hard, she almost came off the bed.

"Lad!"

"Yes, love." He surged up to capture her mouth. "Tell me what you want." He kissed her, tickling the sensitive corners of her inner mouth with his tongue. His hands moved over her body with bold possession. "Tell me. Show me."

She rose up in answer to meet his kiss, like for like, as demanding as he was, and more. With all the strength she possessed she pushed him over onto his back and straddled him as if he were her steed, her strong legs hugging him tightly. Reaching down, she curled her fingers about his hardened manhood, murmuring with satisfaction as he now writhed beneath *her*.

"Do you like this manner of torment?" she asked, her hand gliding up and down the silken length of him.

"Witch," he said with a gasp, moving as she moved.

"Shall I make you my slave?"

"I've been that," he said, halting only to draw in a sharp breath, "since the day we met. Enough." He reached out to grip her hand and pull it to his mouth to kiss it. "Now I get to torment you."

She leaned down to find his mouth. "Yes. Please."

He kissed her long and fully, sliding his fingers caressingly up and down the length of her back, from her shoulders to her hips, until she was incoherent with pleasure. Then he took her shoulders in a gentle grasp and pushed her up to sit upon him.

"Now, ride me, Diana," he whispered, his strong hands closing over her legs, pulling them apart and lifting her. "Ride me as you'll ride Maeva."

"Ride?" she repeated with confusion, following blindly, awkwardly as he guided her open body down onto his own, feeling him coming into her, first with surprise and then with growing understanding.

"Oh," she murmured as he filled her. Her eyes widened with amazement. "Lad . . . can we . . ."

"Yes, Diana." He thrust up into her, hard enough to make her gasp. *"Oh, yes."*

She was insensible at first, only feeling him in this new way, then came to herself as she heard him telling her what to do.

"Ride me," he said, his voice gritty and harsh. "Harder. Yes, Diana. *Harder.*"

She felt—dimly, distantly—him shuddering beneath her, but her own pleasure overtook her more fully, so good, so intense, that she felt it even to the tips of her fingers and toes. Everything else save Lad fell away. The world spun and drifted, rippling, shivering, and then became perfectly calm, until with a replete sigh Diana opened her eyes and found that she was lying atop Lad's warm, damp, sleeping body. They were yet joined together, and her body hummed with the pleasure that she'd learned at her husband's hands. The husband whom she loved. Diana smiled, sighing with a happiness she'd never believed might be possible before knowing Lad, then closed her eyes and drifted into slumber.

"Do you think we've put a baby in here yet?" Lad smoothed his hand over Diana's belly as he asked the question.

"Lad!" She could feel her cheeks growing hot at the words.

He chuckled. "What? Never tell me people in England don't talk about that either. It's a wonder you folks have any kind of conversation at all, the way you go on with what's proper and improper."

"Well," she admitted, "it isn't generally discussed so openly. It's a . . . delicate topic."

Lad gave a snort. "It isn't *too* delicate, I gather, or there'd never be any English babies born year to year. Not that we're going to have that problem." He bent to kiss her nose. "I wouldn't be surprised if we haven't already got the next Walker on his or her way. Not with the way we've been going, anyhow."

"Would you be pleased if that were so?"

"Yes. Very pleased." His hand began to make slow, circular motions on her tummy. "I hope we'll have several children, the more the better. Would it make you happy, knowing you were going to have a baby?"

"Oh, yes," she replied, still blushing. "Very happy."

"It would make traveling kind of difficult, though," he said more thoughtfully. "I hadn't thought about that much before now, but it's true."

Diana gazed up at him with bewilderment. "Traveling? To London, you mean?" It was true that Mr. Sibbley probably had papers for them to sign, now that they'd married, but Diana had assumed that he would make the journey to Kerlain, not the other way around.

Lad's own gaze fell to watch the movements of his hand. "In case we return to the States soon," he said. "It's a pretty long voyage across the Atlantic. I didn't get sick making it myself, but I wasn't a pregnant woman. On the other hand, it wouldn't be any better taking a newborn baby across the sea either."

Diana set a hand over his, stilling his movements. "Return to the United States?" she repeated. "For what purpose?"

He met her eyes, held them. "I can't leave Fair Maiden untended forever, Diana. All the money we have right now comes from that estate, not this one."

She sat up, the covers pooling around her hips, and turned to face him. "But once Kerlain has been made profitable, the gains here will be much greater than those from Fair Maiden."

He sat up too. "It will be years before Kerlain's made profitable again, if it ever is. We can't depend upon that kind of hope, sweetheart, or we'll end up starving along with everyone else here."

"But you went out to speak to The Farrell and The Colvaney about crops this morning," she said in protest. "Surely if the land is made ready to be planted—and I know you've already ordered the lime—"

"It won't make any difference, love," he said, smoothing the hair back from her face with a gentle hand. "Kerlain can't be saved that quickly. It will take time and a great deal more money than we now have."

Diana felt a dread panic rising within. "But, Lad—"

"Shhh." He kissed her mouth, still stroking her hair. "Everything will be all right, in time. You must be patient, Diana, that's all. But before summer comes, I must return to Fair Maiden."

"But why?" she pleaded. "You told me that you'd left your cousin and your uncle to care for your father's farm."

"*My* farm," he corrected. "And I can't just leave Cousin Archie holding the reins forever, waiting for me to return. He's due to marry soon, and his future father-in-law is deeding him his plantation in South Carolina as a wedding gift. He won't be able to run both places at once, and my Uncle Hadley's too old to take Fair Maiden on. Don't you understand, Diana? If I don't go back, the place will fall into ruin, and I can't allow that. I have to return, and I want my wife to come with me. There's so much I want to show you. So many people I want to introduce you to."

"Oh, Lad." She took his hands in hers and brought them to her mouth to kiss, then shook her head mournfully. "I would do anything you asked of me—anything, I vow, save this alone. I can't leave Kerlain."

He pulled back and gave her a slightly bewildered half-smile. "Of course you can. I know how you feel about Kerlain. It's been the only home you've ever had. But you'll love Fair Maiden too, once you're there. In fact, I wouldn't be surprised if you didn't feel that it was just as much your home too."

"Now you're the one who doesn't understand," she said softly. "Kerlain is more than simply a home to me—far more."

"I understand more than you know," he replied, his tone becoming taut. He pulled his hands free and glared down at her. "You're my *wife,* Diana, and your loyalties should be with me, not Kerlain. I gave you my word that I'd do everything I can for the castle and the estate, and I will, but if I say we're heading back to Fair Maiden, then we're heading back to Fair Maiden. There's no other way around it."

Diana abruptly turned away and pushed the bed-curtains aside, sliding from the mattress to the floor and immediately searching for her clothes. Several moments passed before she heard Lad pushing the curtains back on his side of the bed. He sighed aloud as his feet touched the floor, but he said nothing.

"Here are your pants," Diana stated, not looking at him even as she tossed the garment onto a chair near the fire.

"Thanks," he murmured, and moved to put them on.

Diana was nearly fully dressed before she could no longer bear the silence. She strode around the bed to find him standing there, arms crossed over his bare chest, waiting for her.

"I love you, Lad Walker," she told him bluntly, "but I'll not leave either Kerlain *or* England. Not of my own free will, leastwise, though you doubtless have the legal right to tie me up and carry me across the ocean by force." She set her hands on her hips, daring him to make the attempt. "I am the lady of Kerlain, and I'll not abandon it, or the people here. The earl left them to *me,* in my care—and in your care too, if you'd take your responsibilities more seriously. What would become of the Farrells and the Colvaneys if we abandoned them? Kerlain is all they've ever known. And what of the title? The land itself? This is *Kerlain,*" she said meaningfully, praying that he'd finally understand the import of the fact, "not a simple patch of land or a fine house." She took a step nearer him, gazing up into his face, speaking more softly. "It's the history of England itself, of your own family. It's my history as well, all I have to claim for my own. I've no doubt you love the place you call Fair Maiden, but no matter how grand or rich it may be, it cannot ever be what Kerlain is." She searched his eyes, so green and expressive. "Now do you understand why I can't leave, Lad? A visit to Fair Maiden, aye, but not to stay forever, and not until Kerlain is recovered. Then I'll go with you gladly, and just as gladly come back home."

He was silent for a long moment, then, slowly, his arms lowered.

"You love me, Diana?"

She smiled. "All that talking, and that's what you have to say to me?"

His gaze grew intent. He lifted a trembling hand to cup her cheek. "Do you?"

She reached up to cover his hand with her own. "How could I not love you, foolish man?"

The tension in his body relaxed, and he reached out to pull her near, hugging her with a fierceness that almost hurt.

"I love you, Diana. I can't begin to find the words to tell

you how. One thing is certain, though. There's no way on God's earth that I'd ever leave Kerlain without you.''

She pushed away enough to look up at him.

''Then you'll not leave Kerlain for very long, for this is where my children will be born and raised, and this will be our home.''

His expression gave nothing away, but his grip upon her softened, his hands gentle now as they held her.

''Neither of us knows what the future is going to bring, Diana. But no matter what it is, we'll be together, either here or at Fair Maiden. No, love, don't.'' He set a finger against her lips to still the words she was about to speak. ''Let's argue the matter no more. We understand each other, and that's enough for now.''

''Is it, Lad?''

''Yes,'' he whispered, bending to kiss her. ''Because if we love each other, everything else will turn out all right.''

Diana met his mouth with her own, gladly giving way to the passion that flared so readily between them, but though her heart rejoiced in the revelation of his love, her mind was yet fearful.

Love was indeed a powerful force; at last she understood what he had meant by walking over live coals for her, for Diana knew, without a doubt, that she would do exactly the same for him. But honor, loyalty, and tradition were powerful as well and bound Diana to Kerlain as tightly as love bound her to Lad. She prayed fervently, as she felt his fingers unfastening her gown for the second time that afternoon, that he would realize the truth of all that she'd told him and never test the strength of all that constrained her. She would be torn in too many directions if he forced her hand, and she feared, greatly, that what remained would be useless to them both.

Chapter Eleven

"Filthy," Maudie muttered, shaking out the dark coat with an expression of disgust. "Worse than his boots, I vow. How does he manage to get so dirty, day after day, and ruin all these fine clothes?"

"It's from working in the fields," Swithin replied, reaching for one of his brushes. "Like a commoner," he added in a lower but far more meaningful tone. The brush was applied to a pair of equally filthy breeches with great vigor. "I fear that Lord Kerlain doesn't appreciate the quality of this cloth or how easily it may be ruined. As to his boots . . ." He trailed off, giving a sniff of disdain. "I can't begin to speak of the abuse he's shown them."

Stuart, his large, muscular frame hunched into a chair nearby, looked up from his task of carefully cleaning Lord Kerlain's hunting guns, sweeping a few stray strands of blond hair out of his face with the back of his hand as he did so. "I don't tumble about in my good things, nor in my good boots," he murmured shyly, his fair complexion reddening at the words. "Ma would have my head, so she would. And Da too."

"What did he spend such good money on them for—a fortune, if you ask me—if he didn't mean to treat them proper?" Maudie spread the coat on the table near the fire, shaking her head. "I shall have to wash it." She made an unhappy clucking sound. "There's naught else to be done."

"It will be completely ruined," Swithin warned.

"No amount of brushing will take this mud out," she replied. "He must have been rolling about like a pig in the muck, I vow. And him the earl. I should think he'd be ashamed."

Swithin gave a soft, but eloquent, murmur of agreement.

"Working in the fields," Maudie went on, "cleaning out the hearths, and mending things that others should be caring for." She and Swithin exchanged knowing looks. "It's disgraceful, is what it is. Purely disgraceful."

"Certainly very odd in one wellborn," Swithin commented dryly. "One assumes that Lord Charles would teach his son to behave in a fashion far more suited to his station."

Maudie took up one of the brushes as well and, despite her earlier words, set it to the coat. "Poor Lord Charles, God bless his sweet soul. What could he do, with his wife being what she was? I'm sure he hadn't any say in the matter, or in *any* matter, with such a wife as that. But a good and proper young man *he* was, to be sure, and knew what was right. If that heathen he took to wife had let Lord Charles have his way, his son would be a far different fellow than what he is."

"The earl told me they were happy together, his ma and da," Stuart said in quiet tones, only to be pointedly ignored.

"Indeed," Swithin agreed. "Lord Charles was as noble and well-bred as any man could be. A true Walker, to his bones."

Maudie was scrubbing away now, jerking back and forth. "Aye, and wouldn't he be ashamed to see how his own flesh and blood has gone so bad, and here at Kerlain, where it would grieve him so to see it."

Diana, sitting at a table in the far corner of the long, narrow kitchen, finally looked up from the list she'd been writing for what was needed in both the pantry and larder.

She'd spent the past ten minutes striving not to listen to the aggrieved conversation between the longtime servants—though they all three had realized perfectly well that she could hear every word. They'd certainly done nothing to keep their voices lowered. It was bad enough knowing that Maudie and Swithin, and even gentle, good-natured Stuart, spoke disparagingly of their master when she wasn't present, but that they'd begun to cease caring about being overheard was the outside of enough. If this kept up they'd soon be saying the words right to Lad's face!

"The only ones who should be ashamed are the three of you," she informed them with tight anger. "Speaking of the earl in such a manner. I won't have it!" She slammed the ledger shut with loud force. "He works as he does for the sake of Kerlain, doing far more than any earl in recent history—aye, even the late earl!—has done. Would you be happier if he went off to London and gambled away what little we have left? Well?" she demanded, shoving the ledger away and standing. "Would you? Then we could starve and be done with it, the whole lot of us!"

They stared at her in silence, as if she were some shocking stranger who'd suddenly appeared out of thin air. Stuart's face grew so pale that he looked as if he'd faint.

"God help me," Diana muttered, rubbing one hand across her forehead, where an ache had set in. "I'm sorry. I didn't mean to shout. I think I'm just . . . tired." Dropping her hand, she looked at them. They were yet staring at her with disbelief. "Please—I ask this of you in friendship—do what you can to hold your tongues regarding the earl. I know he's far from what you'd hoped he might be, but you might do better to think instead on all that he's done for us. He keeps food on the table when we would have gone hungry otherwise, and fuel burning in the hearths when we would have gone cold. And heaven alone knows that he's already spent a small fortune trying to put Kerlain to rights.

If he adds to all that the effort of his own labors, how can we be so ungrateful?''

"But he's the earl, miss," Swithin said. "No other man of such title would do the same. How can we take pride in that? Knowing that our lord compares so poorly to every other?''

Diana shook her head. "You can't know that, Swithin. And even if it is true, it isn't Lad Walker who's so very different, but Kerlain itself. Look at me, at the way I'm dressed.'' She spread her hands out and looked down at the old, dusty gown she wore, one of the many she'd kept for working in the castle, though Lad had generously bought her a beautiful new wardrobe to match the one he'd ordered for himself. "I'm the Countess of Kerlain, yet I spend my days mending and sewing and dusting and cleaning and writing out lists.'' She glanced at the ledger on the table and sighed. "Yet I do not hear you making complaints regarding my behavior or insisting that I must sit about in my finest silks all day, behaving as a countess should—or as other countesses do.''

Maudie's brow furrowed. "But, miss, it isn't the same. You and the earl—it's all different.''

"Because I'm not a Walker by birth and therefore can't be expected to behave as a proper countess would?'' Diana asked. "Or because I've been at Kerlain since I was a babe and so can do no wrong, while he's a stranger here and so can do no right? Or perhaps,'' she said as Maudie and Swithin exchanged glances, "it's a little of both?''

"Of course you're a proper countess, Miss Diana,'' Swithin said reassuringly. "You're the lady of the manor and ever have been, since you were but a girl. Even the earl recognized you as such.''

Maudie nodded. "You were the most loved and respected woman in Kerlain long before you became the countess. God's truth.''

"Aye," Stuart agreed timidly, blushing.

"Then it seems to me," Diana said, "that you've one standard for the countess and a far different one for the earl, and that's not quite fair, is it?" When they gave no answer, Diana gave a shake of her head and moved to the doorway. Stopping there, she spoke but didn't look back at them. "I know what Kerlain means to you—to all of us. It's the grandest estate in all of England and bears the proudest name. But sometimes I begin to wonder if we've not all us become slightly maddened because of it." She set her hand to the door to open it. "I'll be in the drawing room, Maudie. Bring tea to me there, if you please."

"Viscount Carden, my lady."

Diana hastily set aside her teacup, rising from the chair she'd been sitting in just as Swithin stepped aside to reveal Eoghan's tall figure in the open doorway. She hadn't seen him since their unpleasant encounter on the day of her marriage, for he'd had the very good sense to stay away from her. She knew, though, that he and Lad spent a great deal of time together, always meeting outside of the castle. In the weeks that had followed Eoghan's sudden befriending of her husband, Lad had made only halfhearted suggestions that Diana receive her childhood companion. She had demurred, and he'd not pressed the issue, mainly, she suspected, because Eoghan himself never pushed for a reconciliation.

He was impeccably clad in the highest stare of fashion, as he ever was, and the sight of Eoghan thus, coming right after the conversation that had taken place in the kitchen, only served to show the vast differences between him and Lad. Diana wondered, fleetingly, why Lad couldn't be more like Eoghan in manner and appearance—then immediately crushed the disloyal, hateful idea. What a foolish, stupid thing to allow herself to so much as think! Lad was so far above Eoghan in every way that even dressed as a beggar he'd be superior. She knew that to be true. Why couldn't she make the people of Kerlain understand it?

"My lady," Eoghan greeted in a low voice, stepping forward and making a formal bow. "I hope I do not disturb you?"

Diana gave Swithin an angry look, for he knew full well that he should have asked her if she wished to receive Viscount Carden before showing him up to the drawing room. Swithin raised his chin and sniffed, then bowed to Eoghan and left the room, silently closing the double doors behind him.

"You must know that the earl is out of the castle," she said, "else you'd never have dared to come here."

Eoghan smiled. "Certainly I know he's not here, for it's you I wished to speak to, Diana, and certainly I would have come even if he had been. Your husband is now my dearest, and most frequent, companion. He would welcome me with open arms and pray for you to do the same." He set his hands behind his back and strolled farther into the room. "Lad has even hinted a time or two that I should make the effort to reconcile with my dear childhood friend. Isn't that amusing?" He stopped in front of her, still smiling. "I find it exceedingly so."

"You would," Diana replied stiffly. "I hope you'll not find it rude of me, my lord, if I tell you outright that I want you to leave my husband alone?"

Eoghan chuckled. "I forgive you the break in good manners, Diana, dearest, and hope you'll forgive me as well if I say that I shall be so disobliging as to refuse your request. I find the Earl of Kerlain's company just now far too useful to give up. He's a fascinating fellow. Truly. And he clearly keeps you contented, if the rumors being spread throughout Kerlain are true."

Diana couldn't stop the heated blush that spread across her cheeks, the sight of which clearly only amused Eoghan the more. He wanted to embarrass and humiliate her, but she'd not give him the satisfaction. Holding his gaze, she said with full meaning, "Oh, yes, Eoghan. Lad keeps me very well contented. I was so surprised, and pleased, to discover that a man's touch needn't be repulsive, as you'd led me to believe."

His smile vanished and the muscles in his face hardened. One of his hands shot out to grip her arm and give her a shake.

"You dare speak to me like that!" he said furiously, his fingers digging so tightly into her flesh that she winced and strove to pull free. He shook her again, even harder. "One day, I vow, you'll willingly receive my touch and beg for more. I've a far greater knowledge of how to pleasure a woman than that stupid oaf you took for a husband. Or perhaps that's what you crave." He drew her close, sneering down at her. "Is that it, Diana? You find making love to a gutter-born fool exciting? Some women do, you know. They enjoy coupling with men who are far beneath their station, crude, rough, clumsy men, such as your husband is. I must remember that in future and treat you accordingly."

With an effort, Diana wrenched free.

"What you'll remember in future," she told him, breathing harshly, "is that I'm the Countess of Kerlain *and* a happily married woman. If you touch me again, I'll tell the earl, and you'll shortly discover for yourself what manner of man he is."

"I know full well what manner of man he is," he said in a low, angry tone. "He's a cretin, and no matter what you may tell him about me, I'll have no trouble in turning him about with but a few well-chosen words. He'll soon believe you're the one at fault, not me."

Diana shook her head with disgust. "You and your old

tricks," she said. "You haven't changed much since you were a horrid little boy, Eoghan."

"Why should I?" he countered. "My old tricks, as you call them, work as well now as they did then."

"But not on Lad. At least, not forever. You've managed to cozen him for the time being," she admitted, "but only because he's a good and trusting man and because I've said nothing of your insults to me. But he loves me, Eoghan," she stated firmly, poking him in the chest with a finger, "and you mistake the matter greatly if you think Lad wouldn't wring your neck if he knew the truth."

"Would he?" Eoghan cocked his head slightly and regarded her for a silent moment. At last, the smile grew on his lips again. "But then why haven't you told him? Surely not out of love for my life. Is it because you fear, perhaps, that I would bring him harm instead?"

She gave him a look that could have leveled the castle walls. "Surely, Eoghan, you can't believe such a thing. Lad's muscles weren't padded by his tailor."

He shook his head. "Oh, no, Diana. I'll not rise to your bait again today. You've already made me lose my temper far too many times in the past few months—and much to my regret. I'll admit that your husband has a certain rustic strength that men of his brutish American lineage are probably given to, but that wouldn't protect him from a well-placed bullet, and if that were the case, having seen him shoot, I can assure you that I would be the victor."

Diana struggled to keep her own anger at bay. Playing word games with Eoghan required steady nerves and a steadier temper. Anything less gave him the advantage to twist the conversation to his will.

"I'd see you hang for murder," she told him.

"I'd claim self-defense," he replied, "and the House of Lords wouldn't convict an English nobleman over an American pretender. They'd probably thank me for ridding the British Empire of the fellow.''

"Then I'd kill you myself," she said evenly, "and welcome the consequences for the pleasure I'd have in the doing of it. If you must know the truth, Eoghan, I haven't told Lad about your insults and threats because I don't desire that there be any lasting enmity between you. In time you'll give way with this foolish nonsense you've taken into your head, and once that happens, we can be friends again. All of us, as neighbors should be.''

"Then you should certainly tell him, Diana," Eoghan advised, "for I'll not give way. I shall have you one day for a wife or a mistress—I hardly care which, so long as you warm my bed and my life.''

"Oh, Eoghan," she said wearily, moving to fall into her chair again. "You do exhaust me so with your stubborn ways. I wish you could know how you grieve me. You've been my closest companion, and I've missed you—indeed, I have. But when you go on like this, I don't see how we can ever regain the friendship we once had. I don't want to come to hate you. Please, don't make me do so by pursuing this madness.''

"It's not madness," he insisted. "I love you, Diana, and ever have done. *You're* the one who's ruined things between us, and if anyone has a right to feel aggrieved, it's me.''

"If you truly loved me," she said more softly, folding her hands together on her lap and gazing at him, "you'd wish me happy and leave me in peace.''

"That I cannot do. I will have you for my own, one way or another. What you must decide, I suppose, is whether or not to take the risk of telling Lad what my intentions are. And it is a risk, regardless of what you may think. If he believes you and not me, I shall be forced to kill the man, which I confess I do not wish to do. If he believes me and not you, your marriage will become strained, and more so

day by day as I can possibly make it with my small interfer-
ences, until you'll wish that you'd never set sight on P. Lad
Walker. What does the *P* stand for, by the way?" he asked,
as if they'd only been having a mild, meaningless discus-
sion. "I've asked him, but he refuses to say."

"If he will not, then I will not either," she told him, no
sign of the inner turmoil his words had wrought showing in
either her expression or her tone. "I am not so poor a wife
as to betray my husband's confidences, be they large or
small."

He stared at her thoughtfully, then sighed and said,
"Very well, Diana, if you wish to be stubborn. It matters
not. I'll leave you before your husband returns and finds us
alone here." He smiled. "I'm sure he'd be very surprised,
though pleased, as only a clod like him could be. He'd
assume the best, most likely, rather than the worst, more
fool he."

The words struck Diana deeply.

"Yes," she murmured, rising slowly from her chair.
"That is what Lad does, always. He assumes the best and
not the worst, and, do you know, Eoghan, I believe that may
be why I love him so very dearly? And why I could never
love you, for you think only the worst of all men, ever the
worst, without kindness or compassion. That's why I love
Lad so." She laughed at the wonderful, newfound knowledge. "Because he's not at all like you."

Eoghan's features hardened once more, cold with a
tightly contained rage.

"You may amuse yourself now all you please, Diana, but
you'll have little to jest over in the future, I promise you."

"Our friendship is over, Eoghan," she stated, only
slightly surprised at the lack of sorrow she felt. She had held
him so dear once, but his cruelty and selfishness had grown
beyond any measure of affection. He had never been a truly
good person, but now he wasn't even the man she'd once

claimed as a friend. "There's no hope that it will ever be regained. I'll not receive you at Kerlain again. This is the end. Now be so good as to leave."

He bowed low. "As you wish, Diana," he said, then straightened. "One more thing I must tell you—it's the reason I came, really. Don't let him get you with child. If you become my wife, I'll not recognize any of Lad Walker's leavings as legitimate, for only our children will inherit Kerlain and Lising Park. And if I decide to take you as my mistress, I won't want the useless little brats about. Bear that in mind, will you, darling?"

"Bastard!" Diana swung about and picked up the half-full teapot, ready to throw it at him. "Get out! *Now!*"

He laughed and sauntered toward the double doors, saying, as he neared them, "You lost your temper, Diana." He cast one last glance at her. "Now we're even."

Lad knew that Diana was in a bad mood minutes after he joined her in the parlor, collapsing wearily into the nearest chair. He'd barely gotten a word of greeting out of his mouth before she stood from her own chair and said testily, "Lad, your clothes! Why on earth must you get them so dirty, day after day? Don't you realize how difficult it is for Maudie and Swithin to clean them? I know they're not London-made, but even so, we paid the tailor from Woebley a pretty penny for them."

Lad blinked at her with a measure of surprise but, seeing the honest distress on her lovely face, was careful with his reply.

"Spreading lime out on the fields is dirty work. I'd be glad to wear my old clothes, but Swithin makes such a fuss each morning about what I wear that I've given up making the suggestion."

"He's only trying to make certain that you're properly dressed, as the Earl of Kerlain should be."

Lad sighed wearily. "We've gone over this," he said, rubbing a hand across his face, feeling the dirt and grime there. He should go get cleaned up, he supposed, before she noticed that he was getting the chair dirty. There wasn't much good furniture left at Kerlain, and Diana jealously guarded what little there was. Thinking of that, he stood, then turned to dust the specks of mud from the elegant cloth that covered the chair's cushion. "If I sit around in fine clothes all day, being the proper earl, then none of the work that needs doing gets done." When he straightened to look at her, it was to find Diana standing near the fire, staring at the flames. Her hands twined and untwined fretfully, and her pretty mouth was turned into a pensive frown. What had happened today, he wondered, to set her so on edge?

It was nearly the end of June. Plants had begun sprouting, some blossoming, and the time was ripe for fields to be planted for harvesting in the fall. In his mind's eye he envisioned the rash of activity that would be taking place at Fair Maiden. His cousin Archie had written to say that he'd remain at Fair Maiden long enough to make certain that the planting was done and the various orchards tended and, most important of all, that the many shipments of seeds, seedlings, and saplings were sent out to Fair Maiden's faithful customers. All was well, Archie had reassured him, and Fair Maiden would realize a tremendous profit, as it usually did.

What Lad wouldn't give to be one of those customers just now. An infusion of healthy plants and trees was exactly what Kerlain needed most, but every time he'd brought the subject up he'd been immediately rebuffed by The Farrell and The Colvaney, and by Diana too. There were to be none of his strange new ways at Kerlain—God help him, but he was sick of hearing it—and certainly nothing American. But perhaps it was just as well. Lad wasn't even certain that he could get through the cost and legalities of importing a suitable shipment of such goods and was less certain that enough plants and trees would survive the long overseas journey. And even if, by some miracle, the shipment did arrive, he'd have to single-handedly do the planting, for none of the people of Kerlain would help him, to be sure. They'd done little enough as it was, though Diana assured him, and his own sense of the people told him, that they were the hardest of workers when they wished to be. They'd clearly labored to the utmost for the former earl, but not for the present one. Lad was fighting a futile, uphill battle and was at a loss as to how to change the direction of his defeat.

He'd been at Kerlain and married to Diana for three months now, and nothing he did seemed to please either her or the people there. His manner of speech was wrong, his manner of dress was wrong, all of his ideas were wrong, and God help him if he slipped and made mention of the recent war—which any reasonable man might do, having lived through such a memorable event. Then he got fury from all sides. There were times, more often than he liked, when Lad began to think that everyone at Kerlain expected him to forget who he was, who his mother and brother had been, where he was from, all of his past, and start his life over from scratch with nothing but a title and an estate for foundations.

At being an earl he was a special failure. If he sat in the castle all day twiddling his thumbs, dressed to the teeth and doing his best to be the "lord of the manor," then he was condemned as being lazy and uncaring. As this so offended the people, and as they refused to work for a lord who wouldn't lift a finger to help them, no work for the day was accomplished. If Lad went out to oversee the labor being done in the fields or to give suggestions, he was condemned with glares and mutterings suggesting that he didn't trust his people. The result was that very little work got done. If he worked physically to attend the needs of the estate, as he had been used to doing at Fair Maiden, he was condemned as behaving in a manner unbefitting the Earl of Kerlain. And, of course, the only work that got done was his own.

No matter what he did—short of leaving the estate and abdicating the title—he couldn't make them happy. Diana still seemed to think he could make the impossible happen, and for her sake alone, Lad strove onward. He'd said nothing further to her since the night they'd argued the matter of leaving Kerlain in favor of Fair Maiden. He had hoped, as he still hoped, that the love she professed for him would eventually help her to realize just how wretched he was, and make the idea more amenable to her.

Diana *did* love him. He knew that was true, believed it with every part of himself. When they were alone, just the two of them, centered on each other and not on Kerlain, she was all that a man could ask for in a wife, and more. Tender, loving, gentle, open, and so sweetly affectionate. Those were the moments when he could tell her about his past, about his parents and Joshua, about the rest of his crazy family. She'd listen raptly, as if he were telling her the most wonderful, amazing fairy tale. But perhaps that was what it seemed to her. Diana had told him that she'd not been out of Herefordshire since she'd come to Kerlain as a young child. The knowledge had amazed him, but even more stunning was the fact that she had no desire to travel anywhere else— not even to London.

She stood so still and quiet by the fire, clearly distressed. Lad rubbed the back of his neck and cast his glance downward for a few minutes, gazing absently at his dirty boots and wondering how he should approach her. Women were such mysterious creatures that a man seldom knew whether he was stepping right or wrong. What worked on one occasion would be a disaster the next. But maybe some good news would warm her up a bit.

"Did Maudie tell you about the salmon I brought home this morning? You were busy washing linens, she told me, so I left them with her before going out to the fields."

"Yes," she replied in a soft voice. "She told me. We'll have a wonderful feast tonight. As good as the pheasant we had last night." A moment of silence, then she added, "I can't think how you manage to bring home so much for the larder as you do. My godfather used to hunt often, but he seldom brought anything back." She crossed her arms about her chest as if she were cold and rubbed her fingers over her arms. "He used to say it was because we hadn't any dogs, but I think it must have been because he wasn't a very good shot. You are, clearly."

Lad took a step nearer to her. "Good enough," he said. "Although I really have Eoghan to thank. He's the one who knows the best places to flush out birds and all the best spots to fish."

At last she turned her head to look at him, her dark eyes large in the firelight.

"You were with Eoghan again this morning." It was a statement, not a question. "Just as you're with him far more often than is right. Why won't you believe me, Lad, that you can't trust him?"

He spread his hands out in a helpless gesture. "He's the only friend I've got in England. Man friend, I mean," he amended, thinking that Diana was truly his friend as well as his wife. "We get along real well, and . . . I suppose it's mainly because I like him."

"He only means us ill!" she declared insistently, her tone so desperate that Lad closed the slight distance between them and took her hands in a reassuring grasp.

"Sweetheart, you can't believe that's true. I know you're still angry with him, but he's been trying to make up for what he did on our wedding day. He brought Maeva, and three and four mornings a week he comes just to help me to keep food in the larder, never taking anything for his own table.''

She made a snorting sound. ''He hardly needs it. Eoghan's wealthy and lacks for nothing. But that's beside the point. He isn't being kind because he's a good man, Lad. He's trying to befriend you for his own purposes—none of which are good.''

He was utterly confused. ''Well, what are they, then?''

She gazed up at him, her eyes troubled, but just when she was about to speak, a scratch came on the door.

''Sorry, m'lord.'' Stuart poked his blond head around the open door. ''I've brought more coal for the fire.''

Diana pulled her hands free and moved away from Lad, clearly embarrassed at being caught in such a stance by one of the servants. With a sigh, Lad waved Stuart into the room.

''Bring it in, Stuart,'' he said. ''Here, let me give you a hand,'' he added as the younger man came around the door, toting the heavy bucket.

''No, my lord, I'm all right,'' Stuart replied at once, as Diana whirled about and remonstrated at the same time, *''Lad!''*

Lad threw his hands up into the air. ''Fine,'' he muttered. ''I'll go and get cleaned up before I offend anyone else.''

He was halfway to the still-open doors when Swithin appeared, bearing a silver tray.

''My lord, a rider from Woebley has just arrived with this missive for you.'' He bowed as Lad took the folded documents. ''I shall go and make your bath ready.''

''What is it?'' Diana came up behind him, peering over Lad's shoulder as he frowned at the missive. ''Who is it from?''

''My cousin Archie,'' he replied with equal measures of

bewilderment and concern. "Can't imagine why he's written again so soon."

"Oh, Lad." Diana touched his arm. "I pray nothing's amiss."

"Everything was fine a few weeks ago," he said as he unsealed and unfolded the document. The news that he read there stunned him so greatly that he didn't realize Diana was saying his name until her voice had filled with panic. Hands shaking, he lifted his eyes to gaze at her.

"What is it, Lad?"

"My uncle . . . my uncle Hadley is dead."

"Oh, no," she murmured. "Oh, Lad."

"I wasn't there," he said unsteadily, blinking back sudden tears as the truth of the words washed over him. "He was alone. Archie found him . . . he died alone, Diana."

She threw her arms about him and held him tightly.

"I'm sorry, love."

He released a shuddering breath and buried his face in the softness of her hair, hugging her slender body against himself. In some dim recess he remembered that they weren't alone, that Stuart was standing in the corner of the room, watching, listening. Lad strove to compose himself.

"We have to go back home to Fair Maiden as soon as arrangements can be made." He swallowed heavily. "I never should have left him alone. Not so soon after Mother and Josh . . . after they . . ."

"It's all right." Diana's grip on him became fierce. "You couldn't have known. He told you to come, and you pleased him by doing so. You didn't leave him alone, Lad. Your cousin was with him. And the servants."

Lad shook his head, unable to speak for a time, only able to think that he should have gone home—he and Diana—weeks ago. They might have been with Uncle Hadley at the end. They might have been able to save him. God! If only he'd never come to this cursed place! If only he'd stayed at Fair Maiden, where he belonged.

"Archie was in South Carolina, visiting his bride. The servants . . . they're good folk, but they're not family. There wasn't anyone . . . no family . . . to be with him at the end. Oh, God . . . he was such a good man, Diana."

"I know," she whispered soothingly, stroking a hand over his head. "I know, my love. You mustn't torment yourself. It isn't what your uncle would want. Everything will be all right."

He shook his head. "No." His voice was muffled against her hair. "No." He pulled away, lifting a hand to wipe his damp eyes. The letter from his cousin was lying on the ground. "Except for you, coming to England has been nothing but a disaster. I should have stayed at Fair Maiden and taken care of my uncle and my home, no matter what he wanted me to do." He set his hands on her shoulders and drew in an unsteady breath. "We'll go home to Fair Maiden as soon as possible. You understand that, don't you, Diana?"

She reached up to touch his wet cheeks, gentle and loving. "Of course I understand. But let's make no determinations now. You're overset and need time to grieve. And time to think, as well, on what's best to be done."

A deep shudder ran through him, an almost overwhelming longing to be home again and away from Kerlain, away from England, never to so much as think of them again. He felt as if he'd been playing at some useless game all these months—the game of being "earl"—when he should have been at Fair Maiden, taking on the responsibilities left to him by his parents, by Joshua.

"I know what's best to be done," he said.

"You're overset," she said again, stroking his cheek. "But when you've had time, you'll realize that there's no sense in returning to Tennessee. You've no one there any longer, now that your uncle is gone. I realize that you wish to take care of matters at Fair Maiden yourself, but it's such a long journey, love, and we're needed so very much here. If we were to go now, we'd not return to Kerlain again until harvest time, and then only if we were fortunate in the weather. Surely your cousin can find someone who can be trusted in Tennessee to take care of what must be done, if he's unwilling to do so himself. Did you not have a lawyer there who handled legal matters for the estate, as Mr. Sibbley does for Kerlain?''

Lad felt cold suddenly, as if ice water had been poured over him. He stepped away from her.

''What are you saying, Diana?''

She seemed confused by both his actions and his words and tried to move close again. Lad put his hands out to hold her back.

''What are you saying?'' he demanded.

''Only that you must give yourself a few days before making any decisions about Fair Maiden,'' she said gently. ''You don't know what you may decide, now that you've no one left in Tennessee—no relatives, I mean. You may want to discover if your uncle in Massachusetts—your late mother's brother—wishes to have anything to do with the estate. Or perhaps, even, if it might not be wisest to find a buyer—''

''*A buyer?*''

He almost couldn't believe she'd said it. The words struck harder than any blow—and far more painfully.

''You think I'd *sell* Fair Maiden?''

''Lad, please, you misunderstand me.'' She stretched a hand out pleadingly, and he stumbled away from it, from her.

''No.'' He shook his head, sick with despair. ''Never . . . I'd never sell it.''

''I've spoken poorly. I didn't mean—''

"I know what you meant, Diana," he said bitterly, overwhelmed by the hurt of what he finally understood to be true. "You have no care for Fair Maiden, for what it means to me. It's only Kerlain you care about. God! I've been such a *fool* to think it would ever be otherwise!"

Her face whitened. "No, Lad. Please, only let me explain . . . I'm sorry I said it as I did, especially now, when you've had such terrible news."

"Do you even love me?" he asked, grief and anger driving him beyond all temperance. He felt as if he'd begin weeping again and struggled to maintain the slender grip he held on his emotions. "Or is it simply that I'm the heir to your precious Kerlain? Is that my whole value to you? I regret that I've been such a grave disappointment—to you and the people here."

Tears were streaming down her face now, and she lifted trembling fingers to her lips.

"Oh, Lad," she murmured sorrowfully.

He left, stalking out of the room and out of the castle without looking back. He mounted Maeva and rode out of the castle courtyard into the dusk of early evening, not knowing where he went, not caring.

Chapter Twelve

The lake was cold—freezing cold—but Lad stayed in the water until he was numb all over, until he couldn't feel his fingers or toes, until his teeth were chattering so fiercely that he couldn't hear anything over the sound. Then, and only then, he crawled out and stretched naked on a nearby patch of grass, drawing in great rasping gulps of the still night air to calm the racing of his heart and the shuddering of his body. His skin was chilled with gooseflesh, though he felt warmer now than in the water. When he was dry enough, he pulled his shirt and pants on, then lay back down on the grass, barefoot and exhausted.

He might have slept, despite the cold and the vulnerability of lying as he did, so fully exposed in the dark of night, but his mind was too full of thoughts to rest.

He was familiar with grief and all its attendant sensations. His father, his mother, Joshua—and now Uncle Hadley. Tears couldn't begin to touch the sense of loss he knew. To be here, in a foreign land, without family, without friends, only made it that much worse—an aloneness far beyond being merely alone. Not that it mattered. He could be anywhere now and feel it. Even at Fair Maiden, with all its ghostly memories, though he did wish, so fervently, that he'd been with Uncle Hadley at the end.

He sat up after a while and rested his forehead on his indrawn knees, telling himself that he needed to get up and finish getting dressed, then find where Maeva had wandered off to and go back to the castle. Diana would be worried about him, if not because he was her husband, at least because he was the precious Earl of Kerlain. He had no idea what the morrow would bring, but somehow they would have to come to some kind of resolution on all the difficulties that lay between them. He loved Diana too much to either leave her or let her go, but they couldn't continue on as they were. This madness about Kerlain was just that—a complete insanity. He either had to make Diana understand it or let himself go mad, too, and join headlong in what she felt for the wretched, crumbling estate.

A rustling in the trees behind him told Lad that he was no longer alone, but he made no movement to see who approached. His own personal safety meant naught to him at the moment. He was numb and cared for nothing.

"Lad?" It was Eoghan. "Lad?"

A moment of silence, then Eoghan spoke again, clearly to someone else, "I've found him. Return to Lising Park. Take the other men with you." A soft murmuring followed this, to which Eoghan replied curtly, "There's no need to upset Lady Kerlain any further. I forbid it. Return to Lising—*now.*" The command was given with such taut superiority that Lad couldn't imagine any servant disobeying. Eoghan's servants clearly didn't, for he heard more appropriate mutterings and a good deal more rustling as they obediently departed.

Lad lifted his head and gazed out over the lake, waiting for his friend to join him. He was glad that it was Eoghan who'd found him. He didn't have to pretend with Eoghan. He didn't have to be the Earl of Kerlain with him. He was truly the only man in England whom Lad could trust, and his presence now was a relief, rather than a burden. When Eoghan's hand fell warm upon Lad's bare neck in a brief, comforting touch, he nearly began to weep again, but clamped his teeth together tight and didn't allow himself the indulgence.

"So here you are," Eoghan said, and sat down beside him. "I've been looking for you since I heard. I'm so sorry about your uncle, Lad."

Lad nodded and said nothing. They sat in silence a long while. Eoghan pulled a silver flask out of an inner coat pocket and passed it. Lad drank deeply of the contents, a slightly bitter whiskey that he recognized as one of Eoghan's favorites. It tasted of apples, as everything in Herefordshire seemed to do, and made Lad think of the whiskey Uncle Hadley used to distill every year at Fair Maiden. Uncle Hadley's hadn't tasted of apples, but of berries—the smoothest, sweetest, hardest-kicking whiskey Lad had ever known.

Taking another long sip, he wiped his mouth with the back of his hand and passed the flask back.

"Will you stay out here all night?" Eoghan asked, capping the flask and setting it on the ground between them.

"I need to get back to the castle soon," Lad replied. "Diana will be wondering where I am. Did she send you to look for me?"

"Well, she was worried, wasn't she?"

"Was she?" Lad asked. When Eoghan gave no answer, he sighed and said, "I suppose she was. I wasn't very pleasant to her. She must have thought I'd gone a little crazy."

Eoghan didn't look at him but held his gaze out over the lake.

"She wasn't very pleasant either, though, was she? Asking you to sell Fair Maiden? I can hardly fathom how any woman could ask such a thing of the husband she claims to love."

Lad couldn't precisely fathom it either. When Eoghan pressed the flask into his hands again, he drank from it without thinking. An hour or more passed, of drinking and talking. When the flask was empty, Eoghan rose and brought a fresh bottle of whiskey out of his horse's saddle-bags. And brought something else too.

"What we need to do is take your mind off Kerlain and your uncle," he said, sitting down once more. He held a small silver box in his hands which he showed to Lad, who inspected it briefly in the pale moonlight before lifting the bottle to his lips.

"What is it?"

Eoghan flipped a small clasp open with his thumb and opened the lid. Lad could just make out an ace of spades. A deck of cards. What a strange notion for Eoghan to take just now.

"It's a little dark to play cards, don't you think?" he asked, tipping the bottle again to sip from it. The whiskey was smoother now, tasting less like the cider he'd drunk so much of at Kerlain.

Eoghan glanced up into the night sky, at the half-moon.

"There's enough light to play by," he said, "and the reflection from the lake is helpful. Come, we'll play a few rounds of *poque* just to get your mind off your troubles, and when you've lost all that you own to me, you'll be able to return to Kerlain too miserable to think about anything else."

Lad uttered a laugh and shook his head. "I almost think I'd *give* everything away to you for that," he said.

Eoghan smiled. "Don't be foolish," he chided. "Here, let's play a round and stop thinking of what's happened. I don't mean to make light of your uncle's death, but a few hours of peace will be restful to you, I think."

"Aye, it would be," Lad agreed, feeling a bit sleepy and thinking that he'd probably had too much to drink. "You're a good fellow, Eoghan Patterson, always getting me out of trouble. A very good friend. I can't think why it is that Diana's so angered at you every moment."

"Can't you?" Eoghan asked, carefully taking the cards from their elegant case. "I'm sure I can't explain it either. No, keep the bottle for yourself, old man. I don't want any more. Do you know how to play *poque?*"

Lad shook his head and, when it began to spin, was instantly sorry.

"It's French," Eoghan explained, shuffling the cards with expertise. "Quite entertaining. I'm sure you'll enjoy it a great deal."

"It's too dark to see, just about," Lad told him, feeling too drunk and weary to play at all.

"No, it's perfect," Eoghan said as he began to deal. "The moon's not yet at its midpoint, and will give us light for hours." He smiled. "We'll be just fine."

The moon had nearly finished its nightly journey by the time two servants from Lising Park brought the insensible Earl of Kerlain home. Diana rushed into the courtyard, kneeling to receive Lad's head in her lap as the men pulled him from Maeva and laid him on the ground.

"What's happened to him?" she demanded, uncaring of the tears that betrayed her distress. He was alive, she discovered quickly, sobbing with relief, but he was fully unconscious, as if he'd been grievously wounded. But, no . . . she bent closer, sniffing the strong odor that clung to him. What on earth . . . *whiskey?*

"Where did you find him?" She stared up at the men through the chilled darkness, blinking to clear her vision. They shifted uncomfortably.

"My lord Carden returned to Lising Park but an hour past and told us where we would find Lord Kerlain, my lady. He sent us out to bring him home to you."

Diana shook her head with bewilderment. "Eoghan?" she repeated. "But how could he have known that Lord

Kerlain was—'' She fell silent, suddenly realizing where—rather, *whom*—Lad had gotten the whiskey from. Just how Eoghan had found Lad was another question. She'd sent every able-bodied man in Kerlain out to look for their earl, with no success, and had nearly been ready to go searching herself.

''My lord bade me give this to you, my lady.'' One of the men pulled something out of a pocket and handed it to her. It was a small metal box. Diana peered at it in the darkness, turning it about with one hand while still cradling Lad with the other. Silver, she thought, feeling how cold and smooth it was. A small silver card box.

''Help me to get the earl into the castle,'' she commanded, tucking the box safely inside her gown. ''All but my oldest servants have gone in search of Lord Kerlain. Be careful with him!''

They carried Lad to his chamber, where Swithin awaited, and laid him upon the bed. For the first time Diana saw that he was barefoot, bereft even of shoes and stockings.

''Oh, Lad,'' she murmured, sitting beside his powerless body and rubbing her hands over his cold arms in a futile attempt to warm him. ''Lad, what have you done?''

''Allow me to care for him, my lady,'' Swithin said gently, touching Diana's shoulder. ''I know what's to be done. He'll be very ill in the morn, I fear.''

''I want the fire hotter,'' she said tightly. ''And a warm bath. I shall bathe him if you'll help me to get these off.'' She tugged at the shirt he wore. ''And then we'll have him warm beneath the covers, just as soon as may be, for he's so cold.'' She pressed her hands against the chilled skin of his face, then bent to lay gently over his chest, warming him with her whole self. ''So cold . . . oh, God, what have I done to him?''

''Miss Diana . . . my lady . . .''

She sat up slowly, her trembling hands lingering at Lad's

cheeks, then smoothing down to his neck to feel the life, so precious to her, still within him. "The fire, Swithin," she said, her voice firm if not her hands. "When he's comfortable and resting, I'll go. Not until then."

Half an hour passed before Diana left Lad in Swithin's care, confident that he was as comfortable as he possibly could be, for the time being. He had moaned and groaned in protest as they'd undressed and bathed him, but she knew he'd be in far greater misery in the hours to come, as the liquor he'd consumed took its heavy toll. She'd helped Swithin nurse her godfather through too many similar nights to believe otherwise.

Wearily, she made her way to her own bedchamber, leaving the adjoining doors open so that Swithin could call out if he needed her. Collapsing into the nearest chair, she closed her eyes and allowed herself a few minutes rest before forcing herself to address the next issue at hand.

Eoghan.

What deviltry had he been up to now? she wondered, pulling the small silver box from the pocket hidden within the folds of her gown. A box of playing cards. How foolish, she thought. And how very like Eoghan. A game player to the last.

She undid the clasp and lifted the lid to find a note lying atop the deck of cards. Setting the box on her lap, Diana sat back and unfolded the note. A familiar verse of poetry greeted her—from the Epitaph of Thomas Gray's *Elegy*.

> *Here rests his head upon the lap of Earth*
> *A Youth, to Fortune and to Fame unknown.*
> *Fair Science frowned not on his humble birth,*
> *And Melancholy marked him for her own.*

How often Eoghan had poked fun at her love of poetry. He thought it humorous, did he, to compare Lad to the young man referred to in the poem? Well, the Earl of Kerlain wasn't dead yet, no thanks to Eoghan's cruelties. Or her own.

Beneath the verse, Eoghan continued.

Kerlain is mine now, along with what little honor Lord Kerlain possessed. I hold your husband's vowel for the entire estate, including your beloved castle, all fairly won, no matter how you may strive to find it otherwise.

"Oh, God." For one brief moment, Diana thought she might actually faint. Rivulets of pain shot through her body like jolts from a lightning strike. She blinked to clear her vision and forced herself to read the rest of Eoghan's elegantly scripted words.

My sweet Diana, I am at your service, as ever, and shall await the pleasure of your arrival, which I trust will come sooner than later. It has been, I fear, a wearisome night, though certainly a profitable one. Don't make me wait long, dearest. I can't promise that my present good mood will last until morning.

Diana's hand trembled as she lowered the note to her lap, gazing at the open card case lying there. She couldn't believe it was true. Surely it wasn't . . . surely this was one of Eoghan's stupid jests.

Lad disliked gambling. He'd told her so shortly after they'd married. She knew it was a common pastime among gentlemen—indeed, several previous earls had aided Kerlain's ruin with their love of gaming. But the only games Lad enjoyed were the same she cherished—chess in particular, with which they had whiled away many evenings before the fire.

She lifted one of the cards from the box and turned it about, gazing at it. No, Lad didn't enjoy gambling, and he didn't approve of drinking to excess either, yet he lay only a short distance away, soaked through with whiskey. The card fluttered to the floor, followed by its mates when Diana stood. The note she tucked inside the bodice of her gown, securing it carefully so as not to lose it. She could let no one know of this, not even Swithin and Maudie.

"I'm going out," she said aloud from the door that adjoined her chamber.

From his place beside the bed, Swithin looked up at her. "But, miss! It's the middle of the night!"

"I'll send Maudie up to help you with the earl," she replied, casting a glance to where her husband lay. He was so still and pale, so vulnerable, and her heart knew a pang of grief. He couldn't have done this terrible thing, gambled Kerlain away, knowing what it would mean to her—to them both. Please, God, let it not be true.

"But where are you going, miss?" Swithin asked, his eyes wide upon her, his usual composure gone.

"To Lising Park," she replied. "You may tell his lordship, if he should wake and ask for me, that I've taken care of everything."

"Everything, Miss Diana?"

"Yes, Swithin." Her eyes narrowed. "Everything."

Chapter Thirteen

"How delectable you look, Diana, my pet," Eoghan said, lazily contemplating Diana from head to toe. "All damp and windblown. Has it begun to mist outside? Or is it merely exertion and passion that make you look so delightfully moist? I should love to see you looking the same in my bed. Quite inspirational. It makes me want to lick you. Everywhere." He casually lifted his glass of wine and drank.

Diana was still breathing heavily from her frantic ride, made even more horrifying by the darkness of the early morning hour. It had taken an hour or more to cross both their lands and reach Lising Manor, pushing hard every moment. She had followed Eoghan's butler to this parlor on trembling legs, exhausted and distraught, only to be greeted by the sight of Eoghan freshly bathed, his blond hair combed, lounging indolently before the fire in a silk jacket, sipping wine.

"Is it true?" she demanded.

He set his wineglass aside and stood, his movements slow and leisurely.

"Yes. Quite true." He touched a nearby table, upon which a crumpled piece of paper lay. "See for yourself."

She strode forward and snatched the paper up, pulling it apart. There, scrawled in but a few simple words, she saw the end of all that she cared for, all that was her own— signed away by Lad.

"You f-forged it," she whispered, desperately hoping. "His signature."

"Ask him if I did, once he's sobered up. He wasn't so far gone that he doesn't remember very well what he agreed to. I won Kerlain fairly, and unless you can convince your husband to lie—"

"Nay." She shook her head and dropped the paper to the table again. "He would never do so, and I'd not ask it of him." She lifted her gaze to Eoghan's. "It isn't legal. Lad hadn't any right to give away what isn't his. Only the land belongs to him. Castle Kerlain is mine."

"It hardly matters, does it?" Eoghan asked, leaning against the mantel and folding his arms across his chest. "The law recognizes that a husband controls what his wife possesses and that her properties may be used to satisfy his debts. Aside from that, we must consider Lad's honor— what little there is, or ever was, of it. If he fails to pay his vowels, then the name of Kerlain is permanently soiled. Your husband will have no honor and certainly no respect. He, and you, will be pariahs to any and all who matter, and Kerlain itself will be covered in shame—all of it. The title, the lands, the estate complete."

It was true, Diana thought with despair. She didn't care so much for her own reputation, but a man's honor was his most precious possession, and Lad would suffer greatly if he lost his. At least so long as they were in England, while he was the Earl of Kerlain.

"What do you want, Eoghan?"

"You know very well."

She nodded, her heart throbbing painfully in her chest.

"You want me to spread my legs for you? Here?" She pointed to the floor. "Shall I lie there on the carpet while you take what you desire, raping another man's wife? Your *neighbor's* wife?"

His eyebrows rose. "I hadn't considered it," he said,

seemingly much amazed. "Would you do such a thing, Diana?"

"I have little choice in the matter, have I? Not if I wish to regain Kerlain and all that is rightfully mine."

"And your husband's honor."

"Yes," she agreed. "That most especially."

"Indeed." He gave a slight nod. "And for all this, you're willing to do whatever I wish?"

"No, Eoghan. I'll debase myself for the sake of Kerlain but will bring harm to no one else—and never to my husband."

"I see." He smiled slowly and tapped his chin with one thoughtful finger, gazing at her consideringly. "Well, I must admit, the idea of having you leap to fulfill my bidding here and now is tempting. There are a great many things I should like to have you do—for me and to me. Most of them on your knees . . ."

"I'd hate you every moment," she vowed tightly. "And consign you to the devil ever after. You know better than anyone, Eoghan, what that means."

"Certainly I do," he said affably. "For no one knows you better than I, Diana, my sweet. But you needn't think I should ever debase you in such a manner. When you give yourself to me, you'll do so willingly, regardless of whether you hate me or consign me to the devil. I don't desire a martyr for a wife."

"Wife?" she repeated. "You've lost your wits, Eoghan. I'm already married and intend to remain so. If you think to add murder to your list of accomplishments, then I pray you will think again."

He laughed. "It will hardly be necessary to go to such extremes now, Diana. You've asked me what I want in return for Kerlain, and I'll tell you. You're to divorce your husband and send him back to his beloved America. That's all. Quite simple, really."

Diana didn't need to consider the idea—not even for all the love she bore Kerlain.

"No," she said. "I'll not do it. You can keep Kerlain—all of it. I'll go with Lad to America, and we'll begin again at Fair Maiden. I wish to God I'd said those very words to him this afternoon, before you tricked him with your deviltry."

She managed to say the words without hesitation, but within, her heart felt as if it were crumbling to tiny, jagged pieces. She wanted to weep for what she'd lost—Kerlain, her home, the people she loved—and for breaking the solemn vow she'd given her godfather. But there was nothing else that she could do. She and Lad were *one,* and nothing could come between that. It had been her own foolishness that had driven him to wager Kerlain against Eoghan's wiles—now she would pay the price.

"We'll be gone within a month," she said, reaching with numb fingers to pull her cloak more tightly about her. "I'm sorry to ask for so long, but there will be much to attend. I'll send a missive to let you know when you may take possession of the castle and . . . everything else. Goodbye, Eoghan."

He was across the room before she had a chance to take more than three steps, barring her way to the door.

"Diana, this is *Kerlain* we speak of. You could never give it up. It's . . . it's impossible."

"Oh, yes, Eoghan, it is possible—for Lad. Move, please. I'm weary of your company."

"You'll not leave England," he stated. "Nor Kerlain. If you do, I'll destroy not only the castle but the people as well. The Farrells and the Colvaneys. All of them. They'll suffer so greatly that they'll pray for death—and set their curses at your door."

"Why?" she demanded furiously. "Your quarrel is with *me.* They've done nothing to you!"

A grim smile curved his lips, and his breathing heightened. "Even the children. I'll see them starving—I vow before God I will. Babes in arms, the young and old alike. They'll have nothing from their new master but misery and sorrow. But not if you stay, Diana. Not if you'll do as I tell you."

"*Bastard!* I'll have none of you! I *will* leave Kerlain, even if I must take every man, woman, and child with me!"

He laughed again, but now it began to sound almost crazed. "What will you do, Diana? Ship them all across the sea to live at Fair Maiden? Will you?" He laughed harder, as if the notion tickled him immensely. "Can you not see The Farrell and The Colvaney in the accursed United States? Oh, God, just to think of it!"

Diana frowned. "Move aside, Eoghan."

"They'd never leave, anywise," he went on merrily. "Generations they've lived on Kerlain. It's as much in their blood as it is in yours. More, what with all their loved ones from hundreds of years back buried there. You might as well try to take their souls away as to make the Farrell and Colvaney clans leave their beloved land."

It was the truth, Diana knew. Completely and absolutely the truth. The Farrells and the Colvaneys would rather wage war, and face death, than leave Kerlain.

"Move aside," she repeated firmly, "and let me pass."

"No, wait," he said, calming, grinning at her, wiping his face with his fingers. "Wait a moment. I can see that you're in earnest, Diana. I'll make no more demands of you, for you'll clearly have none of them, not even at the cost of Kerlain and its people."

"Nay, I'll not."

"But what of a wager? You'd consider wagering for Kerlain, would you not? A fair wager, mind you. No tricks. I promise."

"Your promises mean nothing."

"I'll put it in writing—a contract between the two of us. I'll let you write and keep it, just so you'll know it's always safely taken care of."

Diana regarded him suspiciously. "What manner of wager?"

"A perfectly reasonable one. You agree to remain at Kerlain, and I'll give you the chance to buy it from me at a fair price, say . . . seventy thousand pounds?"

Diana's knees nearly gave way. Seventy thousand pounds! It was an enormous sum of money. And yet it was probably as close to being what Kerlain was worth—even in its great disrepair—as it could be.

"Of course, that's something of a bargain," Eoghan went on, "considering that I could sell an ancient estate like Kerlain for a great deal more to one of those rich nabobs who love to boast about such possessions. Even in its dilapidated state."

Diana backed away a few steps until she felt a chair at the backs of her legs. Carefully, she sat down, staring at him.

"Seventy thousand pounds," she murmured. "We might be able to pay the money in installments, but we'd need time. Once the fields have begun to produce again, I'm sure we'd be able to—"

"Three years," Eoghan stated curtly. "I'll give you three years from the day after tomorrow to make payment in full. If you don't, you'll cede the wager—on my terms."

"But that's impossible!" Diana told him. "It will be three years before the fields have even begun to produce decent crops, let alone that kind of profit."

"Then the earl must find another way, mustn't he?" Eoghan said. "I don't particularly care how or where, even if he must return to his beloved United States, so long as you remain at Kerlain, Diana. You might send him to London," he added more thoughtfully. "Many a fortune's been won and lost in that great city's gaming hells."

"You dare to speak to me of gambling after what you've done?" Diana asked with narrowed eyes.

Eoghan smiled. "It could hardly do the fellow any harm now to attempt his hand at gaming. He's little left to lose, after all."

"Lad has his title," she told him, "and his honor."

"The title he may keep," Eoghan said carelessly. "His honor is only his if he manages to repay his debt to me— either by keeping his word and giving me Kerlain, or by winning our wager. Now, perhaps we should discuss what my prize will be should you lose."

"I haven't accepted the bargain yet," she reminded him.

"Oh, but you will, Diana, my sweet," he said with certainty. "You will. It's the only chance you'll have to regain your precious Kerlain and to keep its people safe from such a misery as I'll visit upon them. Three years is a long time for a man to acquire a mere seventy thousand pounds. He might become involved in some kind of trade . . . only think of how many merchants have become wealthy in a far shorter amount of time in imports."

That was true, Diana thought, almost afraid to let any kind of hope take seed in her heart.

"Or it may very well be that the earl's estate in America will provide the necessary funds." He shrugged lightly. "I have no notion of these things, but it seems likely. So, you see, Diana, my offer isn't an impossible one. Merely difficult enough to give me a sporting chance at winning what I truly desire."

"It would be too much to assume that you'd give me the chance to win back Kerlain for the sake of the estate alone," she said dryly.

"I don't know why I should," he replied. "I already hold the estate in my grasp. But it's not what I want. I've already told you what that is. You, as my wife."

"And I've already told you," Diana said, standing, "that I'll not divorce my husband. I love Lad."

He gazed at her for a long, silent moment, then lifted a hand toward the door.

"Then perhaps we have nothing left to say to each other. Only remember this, Diana," he said, stopping her before she took a step, "that I gave you the fair opportunity to save Kerlain and its people. You promised your godfather, the late earl, on your very honor, that you'd take care of his people—and his ancestral home."

"Yes," she murmured, immediately stricken to the core. Only Eoghan would be so cruel as to remind her of what she'd been so desperately trying to forget. "That's true."

Eoghan's handsome features softened, and his voice grew gentle. "If you accept my bargain, I will give you this added promise, made upon my own honor. Even if you should lose, and thus become my lady wife, I'll yet keep Kerlain and its people well. I'll rebuild the castle and make repairs to the estate—and will make it profitable again so that one of our sons will be proud of the inheritance."

Diana closed her eyes, sickened at the words. "I can't . . ."

"Surely you can," he said in that same slow, gentle tone. "Either way, win or lose, once you've accepted our bargain you've saved Kerlain. Only if you turn aside have you lost all and made your vows to your godfather as dross. Not that I suppose you'll think on it much, happy as you'll be with your dear husband in the United States. But that's all that matters, isn't it? Your own happiness in being with the man you love? Whatever suffering the people here would know wouldn't compare."

She would think of Kerlain every moment of every day, Diana knew. She would go to her grave knowing what she—and Lad—had lost. Their marriage would suffer from the guilt and anger she would ever carry. It would be impossible to put aside, knowing that the people of Kerlain were suffering so. And suffer they would, if Eoghan was their master. He'd make good on that vow, just as he would have the castle destroyed and the land laid bare. Kerlain would become a wasteland, because of her—because she'd been too selfish and fainthearted to save them from Eoghan's wickedness.

"If I accept this wager," she murmured, "and if I win, you'll return all that Lad lost to you and you'll leave us in peace. Forever."

"Very well," he said solemnly. "Agreed. And if I win, you'll find the way to divorce Lad and send him away. Forever."

Tears pricked Diana's eyes at the very thought. Life without Lad wouldn't be a life at all. She'd have only the knowledge of the safety of her land and people to keep her sane for the rest of her days.

"Agreed," she whispered.

"You'll become my wife with full acquiescence," he added. "I want no martyrs, just as I said. I don't ask that you love me, Diana, but you'll be a wife to me in every way that God and the law demand—and that includes receiving my touch without shrinking away and openly pleasuring me in our bed as I shall likewise pleasure you. All willingly. Give me your word on it."

She shuddered within but said, "You have it. If you should win, it will be as you say."

"Give me your hand then, to seal our wager."

He lifted one of his elegant, perfectly manicured hands toward her. Diana stared at it a moment, then at last lifted her own hand and set it in his, disgusted by even this simple touch. He squeezed her fingers, attempting to lift them to his lips. She pulled her hand free at once, resisting the strong urge to wipe it against her damp skirts.

"You'll not tell your husband of our wager, will you?" he asked, watching her intently.

"What I tell Lad is none of your concern," she replied acidly. "Though you may be certain I'll not speak of what will occur should we fail to raise the money you require. If he knew your intentions toward me, Lad would shortly afterward arrive at Lising Park to kill you. A thought, I admit, that dismays me only in that he'd suffer for it."

Eoghan chuckled at her words. Diana itched to slap him.

"Such a passionate creature you are, my sweetest love, and ever have been," he said, standing aside as she swept past him. "How I shall enjoy having you beneath my hand. Three years will be an eternity to wait. By the by, I'd take care, were I you, to control your affections for your husband before he takes his leave. I've already told you how I'd greet any child of his."

"Eoghan," she uttered with pure exasperation, turning at the door to face him. "I don't give one good damn about what you want or think or feel. You may take yourself off to hell with my every blessing."

"Can't," he said, holding his hands up in a gesture of helplessness. "I must remain close at hand to keep an eye on my property. And you."

"Then God help us both," she said. "If I don't kill you myself before the next three years have passed, it will be a very miracle."

Chapter Fourteen

Lad had never been so sick in all his life, not even as a child stricken with the fever or as a soldier eating bad food and drinking bad whiskey and spending his nights sleeping in freezing mud, rain, and snow. Never. His head felt as if some tormenting demon were repeatedly—and gleefully—plunging a pickax in the spot between his eyes. His mouth was relentlessly dry, his eyes burned as if acid had been thrown in them, his every muscle ached painfully, and his stomach refused to believe that it hadn't anything left in it to toss up.

Swithin nursed him as stoically as an army sergeant, earning Lad's eternal gratitude for his patience and silence. Two hours after he'd come awake, ill and bleary, to find Swithin ready with a bowl, Maudie had delivered an awful-tasting brew laced heavily with herbs, assuring Lad kindly that it'd be just the thing to make him better. He'd been too weak to resist as Swithin held the cup to his lips, but at least the wretched potion—which put him very much in mind of a similar concoction that Uncle Hadley swore by—had given him the gift of sleep.

He had no idea what time it was now, though light streamed through the windows, hurting his eyes. Why hadn't someone mercifully closed his bed-curtains? he thought grumpily, groaning with the effort to lift a hand to set upon his throbbing head.

God, he would never drink again. Never, ever again. It wasn't worth the little pleasure it gave, drinking. Not when a man woke up feeling like he'd rather be dead than alive. Lord, but his head ached. Damn Eoghan Patterson to hell! What kind of a friend gave a man pure poison to drink? And kept giving it to him, over and over and over . . . He groaned again just thinking of it.

"Lad?"

Even Diana's soft voice made him wince in pain.

"Are you going to be ill? I have a bowl ready."

God help him, he wished he *was* dead. It was bad enough to be sick in front of Swithin and Maudie, but he couldn't bear the thought of being so disgusting and helpless in front of Diana.

His stomach rumbled threateningly, and he prayed that she would simply go away.

"Here, I have a cool cloth." She took hold of his hand and gently pulled it from his face. With even greater care she laid the cloth across his forehead. It felt like pure heaven.

"There," she murmured, stroking the hair from his face, clearly unaware that even the simple caress hurt as if she were probing a raw, open wound. "I'm sure you're feeling dreadful, but you must let me get some of this into you. It's Maudie's special remedy for the drink. The late earl swore by it. Come, Lad, sit up just a little and I'll hold it for you."

Groaning the while, he did his best to sit up and drink the same brew he'd taken earlier. More sleep would do him good, and he felt the concoction's soothing effects almost at once. Even his stomach seemed to settle as Diana helped him to lie back down on his pillows. He was going to kiss Maudie soundly the next time he set sight on her.

"Curtains," he managed to murmur before Diana moved away.

She lightly touched his cheek and said, "I'll close them."

Darkness shrouded him within moments, and Lad gave a relieved sigh. Diana returned to sit beside him, pulling the final curtain shut to blanket them inside.

"Rest now, if you can," she murmured, lightly touching his fingers. With what strength he possessed, Lad curled them around her own, wanting her to stay. "I'll be here if you need me."

It was nighttime when he woke again, feeling much the better for the sleep he'd had. The bed-curtains had been pulled aside, and he sat up slowly, rubbing a hand over his face and through his hair, thanking a benevolent God that his pounding headache had gone at last.

The room was lit by a fire in the hearth as well as a candle on a nearby table, beside which Diana sat in a large chair, reading. When he yawned and stretched she looked up at him, then set the book aside and rose, hurrying across the room.

"Are you feeling better now?" she asked, sweet concern in her tone. She set a hand on his forehead and murmured, "You're neither cold nor overwarm, thank a merciful God."

Lad reached out and lashed both arms about her slender waist, drawing her near, pressing his face against her belly and holding her there for comfort. Her hands moved lightly over his hair, and he felt her drop a kiss there too.

"I'm sorry I got so sick, drank so much," he said, his voice hoarse and filled with slumber. "It won't happen again, I promise."

"No, it was my fault," she murmured gently, her touch loving and gentle. "I drove you away with my thoughtless tongue and foolish words, at a time when you needed sympathy, most especially from me, your own wife. I'm so very sorry for it, Lad.''

"Sweetheart, none of the blame is yours. Eoghan found me and shared his liquor—it's the way men offer comfort, I guess. I didn't have to accept it."

"I know that, but if I hadn't driven you away, none of what occurred would have happened. Do you remember all of it? I know that drink can rob a man of his memory, as well as his senses. Do you remember gaming with Eoghan?''

"Gaming?'' he repeated, hugging her a bit more tightly, closing his eyes as he pressed against her. "I remember that he had a deck of cards. We played some odd game . . . French game of some sort.''

Gently, she disengaged from his embrace and stepped back. He looked up at her, thinking how very beautiful she was, feeling the endless tide of love she wrought in him and knowing how awful he must look at the present moment. Her expression was grave, unhappy, and he knew himself as the one who'd made her thus.

"Let me send Swithin in, to help you bathe and dress. You'll feel better afterward and will want something for your stomach, I think. I'll come back and share tea with you, once you've had some soup and bread.''

"Diana—"

She bent and pressed a light kiss to his forehead.

"We'll speak when you're feeling better. I'll send Swithin in."

He was sitting by the fire when she returned, feeling much the better for Swithin's ministrations. He felt human again, well on the way to recovery and able to shake his head at the folly that had driven him to such foolishness the night before. Much of what had passed between himself and Eoghan was a blur, but he had the unsettling feeling that something of import had passed. Diana's face, when she joined him again, carrying a tea tray, told him that he was right.

He stood to take the tray from her and set it on the table between them. She poured and handed him a cup, and soon they were sitting before the fire, in chairs facing each other, as outwardly cozy as they'd been on many a night before. But now there was a difference. Lad could see it in Diana's movements, hear it in her voice. Something was dreadfully wrong, far beyond what he'd done in getting so stupidly drunk.

"Eoghan said last night that you'd sent him to find me," he said after a long silence had passed. "Is that true?"

"No," she replied softly, and sipped her tea.

That gave him pause.

"Are you certain? Perhaps I misunderstood him."

"Eoghan probably made sure that you did," she said, her tone more bitter now. With a purposeful movement, she set her teacup aside, then sat forward and folded her hands. "There's no putting this off, Lad. I must tell you, if you've not yet remembered. Last night, when you were drunk, you gambled Kerlain away. The entire estate . . . even the castle."

"What?" He nearly dropped the cup from his hands. "That's impossible."

She lowered her gaze. "I only wish it were, but I've seen the paper with my own eyes. The vowel you signed away to Eoghan. Whether he won it fairly or not, you put your name to the debt, and now it's a matter of honor that payment be made."

"But I don't even remember signing a paper. Besides, it was dark," he protested, setting his own cup of tea aside so quickly that it sloshed onto the table, "and I was six sheets to the wind. Even if I unknowingly wagered Kerlain, it couldn't mean anything. No decent gentleman would hold such a debt as being true—certainly not in the States." He was beginning to feel sick again. "Look, I'll ride over to Lising Park and speak to Eoghan in the morning. We'll have a good laugh and that will be the end of it. You can't think he means to maintain such a thing as valid?"

"He does," she said, meeting his gaze fully. She was stiff now, a bit colder, as if she'd put a distance of emotion between them. "I spoke with Eoghan yesterday, and if we cannot make repayment for the debt in another way, he intends to take Kerlain. I tried to warn you about what he was like, but you wouldn't listen." Her tone grew bitter, angry. "He's the worst sort of snake, playing at being your friend in order to trick you into trusting him. Why wouldn't you believe me when I told you that he meant us no good?"

Lad was still disbelieving. "I'll speak with him, Diana. He'll laugh the matter off and return the vowel. I know he will."

Her lovely features hardened even further, and she drew herself up straight, as if turning into a beautiful statue.

"Lord Carden has been good enough to offer us the chance to repay our debt to him. For the sum of seventy thousand pounds, he'll return your vowel and Kerlain will be ours again."

She spoke so formally, so coldly, that Lad began to feel at a loss. She was *serious,* he realized with a deep, inward tightening of pain. Utterly serious. This matter was of the gravest nature, and her response was to withdraw, to pull away from him. Lad struggled to remember what had passed between himself and Eoghan, striving to recall every word, everything that either of them had said or done.

Eoghan was his friend. He'd been so sympathetic about Uncle Hadley, about Diana and the people of Kerlain and the way they'd treated Lad from the start. He'd even given Lad advice about how to be a proper lord. If his behavior hadn't been genuine, then either Viscount Carden was the greatest actor on God's earth or Lad was the most gullible man alive.

He was afraid—very afraid, all of a sudden, thinking on all that had passed—that the latter was true. And now he had lost Kerlain, because he was such a stupid, God-cursed *fool*.

"I lost the estate," he murmured, stricken by the enormity of what he'd done.

"And the castle," she added softly. "Though it's legally mine, I must honor your debts as if they were my own."

The castle, he thought sorrowfully. She loved this wretched old place, though he'd never truly understood why. She would never forgive him for losing it.

"Diana, I . . . I don't know what to say to you. I was drunk, out of my mind with grief, and . . . angry with you too. I'm sorry. So very sorry." He let out a breath, desperately casting about for a solution to the mess he'd made. "I guess we'll have to return to Fair Maiden, now that this has happened. I'm sorry, sweetheart. I can't begin to tell you how much. I know how greatly you love Kerlain, and I'd do anything to undo what's happened, but—seventy thousand pounds! It's impossible . . . unless Eoghan means to give me some time to come up with the money."

"He's given us three years to make payment in full. Three years from tomorrow."

Lad shook his head. "If he'd give us five years, we might be able to do it, but until the fields are making a profit, Kerlain will be far more of a drain than a source of income."

"What of Fair Maiden?"

"It clears twenty thousand a year in profit," he said, "but most of this year's profit has already been paid out on improvements for Kerlain and the rest put back into Fair Maiden. And without a manager, the farm won't make even that next year."

She stood slowly and, saying nothing, moved to face the fire.

"There's nothing to be done for it, Diana," he said at last. "We'll have to turn Kerlain over to Eoghan and go home to Fair Maiden. I'm sorry, love." With an effort, he stood as well, fighting down the dizziness that assailed him. When he reached out to touch her shoulder, she moved away. "I don't expect you to forgive me, but what's done is done."

"I can't leave Kerlain," she said, turning to look at him. Her dark eyes were large in the firelight. "Lad, we have three years to come up with the full sum. You must . . . somehow, you must find a way to get it." She hesitated before adding, "I'll remain at Kerlain and keep the people and the estate, as I've ever done, and you must leave for London, or America, and do whatever you must to gather the full seventy thousand."

Lad stared at her. "Leave Kerlain? Without you?"

She neither smiled nor frowned as she spoke. "Aye. I'll not go with you. I cannot leave Kerlain, just as I've told you time and again, though you've never understood. You've gambled away what was dearest to me, Lad Walker, and now I ask that you do everything in your power to set matters right. Indeed, I demand that you do."

"I will," he vowed fervently, moving nearer to her. She backed away, as unapproachable, untouchable, as if they were strangers. "Darling, surely we can find a way together. If you'll come with me to Fair Maiden, I know I can figure something out. And then we'll return to Kerlain and start over again. I promise, Diana. We'll begin again here as we should have done."

"No, Lad. You must do it on your own, just as you lost Kerlain on your own. I want you to leave Kerlain tomorrow morning . . . and not return until you have the money. All of it. No, I'll not argue with you." She held up a hand when he tried to speak. "It has to be this way or . . . or no way at all. If you won't do as I ask, then we should divorce at once so that you can return to the United States and go on with your life."

"Divorce?" he repeated, stunned. "Never, Diana. That's . . . just plain ridiculous! We love each other, even if you are so mad at me right now that you'd like to disagree."

"No," she murmured, tears filling her eyes. "I love you, Lad. I'd never deny that. But love makes little difference now. If you can't earn the money to repay Eoghan before the end of three years, then I don't want you coming back to Kerlain at all. Ever." A lone tear spilled onto her cheek, coursing downward.

"Diana, please, love, don't speak of such things. Look, I made a dreadful mistake, but that's all it was—a mistake. I didn't purposefully lose Kerlain. I know you're angry, but you can't truly mean what you're saying."

"Can I not? And did you truly not intend to gamble Kerlain away? You've never cared for the estate, or the title. In truth, I think you've been doing little more than humoring me since you arrived, biding your time until the land fails and we were forced to return to that place you do love—Fair Maiden. You've always hoped we'd have no choice but to go there, haven't you, Lad?"

He had nothing to say to this, because it was true. Diana sobbed and closed her eyes, but not before he saw the pain in them. In that moment, he knew that he'd lost not only Kerlain but her as well. The only way he could regain them both was for a vast sum of money—seventy thousand pounds.

"Very well," he said. "It will be as you've said. I'll leave for London in the morning."

When she opened her eyes more tears spilled out of

them, but she seemed to have no care for that. With an effort she mastered her voice.

"You'll not return to America?"

He shook his head. "No, love." He couldn't bear the thought of being parted from her, but at least in London there'd be no endless ocean separating them. When he finally had the money he would be but days, and not months, away from her. "I'll speak to Mr. Sibbley in London and we'll work something out. Perhaps a loan of some sort. Noblemen are able to do such things, I understand."

"Perhaps," she said, though her tone was yet cheerless. "I pray it will be so."

"I'll write to let you know what's occurred and where I'll be staying. And I'll have Mr. Sibbley forward funds from the bank—"

"Oh, no, Lad, don't," she said. "Everything now must go toward repaying the debt."

He would have reached out for her again if she'd shown any inclination toward receiving his touch, but she was still so distant in manner that he dared not.

"You must have something to live on," he told her. "I don't suppose I'll be able to send enough to be of any good to the Farrell and Colvaney clans, but perhaps the crops will yield enough this year to feed them through the winter. But I'm sure I'll be back before then."

"Yes," she said, wiping her tears away and straightening her stance. "I'll leave you to rest, then. You should sleep before beginning your journey. You'll take Maeva?"

"No." He could scarce believe they were speaking to each other in such a manner, so stiffly, so formally. "I'll leave her for your use."

"I want you to take her. You'll have far greater need of a fine horse in London than we'll have here."

He didn't particularly care whether he rode or walked.

The future loomed before him as a hopeless, miserable journey.

"Lad, promise me you'll not try to speak to Eoghan before you go. He'll not change his mind, and I fear you may come to blows if you meet."

"I believe you may be right." Lad uttered a hollow laugh. "I'll not speak to him, if I can avoid doing so."

"Thank you," she murmured.

"Will you come to London once I've settled, even for a few days, if I send for you?" he asked more hopefully. "Or perhaps I could come home for a week or two, once Sibbley and I have worked something out."

She shook her head. "No. Only come home when you have the money in full, Lad. I'll remain here, waiting for you, and will look for you every day—every day, I vow—to come back home to me."

Diana backed away toward the door, her heart shattered by the look of hurt she'd put upon his handsome face. She had to leave now or give way, as she'd nearly given way every moment since telling him that he had to go. How she wished that she could tell him the truth, of the devil's wager she'd made with Eoghan, but she couldn't. All would be lost. Their only hope lay in his believing what she had so coldheartedly said.

"I'll bid you good night, Lad. I know it will be difficult, but sleep if you can. I'll have Swithin wake you before sunrise."

"Diana." His voice was a pained whisper, pleading, desperate. "Don't go, love. Spend these last few hours with me. Give me the memory of a sweeter parting than this."

"No," she said, forcing the word firmly past trembling lips. "I'll not be a wife to you, Lad Walker, until you've returned with the money—all of it, every penny. I can't be a wife to you until then."

Not because Eoghan had threatened her, she told herself,

swallowing down the sob that rose up in her throat, but for the sake of any child Lad might give her if they came together on this night. If Lad never returned, Eoghan would treat the child cruelly, and that she would not allow. Never would she put a child of hers in Eoghan's power. Never.

Lad said nothing, only stood where he was, gazing at her in numb shock, and Diana fumbled for the handle to the door that adjoined their rooms, leaving him before the tears she'd striven so hard to hold back began to flow.

"Oh, God," she whispered, standing on the other side, in her own chamber. "God."

She wanted to fling the door open again and run back inside, to throw herself at Lad and beg his forgiveness and tell him how very much she loved him, that nothing else— not even Kerlain—mattered. But it would be the worst thing she could do, for him, for her, for everyone at Kerlain. Lad mustn't think of her in the days to come but only of the task at hand, so that he might come back to Kerlain, and to her. To that end, Diana steeled herself, determined that on the morrow he would see no weakness in her but only more of the anger and coldness that she'd tried to show him this night. There was no turning back now. He must find the money or never return, and sending him on his way knowing that was perhaps the best, and most loving, gift she could give him.

Chapter Fifteen

Kerlain, 27 June
To Lad Walker, Earl of Kerlain
London

Lad, my love,

You've only just ridden away from Kerlain. I ran to the highest window in the north tower and watched until I could see your figure no more, praying every moment that you would turn around and come back to me, knowing that such a hope was foolish and utterly selfish. Now I have come to my bedchamber to hide my misery and tears. As wretched as I am at the loss of you, my darling, I know that you suffer far more—because of me. My coldness and distance last night and this morning are what put such sorrow in your eyes. Will you ever be able to forgive me? Can I ever find the words to ask for such forgiveness?

One day, I vow, I'll have to freedom to tell you why I behaved as I did. I meant to strengthen you, to fortify you— and myself as well—for the daunting task ahead. Yet perhaps it was far more for myself, for you cannot know how I wavered as I stood beside you in the courtyard, telling you good-bye.

I don't know if I will send this to you or keep it as my own silent confession. Even if I did post it, I don't know

*where it might find you, though perhaps Mr. Sibbley would
forward it for me. Surely he'll know where to find you.*

*I love you, Lad. Despite my foolishness and the pain I've
given you, always know that I love you and will do so until
the day I last draw breath. You are my life—far more than
Kerlain ever has been or could be. Unless you come home
to me, the love I once bore this land will turn to the bitterest
hatred any being could know.*

*Write to me soon, I pray, and let me know where you are,
and if you're well.*

Diana

London, 1 July
To Diana, Countess of Kerlain
Castle Kerlain, Herefordshire

Madam,

*I think it might be best, for a time, to post whatever
missives you may desire to send me to Mr. Sibbley. I've
taken lodgings above a certain establishment that, while
perfectly suitable for my needs, would doubtless fall far
short of what you'd think right for so grand a personage as
the Earl of Kerlain, and I'll not divulge the address in deference to your tender sensibilities—tender, at least, where
anything involving Kerlain is concerned.*

*You need not fear that I've soiled your precious title in
taking such lodgings. I have given my name as Lad Walker
there and am certain this will meet with your approval, if
nothing else does.*

*I will let you know what transpires from my meeting with
Mr. Sibbley. You will doubtless be interested in knowing the
details of that, but you needn't fear that I shall bore you
otherwise with news of my own personal doings. It was*

quite clear from our parting a few days past that you neither care about nor wish to know of them or of me.

The Earl of Kerlain

London, 1 July

To Diana,

My darling, please toss straight into the fire the foolish missive I so regretfully posted to you earlier today. I wish to God that I'd destroyed it myself before ever sending you such a bitter, unwarranted attack. Forgive me, I pray, a thousand times over. It was only my stupid anger at myself and you and, most especially, Eoghan Patterson, that made me write such cold and hateful words. Although that's not the whole truth, I suppose. I know what it was—the way we parted, and what you said to me, your very last words before I mounted Maeva to ride away. Not "I love you," or even "Take care," but "Always remember that you're the Earl of Kerlain."

I knew, even as you said them, that you only meant to make me certain of how serious our situation is. I could hear the desperation in your voice, love, but chose not to think of that as I rode away. I let myself grow angrier every hour as I journeyed to London, and what I wrote you this morning was the culmination.

Now I know myself for a fool and deeply regret taking my ire out on you. I love you, Diana. No matter how foolishly I may behave, never forget that. I love you and will always love you, and we will be together for the rest of our lives, just as soon as may be. I promise you that. Don't lose faith in me, darling, for I need your faith so very much. Especially now.

I've just finished meeting with Mr. Sibbley, and it appears that he won't be able to arrange a loan for us with any of London's banking institutions, but he's doing what he can to discover other avenues that we may take. He mentioned that I might be able to obtain a partnership in one of the many prosperous shipping businesses hereabouts, but that would require a longer stay in London than I'd hoped, and I'm praying that he'll find a better answer to our troubles. He must, for I'll go mad at being parted from you for so great a time.

For now, I've settled into my rooms, and Maeva has been well stabled. I fear I should send her back to Kerlain, as it's far more expensive to keep and feed a horse in London than to keep and feed a man. Hopefully, I'll return to Kerlain long before we must become so economical as to think of such things.

Write to me soon, Diana, I beg it of you, and tell me that you forgive me for the unfortunate missive I earlier sent you. Send your letters to Mr. Sibbley. I should have admitted to you previously that I'm simply too ashamed for you to know the place where I've taken lodgings. They're not shabby, but the location is . . . well, I think you might be distressed. There's not the least need to be, for I doubt I'll be here long—only so long as I must, until matters are more settled—and will send you a proper address to write me in the near future.

Promise me that you won't begin to use the food and coal sparingly just yet. I want you warm in your bed at nights, not missing me so very much as I know I shall miss you.

Write soon,
All my love,
Lad

Kerlain, 12 July 1815

Dearest Lad,

So many days you've been gone, and still no word from you. I worry so that you've not yet forgiven me for the manner in which we parted, but I pray that the reasons for your silence are otherwise.

I know how busy you must be, getting settled and meeting with Mr. Sibbley. And, too, it may be that my own letters to you haven't yet reached you, as Mr. Sibbley perhaps hasn't had a moment to forward them to whatever lodgings you've taken.

I pray that all has gone well for you, and that you've found the way to meet our debt. It is foolish of me to hope so much that you'll be coming home soon, I know, but I do hope it, fervently, and pray for it and look for you each day—every hour—to come riding into the courtyard. When that time comes, my love, I fear you'll need to change your clothes within but minutes of your arrival, for I shall have soaked you through with my happy tears.

I suppose I should tell you some of what has gone on at Kerlain since your leaving—though, indeed, there has not been much. The weather has begun to warm, and the nights have been filled with summer's blessed light, all of which make it easy to maintain a strict accounting of both coal and candles. The Farrell and The Colvaney have finished overseeing the liming of the fields, too late, I know, for planting, but I'm not certain I could have prevailed upon them to do as you had desired with the bringing of new crops. They are so stubborn and set in their ways that I'm sure they'd rather starve than allow changes at Kerlain. I've begun to think back to how easy the people were with my godfather, the late earl, and have suddenly realized why they loved him so. It is because he seldom, if ever, interfered, and left The Farrell and The Colvaney to fight each *other alone in the managing of the land. I, too, have earned their affection because I've sought to protect their dignity and pride, rather than that of the one person whose dignity and pride I should have set above all others—your own. Not only because you are the Earl of Kerlain but because you are my husband. I've failed you miserably both as your countess and as your wife, but it shall be no more. When you come back to me, Lad, you'll see the truth of what I say. I'll never again take the side of anyone apart from you. We will be as one, just as we should have been from the start.*

Write soon, Lad, please. If you could only know how wretched I am without you—so that I wonder every moment how I ever knew happiness before you came into my life— you would take pity on me and write, even just a brief sentence or two, and every word I would cherish.

All my love,
Your Diana

London, 20 July 1815

My Darling Diana,

There's been no missive from you yet, and I can only believe that you're yet angered at me, not only for the stupid letter I sent you two weeks past but for this entire, wretched mess I've gotten us into. I can hardly blame you. Not a day—nor a moment—goes by that I don't feel the same anger. Your silence is fully justified, and I only blame myself for it.

I hope, however, that you'll not find it an unpleasant occurrence if I continue to write to you. I'm so lonely for you, Diana, that I can scarce find the words to tell you how much. It presses in all about me, this dread loneliness, when I think of all those whom I loved so well who are gone from me now. My lone comfort is that you are but miles away, safe in Kerlain, and not cold in the grave as all my family is. But I won't trouble you with such morbid thoughts. I've done enough to dim your life with my foolishness. Now I can only pray for a second chance to fill your days with the love and happiness that you deserve.

London is hot and muggy now, and many of London's finer families have begun to leave Town for their country estates. I've discovered that my grandfather, the late earl, once owned a grand town house here—a family home of long-standing, or so it seems. I try to imagine Walkers of previous generations coming to Town for the season, then packing up and returning to Castle Kerlain for the rest of the year. It's a pity Grandfather decided to sell the London house; I would have liked to have a ready home here and to be able to bring you to Town once our difficulty has been settled.

You've never been to London, have you, Diana? Not even for a proper season, which the late earl owed you, surely. It's not the sort of place I'd ever want to live, mind you, having been raised in the country, but it's interesting, in its way. So many people, so much activity. But the smells, Diana, and the filth, are beyond anything you could ever have imagined. If you've ever dreamt that London was a grand, fine place, then you'll have to adjust your visions before ever coming, else you'll suffer a real shock. Some parts are nice enough, where the nabobs live, mainly, but overall it's something of a challenge. If it weren't for having Maeva to gallop in the park each morning, I'd probably have gone insane by now.

As to our situation, I wish I could lie and tell you that I've had even a small measure of success in securing some way to repay our debt, but I can't. Matters remain almost as they were when I arrived, despite Mr. Sibbley's help. However, I've sent a letter to my man of business in the United States, also to my cousin Archie, and can happily report that

*fresh funds will soon arrive in London to provide me with a
greater measure of influence among the local business lead-
ers. Mr. Sibbley has taken pains to explain that the Earl of
Kerlain can't be seen as having "soiled" his hands with
any connection to trade, but there are ways, evidently, to get
around these stupid society strictures. If not, I shall proceed
as I see fit, strictures or not. I don't particularly care what
society thinks of me; I only want to get home to Kerlain, and
to you.*

*I am well and pray that the same is true with you and all
those at Kerlain. I know that I don't deserve your kindness
now, love, but if you could bring yourself to write to me
. . . even a few lines, a few words, to tell me that you're
safe and well, I would be so glad of it, and thankful as well.*

I love you always,
Lad

Kerlain, 10 August 1815

Dear Lad,

*I've begun to give up believing that you will ever write to
me. Days come and go, and I hope for word to arrive, but it
never does—not from you, or even from Mr. Sibbley. Stuart
rides into Walborough almost daily to see if there is anything, also to post my own letters to you, but ever returns
empty-handed.*

*Perhaps this is for the best. I tell myself it is so. You will
be busy with money matters, and I remember well how many
hours you labored to craft letters for your various relatives,
perfecting them with the greatest care and consideration
before announcing yourself satisfied.*

*The weather grows hotter now, but the nights are most
pleasant. Stuart and some of the younger men among the
Farrells and the Colvaneys have taken to hunting in the*

mornings and fishing at night, and they always share what they catch with us at the castle. I am amazed, at times, to think that it took your coming to put us in mind of such a simple solution to filling our larder—though, of course, the families always hunted for themselves. It will be harder in the winter, I know, but the few crops we planted are showing well, and I expect what we gain from the harvest will be more than plenty to keep us through the cold months. And, though I did not ask it of them, Stuart and the younger men have felled several trees as well, chopping them up so that for the first time in many and many a year, we will have wood for fuel at Kerlain rather than coal. I think I shall like the change, though Maudie complains that the dryness that comes with wood will give her the headache.

I'm sorry this is so short a missive. I'll write again soon, and again and again, until you write back and tell me to stop, and will send you my love, as I do now.

Yours, faithfully,
Diana

London, 31 August

To my wife, Diana,

I shouldn't be writing to you in my present mood. No good can come of it. I've spent the day walking, just as I spend every day walking, aimlessly, without course or reason. I feel lost here, Diana. Lost and so alone. I walk everywhere, searching for God knows what, but never find the face of a friend or even the assurance of a smile and a nod. I might as well be a mongrel running about, masterless, for all the interest anyone gives me—save those few measured expressions of distaste and disgust. Perhaps I am such a creature. Here, in England, I cannot seem to find the way to be human.

Diana, I can no longer summon up either the energy or the desire to put a face of hopefulness on our situation, not even for your sake. I'm no further ahead in solving the problem of my debts than I was when I arrived. In fact, if anything, I'm further behind, having clearly made the title of Kerlain a source of laughter. I'd recount my several attempts to gain entrance to the kinds of places where the so-called ton *congregate, where I had assumed the Earl of Kerlain would be welcomed, but the pathetic tales would only depress you. I can't even get into the House of Lords, where I understand the Earl of Kerlain is supposed to occupy a seat. Mr. Sibbley is reluctant to advise me in these particular matters, as he clearly doesn't wish to be associated with me any more closely than our business matters necessitate. I've given up going to his place of business to see if any letters have yet arrived from Kerlain. None ever do, and I can only humiliate myself so many times before finally giving way. Mr. Sibbley has kindly promised to forward any future missives to me, though I much doubt that he'll ever be put to the trouble.*

I long to leave this land and return to America. I dream of doing so, of forgetting England and all that's occurred here as if it had only been some awful, unreal fantasy—even you, Diana. In the worst moments of despair I try to imagine what it was like to be greeted by a neighbor with a smiling face and outstretched hand, to be embraced by my family and friends with both love and genuine affection. Even with all those I loved most being now dead and gone, with all their ghosts surrounding me there, I could live at Fair Maiden in peace. Except for this one thing . . . knowing that I'd abandoned my heart at Kerlain in the form of a beautiful, delicate woman whose face haunts me now as it will haunt me forever.

I'll not abandon you, Diana. I don't know what I'll do, but I'll not abandon you.

Chapter Sixteen

London, September 1, 1815

Sir Geoffrey Vear seldom walked through London's dark streets at night, not when he disliked walking great distances and certainly not when his pockets were heavy with fresh winnings earned at the tables of one of his favorite gaming hells. But this evening, as circumstances would have it, there were no hackneys present to be hired, and he had long since learned that a man who made his livelihood by gambling had better make haste from any establishment where he'd won such a large bankroll—or else suffer the consequences. His lone manservant, Lloyd, who was a rough and ready fellow, would prove insufficient protection against a half dozen drunk and unhappy fellow gamesters who wanted their money back.

And so tonight Sir Geoffrey walked, picking his way carefully along the dark avenue in what was indisputably one of London's shabbier districts, Lloyd close behind him, hoping that a cab for hire would shortly present itself. And sooner than later, please God, before they were set upon by scurrilous villains intent upon doing them harm.

"Gads, where are all the hacks tonight?" he muttered aloud, striking the ground with his walking stick far more heartily than need be as he moved along. "You'd think they'd vanished from the face of the earth."

"Probably some fancy doings," Lloyd said in his usual blunt manner. "All hired out. Turn north here, m'lord."

Sir Geoffrey deftly changed courses, heading north up another street, grateful that Lloyd knew the city so well. Every step led them toward the more civilized part of London, but they were yet far from being safe. It was always a risk visiting the hells near the docks, but for a man such as himself, who seldom visited the better establishments, the odds for coming away with richly lined pockets usually won out against danger.

The night was damp and chilly—he'd pay a heavy price come morning for being out in it—and several small fires lined either side of the street. Groups of people huddled around each one, men, women, and children alike, speaking in a low din among themselves but gazing at Sir Geoffrey and Lloyd as they passed. A few of the women called out offers of pleasure, and Sir Geoffrey tipped his hat in their direction and smiled, moving onward and regretting the loss of his youth and the days when he'd most certainly have replied to their propositions in a far more eager manner. Behind him, Lloyd sighed loudly, causing Sir Geoffrey to smile.

"Only get me and our winnings home safe, m'boy," he said congenially, "and you may return to seek out your own pleasures."

"Be too tired if we walk all the way," Lloyd muttered.

"The devil! Perish the thought," Sir Geoffrey said with feeling. "My feet already feel as if they're about to crumble into dust and bones. Surely we'll find a cab soon."

"It's them shoes you wear, with them heels," Lloyd said with a measure of amusement. "Silly things, they are. Told you a hundred times or more, but you always wear 'em."

Sir Geoffrey sniffed through his long, aristocratic nose, pulling his elegant cape more closely about his neck and mincing upon the aforementioned heels with even greater delicacy.

"Little though you would know about such things, Lloyd, these shoes were the height of fashion in my day, and no well-dressed gentleman would be seen publicly wearing anything but—" He came to a stop. "What the deuce have we here? Lloyd?"

Lloyd peered over Sir Geoffrey's shoulder, then quickly scooted around to kneel beside the insensible figure lying on the ground. "Robbed," he said, setting a hand against the man's neck.

Sir Geoffrey recoiled. "God's mercy. Is the fellow dead?"

"Not yet." Lloyd touched a bloody spot on the man's golden head. "Roughed over more'n a bit. Bashed on the noggin." He ran a hand over his coat. "Pockets emptied. Did a proper job on him, they did. Good cloth. Gentleman's clothes."

"God save us," Sir Geoffrey muttered. "What's the fool about, coming to this part of the city unaccompanied? Will he live?"

"Mebbe."

Sir Geoffrey cast a glance about, but they'd walked beyond any living souls and there was no one to help. A distant sound caught his attention. "Listen!"

Lloyd cocked his head, identified the sound of an approaching carriage, then nodded. "Coming this way," he said. "Be here in a beat. Take him home, will we?"

Sir Geoffrey had never featured himself playing the role of Good Samaritan, but if the man was a gentleman, as indeed his attire indicated, then only a dishonorable fiend would leave him to die in such a horrid, filthy place. Sir Geoffrey wasn't necessarily kind, or even concerned about his fellow man, but if he lacked a great many noble qualities, no one could have rightly claimed that he lacked honor.

"Of course," he told Lloyd, offense in his tone that there should be any question of such a thing. "And once we've got him there, you'll fetch a doctor."

"Won't have my night of pleasure after all, will I?" Lloyd muttered, setting his arms beneath the insensible stranger to lift him from the ground.

"I do believe he's coming to, Lloyd. Yes, look—at last! He's opening his eyes."

Lad struggled to pull his eyelids apart, but the effort was beyond him. Turning his head minutely toward a source of light, he parted his lips and drew in a long breath, managing to make a thin wheezing sound.

"Hello, sir!"

Some curst fool was shouting at him as if he were deaf. Lad groaned in reply.

"Hello, I say! Come, sir, you've slept two full days, and the physician assures me you'll be well enough in time."

"Mebbe all your shouting's got him rattled," someone else said in a deeper, softer voice.

"Shouting's the only remedy left us," the other voice, far more imperious, replied. "God alone knows we've tried everything else, and I'm out of my wits to discover who this Diana is that he keeps calling for."

"Too curious by half, you are," the low voice chided. "Here, move aside. Let me give it a try." A cool, damp cloth padded about his face, then a strong hand slid beneath his neck and lifted Lad up with ease. "Try some of this, sir," the low voice prodded gently. A cup was pressed against Lad's lips and after a moment's confusion, he realized that it contained nothing more dangerous than warm, weak tea. He drank gratefully.

"There." The cup was taken away and he was laid back down upon cool pillows. "He was thirsty, poor fellow. He'll come to now, won't you, sir?'' The cloth, wetter now, washed over Lad's face again, lifting him to greater consciousness. He managed to crack his eyes open.

A rough, swarthy face was staring down at him, lips pursed, and regarding him intently.

''He's awake,'' he stated, then gave Lad a reassuring smile. ''Hello, sir. You're in a safe place.''

Abruptly, the man stood and moved away, to be replaced by what seemed to Lad an apparition. He blinked, but the apparition only grew clearer, came closer, eagerly gazing down at him with open interest. It was a man, Lad thought—though a decidedly feminine one—who looked as if he'd stepped into the present day from an earlier era. He was tall and slender, with perfectly powdered hair and a face so stark and white with makeup that he might have been a wax figure rather than a living being. His eyes were startlingly blue, his nose bony and aristocratic, and his features as thin as the rest of him. He was a handsome figure, nonetheless, this older gentleman of clear refinement, dressed in the same kind of elegant, old-fashioned clothes that Diana had dug out of the late earl's closet for Lad to wear on their wedding day. At present the man was a golden vision, dressed in that shining color from his heavily embroidered coat and matching vest to his silk breeches. It made Lad's already burning eyes ache all the more just to look at him.

The golden man drew up a chair near the bed upon which Lad perceived he was lying and leaned close to say, ''So, my good sir, you come awake at last! We—my manservant, Lloyd, and myself—have been hovering about on tenterhooks these past two days, waiting for our Sleeping Beauty to rouse himself. How do you feel?''

''Like death,'' Lad murmured, his voice raspy and weak. Tentatively, he lifted a hand that felt as if it weighed twelve stone to touch his aching head and found that there were bandages there. "What happened to me?"

"Robbers, I'm afraid," the vision told him, then gave a *tetch*. "You never should have gone into that part of the city alone, my friend. If Lloyd and I hadn't come across you when we did, you'd presently be singing with the angels—or at least one may hope that it would be angels." He smiled in a genial manner.

"Robbers?" Lad repeated, confused. "I don't remember . . . I'd met a man . . . God help me, what was his name?" He closed his eyes briefly, striving to recall. "Met him in a tavern. He said he knew a good place to make money . . . a gaming hell . . ."

"Set you up for it," said the other man, who had moved too far away for Lad to see. "Took you for a soft touch."

"And he was clearly right," the vision agreed, "for here you are, victim to one of the oldest games in the book, with all your possessions lifted and yourself left for dead. I do hope that you've learned your lesson. Or lessons, rather. I'm Sir Geoffrey Vear, by the by, and that rascally looking scoundrel over at the basin is Lloyd. Do you happen to remember who you are?"

"Lad Walker," Lad replied wearily, lifting his hand up to offer it to Sir Geoffrey. "I'm in your debt, sir. And yours, Lloyd," he said in the general direction of where he hoped the basin was. His vision hadn't yet cleared to give him any precise idea of his surroundings.

"My lord, it's a pleasure." Sir Geoffrey gripped Lad's hand carefully; when he released it Lad gave a sigh of relief and dropped it back to the bed. He felt weak as a half-drowned kitten, as if he'd suffered a long, deadly illness from which it would take a long time to recover. Grimly, he thought of what Sir Geoffrey had just told him.

"Everything was stolen?" he asked.

"I'm afraid so, my lord." Sir Geoffrey gave him an

apologetic look. "Your pockets were completely empty. Lloyd cleaned your clothes thoroughly and found nothing within, and you may believe that he's as honest as the day is long, despite the manner in which he once earned his keep." At Lad's blank look, he added, "A wonderful pickpocket Lloyd was, in his day. That's how we became acquainted, you see. I thought I'd never meet the man to better me at lightfingers, but Lloyd's a master at the art. He's also an invaluable font of knowledge regarding every manner of crime and criminal, such as the men who gulled and robbed you."

"Did a good job of it, they did," Lloyd said in a definitive tone from the other side of the bed now. "Knew what they were about. Knew a noddy cock bloke when they saw one."

That just about summed him up, Lad thought dismally. An idiotic, noddy cock bloke. Three months he'd been in London, and never in his life had he held such a low opinion of himself. In Tennessee, he'd known his worth as a son, as a brother, and as a captain in General Jackson's army. He'd been a wealthy landowner when he'd boarded the ship that took him to England, a man well liked and respected by his many acquaintances, and even, it might be said, a man with a measure of influence in the state of Tennessee. Since arriving in England, he'd lost all touch with the man he'd been. Things had been bad enough at Kerlain, but here in London—God's mercy, he might as well have been a chimney sweep as a blasted nobleman.

He'd been so certain that as the Earl of Kerlain he could at least command enough respect to secure a loan for the sum he needed, or even part of it, but Mr. Sibbley had quickly dispelled the notion. No one approved of the ancient title Kerlain being given to an American—especially one who'd fought against Britain in the recent war, which, Sibbley had reminded him, had only officially ended a few months before. Feelings were high on all sides, and, truth to tell, he might have done better to be Napoleon Bonaparte than an American pretender to the title of earl. At least Napoleon was admirably European and considered quite fascinating. Americans, on the other hand, were ill-mannered, foolish, churlish, and *ungrateful* upstarts who didn't even have the sense to retain their loyalty to England. Apart from that, they also didn't have any idea of fashion, which was evidently a sin far more unforgivable than the rest.

As that was the case, none of the lending institutions Mr. Sibbley was associated with would give Lad a loan on the basis of his own honor—Americans clearly didn't possess any. If he could provide some form of security against the loan, that would be a different matter. Kerlain, however, couldn't be used so long as Lord Carden already held its value by virtue of Lad's vowel, and Fair Maiden was not only too far away but also completely unknown. For all Mr. Sibbley knew, it didn't even exist. And if it did, how could he possibly convince any lenders of the fact without some proof of a deed? In that regard he'd been a little more helpful, offering as Lad's man of business to send to the States for proof of the deed. Lad had told him not to bother.

Since then he'd approached several different businesses, striving to buy a partnership, to find every door closed in his face. He'd tried to meet other noble gentlemen, as Diana had advised he do, to seek guidance and help, but had been only more firmly rebuffed. White's, Almacks—even the House of Lords—all took one look at him, laughed at his American-accented pronouncement that he was the Earl of Kerlain, and turned him aside. He had no cards with his name on them and little idea of how to get such things made. His clothes, which had seemed outrageously fine in Herefordshire, looked decidedly countrified against the spotless elegance of London's dandies.

Days came and went, and Lad made no progress at all.

He wandered the streets, striving to think on what he must do, to chart some course, to find some solution, by turns dejected and desperate. He'd always been a man of action, but in London—indeed, in all of England—he felt as if he were striking uselessly out against dancing shadows or swimming round and round in thick, exhausting mud, never getting anywhere, never finding the way out.

And always there was the great aloneness that had settled so impenetrably upon him, causing the world to take on a darker hue yet.

Each night he returned to the dingy room he'd rented above the coffeehouse in Billingsgate, thinking of Diana, wondering if she was all right, writing endless letters that never had any reply. He'd sit in the coffeehouse itself for long hours, striving to ignore the heavy, ever-present stench of salt and fish in the air, drinking the bitter ale they served and eating the cheapest meals he could buy, and thinking of returning to Tennessee.

How easy a thing it would be to return, to embrace again all that was familiar and welcome, to put his entire journey to England behind him as the worst nightmare he'd ever known. His immediate family was gone, but he had uncles and aunts and cousins, and friends—aye, good friends, each and every one. He thought on them with such longing during the darkness of his present days that he could scarce contain the feeling. What wouldn't he have given to be hailed by one of them now with smiling face and open hand? To be embraced and welcomed and wanted—to see his own worth reflected in the heartfelt manner of someone who cared for him even a little?

That was how it would be if he returned to Fair Maiden. He could almost envision it if he closed his eyes and dreamed. Neighbors on every side would throw balls and grand parties to welcome him back home. There would be music and dancing and merriment, and all his father's dearest friends would set their pretty daughters before him, just as they'd done in the past when he and Joshua had attended such assemblies. Lad had spent plenty of time sparking some of the local beauties but at his mother's insistence had never become serious with any of them. The conflict with England had loomed too threateningly, and she'd told him that only a man who held no honor would bind a woman to himself when he knew that he might march off to war. He wished now—God above, how he wished it!—that he'd not listened to her. He might have already had a wife, then, to yoke him to Fair Maiden, to keep him from ever coming to England—and from meeting Diana and loving her with such blinding madness.

There was no hope for him now. He couldn't leave her behind, loving her as he did, and he couldn't return to her unless he somehow found the way to make a fortune in three years' time.

It had been an equal madness to listen to the fellow he'd met in the tavern near the Strand. He'd never have done so if he hadn't felt so desperate and if the man himself hadn't been so amicable. The memory was daunting, and Lad knew himself for a pathetic creature, being so hungry for a friend that he'd let himself be taken in by the veriest trick. *Of course* it had been a setup for robbery. Looking back on it now, he could see it so fully that he was amazed. And saddened. God help him, but he'd sunk low. And if it hadn't been for the kindness of these men, he might be dead. How ironic it was. King George's soldiers hadn't been able to kill him on the battlefield, but Lad's own stupidity had given the British Empire a second, and far better, chance at doing him in.

A thought occurred to him, and he looked into Sir Geoffrey's kind, patient face and asked, "How did you know I was a lord? You called me that . . . 'my lord.' "

"You're the Earl of Kerlain, aren't you?" Sir Geoffrey

remarked. "If you're truly Lad Walker, that is. And the Diana you spoke of while you were yet insensible must be the late earl's goddaughter, who is now your wife, Lady Kerlain."

"Yes, but how—"

Sir Geoffrey gave a wave with one elegant hand. "My dear boy, I'm a dreadful gossip. I know *everything* about *everyone* in London."

"In *England*," Lloyd corrected dryly, suddenly appearing in Lad's line of view, bearing a cup in one hand that Lad feared was meant for him.

"Well, yes," Sir Geoffrey allowed. "That's probably so. Sharp ears, a sharp mind, and a horrid curiosity tend to make one knowledgeable. Oh, yes, my lord, I've heard a great deal about the Earl of Kerlain these past many weeks. Mostly spoken of in jest, mind you, although I see that it's true about the accent. Dreadful, if you'll pardon my saying so." Sir Geoffrey withdrew a brilliantly white handkerchief from a pocket and dabbed carefully at his rouged lips. "Truly dreadful. An outright murdering of the King's English. Doesn't it make your head hurt to hear it so much in your native land?"

Lad closed his eyes wearily. "What else do you know?"

"About the Earl of Kerlain?" Sir Geoffrey asked. "Not much. Only that you've been trying to gain a large sum of money and haven't had any success. I suppose that was the reason for the visit to the gaming hell?"

"Yes," Lad said, groaning. "Thank you, by the way, for saving me. I'm in your debt, sir."

"Not at all," Sir Geoffrey said dismissively, as if it had been the merest thing. "It was the least I could do for my fellow man." Lloyd cleared his throat loudly, prompting Sir Geoffrey to add, "And Lloyd as well, of course. He did help, you see."

"Can you drink some of this, my lord?" Lloyd set his

free hand behind Lad's neck once more to pull him up to drink from the cup. "Help to clear your head a bit. Get your strength up."

The drink was bitter, tasting of some strange chemistry that Lad couldn't identify, but it wasn't as awful as the brew Maudie'd fixed for him when he'd gotten so drunk at Kerlain. His head throbbed painfully as Lloyd lowered him to the pillows again, and for the first time Lad noticed the bandages on his arms.

"I've been bled," he murmured stupidly, amazed to think that he'd been so completely insensible for two full days.

"The doctor felt it necessary," Sir Geoffrey informed him. "Lloyd would have argued the matter—"

"Already lost plenty of blood, so he had," Lloyd muttered.

"—but for myself, I've always found a good letting to be exceedingly beneficial. Now, if you're not too weary, my lord Kerlain, pray tell me the tale of how and why you came to London. I confess to being painfully curious."

Lad gave him a wan smile. "It seems a poor way to repay your kindness, telling you my troubles."

"You must let me be the judge of that, my lord. Perhaps, after you've finished, we may together devise a plan that might be of use to you . . . and also to me. Now," he said, settling more comfortably in his chair, "proceed."

The telling didn't take very long. Sir Geoffrey and Lloyd both sat in silence, save for the occasional nod and the exchanged glance. Sir Geoffrey was acquainted with who Eoghan Patterson was, as well as with the other major players in the tale. He required little elaboration and at the end seemed satisfied that he knew the full of it.

"Viscount Carden is certainly a fellow to be wary of," he commented when Lad had finally fallen silent. "And *poque* was undoubtedly a choice of game meant to give him the greater advantage. I have no doubt you'd never even heard of it before coming to England, and it's not really played here with any frequency. One of the most important lessons any gamester must learn, my lord, is never to join in any game that he hasn't fully mastered.''

"I thought it was just a friendly game," Lad said wearily, yawning. The throbbing in his head had disappeared, thanks to the effects of Lloyd's potion, but he felt as if he might sleep for a fortnight. "I didn't know we were going to wager anything.''

Sir Geoffrey gave an elegant snort. "There's no such thing as a friendly game, my boy, but you'll soon learn that well enough.''

"I don't want to learn it," Lad grumbled. "I *hate* gambling. I don't know what possessed me to even consider it. Look where it's landed me—I've lost the very thing I was striving to gain, and I'll have to dip into what's left of my funds in order to start fresh.''

"And then what will you do that you haven't already tried?" Sir Geoffrey asked. "The banks have turned you aside, as have the more proper men of business. You could secure a loan for a smaller amount from any of the less savory establishments, but I doubt you'd enjoy the interest they'd charge. Or you could become a thief and hope that you're not caught and hung before gaining the fortune you require. Or, if it wouldn't distress your sense of morality, you could hire yourself out as a whore.''

"What!" Lad's eyes, which he'd closed, flew open.

Sir Geoffrey regarded him steadily. "You're a handsome fellow, and there are a great many wealthy men and women who'd pay a pretty penny to obtain your favors.''

Lad struggled to sit up, ignoring the pain that knifed through his head. *"Men!* What in God's name are you—''

"Now, now, don't fly up into the boughs," Sir Geoffrey said calmly, waving Lad back down with a hand. "How emotional you Americans are, and how entirely lacking in Continental sensibilities. We are speaking of making money, my lord, and therefore we are speaking plainly. You require a fortune; I'm merely pointing out your options. A great many individuals—females, on the main, I grant you—have made a good deal of money in such a manner. But I do think we'd best leave that aside, for I can't think such employment worthy of the Earl of Kerlain, especially as entertaining other men for money usually involves an activity that's a hanging offense. Apart from that, it's plain that the idea distresses you somewhat.''

"Greatly," Lad corrected him stiffly. "The idea distresses me *greatly*.''

"Very well.'' Sir Geoffrey gave a nod. "We'll put that aside, then. And, doing so, that leaves you with very few choices. Indeed, my lord, if you have any real hope of acquiring the funds you need in order to regain your wife and estate, I'm afraid you must reconsider—and overcome— your objections toward gaming.''

"It's impossible. I've never been any good at cards or dice. I'd end up losing what little else I have left.''

Sir Geoffrey's smile was angelic. "But that is precisely why I believe that Fate, in all her grand and glorious wisdom, has brought us together.'' He turned his gaze to Lloyd, who had observed the exchange in silence. "He'll answer splendidly to my little problem, don't you think, Lloyd?''

Lloyd gave Lad a considering look. "Suppose so. Once he's cleaned up and dressed right.''

"Answer?'' Lad repeated with confusion. "Problem?''

"Yes, my lord,'' Sir Geoffrey said, standing and sketching him an elegant bow. "A little problem, for which I would be most grateful of your aid. In return, I shall make you into a proper nobleman and tutor you in the fine art of gaming. I see that the idea leaves you speechless, but I promise you, sir, that before too many months have gone by, you'll realize how exceedingly fortunate you've been to make my acquaintance.''

Lad was too weary to argue, but said, ''I owe you my life, and I'll be glad to do whatever you ask of me in return. But it's not necessary for you to do anything else for me.''

''Oh, but it is,'' Sir Geoffrey countered. ''My troublesome matter must be addressed by a proper nobleman—someone other than myself, I fear. And by the time I've finished with you, Lad Walker, Earl of Kerlain, you'll not only be the downiest gamester in all of England but a creature of such aristocratic perfection that the *ton* will reel in your presence.''

Lad uttered a laugh and closed his eyes, exhausted beyond measure. ''Then you'd better be some kind of miracle worker, Sir Geoffrey, because I'll tell you right now the whole thing's impossible.''

Lloyd, from across the room, made a snorting sound. Sir Geoffrey chuckled with clear amusement.

''Return to your slumbers, my dear earl,'' he said. ''Before the week is out, when you've regained your strength, we'll see about working a miracle or two.''

Chapter Seventeen

London, 15 September 1815

My darling Diana,

Forgive, I pray, the length of time between letters. Matters have changed so drastically over the past several days that I hardly know how to describe them to you, but it seems that, at last, I've stumbled onto the way out of our difficulties. Either God or Fate, I'm not sure which, has seen fit to smile down upon us and has brought help in the form of a new friend, Sir Geoffrey Vear.

I don't know if you've ever heard of Sir Geoffrey or not. He claims to have known my grandfather, the late earl, but that's not surprising. He seems to know a great deal about everyone in England, especially members of the aristocracy. Gossip is Sir Geoffrey's favorite pastime, and since I've been in his company I've learned all sorts of interesting and unusual facts about my fellow peers. Sir Geoffrey seems to think that I should know as much as possible about the ton *and insists it's essential if I'm to have any success in making the money we need.*

I'll not tell you every detail now, Diana, for I fear there is neither the time nor space, though I promise to write at greater length when I can. Sir Geoffrey means to keep me busy with "training," which sounds rather dire, but I'm willing to try anything to attain our goals. I do want to let

you know that I have, at last, a proper address at which you
may write me. Sir Geoffrey has been kind enough to invite
me to share his rooms on Stratton Street, where he lives with
his manservant, Lloyd. (I shall have to write a fully separate
letter to you about Lloyd sometime. A most interesting fel-
low, he is.) If you'll address your letters—if you decide to
write to me at all—to The Earl of Kerlain, Stratton Street,
London, they'll find their way to me here.

I hope to send money to you soon, Diana, so that you can
stock the pantry and the larder for the coming winter. I'll
instruct Sibbley to pay for a supply of coal and have it
delivered to Kerlain by wagon.

I must close this now, as Lloyd informs me that Sir Geof-
frey is growing impatient to be on our way. We've an ap-
pointment with a tailor named Weston, who is evidently the
only suitable tailor in London for a true man of elegance.
I'm still laughing about how foolish that sounds, but I've
promised to let Sir Geoffrey have his way in these matters. I
owe him my life, and, before very much longer, we may owe
him far more than that.

All my love,
your own Lad

Kerlain, 24 October 1815

Dear Lad,

You've been gone almost four months. It seems more like
four years. Still there has been no word from you, no matter
how often I write, so that I almost might believe that you
had died, save that Mr. Sibbley wrote to me briefly, explain-
ing that you've given him instructions to purchase coal and
send it to us here. We may expect it to arrive within another
week, well before the weather begins to turn cold. Maudie is

glad of it, though we had gathered a goodly supply of wood, as I told you.

I'm thankful that you still think of our comfort here, even if you can't bring yourself to write. I'll no longer ask you to do so. Such pleading is humiliating to me and, I'm certain, unwanted by you.

All is well here. The crops that were planted were harvested three weeks past and, though we'll see no profit from them, there will be enough to get us through the winter, and there will be money to buy seeds for next year. If we can but continue on this course, we shall do very well until you've returned to Kerlain.

Rhosyn Farrell and Garan Colvaney were wed two weeks past, and we did have such a fine celebration in the Castle's great hall. Eoghan Patterson was invited by the groom, much to my fury, and so I could not throw him out, but he behaved himself tolerably well and gave the newlyweds a rare gift of two pigs, six laying hens, and a young milk cow. He also brought several bottles of wine and champagne, which saved us the trouble of raiding our own dwindling supply. I did not speak to him during the celebration nor look at him even when he strove to gain my attention. I cannot forget that if it weren't for him—and my own foolishness—you would be here with me, and all would be well. Take care in all things, my lord, and come home to me soon.

My love to you always,
Diana

Kerlain, 7 November 1815

My lord,

I have just now received the sum of money that you forwarded to me through Mr. Sibbley's office and must profess my great astonishment. Though I am certainly grateful *for your consideration, I must protest that the funds would be far better used if put toward the debt that we owe for Kerlain.*

Lad, you mustn't send me anything more. Only do your part while you're in London and trust me to take care of Kerlain and the people here within our own means. We've done it for many years before you came and can certainly continue on for a few years more. You must have no worries for us—for any of us—but only do whatever you can to come home to us soon.

Diana

London, 15 December 1815

My darling Diana,

London is nearly empty of fine company now, and winter has come hard upon us. It's snowing even as I write, covering the street outside my window with a light dusting of snow. It makes me think of Tennessee, and Kerlain, and the cold, snowy day when I first met you.

I miss you more than I can say in moments such as these. Sir Geoffrey teases me about writing so many letters that ever go unanswered, but he understands, too, about love and hope and seems equally pleased to find both in me.

Sir Geoffrey's kept me busier than I ever might have imagined with his endless training. We're both exhausted by the end of each day, but that, of course, is when we must go out to the most godforsaken places so that I may learn how to gamble. He's determined to make me into a proper nobleman, no matter how hard the going—though it is certainly far harder than he thought it would be. He's taken to rapping me on the knuckles like my old schoolteacher back in Tennessee used to do—though Sir Geoffrey uses his cane, and not a ruler—whenever I lapse into what he calls my "awful American speech." He has but three months, he claims, to break me of my natural manner of speaking—indeed, of all my own nature. In March he intends to "launch" me, the Earl of Kerlain, as his own new and perfect creation. Hopefully, by that time, everyone in London who heard of my earlier failures at striving to gain access to the ton will have forgotten them. Sir Geoffrey says it doesn't particularly matter if they do or not. He has ways and means of making them forget, or so he claims. At this point, I'd believe him capable of almost anything.

I want to tell you about one of his particular "lessons," Diana, because you alone will be able to appreciate it as I did.

Two weeks ago, Sir Geoffrey took me to a certain studio where lessons in swordplay are given. The master there put me through my paces and Sir Geoffrey watched, pronouncing himself satisfied with the small measure of skill that I possess. He asked the master to pair me with another student—a man who is clearly the master's prize pupil. I never even saw the other fellow's face, for he wore a mask into the hall where we matched swords. Before we set to, Sir Geoffrey took my sword from me and laid it upon a nearby table beside a small dagger.

"You've little regard for the title of earl," he said, stepping back, "because you feel you've little use for it."

I agreed to this. Heaven knows I could hardly deny it.

Sir Geoffrey indicated my sword. "This," he said, "is your title, the Earl of Kerlain, nobleman of England, and this," he pointed to the dagger, "is Lad Walker of Tennessee. That gentleman over there," he nodded toward my waiting opponent, "is England itself. Begin with the dagger, my lord, and defend yourself just as you've been doing since you arrived here, with naught but your one self." To give me no choice in the matter, he took the long sword away.

I began to protest, but my opponent charged me so suddenly that I grabbed up the dagger and did what I could to fend him off. He fought like a madman, completely outside of the rules of proper swordplay, as if he meant to kill me. Before very long I shouted to Sir Geoffrey that I needed the sword, that he must give it to me. He replied, very calmly in the midst of the noise of the fighting, that he had laid it upon the table the moment after I had snatched up the dagger and that it had been there all along for me to take up and use.

I tossed the dagger aside and took the sword up at once, and though I can't say that I won the match with my opponent, I certainly kept him from running me through.

Sir Geoffrey had spent many an hour striving to make me understand just how important my title is—and you, Diana, spent many more. All futile, thanks to my own stubbornness. Until that moment in the fencing academy, I couldn't understand what you were trying to tell me. Now I'll never forget. No matter what I may feel personally for being the Earl of Kerlain, it's my only protection here in England, and perhaps not only mine, but yours and that of the people of Kerlain as well.

As to the gambling with which I have become engaged, and which I think will worry you a great deal, be reassured. Sir Geoffrey is a strict and severe master and has already shown me a number of methods by which I have increased our fortune. Every spare penny that isn't required for my keep or my gambling stake goes to Mr. Sibbley, and you may write to him if you like to have an accounting of the funds I've lately been able to put away toward our goal.

I'm far from being what Sir Geoffrey is as a gamester, mind you, but I've learned a great deal. Indeed, I can recite, in my sleep, the two main tenets of every professional gambler. They are thus: First, you must ever be patient for luck to fall your way—far more patient than any of your opponents—and second, never accept any bet, no matter how good it may seem. *A professional gambler only ever makes wagers; he never accepts them. And to this I suppose a third stricture might be added: Never make any wager that is so unfair as to make yourself the certain winner. Not only is this dishonorable but also dangerous, causing revenge to lurk behind you every moment of the day. This particular knowledge is especially dear to me, for now that I've become familiar with gaming in its many forms, I've also become far more aware of just how treacherous Eoghan Patterson was in his dealings with me. To get me drunk and propose a game in the dark of night was a breach of honor too severe to set aside. One day, I vow, my lord Carden will know the truth of that as well.*

The snow grows worse as I look out my window, covering the street and rooftops more thickly. I would remain indoors by the fire this night, but Sir Geoffrey insists that we must go out again to game.

I have given Mr. Sibbley a present to forward to you at Christmas, my love, and pray that you'll not think it too extravagant for our current circumstances. As I said earlier in this missive, every spare penny has gone toward repaying our debt for Kerlain, but the small gift I've sent cost me very little. Please don't turn it away for the sake of the few shillings it cost. I cannot rest easily this Christmastide—the first we should have spent together as man and wife—without giving you some small token of my love.

Wishing you a blessed Christmas Day, my dearest, I remain, your own——Lad

Chapter Eighteen

Late April 1816

Nearly everyone at Kerlain attended the funeral, crowding about the small grave where the snow had finally melted away.

It was a warm day now, with the sun shining gently over the land, and far different from the bitterly cold night three days past when young Josee Colvaney had died. Diana had been at the five-year-old's bedside when the end had come, having spent two full days there beforehand, doing all that she could to save the child's life. She had dipped into the precious funds that Lad had so stubbornly continued to send her, calling Doctor Rushford to attend Josee as soon as she'd fallen ill, but to no avail. The only child of Hugh and Jennie Colvaney had slipped away despite every effort made to save her, and now she lay cold in the ground on the first true spring day that Kerlain had seen in the year 1816.

There had been no resident minister at Kerlain since before her godfather's time: his father, the fourth Earl of Kerlain, a famously profligate man, had banished religious men from living on the land for all eternity—and had put the command in writing, no less. Parson Moore, of Woebley, had been good enough to make the journey to Kerlain every few days to perform services, as well as for special occasions such as marriages, births, and funerals.

But Parson Moore was presently absent from his usual post, taking a long and much needed rest, and his temporary replacement had been too overwhelmed with the wealth of his new duties to tend so small a matter as the funeral of a poor child from the poorest of estates beneath his care. In the end, Diana had been forced to give way to the pleading of Josee's parents and had sent a request to Eoghan, asking if he might loan her the use of Lising Park's resident cleric. Eoghan had, of course, not only agreed but had personally visited Hugh and Jennie in their humble dwelling to offer both his sympathies and a small measure of gold to aid them in arranging their child's funeral. The young parents had been filled with gratitude, and Eoghan had succeeded in increasing the admiration that the people of Kerlain already held him in.

The knowledge sickened Diana, just as the fawning and reverence with which Eoghan was treated by both the Farrell and Colvaney clans sickened her. She longed to tell them of the threats Viscount Carden had made concerning them, that he would make them suffer greatly if she dared to leave Kerlain. How amazed they would be to know the truth—if they believed it, which perhaps they would not. It had become clear to Diana that the people of Kerlain hoped that Viscount Carden might one day take Lad Walker's place as their lord and master. Rumors had spread—started, most likely, by Eoghan himself—that the Earl of Kerlain had abandoned not only his wife but his estate and people too. Divorce, it was whispered, would soon follow, shaming both Diana and the title, and after that only Lord Carden could be their salvation.

Eoghan happily made the most of such admiration, but he'd ever enjoyed pulling the wool over the eyes of those he deemed "inferior." Now he was in his happiest element, playing the people of Kerlain as fools to suit his own purposes, smiling to their adoring and grateful faces and laughing the very moment their backs were turned.

Diana let it continue without a word. Telling the truth now could only prove a disaster for Lad and her—indeed, for all of Kerlain. Eoghan would sell the deed to the estate in but a heartbeat, despite all his promises, or, worse, gamble it away to the lowest, meanest gamester he could find—someone who would promise to never give Lad the chance to buy the estate back. Diana could almost hear Eoghan now, promising the fellow that he'd match any offer that Lad made, a promise Eoghan could make good on, being so damnably wealthy.

No. Until Lad was safely back at Kerlain with the funds to redeem the estate in full, Diana knew that she must work against Eoghan far more quietly, and intelligently.

She'd begun her campaign already by making it known—quietly—that the Earl of Kerlain had not only kept Castle Kerlain warm throughout the winter with deliveries of the finest coal but had also regularly sent money—the very funds with which Diana had fed those who would have otherwise gone hungry throughout the winter, bought shoes for the children who would have gone without, and paid for the doctor to come when Josee Colvaney had fallen ill.

The Earl of Kerlain had not quite abandoned them.

Not quite.

There were days—many of them—when Diana had trouble believing that herself. But no matter what her personal fears were, she'd *never* make the mistake of revealing them, especially not to the people of Kerlain. It would give Eoghan too much satisfaction.

When Josee Colvaney's tiny coffin had been lowered into the ground and covered with three fistfuls of dirt, one each from her parents and one from Diana, who stood as representative of the Earl of Kerlain, the assembled began slowly and silently to make their way back to Castle Kerlain, where

Josee's short life would be celebrated with a proper wake. Eoghan, who had attended the funeral—much to the gratitude of Josee's parents, for it was considered a great honor that such a nobleman would deign to recognize the passing of so poor a child—walked beside her. He tried once to take Diana's elbow in his hand, to guide her as any true gentleman would rightly do. Diana stiffly freed herself and, speaking to him for the first time in nearly a year, uttered three words: "Don't touch me." He wisely made no further attempt to do so.

He was less wise by the time the wake had come to an end several hours later, when most of those in attendance had taken note of the waning sun and begun to make their way home. Eoghan politely excused himself from the company of a few who had lingered behind and resolutely made his way toward Diana. She'd kept a clear distance between them throughout the wake, and now, seeing his approach from the other side of the great hall, steadied herself to meet his brazen opening head on. Hot anger tightened her throat as he stopped before her, making an elegant bow. She stared at him with all that she felt for him and said nothing.

"My lady," he said. "I must thank you for your kind hospitality of the day, though one might wish for a happier occasion upon which to visit Castle Kerlain."

"Sir," she replied stonily, "this is so. For you, however, there can be no such occasions. I bid you good day."

She turned to go, but he moved to close the space between them.

"Diana—"

"Sir." She turned to face him, striving mightily to keep the fury she felt from her tone. "I said *good day.*"

"I've brought something for you," he said, following her when she began to walk away again. "From London. I've given it—them—to Swithin."

Diana drew in a sharp breath but only lifted the hem of

her skirts an inch higher and walked more quickly toward the doorway that would allow her to quit the great hall and leave Eoghan behind.

"You'll find news of your husband in them," Eoghan told her, still following. "I thought you'd be interested to know how the Earl of Kerlain occupies his time there."

There wasn't the least hesitation in Diana's step as she continued on her way, head held high, nor any sign of the distress she felt at Eoghan's words. She made her way through the passage that led to the West Wing, thankful that he at least retained enough manners to keep from following her any further.

Swithin met her at the entryway, bowing.

"Miss Diana—"

"Lady Kerlain!" she snapped tightly, glaring. Both he and Maudie insistently addressed her as if she'd never been married, and she had long since ceased believing that they were merely forgetful. "The *Countess* of Kerlain, and wife to your lord. I pray you'll not forget it again."

Swithin betrayed his surprise at her terse words only by blinking more slowly than he normally did. Diana, knowing him since she had been but a babe, also recognized the particularly stony set of his features that told of his well-hidden aggravation.

"Yes, my lady," was his stiff, but perfectly proper, reply. He gave a low bow. "I humbly beg your pardon."

Diana made a scoffing sound. "You've never done anything humbly in your life, and I've reason to doubt that you'll begin doing so now. Viscount Carden gave you something for me?"

Swithin nodded once. "Several London newspapers, my lady. I've taken the liberty of putting them in the parlor."

"Thank you," she said, moving toward the stairway. "And, Swithin?"

"Yes, my lady?"

"If Viscount Carden brings anything else to Kerlain, no matter what it may be, you're to throw it straight into the fire and bid the viscount to the devil."

She meant to take her own advice as soon as she gained the parlor. Whatever the newspapers had to say about Lad, Eoghan wouldn't have brought them if they hadn't served his own cruel purpose. They would be pure poison, and she'd been tricked too many times by her former playmate to trust anything that he brought her now.

They lay on the low table near the fire, a thin stack of perhaps two or three papers, neatly folded. Her godfather had sometimes brought home the less political London newspapers for Diana's entertainment following one of his visits there. She'd always looked forward to these gifts with unmitigated delight and had spent hour upon hour scouring each page, reading the announcements and anecdotes and bits of gossip over and again and dreaming of what it might be like to have a season in Town.

But she took no delight in these that Eoghan had brought. It crossed her mind that he must have gone to London himself to bring them back. Had he seen Lad? Spoken to him?

Diana hadn't had so much as a word from her husband since he'd been gone. No matter how often she wrote, or how seldom, or even how pleadingly, there was never a reply. Lad was punishing her for sending him away—perhaps even for calling him to Kerlain in the first place. Whatever love he had once felt for her had clearly turned to hatred, and all that kept him in London was his sense of duty and the promise he'd given her to gain the money to buy back Kerlain. It must be the truth. Diana could think of no other reason for his cold and constant silence.

Though perhaps it could not rightly be called a total silence. There had been the money, a small amount assuredly, but sent once each month since September, and the precious coal before the winter, without which they would have nearly frozen from cold. And two small gifts, which had surprised her beyond measure: a pair of gloves at Christmastime, and a small silver brooch on the date of their one-year anniversary. These—all of them, even the gifts— had been forwarded to Diana through Mr. Sibbley's private courier, with mention only that they were from the Earl of Kerlain, but with no personal note from him. She fingered the brooch now, wearing it, as she had done since it came, over her heart.

She was his wife, yet she had no idea how Lad was, what he had been doing, even where he had been living.

But, oh, how she longed to know. So many nights had ended in private tears as she'd lain upon her bed, lonely and sorry—both for what she had done and for herself—and wondering. She loved Lad with a fullness that had completely overtaken her, and he had once loved her. Being parted from him was the worst living hell she ever might have imagined; but never hearing from him, not knowing where he was or whom he was with—her handsome, charming husband, whom every woman fell in love with—was a pure torment.

Diana moved swiftly, snatching up one of the papers and unfolding it. Her heart beat loudly in her ears, and her mind told her fiercely not to read anything Eoghan had brought— that she must throw it straight into the fire at once. She must. She would.

With trembling fingers she began to crush the blur of words to consign them to the flames—then stopped. *The Earl of Kerlain.* His name. There it was, upon the page. Slowly, shaking everywhere, she pulled the page open again.

Lady Queensley's annual ball, held Thursday last, was the season's greatest success to date, made more so by the attendance of the much sought after Earl of

*Kerlain, whose presence in London this year has set
female hearts to thrumming and mouths to chattering.
The as yet unmarried earl, having assumed the title
only recently, has quickly become the talk of the* ton.
*Despite the fact that he's an American and inherited of
one of England's poorer estates, Lord Kerlain's manner is perfect, his dress impeccable, and his charm
estimable. Taking special interest are the mothers of
available daughters, who would do well to seek Lord
Kerlain's notice at those quieter affairs he may deign to
attend and thereby avoid being trampled by the throng
of females—married, unmarried, and otherwise—who
are currently rushing to throw themselves at Lord
Kerlain's feet.*

"Unmarried," Diana murmured, lowering the paper.
"How could they think him unmarried?"

She tossed the paper aside and took up the next, scanning
the pages for mention of the Earl of Kerlain. When she
finally found it and began to read, her heart sank. It was
much the same as the first paper. Only worse.

Half an hour later, Diana had at last set the newspapers
into the hearth and stood before the flames, watching the
pages curl and glow, turning to ashes. Her eyes ached with
unshed tears, and her chest was tense with both the hurt she
felt and the fierce need to cry. But she pressed her lips
together tightly and refused to give way to the misery
within. She'd wept rivers of tears for Lad Walker. Now she
wouldn't waste another breath of sorrow on him.

So. Now she knew why he hadn't written. He'd been
rather busy enjoying himself and becoming the toast of
London. And being pursued by the beautiful, elegant
women of the *ton,* allowing them to believe that he wasn't
already married to a plain country mouse who had never
once even been outside of Herefordshire.

It was the last thing—the very last thing—she ever would have believed him capable of. Indeed, even having read the truth of it with her own eyes, she yet had difficulty reconciling such behavior with the man she'd fallen in love with. Lad hadn't even liked wearing the fine clothes that the tailor in Woebley had made for him, yet now he was actually considered a *leader* of fashion in London? How could it possibly be?

"Oh, Lad," she murmured, struggling against the sorrow that threatened to overwhelm her. How could he have betrayed her so? Had she lost him forever when she'd sent him away? But he had admitted that it was as much his fault—more—as hers that he'd had to go. Now he clearly didn't care at all for regaining Kerlain. He was too busy being feted in London to make the money they required. Or to ever come back to her.

He had abandoned her and hadn't even had the courage to write and tell her so. She would lose Kerlain—everything. Not that it would matter now, for she had lost Lad, and with that loss, nothing else could truly touch her heart or give her pain.

She fingered the brooch again, as she had been in the habit of doing since it had arrived. What a foolish hope it had given her, this small, inexpensive piece of jewelry. Just as the gloves had done. And how precious it had become, just as if it had been made of the finest diamonds instead of such plainly wrought silver.

Diana closed her eyes. Two tears, victorious at last, spilled out upon her cheeks. With an abrupt movement, she unclasped the brooch and pulled it free, setting it on the mantel above the hearth. Her mouth quivered and she blinked, allowing more tears to escape. Grief welled up hot and sharp, and she strove to push it down again.

A tap fell on the door, and she drew in a hard breath, furiously wiping the tears away.

"Come!" she called, glad to hear that her voice, at least, was strong and steady.

The doors opened, and Swithin said, in an odd voice, "My lady, several gentlemen have arrived. . . ."

Wonderful, Diana thought. Just what she needed.

"Who are they?"

"I'm not sure, miss—my lady. The one speaking for them claims to have been sent by the earl."

Diana uttered a laugh. "That's impossible."

"I agree, my lady, but he insists upon speaking to you. He says that he has a missive for you from Lord Kerlain."

Diana whirled about and headed for the door. This was clearly another of Eoghan's cruel jests.

"Does he, indeed?" she said angrily. "We shall see about that."

A dozen or more men stood in the castle courtyard, and a scruffier, more ill-looking lot Diana had never seen. Most of them were dressed in tattered army uniforms, soldiers who'd come down from the wars. They were pale and undernourished, and four of them, at the least, had been grievously wounded. One of these, a young man with straw-colored hair, limped forward to speak to Diana. He was missing one arm entirely, and the right side of his face had been heavily disfigured by a terrible scar. Despite this, he made her a low and elegant bow.

"You will be Lady Kerlain," he said in a voice that sounded far more cultured than what Diana had expected. "Lord Kerlain told me that you'd be the most beautiful woman I had beheld in my life, and he spoke the truth. Forgive me," he added quickly when Diana gave him a stern look of disbelief, "if I've spoken in too forward a manner."

"I am the Countess of Kerlain," Diana told him. "You wished to see me?"

"Yes, my lady. We"—he swept his remaining arm backward to indicate the men who stood behind him—"have come to Kerlain at the invitation of his lordship, the earl, in order to begin repairs to the castle. My name is David Moulton. I'm an architect," he said, adding, as if he was embarrassed by the fact, "or rather, I was, once, before the war."

Diana had ever prided herself on being able to conduct herself with a certain measure of polish in any situation. It was, after all, the manner in which her godfather had raised her to behave. But at David Moulton's words, she could only stare, wide-eyed, and shake her head with disbelief.

This reception had a sorrowful reaction on the men. They had already appeared to be fully wretched, both physically and mentally, but there had been a certain hopefulness in their eyes, a gladness at having arrived at Kerlain. At Diana's reaction, their expressions fell, each and every man, and desperation took the place of hopefulness.

David Moulton was the exception. Diana's shock seemed only to steel his resolve. He fumbled with a pocket in his jacket to pull a folded packet out.

"Lord Kerlain hired me to oversee the work that's to be done. I'm fully qualified, I promise you. Before the war, I studied with Mr. Beacon of Wainsright. I'm sure you've heard of him? And before that, of course, I had my degree from Oxford."

Diana kept shaking her head. David Moulton began to redden. He held the packet out to her.

"I have my papers in my bag," he said insistently, as if she couldn't believe that a man so horribly maimed could be speaking the truth. "My degree and a letter from Mr. Beacon, which I shall be glad to show to your ladyship for further proof. Please, here is the missive that Lord Kerlain sent for you, my lady, which I believe contains his instructions."

She took the missive and lowered her gaze to stare at it, instead of him. Before her, she heard the men nervously shifting and murmuring. David Moulton cleared his throat and said, "If your ladyship is concerned that we're unfit for the task, let me reassure you that we're all of us far more able than we may appear, and also willing."

"And 'ungry!" one of the men in the back added, which made the others laugh.

"Yes, that too," David Moulton admitted. "We've walked from London these past three days, Lord Kerlain having sent us with the promise of gainful employment. I'm sorry that he had no chance to warn you beforehand, my lady. I can see that our coming is something of a surprise to you, though I may hope not an unwelcome one. From what I can see of the castle thus far, it requires a great deal of work before it can be truly habitable."

Diana blinked several times, only half-hearing him, and at last broke the seal to the missive to read it.

Diana, I apologize for not finding the way to warn you that Lieutenant Moulton and the men with him would be arriving at Kerlain, but their situation was dire, and time was of the essence. These men fought in the Peninsula, were wounded, and thereafter discharged, but they've no hope for employment and many of them who were grievously injured—like Lieutenant Moulton—aren't yet ready to return to their families. The army casts such brave men away, either unable or unwilling to offer them any measure of support, so that they've nowhere to go but the lowest part of society, to beg or steal, often to starve and die. I will not tell you how I came to meet Lieutenant Moulton and the others, but you must believe me when I say that they were rapidly heading down the path to the latter.

And so I have sent them to Kerlain, with the promise

of food and a bed covered by a roof—if a rather dubious one—in exchange for labor. House them in the great hall of the castle, where they should be warm enough throughout the summer. When winter comes, they'll either have proven their worth by making that part of the castle livable or suffer the consequences.

There is no need to coddle them, Diana. They are soldiers and used to hard living, to sleeping on the ground with but a blanket to cover them, to cooking their own meals and caring for their own clothes. Their needs are very simple, and they will work hard for you. Lieutenant Moulton will be in charge of the men, and you need only tell him what you desire, just as if you were his superior officer, and he will make certain that they carry out your wishes.

I'll instruct Mr. Sibbley to send additional funds to cover their needs, so that you will not have to stretch the meager limits of Kerlain itself more thinly. You needn't worry that this will negatively affect our own efforts toward regaining Kerlain. I've begun to make a steady living with my gaming, just as Sir Geoffrey promised, and the amount it will take to keep these men will be small and worthwhile. In truth, we could never have hired other workers so well or so cheaply. I hope that this beginning on the repairs of the castle will please you, Diana. I have told myself, and believe, that it will.

If you've any concerns regarding this new arrangement, you need only write and tell me. If you still cannot bring yourself to do so, inform Mr. Sibbley and he will be good enough to pass them along to me.

My love to you, as always,

Lad

Diana read the entire missive through once more, very aware of the silence of the men in the courtyard. At last, she lowered the page and lifted her gaze to David Moulton.

"It seems that my husband has hired you to rebuild the castle," she said softly. "Welcome to Kerlain, gentlemen."

Their relief was a palpable thing, with smiles and grins and patting each other on the back. They nodded deferentially to Diana, and David Moulton made another bow.

"Thank you, my lady. We're very glad to be here, and hope that we may be of the greatest service to you."

"I'm sure you shall be, Lieutenant. Lord Kerlain clearly thinks so, else he'd never have sent you."

"There's no need to call me by my rank, my lady. I've been discharged from the army."

"It is how you are addressed in the earl's letter," she told him, "and it is how you shall be addressed at Kerlain. If you gentlemen will be so good as to collect your things and follow me, I'll show you into the great hall. We've just had a wake this afternoon, which is, of course, a sad occasion, but some good may come of it on this instance, for there's a great deal of food and drink remaining and not yet cleared away. After your long journey," she said, looking at each man more fully and seeing, with a pang of distress, how thin they all were, "I think you'll be glad of some sustenance."

It was another hour before Diana was able to steal back to the peace and quiet of the parlor in the West Wing. She'd personally seen to the settling of the men, thankful that the old part of the castle where the many servants had once been housed yet contained enough pallets to provide the men a greater measure of comfort. These were all carried to the great hall and set up at one end in rows, causing that part of the hall to look like a soldier's barracks. David Moulton promised to build a set of screens, as were used in ancient times, to section the area off into its own room, and this pleased Diana greatly. It would be good to see the great hall occupied once more, just as it had been occupied long ago by knights and soldiers.

Once she was satisfied that the lieutenant and his men were sated with food and drink and comfortably settled, she tackled the exhausting task of soothing Swithin and Maudie's frayed nerves. The elderly servants were aghast at the unholy invasion of the newcomers—men who had no claim to Kerlain in any way, save that they were acquainted in some manner with the new earl. They were strangers, perhaps criminals, even murderers! And no stranger should have a hand in rebuilding the castle. That should be done only by Farrells or Colvaneys, and if the earl had wanted men to do such work, he need look no further than his own people—if he ever deigned to return and look at them at all.

Diana had calmly listened to their complaints, then told them just as calmly that the newcomers had been sent to Kerlain by the earl and that there was nothing that she, or they, or anyone, could do to change that. He was the earl, and his word was law at Kerlain. That was that. When they began to argue anew, she smiled and shrugged and walked away.

In the parlor she read Lad's missive through once more, slowly and wonderingly, her brow furrowed with bewilderment. He wrote in such a dear, familiar tone, as if he'd not changed in the least, as if there hadn't been such a lengthy break in communications between them. But he'd not answered one of her letters in the past year, and the London papers gave evidence that he had changed a great deal. And who was this Sir Geoffrey that he spoke of, as if she would know who he was? Diana shook her head at the words that spoke of his gaming, especially distressed by this. How could he possibly have taken up the very sport that had lost them Kerlain? Yet this, too, he wrote of in such a manner that indicated she should be aware of what he had done. It made no sense.

Despite that, the pace of her heart quickened at the final words he wrote—words of love. Perhaps it was a lie; she hardly knew what to think any longer, but if it was, then it was the sweetest lie she'd ever known.

Most telling of all was that he'd sent David Moulton and his men to Kerlain to begin the much-needed repairs, and he'd not have done such as that if his intention was never to return. Indeed, he had written outright of their *efforts toward regaining Kerlain.* And he spoke of pleasing her, knowing full well what it meant to Diana to have Kerlain built again to its former glory. It could only mean—truly, there was no other explanation—that he yet cared for her, even a little.

Diana folded the missive, tucking it into a pocket hidden in the folds of her skirt. Reaching out, she retrieved the brooch that she had set upon the mantel and deftly refastened it in its place upon her dress, then ran her fingers lightly over the filigreed design and smiled.

Chapter Nineteen

Late November 1816

The coughing was bad today; Lad woke to the sound of Sir Geoffrey's rough, painful hacking before the sun had risen in the sky—not that he would be able to see it when it did finally rise. The day would be cold and overcast, just as it had been all week. A second, weary November spent in London, away from Diana and Kerlain. Lad looked out the window as he pulled his dressing gown on and gave a sigh. What he wouldn't give to be done with all this.

He had become a successful nobleman at last, thanks to Sir Geoffrey and Lloyd. He was a successful gambler, a successful wagerer, and a successful charmer—especially of women. He'd made friends of men who had at first been his enemies, fellow noblemen who had despised him for his American heritage but who had now brought him into their inner circle and made his life in London bearable.

Any other man would probably be content with such a life, but Lad merely abided it. Gambling, he had discovered, was a horrible, mentally and physically exhausting way to earn a living. Having learned nearly every trick to the art of both gaming and wagering, Lad had also begun to realize, to his dismay, that success in such a career was merely a matter of a wiser man taking advantage of those who were less wise. All the little tricks, the mannerisms, the careful facial expressions—it was all like being an actor in some awful play. There had been a few nights when Sir Geoffrey had taken him out and Lad had been unable to continue with a game, especially when foolish, hot-blooded young noblemen were involved. If they were going to throw their fortunes away and bring distress to their families, they were not going to do so with his help. Sir Geoffrey said that a gambler couldn't afford to be squeamish, but Lad knew in his heart that his parents, and Joshua too, would have been deeply disappointed in him for being involved in anyone's ruin, and he couldn't bring himself to participate.

He liked wagering far more than outright gaming, at least with the few wagers that Sir Geoffrey had so carefully guided him through. The winnings were just as substantial and the outcomes far more satisfying.

His first truly important wager, in fact, had only just been successfully completed and had gained him ten thousand pounds, as well as new and very dear friends and an immense satisfaction that no minor gaming win could bring. At Sir Geoffrey's instruction, he had wagered with one of the *ton*'s most reprobate noblemen, Lucien "Lucky" Bryland—Viscount Callan—that he would fall in love with his rather plain bride, Lady Clara Harkhams, within six months of their marriage. Lord Callan, fully affronted by the idea of this, countered that he would have Lady Clara pregnant and put away at his country estate within those same six months and had readily accepted Lad's wager.

It had been an almost-certain win for Lad, having as he did Sir Geoffrey's inside knowledge that Lord Callan had been head over ears in love with his country-bred betrothed since they were both quite young. If a distance had sprung up between them during the years they'd been apart, it only needed some help from an interested party—Lad, as it happened—to make them realize that same love once more. Lady Clara had indeed been expecting a child at the end of six months of marriage, but Lord Callan was so deeply in love with her that nothing on earth could have parted him from her side. He'd gladly ceded the winning of the wager to Lad and even thanked him for helping him to see the error of his ways. What a wonderful thing it had been to see Lucky and Clara off to their country estate—together—only a few days past, and to know, as well, that he was ten thousand pounds closer to returning to his own love.

If she was indeed still his love. There had been but one note from Diana in all this time since his leaving, and this had been delivered by a friend of David Moulton's, who had brought it directly from Kerlain as he had passed through on his way to London. She had thanked him for sending David and the other men, also for the coal and the money, all practical things. At the end, she had thanked him for the small gifts he'd sent her through Mr. Sibbley and expressed what was to him a bewildering hope for a letter, just as if he'd not sent her dozens upon dozens from his first day in London. Somehow, Lad began to think, she had not received anything that hadn't been sent directly from Mr. Sibbley and he suspected Eoghan Patterson's hand in the matter. It would explain a great deal. Sir Geoffrey, when Lad had put forth this theory over their supper one night, had nodded in his usual sage manner and said, "Know your opponent, Lad. Always know your opponent."

The door to his bedchamber opened. Lloyd stood in the hall, holding a bowl that Lad knew was filled with the morning's blood.

"He's very bad today," Lad said, a statement, not a question.

Lloyd's face gave nothing away. He was very like Swithin that way, Lad thought.

"He's bad" was the answer. "Shouldn't have been out in the cold last night." He gave a slight shrug. "Told him. Both of us, so we did."

Yes, they'd told him. Night after night for months, since his fits of coughing had begun to bring up blood. Long before that, Lad had realized that Sir Geoffrey wasn't wearing makeup to whiten his skin; he was simply deathly pale from the consumption he'd been suffering for so long.

Sir Geoffrey had been dying since before Lad had met him and had refused to do anything about it. He certainly had no intention of ending his nightly journeys, though he no longer gambled, not having the strength for it. Instead, he oversaw Lad's ventures, watching him from a certain distance, then making observations and giving advice and correction as they made their way home. Lad had repeatedly told his benefactor that he needn't continue to exert himself in such a manner, though secretly, and selfishly, he was glad for Sir Geoffrey's presence. On those few nights when the older man hadn't accompanied him, Lad had felt vulnerable and exposed and had sat in his place at the gaming table waiting to make a mistake so dire that complete disaster would surely follow. He'd not yet stumbled quite that badly, but he still dreaded the knowledge that one day—perhaps one day very soon—he would no longer be able to feel Sir Geoffrey's comforting presence lurking somewhere behind him in the dark hells where he must continue to seek out fresh sport.

"I'll sit with him while you take care of that," Lad said, nodding toward the bowl Lloyd held. Lloyd sighed wearily, offered a rare and fleeting smile of gratitude, and left without a word.

"Causing trouble early this morning, are you?" Lad murmured in a teasing jest as he took the chair beside Sir Geoffrey's bed. The older man's skin was as white and waxy as one of Madame Tussaud's figures. Fine droplets of blood had sprayed over the bedsheets, but Lad neither gazed at nor mentioned them. Sir Geoffrey's dignity required such occasional feigning of ignorance. "Now perhaps you'll listen to Lloyd and me when we tell you it's far too cold for you to be going out in the evenings.''

Sir Geoffrey smiled faintly from where he lay among the many pillows Lloyd had propped him up with.

''I'm beginning to think that perhaps you may be right, Lad,'' he said, and Lad hid his distress at how thin and weak Sir Geoffrey's voice was, so different from the vibrancy it had held only a year ago, ''though I dislike the thought of leaving you to the wolves without a friend near at hand. Still, you've come a long way since first we met. I should be terrified to meet you across a table now.''

Lad uttered a laugh. ''You jest, surely. I shall never attain your skill, no matter how long I may make the attempt.''

''Nay, you're wrong, Lad. Sooner than you think, you shall not only match me but perhaps even surpass me. You've an innocence in your face that I never possessed, not even as a boy, God knows. And more charm than a man has a right to, though I'm dreadfully glad you do possess it.'' He reached out a hand. ''Lad?''

Lad took the frail hand gently. ''What is it, Geoff?''

''You'll watch over Christabella, won't you? On your honor?''

''Yes. On my honor. I gave you my vow long ago, didn't I?''

Miss Christabella Howell, a strikingly beautiful young woman known to be the daughter of a famous chemist, Viscount Howell, was in truth Sir Geoffrey's daughter. No one, including Viscount Howell and Christabella, knew the truth, and that was just the way Sir Geoffrey wanted it. The secret love that Sir Geoffrey had shared with Lady Howell had come to an end only at her death, though perhaps not even then. Hardly a day went by that Sir Geoffrey didn't open the false backing in his precious pocket watch and gaze long and adoringly at the picture hidden within—of Lady Howell.

Miss Howell herself looked so much like Sir Geoffrey that Lad understood perfectly why his friend had almost completely disappeared from polite society shortly after her birth. In the beginning, he had spent years abroad, returning to England occasionally to make certain—from a careful distance—that all was well with his daughter and his love. When Lady Howell had died, Sir Geoffrey returned to England permanently. He had lived on the outskirts of the *ton*, meeting only with his closest friends and careful never to cross paths with his beloved Christabella, knowing full well any rumors regarding her birth would stain her permanently and ruin her chances for a decent marriage. He'd been glad to see that Viscount Howell had no idea that Christabella wasn't truly his own daughter and treated her well. In that regard, Sir Geoffrey had no fears.

What worried Sir Geoffrey was Christabella's fiancé, Wulffrith Lane, Viscount Severn—or Wulf, as he was known to his intimates, among whom Lad was now counted. Lord Severn was a young and promising chemist who had studied beneath Viscount Howell's tutelage. He was wealthy, of good family, and madly in love with Christabella. He was also one of the biggest, most frighteningly muscular men that Lad had ever known and, if he hadn't been such a brilliant scientist, could easily have gone on to become one of England's most successful boxers. But Wulf, for all his attributes, was possessed of one exceedingly grave flaw.

He was a complete, total, and absolute blundering fool.

Viscount Severn could calculate an impossible mathematical problem in the beat of a heart, but he seldom knew where he was, why he was there, or what was occurring about him. He could figure scientific equations with ease, yet he bumbled about in a ridiculous manner when faced with the most minor social event. He could be the most endearing fool to those who knew him, and yet his temper, where the beautiful Christabella's many admirers were concerned, was explosive and deadly—Lad had fallen prey to it a time or two, much to his detriment. But despite both the love he clearly bore his fiancée and the numerous years that had passed since their betrothal, Lord Severn showed no sign of formalizing their union. He seemed content to go on as they were, and this, as it had turned out, was what constituted the "little problem" that Sir Geoffrey had wanted Lad's help with in return for saving his life.

"I do worry about her so," Sir Geoffrey said, closing his eyes wearily, still holding Lad's hand in his frail grip. "You can't know what a relief it is to me to know that you'll watch over her, Lad."

"I'll not leave London until she's safely wed to Lord Severn, Geoffrey. I'll find the way to bring the matter to a close, I promise you."

Sir Geoffrey made a scoffing sound. "He's such a clumsy buffoon. I can't begin to know what she sees in him. Her mother—ah, Lad, if you could but have seen my darling Caro. She was the most magnificent creature."

"She must have been," Lad said. "Christabella is too stunning for it to be otherwise."

"Indeed," Sir Geoffrey murmured. "Indeed."

"I wouldn't worry overmuch about her alliance with Viscount Severn. He truly loves Christabella, despite his aversion to marriage."

"And she loves the fool as well, that's plain enough," Sir Geoffrey muttered. "How I wish it might be otherwise. She deserves so much better." He opened his eyes and smiled at Lad. "I do wish you weren't married, my boy. I should love to have you for a son-in-law."

Lad grinned. "You should thank the heavens above that I'm well and truly married, my friend. You don't want a gambler for a son-in-law."

"True." Sir Geoffrey chuckled faintly. "I suppose a

chemist will have to suffice." He wearily closed his eyes again. "I'll sleep for a bit, I think. Will you tell Lloyd to wake me before noon, please? I don't want to miss seeing my Christabella."

"You shouldn't go out today," Lad said, gazing at him with concern. "It's drizzling and cold. If you don't take more of a care for your health—"

"I'm dying, Lad," Sir Geoffrey said bluntly. "Staying by the fire day in and day out won't change that. I want to see my beautiful girl. She's all I have—all that I love in this world."

"Very well," Lad murmured, taking the hand he yet held and placing it carefully under the sheets. He pulled the covers up until he was sure the older man was warm. "You'll have the devil of a time convincing Lloyd, however."

"Lloyd wouldn't be happy unless he could fuss over me like a hen over one of its chicks. He'll give way in the end."

"Yes, he'll give way," Lad said gently. "He always does. And so do I. You're a horrible, managing fellow, Geoffrey Vear."

Sir Geoffrey smiled, his eyes yet closed. "I am indeed, Lad Walker. Never think otherwise."

Fortunately for Sir Geoffrey, his daughter lived a punctual, predictable life. Every Thursday at noon, weather permitting, she could be found exiting Hookham's lending library on Bond Street, usually accompanied by Viscount Severn, with a week's worth of new reading. Across the street each Thursday, in The Jolly Rogue coffeehouse, Sir Geoffrey took his regular table near the window, always accompanied by Lloyd and occasionally by Lad. Today, all three men sat together, sipping strong, hot coffee in deference to the cold (save for Lloyd, who drank his customary ale), waiting for Christabella to make her appearance.

Sir Geoffrey's color was as poor as it had earlier been, though two bright spots on his cheeks made Lad worry that he was feverish, despite the chill of the day. There was no good telling the fellow that he should see a physician; indeed, there was no good telling Sir Geoffrey anything.

"You've had no word from your wife yet, Lad," Sir Geoffrey stated.

As always, talk of Diana, which Sir Geoffrey loved, made Lad tense and unhappy. His misery where she was concerned was as raw and painful as an open wound. He hardly needed salt poured into it.

"No" was his curt reply.

Sir Geoffrey sighed. "Will you send the cattle, then, after what David Moulton wrote to you?"

"Indeed I will," Lad told him. "David and his men have weathered the storm at Kerlain, and the cattle will too. Nearly every other estate in Herefordshire turns a good yearly profit from cattle sales, and there's no reason why mine shouldn't."

Delicately taking a sip of his coffee, Sir Geoffrey murmured, "Aren't you afraid of angering The Farrell and The Colvaney and making trouble for your good lady wife?"

There had been a time when Lad would have worried about nothing more, but Sir Geoffrey had long since taught him better.

"It hardly matters what the people of Kerlain do, say, or think. I am the lord of Kerlain and wish to raise a small herd of cattle. Diana may consign me to the devil for a time after their arrival with the herders, but she knows how to handle the Farrell and Colvaney clans. David reports that she fought for him quite fiercely when the people of Kerlain came to register their complaints about such newcomers invading the castle, and there has since been no trouble.

She'll do the same for the cattle, once they've arrived, regardless of what she may think about them. She may hate me,'' Lad told him, ''but she's a very proper countess, you may be sure, and she'll not turn aside anything that would be so profitable to Kerlain.''

''Eh, she don't hate you,'' Lloyd told him. ''Would've sent you back to America if she hated you. Just mad, she is, and you know what women are when they're mad.''

''Did Lieutenant Moulton have anything to say regarding Viscount Carden?'' Sir Geoffrey asked.

Lad gave a curt nod. ''Carden's at Kerlain often, using every excuse under the sun to keep from being thrown off.''

''Ah,'' Sir Geoffrey said knowingly. ''Lady Kerlain refuses to formally receive him still?''

''So it would seem.''

''She don't hate you,'' Lloyd said again.

Lad shook his head. ''But she accepts his gifts, of which there are many. Wine, food, clothes.''

''Hmm.'' Sir Geoffrey looked thoughtful. ''That's not a good sign, I fear.''

''Getting lonely, she is,'' Lloyd stated. ''Won't be long afore she's receiving him formally. Just for company, mind you. Conversation.''

''It won't be only for conversation if Carden has anything to do with it,'' Lad muttered. ''I can only hope that Diana won't fall for any of his trickery.''

''It's what you fear most, is it not?'' Sir Geoffrey asked. ''And it would be understandable, of course. Lady Kerlain is human, and lonely, just as Lloyd says. And Viscount Carden has a gift for treachery. Our suspicion that he may have interfered with your correspondence to Kerlain isn't entirely implausible for such a man as that.''

Lad nodded. ''There's a difference, though, for Diana. She's known Viscount Carden since they were both children, and she's wise to his devious nature. When I think of how often she tried to warn me about him . . . it makes me feel like such a *damned* fool.''

Sir Geoffrey reached out to pat Lad's hand reassuringly, a gesture of kindness that Lad was well used to from his patron. Today, however, he felt only a measure of renewed distress at how cold and frail Sir Geoffrey's fingers felt.

''The ability—and desire—to trust our fellow human beings is a gift, Lad, never a curse. It is only blind trust coupled with ignorance and too much self-confidence that makes for a fool. You've discovered this from what you've learned of gaming, most especially about the self-confidence. Now you need never fear that you'll fall prey to such a man as Viscount Carden again.''

''And what of Diana?'' Lad asked.

Sir Geoffrey smiled, looking very weary. ''You must pray that she remains strong against his wiles, and if she does not, you must be ready to understand and forgive.''

''And then afterward kill Eoghan Patterson,'' Lad said.

Lloyd laughed and raised his tankard in a salute. ''Amen,'' he said, ignoring Sir Geoffrey's look of disdain. He took a long sip, then wiped his lips and nodded toward the window. ''Here comes Miss Christabella.''

Sir Geoffrey eagerly turned to follow his manservant's gaze. ''Ah, indeed. And with Lord Rexley this afternoon, rather than that oaf Severn. What a handsome pair they make, my darling girl and the Earl of Rexley. 'Tis a pity she isn't engaged to him instead. She'd make the most marvelous countess, don't you think?''

''She would indeed,'' Lad agreed sincerely. It was difficult not to gaze at Christabella. She was English perfection, the ideal British female, though perhaps rather taller than what most men might prefer. Blond, blue-eyed, with a face and form that made other women weep with jealousy, she was utterly beautiful but possessed of a sweetness and shyness that kept her from realizing it.

"Look at the number of books she's taking out today!" Sir Geoffrey said with love and admiration heavy in his voice. "As bright as she is beautiful, just as her mother was. Oh, God, how I pray Howell knows what treasures he's been blessed with. Hurry, Lad!" He nudged Lad with his cane. "Hurry, run out and engage them in conversation for a moment or two, so that I can have a good, long look at my girl."

Lad was on his feet, snatching up his hat and gloves even as Sir Geoffrey spoke, and the next moment was making his way out the door. It was indicative of how well Sir Geoffrey had trained him that Lad was able to mold his features into the cheerful, relaxed expression he wanted as he approached Christabella and Lord Rexley. His stride was equally controlled, as easy as if he had merely been out strolling for pleasure.

"Jack!" he called out happily. "Bella! What a welcome surprise!"

They had been about to walk away, waiting only for Christabella's maid to exit the library, but turned at the sound of Lad's voice. Christabella blushed and smiled shyly at his approach, while Lord Rexley surveyed him with proper British reserve. He had once been Lad's most vocal enemy in London, bearing a strong dislike for all Americans due to his younger brother's death in the States in the midst of the war. But they'd eventually become friends during the wager that Lad had made with Lord Callan, who was Lord Rexley's dearest friend. Having lost Joshua during the same war, Lad was able to understand Jack Sommerton's loss far better than his other acquaintances, and they shared yet a far deeper grief: the death of not only their brothers, but also of their parents within but the space of a few years. Apart from himself, Jack Sommerton was the most solitary man in London, and he and Lad had found themselves drawn together in welcome companionship.

"Lad," he said now, touching the brim of his hat, "well met."

"Indeed, my lord," Lad returned the greeting. "But what a great and unexpected pleasure this is on such a dreary afternoon." Lad made his most elegant bow to Christabella. "Miss Howell, you could brighten even the darkest day. Have you just come from the lending library?"

They conversed easily for a few minutes, until Lad was certain that Sir Geoffrey had been able to look his fill. Then he sketched them a proper bow and said, "I'll keep you no further, as I'm sure you wish to escort Miss Howell home."

"Perhaps I'll see you this evening," Lord Rexley suggested, "at White's?"

Lad nodded. Since most of the *ton* had left London to rusticate in the country over the next several months, Jack depended upon him even more greatly for company. "I intend to dine there and perhaps enjoy a game or two."

"I'll meet you for supper, then. Say at eight? I'll send a man round to reserve a table for us." Lord Rexley touched the brim of his hat once more. "Good day to you, Lad."

Lad remained where he was until they moved away, then strolled half a block in the opposite direction before changing course and returning to the coffeehouse. Sir Geoffrey was still gazing out the window to where Christabella and Lord Rexley had disappeared. With a sigh, Lad took the seat across from him, meeting Lloyd's knowing gaze. Several silent moments passed before Sir Geoffrey shook away the spell that held him so entranced and turned to his companions with a weary smile.

"I have never seen her in such good looks," he murmured. "Thank you, Lad."

"It was a pleasure," Lad assured him.

"Lloyd." Sir Geoffrey looked at his manservant. "Will you be so good as to run down to Stapley's and buy an

ounce of my favorite snuff, please? We may as well take
care of the chore while we're so close at hand."

Lloyd stood, exchanging another look with Lad. He was
being sent away so that the other two men might speak
privately, and he knew it.

"I'll have Stapley put it on your tab, then," he muttered,
looking rather aggrieved, and left.

"Now I've hurt his feelings," said Sir Geoffrey, leaning
back in his chair and closing his eyes. "But it can't be
helped. There isn't much time left, and I need to speak to
you alone, Lad. About Lloyd."

"Yes, Geoff? What about him?"

Sir Geoffrey opened his eyes and sat forward.

"He'll be a rich man when I've gone. I'm leaving everything I have to him, including a small estate in Sussex. The
trouble is, Lloyd won't know what to do with any of it, and
he won't be happy if he should suddenly find himself on his
own, rich or not." Sir Geoffrey's expression filled with
deep affection. "He's been with me since he was but thirteen—just a boy, really, though circumstances required that
he mature more quickly. He had no family and only a gang
of other young thieves for friends. When I gave him the
chance to leave his life in the streets, he gladly took it and,
with the little I was able to teach him, transformed himself
into the fine young man he is today. But you know, Lad,
better than anyone else could, how unfriendly a place the
world can be to one not born into the nobility, much less
without wealth and property."

"Aye," Lad murmured.

"No matter what I'm able to leave him with, Lloyd will
be like a ship cast out upon the sea without an anchor once
I've gone—unless you'll keep him with you."

"Of course I'd be glad to," Lad said, "but as a friend.
An equal."

Sir Geoffrey shook his head. "He'll not stay if you put him in such a position. He'd be dreadfully unhappy."

"But I can't ask him to continue on as a servant."

"Whyever not?"

"Because he's . . . well, for one thing, he's your servant, not mine. I could never presume—"

"Well, don't *presume* the thing, of course," Sir Geoffrey told him. "In fact, don't even speak to him about the matter once I've gone. It would make the poor fellow uncomfortable. Only make it plain by your actions that you're willing to let things go on as they have. Lloyd will let you know what he wants to do."

"I don't know, Geoff," Lad said doubtfully. "It doesn't seem right that Lloyd should continue on as a manservant when he's a wealthy man in his own right. He should have servants of his own and spend his days doing as he pleases."

"Lloyd won't be happy unless he's being useful, Lad," Sir Geoffrey said, "and if he's not being useful to me or to you, he'll find someone else—and that person may be someone who abuses his trust or even turns him back into the harsh embrace of the streets. Please. I know I ask much of you, but Lloyd has been as my own son these many years. There's no one else I could trust to keep him safe."

Lad couldn't deny that Sir Geoffrey had a point, and, in truth, he was relieved to think that Lloyd would stay with him. He was going to feel lost, too, when Sir Geoffrey at last succumbed to his illness.

"Take him to Kerlain when you've made your return," Sir Geoffrey said after Lad nodded his agreement. "You'll be glad to have someone you can so entirely trust there and who'll stand with every decision you make. Your position will be much stronger with Lloyd beside you."

An ineffable feeling of sadness enveloped Lad, much like the dark despair that he'd known after leaving Diana.

But he was far stronger now than he'd been then and had gained an enormous measure of self-confidence—all because of Sir Geoffrey. How could he do less than what this man asked of him? "You have my word that I'll keep Lloyd with me, if that's what he also desires."

Sir Geoffrey's pale, tense expression relaxed. "Thank you, my boy. You relieve my mind, just as you've done with Christabella. Now, I shall give you a few last pieces of advice and ask you to consider them well."

"Of course."

"You did well with the wager concerning Viscount Callan and his bride, Lady Clara."

"Because of you," Lad said. "I never could have done it on my own. You knew the wager would come out in my favor because you knew the history of all those involved. You knew that Lucky Bryland loved his wife."

Sir Geoffrey gave a gracious nod. "I've told you many times that this is what comes from the art of listening to all those around you. Listening, and remembering. Now the time has come for you to put forth a wager of your own, with but a little guidance from me."

"Another wager?"

"You've already earned more than half of what you require for your triumphant return to Kerlain, and I've no doubt you'll easily win the rest before the time has come. But your needs exceed the mere repayment of the wager, my lord the earl. You must have much more when you return if you wish to rebuild the estate and regain the heart of your wife. To this end, you must not only continue your nightly ventures but set in motion another wager—one for which the odds will be in your favor. I can but give you a small measure of guidance now, but on the main, you must rely upon your own good sense and all I've taught you regarding such matters." He stopped and sipped at his coffee, then set the mug aside. "I want you to engineer the means for a wager regarding the Earl of Rexley. It's high time the boy was married, and I know his family would be relieved to see the name of Sommerton carried on, not to mention the title."

Lad stared at him. "You want me to propose a wager involving Jack Sommerton," he said dumbly.

"Yes."

Lad blinked several times. "A wager regarding his being married."

"Not just that, but to a specific woman. And I have one in mind too. Your cousin, Gwendolyn Wells."

"My c-cousin?" Lad choked out. *"Gwennie?"*

"Just so. She's the ideal choice. From what you tell me she's beautiful, charming, witty, and highly intelligent. And her father is a renowned chemist whom Viscount Severn is frothing at the mouth to meet, which provides you with the perfect excuse for bringing them to England. Once they've arrived, you must merely arrange for Lord Rexley to meet your cousin and thereafter do whatever you can to put them in company with each other as often as possible. Wait only long enough to make certain that they'll do before making your wager, and all will be well."

Sir Geoffrey must be more ill than he'd realized, Lad thought. He was clearly delusional to even consider such an idea.

"Jack Sommerton hates Americans," Lad said. "Hates them with a passion. He'd still hate me if it hadn't been for what happened with Lucky and Lady Clara. The last woman on God's earth that he'd take for a wife would be an American."

Sir Geoffrey gave him a curious look. "There's a great deal you don't know about the Earl of Rexley, my boy, and a great deal that he has yet to discover about himself. You must believe me when I tell you that an American wife will suit him far, far better than an English one.''

Lad's curiosity was more than a little aroused by Sir Geoffrey's words, but he strove to keep his thoughts on the topic at hand.

''But surely there are other wagers I might embark upon that would be just as profitable, and certainly far safer. Meddling in Jack Sommerton's affairs is a chancy gamble in and of itself.''

Sir Geoffrey gave a single shake of his head. ''It must be Rexley. He and Viscount Callan are Lord Severn's closest companions. Once both of them have happily embraced the state of wedded bliss, as Callan has already done, Severn will shortly thereafter follow suit and at last take my darling Christabella to wife, as he should have done long ago.''

''You can't know that for certain,'' Lad returned doubtfully. ''Wulf's just as likely to continue on as stubbornly as he's ever done.''

''We must pray that he does not,'' said Sir Geoffrey, ''for both your sake and his. You've given me your promise to see Christabella safely wed, but you must not lose Kerlain, or your dear wife, in the doing. See Rexley wed to your cousin and you'll soon thereafter be free of your debt to me.'' He reached out a thin, brittle hand. Lad took it in a light clasp. ''You must trust me in this matter, Lad, as you've learned to trust me in so many others. I know the players in this game far better than you may believe, and the odds are greatly in your favor for success.''

Lad couldn't find the words to answer. It seemed an impossibly foolish quest, and yet Sir Geoffrey had never before led him astray.

''I'll write Gwennie and my Uncle Philip tonight,'' he said. ''And have the letter on its way across the Atlantic by tomorrow.''

Sir Geoffrey smiled and faintly squeezed Lad's hand.

"Good. Now, here is Lloyd, come back with the tobacco," he said, and suddenly looked older and far more frail than he had only moments before. "It is well. I believe it's time we made our way home."

Chapter Twenty

June 1818

"They've been married," Diana murmured faintly, lowering the paper from which she'd just read the announcement. "Gwendolyn Wells and the Earl of Rexley. It's . . . unbelievable."

Eoghan reclined more comfortably in his chair and set aside the glass of whiskey he'd been sipping.

"But true. And your dear husband in attendance to oversee the success of his latest wager. What a happy time they must have had together, as families usually do. A pity the earl didn't take the trouble to have his wife in attendance, but, then, he hasn't taken the trouble for years now, has he?"

"Don't," Diana warned him between set teeth.

"I wonder if he even told his uncle and cousin that he's married? Probably not. After all, no one in London knows. He's made very certain of that."

"Don't!" Diana shouted furiously, balling the paper in her hand and tossing it into the fire. "God help me, you're the very devil, Eoghan Patterson. Always bringing me your poison." She wished, vehemently, that she had the power to resist it, but she'd long since given up the battle. She had become addicted in the most sickening manner to reading of the Earl of Kerlain's many London adventures, from the entertaining wagers he made to the shocking amounts of money he gambled for to the number of women whose hearts he'd broken. He was like some kind of fictional character come to life—certainly not the man she'd married but a stranger who'd taken the face and form of Lad Walker.

"Oh, no, my love," Eoghan countered smoothly. "Not *my* poison. Your husband's the source of what gives you pain." He sighed aloud. "It's rather amazing that he doesn't seem to be in any hurry to return to Kerlain, is it not? Tomorrow, after all, is the day that our wager becomes final—one way or another."

It was true. Diana couldn't deny it, no matter how desperately she wished she might. Tomorrow would mark three years since the day Lad had left Kerlain. Three long, horrible years. She knew she should accept that he wasn't going to return to rescue either her or the estate, but somehow Diana couldn't make her heart do so. He'd as good as betrayed her trust, had been unfaithful and cruelly silent, but he continually sent money and goods for her benefit and that of the people of Kerlain. And these were usually delivered by someone whom he'd hired as a new servant for Castle Kerlain, or even a group of servants, a vast assortment of unfortunates whom he'd met in London and decided to send to Kerlain for gainful employment. This being the case, the castle was now fully staffed with maids and footmen who, if not perfectly clothed in the expensive uniforms that servants on great estates usually wore, were, unlike Maudie, Swithin, and Stuart, entirely devoted to the long-absent earl. They were also ready and willing to work hard for the small wages that Lord Kerlain forwarded through Mr. Sibbley's office each month, with the result that Castle Kerlain was beautifully spotless and, with each passing day, increasingly livable. Diana herself had moved into the countess's chambers several months earlier and had been perfectly comfortable even during the winter.

Everywhere at Kerlain there were changes that Lad had wrought, despite his absence, and all much to his favor. Over a year ago he'd sent a fine herd of cattle to Kerlain, along with the herdsmen to care for them, and a note instructing Diana to make certain that neither The Farrell nor The Colvaney made any trouble for the new arrivals. She still had the note and sometimes read it through, always shaking her head in amazement at how firm and sure Lad's tone was.

For if they cannot bring themselves to accept the changes that are and will be made to Kerlain, they may choose among the only two solutions open to them: staying in their cottages and keeping silent, or packing their things and leaving.

Could he have written in such a manner if he hadn't meant to be the Earl of Kerlain? Or done all that he had, even though he remained absent and silent? Oh, she shouldn't hope, Diana told herself again, moving to gaze out the parlor window at the courtyard below, where David Moulton and some of his men were mixing one of their endless vats of mortar. The afternoon was beautiful and warm, and one of his workers was helping David to roll up his single useful sleeve.

She knew she shouldn't hope. Even if Lad did come back, how could she be glad to see him, knowing that he'd broken his promise to be faithful to her alone? His many affairs had been vaunted in the London papers so often and with such detail that Diana could no longer deny that they had occurred. But her heart had grown cold after two years of knowing the truth, and the pain that had once held her relentlessly captive was now but a dull, long-accepted, ever-present ache.

''I doubt he'll give us much trouble when you request a

divorce,'' Eoghan said, his tone conversational. "Indeed, I can't help but think he'll be somewhat relieved to be rid of his wife. There'll be nothing then to keep him from fully enjoying his many affairs.''

"You were wrong about Miss Howell,'' Diana murmured. "She married her fiancé, Lord Severn, a month ago, with Lad in attendance. She'd never have allowed the Earl of Kerlain to be at her wedding if she'd been in love with him or dallying with him, as you insisted was so.'' She glanced at Eoghan over her shoulder. "You've been wrong about many things, and you could be wrong about this.''

"Don't be a fool, Diana,'' Eoghan chided, rising from his chair with slow, easy elegance. "He's spent the past three years enjoying every pleasure that London and life have to offer, having next to nothing to do with you and the estate. What little he has done has merely been an effort to assuage his guilt and give him something to point at should anyone learn of his neglected wife. 'You see,' he'll say, 'I haven't ignored my wife and estate. I've sent men to fix the castle, a host of gutter-born servants, a few shaggy cows, and just enough money to make certain that none of them starves to death while I'm living a life of luxury among the most beautiful women of the *ton*. I've not neglected them in the least.' ''

Diana returned her gaze to out the window, her heart so cold that even Eoghan's darts no longer had the power to harm. She'd been overset by the news that Lad's cousin had been married, but that was because, despite what Eoghan said, Gwendolyn and her father, the famous American chemist, Philip Wells, knew that Lad had a wife. They'd written a lovely letter to both Diana and Lad after he'd informed them of his marriage, warmly congratulating Lad and expressing a sincere hope of one day visiting Kerlain and meeting Diana. Gwendolyn Wells had even gone so far as to call Diana her "cousin" in the letter and said how delightful it was to have an Englishwoman in their family. And yet, knowing she existed, they'd made no effort to see her during the months they'd been visiting in England, nor had Gwendolyn sent Diana any missive regarding—or invitation to—her marriage to the Earl of Rexley.

"He would still be here if you hadn't so utterly deceived him," she murmured, her gaze held on Lieutenant Moulton below. What a wonderful source of help he'd been these past two years, and all the men with him. Diana didn't know what she would have done without them all.

She both felt and heard Eoghan coming up behind her.

"You blame me for sending him away," he said softly, "but his behavior since leaving Kerlain has been such that perhaps you should thank me for that rather than continually professing your hatred."

"Hatred?" she repeated dully. "There are days, Eoghan, when I feel even less than that for you. Often, I feel nothing at all." When he touched her shoulder she shrugged away. "Until tomorrow, you've no right to touch me."

There was a tense silence. Diana could almost feel his anger, though he said nothing for a long while.

"When I have you safe at Lising Park, you'll receive far more than my touch," he told her. "And you'll receive it gladly, just as you agreed. I've waited three years and will not be denied."

Diana's stomach lurched sickeningly at the thought of being so intimately possessed by him, just as it always did. She was an honorable woman and meant to keep the vow she'd given him and willingly accept his embraces, but she couldn't imagine how she would be able to make her body behave and deny its complete repulsion. On the other hand, the thought of throwing up all over Eoghan as he attempted to bed her gave Diana an immense feeling of satisfaction.

"You've delivered what you came to bring me," she

said. "Now, why don't you go home to gloat and leave me in peace?"

But it was her own fault that he was here, Diana knew. She should have been strong enough over the years to keep her resolve at having nothing to do with him. For more than a year she'd been successful in the determination, neither receiving nor even speaking to him, but time and Eoghan's persistence and her own loneliness had eventually worn her down. He came to Kerlain every chance that he could—aided and abetted by the people of the land, who yet held him in the greatest esteem—always bearing some item that Diana happened to have a particular need for but couldn't afford, such as a medicinal rub for Maudie when she developed a croupy cough during the winter, or a heavy woolen jacket to replace the one that Swithin had worn through. Pride told Diana to spurn such gifts; practicality made her accept them. In time, and very slowly, useful items gave way to those that were far more luxurious. Cakes of fine, scented soap, bottles of delicious wine, salt and sugar and expensive spices for the pantry, yards of beautiful cloth and patterns for the latest new fashions. These Diana had turned away—for a time. If Lad had written to her even just once—personally written, and not simply sent notes through others—she would have continued to do so. But in time she began to wonder what the purpose of such righteousness was. Lad was living in London in obvious luxury, denying himself nothing. Diana eventually decided that she'd no longer deny herself either.

The trouble was, in accepting Eoghan's gifts, she also had to accept his company. That he strove to make himself as agreeable and charming as only Eoghan could was helpful. Diana wasn't happy to be with him, but at least he was someone to talk to, and she didn't feel her loneliness quite so fully when he was about. It was far more pathetic than Diana had ever thought she could possibly be—accepting the company of the man who was largely responsible for all her woes—but loneliness, as she had discovered, was the hardest misery in the world to endure, day in and day out, year after year. She had not been proof against it. Her single consolation was that she did not forget Eoghan's sins, or forgive them.

"As you wish," he replied, his tone still heavy with aggravation. He was looking out the window at David and his men. "The first thing I shall do once I've got you at Lising Park is get rid of Moulton and install a proper architect to finish the work at Kerlain."

"David is a proper architect," Diana told him, stiffening with anger. "He's a marvelous architect."

"I'll find a better one," Eoghan said tightly.

He had never liked David, Diana knew, though she couldn't begin to understand why. The two men seldom saw each other, much less spoke to each other. But it was often difficult to know what set Eoghan off. His fancies and dislikes were as flighty as a tempest-tossed leaf. David, having benefited from the Earl of Kerlain's kindness, was firmly in Lad's camp and was constantly speaking on his behalf in encouragement to Diana, but she felt certain that Eoghan could know nothing of this.

Only a few days past, indeed, David had commented to Diana that he wouldn't be at all surprised to see Lord Kerlain riding toward the castle very soon. He'd sounded so certain that Diana had asked him what he meant, but he'd merely smiled and bowed and walked away.

"I would prefer to keep David," Diana told Eoghan. "It would be foolish to bring in another architect when he's already well familiar with the castle. And I doubt that his men would follow anyone else's direction. Or do you mean to cast them all aside as well, in your usual brutal and heartless manner?"

Eoghan responded to this with low laughter. "I shall be

delighted to keep him, my dearest, if you can but convince me to do so. I'm certain you'll be able to think of the way. And if you can't . . . I'll be more than glad to give you a few hints.''

Heat crawled up Diana's cheeks at the meaning of his words, and she had a fulsome vision of just what her future would be like, living beneath Eoghan's hand. It would be game-playing and crawling and begging and shameful humiliation—and she couldn't really hate Lad for it, even though he had as much as abandoned her to such a dreadful fate. No, the fault was all her own. She had sold her soul for the sake of the promise she'd given her godfather, for the sake of the people of Kerlain, and for her own desires. Lad's sins were toward her alone, and she felt the betrayal deeply, but for what she would suffer once the morrow had passed, she had no one to blame but herself.

''I'll send several footmen over in the morning to lend you aid in packing what you'll need,'' Eoghan told her. ''I'll arrive myself some hours later to personally collect you and escort you home to Lising Park. I believe Lord Kerlain left early three years ago, did he not? Shall we agree that the wager will become final at ten o'clock?''

It was more than fair, she supposed. Lad had, in truth, left much earlier. At least by ten she'd be somewhat composed—she hoped.

''I'll not need the aid of your servants. I've more than enough here to do the work.''

''That's true,'' Eoghan said lightly. ''But you'll require the use of several carriages, and I prefer to use my own people for the task. The riffraff your dear husband has chosen to fill Kerlain with are hardly trustworthy. I'll get rid of them on the day I empty Kerlain of the rest of its filth.''

Diana drew in a long, slow, calming breath, biting down the hot words that rose up in her throat and making herself think clearly on what she wanted to say. It came to her at last. When she spoke, she spoke very clearly.

"Eoghan, I hold myself as an honorable woman and therefore mean to honor our bargain, but I will do so only as long as you are likewise honorable. I'll have not the least moment of guilt in behaving badly toward you if you behave badly toward the people of Kerlain—or even toward Kerlain itself." Turning from the window, she looked him full in the face. "I've thought long and hard on the matter and know I'm right in this. You'll have me for a willing wife—and as the mother for your children—but only so long as you don't betray both my honor and your own. It seems to be your nature to be cruel to one and all, but I'll not stand by and see others suffer for a mistake that was purely my own."

"Diana—"

"If you throw any of the people of Kerlain—*any* of them, Eoghan—off the estate without some reasonable expectation of work, I will no longer be willing for you in *any* manner."

"You gave me your word!" he protested.

She moved farther into the room, away from him. "God will judge me, whether I do rightly or not. And it cannot be right to be so submissive to a man that one becomes blind to wrong or allows him to commit such grievous sins. That is the way it will be with us, Eoghan. Believe what I say, for I swear by God above that I speak the truth."

His face reddened and his hands fisted, but when he spoke, his voice was controlled.

"So be it, Diana. I have no wish to wage yet another war with you. Kerlain may go on as it has done, filled with servants who have no one to serve. Only be ready tomorrow when I come to fetch you. Ten o'clock and no later. Be ready," he warned again, more softly. "You're mine after that, and I vow I'll wait no longer than I must to claim you as such."

"No more packing tonight, Maudie," Diana said, casting a glance about her chamber at the many opened, half-filled trunks. "Lord Carden won't be arriving until ten tomorrow morning. We'll have plenty of time to finish then."

"Yes, miss."

"My lady," Diana corrected automatically.

"My lady," Maudie repeated obediently. "For soon you will be Lady Carden, won't you, miss? And he'll not treat you as Lord Kerlain has done. He's a proper nobleman, is Viscount Carden."

Diana sighed wearily, giving up the fight. It hardly mattered now whether Swithin or Maudie or any of the older citizens of Kerlain addressed her as they should.

"Maudie, there's something we must speak of," she said gently, sitting in a chair near the fire and drawing her robe more comfortably about her. "Please, sit down a moment." She indicated the chair beside her, grateful that there were still a few pieces of decent furniture in the countess's chambers.

"What is it, miss?" Maudie asked as she obediently sat down, gazing at Diana with concern.

"I know that everyone at Kerlain is aware of the wager that I made with Lord Carden. It would have been impossible to keep it from you these many years. After tomorrow, if the earl doesn't return to Kerlain, I will indeed leave with Viscount Carden and go to live at Lising Park. I wanted to reassure you, however, that you and Swithin and everyone else here will remain at Kerlain and that this will continue to be your home. The viscount will make certain that every need is well met, and, of course, I'll be here often to make certain that this is so."

"But, miss," Maud protested, "that's not the way of it. Swithin and me are to go with you to Lising Park."

"No, Maudie," Diana murmured sadly. "I'm afraid you're not." Eoghan had been quite plain about that earlier. He would abide no servants from Kerlain at Lising Park, fearing rightly that they would ever take her side over his own. And Maudie and Swithin, he had argued, should be made to retire for their own good. Diana had been hard-pressed to disagree. The two older servants had worked hard nearly all of their lives and deserved to enjoy a greater measure of freedom and ease.

"But we are," Maud insisted. "Lord Carden promised that we would. He *did.*"

Diana gave her a curious look. "Lord Carden? When was this, Maudie?"

Maudie suddenly seemed to realize what she'd said and looked instantly distressed. "Oh, miss. I'm so very sorry. I wasn't to say anything of it."

"Of *what?*"

"Please don't ask, my lady," Maudie pleaded, shaking her head and rising. She bobbed a quick curtsy to Diana and began to back away toward the door. "Lord Carden would be full angered, and I don't want to be kept here at Kerlain once you've gone, just for that. He *did* promise that me and Swithin were to go to Lising Park, Miss Diana, and such a fine, proper gentleman as the viscount wouldn't speak false-hoods. I know he'd never do so."

Diana stared after the older woman as she left the chamber, her heart heavy with a depthless sorrow.

Eoghan had truly sunk low if he'd taken to deceiving such innocents as Maudie and Swithin to benefit his own aims. She wasn't surprised that he would do so, only disappointed in herself for being unable to keep her most beloved servants from his cruelties. But even if she'd tried to warn them, they'd not have believed her, for they thought him a fine and proper nobleman. How could they begin to know what Viscount Carden was really like?

But, oh, how wretched and foolish Maudie and Swithin would feel on the morrow, when Eoghan left them behind at Kerlain. There was nothing Diana could do to save them from the betrayal they'd feel. But that was the price they'd have to pay for trusting Eoghan Patterson, just as everyone who trusted him eventually had to do.

Diana stood and walked slowly about the grand chamber, which so many of her predecessors had occupied. She had only been in the rooms for a few short months, once David Moulton and his men had made them livable, and had grown to love them dearly. The chambers she would occupy at Lising Park would no doubt be far finer and more luxurious, but Diana knew that she could never love them—or anything at Lising Park—as she loved these at Kerlain.

She'd not sleep tonight, she decided as she took to her chair again, gazing at the great clock that stood not far away. There were two hours until midnight, and then a few hours until dawn—the last dawn she would know at Kerlain. She would be awake to see it, to remember, and to accept the fact of her future.

After three years of waiting and hoping, it was time for her to put aside her foolish dreams and believe that her husband wasn't coming back. Perhaps Eoghan was right, and it had only been guilt that had driven him to send the servants and the workers and the cattle and everything else. Without communication from him, she couldn't possibly divine his reasons. All she knew was that three years had come to an end, as had all her hopes. She was done with Kerlain, and she was done with Lad Walker.

Chapter Twenty-one

Almost midnight, and only a few windows were shining with dim light at Castle Kerlain. It wasn't much of a welcome for the lord of the land who'd been away for three years, but the sight was indeed a sweet one to Lad's way of thinking.

He'd not expected to be so glad at returning to the place he'd once have happily given away. But glad he was, and even felt a certain pride. He was the Earl of Kerlain, and this was his land, the source from which sprang his noble identity. It was his home. And Diana's.

Diana.

Thinking of her, he felt a twinge of panic and wondered what manner of greeting she would give him. The various scenarios that ran through his mind—most of them unpleasant—made him pull Maeva to a slow halt.

"Jittery, eh?" Lloyd said, coming up beside him. Gazing at the huge castle in the distance with the bright moonlight revealing every tower and turret, he added, "Don't blame you. Bloody big mausoleum, ain't it? Get lost in there, I will. God help me." He let out a rough sigh, filled with disgust. "Figure we'll get much of a welcome?"

"I don't know," Lad replied honestly. "It hardly matters."

Lloyd gave him a sidelong glance. "That it doesn't,

m'lord. It's what Sir Geoffrey would have told you. And don't forget.''

Lad smiled. ''I won't.''

He knew who he was. Knew it now so well and so firmly that he'd never forget. Thanks to Sir Geoffrey. No, it didn't matter what kind of welcome they received from the servants or the people of Kerlain. They would be treated with respect, if not with warmth.

But Diana . . . how would she receive him?

''Don't look so bad from here,'' Lloyd commented, still contemplating the castle. ''Not so tumbledown as you made out.''

''It's far, far improved from what it was,'' Lad told him. ''David Moulton and his men have clearly done their jobs well. When I first set eyes on it . . .'' The words drifted as he remembered that cold winter afternoon and all that he'd felt upon seeing the ruined castle. How foolish he'd been to believe that the grand structure could never rise again to its former glory. Bricks and mortar and human sweat had made it, and the same were now rebuilding it. But this was not the essence of the place or what made it so important. Diana had striven so hard to make him understand the truth: that Castle Kerlain would always be glorious, whether it stood as new or fell to the ground. Its history was already written, filling many chapters of England's past, and there it would remain, safe and secure from the ravages of time, regardless of whatever the future might bring.

''When I first set eyes on it,'' he said once more, ''I thought it the most ramshackle thing I'd ever seen. But, then, I've never been much of a visionary. My wife has to do all the dreaming for both of us, I fear. Fortunately, she's very good at it. Or once was, three years ago.''

What was she going to say to him when he saw her? He shouldn't have left coming back to the last moment. He should have found the way to come earlier, or to let her know, somehow, that he was coming. But except for the few notes he'd sent to her through the people he'd dispatched to Kerlain, there had been almost no communication between them at all. This last year he'd written only two letters and was convinced that, like all the others he'd written, they'd never reached her hands.

"Come on, then," Lloyd said, nudging his horse forward with clumsy movements that told how greatly he hated riding. "No sense waiting. Let's get it over with."

Lad led him through the castle gates and into the main courtyard, straight to the castle doors. From the direction of the stables a tall figure strode toward them, having been roused from his slumbers by the sound of horse hooves.

"Who goes there?" he called out.

"The Earl of Kerlain," Lad replied.

He swung down from his saddle with ease. Lloyd, making the same attempt, got his foot stuck in the stirrup and nearly fell to the ground, holding on at the last moment and hopping about madly until Lad reached out and took hold of his horse's head.

"Bloody horse," Lloyd muttered, just freeing himself by the time the figure from the stables reached them.

"Lord Kerlain?" the man said, squinting at Lad in the darkness. "Is it you, sir?"

"It is."

"Do you remember me, my lord? Jerry Kane from Totham Road? The Earl of Rexley gave you my name."

"Of course," Lad said warmly, extending a hand, which the other man took and shook. "I'm glad that you found your way to Kerlain after all. You've been here almost a year now?"

"Aye, m'lord," Jerry Kane said, reaching out to take the reins of both horses. "Lady Kerlain took me in on the spot, having read the note you wrote for me to give her. She's been most kind to all us new ones."

"I'm glad." Lad began to remove his gloves. "Will you take care of the horses and have our things brought into the castle, then, Jerry? Thank you."

The groomsman bowed. "Welcome home, Lord Kerlain."

Several long moments passed after Lad tugged upon the bell rope before the half gate set inside the mighty doors of Castle Kerlain swung open. The tousled, bare-stockinged boy who opened it, upon seeing who stood there, then pushed the great doors themselves wide.

"My lord!" he said with surprise, rapidly buttoning up his shirt and tucking it into his breeches. "And Lloyd!" he added upon seeing him.

Lad remembered the young man at once: a skinny, pock-marked scalawag who'd threatened Sir Geoffrey and himself one night with a knife as they'd made their way home from a certain unsavory gaming hell. Sir Geoffrey had handily disarmed the boy with a flick of his cane and then, while Lad held the defiant boy by the scruff of his neck, read him a sermon that shortly had him quivering with fear. He'd begged for mercy; Sir Geoffrey had sighed and said that they'd best take him home and do something with him, else he'd only attempt to rob someone less kind. And so they'd taken the filthy creature back to Stratton Street and given him over to Lloyd to wash and scrub. Two days later, he was on his way to Kerlain in the company of a few other boys who'd decided to attempt a life in the Earl of Kerlain's employ rather than one of London's rookeries.

"You look well, Christopher," Lad said, smiling.

"Fattened up nice," Lloyd said. "Not pulling knives anymore, eh?"

The boy blinked at them both. "My lord, we've been waiting for you all this time—all of us that you sent here. You said you'd come!"

"And here I am," Lad said, holding his hands out as if to demonstrate the fact. "As promised."

"Welcome home, my lord," the boy said, bowing and moving aside to let them enter. "Welcome to Kerlain. Wait until everyone sees you're here!"

"Don't wake them now," Lad said, stepping across the threshold. How different this coming was from the first he'd had at Kerlain. He took in the familiar grave coolness of the castle as he entered it, the musty smell of its age and size. The entryway was spotlessly clean; the few pieces of furniture well-polished. But there was a difference now that he detected at once. There was a sense about it that it was occupied once more, not just lived in but also alive with daily activity. The emptiness, the abandonment that had once made Castle Kerlain seem hollow as a cave was gone.

"Sweet livin' days," Lloyd muttered as they came to the great hall. Slowly, he removed the hat from his shaggy hair and stared at the vast room, lit now only by the fire in several hearths. "Never in my life . . ." He shook his head and gave a low whistle. "Sir Geoffrey would've liked to have seen this."

It was astonishingly changed from what it had once been. All of the fires were working, the furniture gleamed, the floor beneath his feet was freshly swept, and the banners and tapestries had all been repaired and cleaned until they looked new again. At one end of the hall, a long, high screen had been erected, partitioning off that part of the room into a private area, and Lad realized that it must be the small apartments that David Moulton had built to house his men and himself. An open door stood in the middle of it, and even through the dim glow of firelight Lad could see several figures standing there, stumblingly pulling on clothes, staring back at him.

"It appears we've waked the castle," Lad murmured regretfully. He cast a glance up the long stairway, knowing that Diana was above in the chamber that properly belonged to the Countess of Kerlain. She'd not lived in the West Wing for many months. He knew the very day that she'd made the move, just as he knew almost everything that she'd done for the past two years. Almost. He hoped, desperately, that she wouldn't be waked from her slumbers and come below-stairs. He didn't need an audience to greet his wife after three years of absence; he wasn't even certain yet what he would say to her or if his pounding heart wouldn't fail altogether at the sight of her.

"What's this? Who's come at this hour?"

Lad turned at the sound of Swithin's taut, angry voice. The elderly servant was little changed after three years, save that Lad had never seen him in his shirtsleeves before, without his formal jacket. He'd clearly been waked from his slumbers, for his hair was all on end and his usual stoic demeanor was marked with irritation. He fairly stomped his way toward them. When he was close enough to see Lad's face, he fell still. And stared, with his mouth hanging slightly open, in a thoroughly un-Swithin-like manner. If Lad had been forced to put a name to the expression on the older man's face, that name would be panic.

"Swithin," Lad greeted with care. "I'm sorry that you were disturbed from your slumbers. You needn't have roused yourself. One of the other servants is taking care of my things."

Swithin took another hesitant step, struggling to regain his composure. "My lord. You've returned." He sounded far from pleased at the fact.

Lad smiled thinly. "Yes."

"But—"

"I intend this to be rather a long stay," Lad informed him. "A coach will be arriving sometime tomorrow with the remainder of my belongings, as well as a number of new garments for Lady Kerlain that I had made for her in London, but we can discuss all that in the morning. I shall want my chambers readied as soon as possible, but for tonight I'll share with the countess. She has taken the formal castle chamber for herself, I understand."

"The countess?" Swithin repeated, as if he didn't know who Lad was speaking of. Momentary confusion crossed his craggy features, then cleared. "Of course, my lord," he said with more of his customary propriety. His features took on the look of veiled disdain that Lad had once been well used to, which had made him know how fully the proper servant had disapproved of his improper master. "I'll send a maid up to Lady Kerlain to inform her that you've arrived."

"There's no need," Lad replied, gladdened by how sure-footed he felt. "I'll inform her myself."

How he wished, as Lloyd had earlier said, that Sir Geoffrey could see him as he was now, the Earl of Kerlain down to the soles of his feet.

Swithin took note of the change in both his lord's command and tone—also, for the first time, of his dress, as his gaze traveled slowly from Lad's perfectly coifed hair to his perfectly wrought cravat down the length of his perfectly fashionable clothes and finally to his perfectly polished boots—and the expression of disdain transformed into bewilderment.

Lad lifted a hand in a dismissive gesture. "Return to your slumbers, Swithin. We'll speak in the morning—though not too early, for I expect to sleep in. Good night." He turned away, just in time to greet David Moulton and some of his men, who'd left their beds to welcome him home.

It was an hour before the commotion in the great hall abated. Lloyd accepted the offer of a spare pallet among David Moulton's men, and Lad turned toward the long stairway that led to where Diana was.

"I'll not let the old bugger get up there before me in the

morning,'' Lloyd promised him in a private word before they parted. "You rest easy about that."

Lad couldn't hold back a smile. "The old bugger," he told Lloyd in an amused tone, "is named Swithin, and you'd do far better to gain his friendship than his enmity."

"See about that, I will," Lloyd replied, and turned to swagger away with David Moulton and his men.

The stairway loomed before Lad like the long march to an executioner's ax. But even if he'd known for certain that Diana would greet him with hatred and vitriol, Lad couldn't have turned away. For three long years he had dreamed of her, been driven by his love and longing for her. For three long years he'd remained celibate, faithful to the vows he'd given her. His body had ached for the release that only Diana could provide, until hardly a night passed that he didn't dream as a raw boy dreamed, haunted by lustful visions of his beautiful, passionate wife that left him painfully aroused and wanting—and often beyond even that. The matter had only been made worse by the number of women he'd met in London who'd flirted and teased and whispered offers into his ears of doing far more. He'd spent the final few months of his time in London in what seemed to be a near constant state of arousal, made the more painful by knowing he'd soon be with Diana again.

Even now, as he made his way up the stairs, step by step, he felt his traitorous body hardening and felt a measure of shame for it. He loved Diana far beyond the physical, but he could not help what he was—a man, weak of the flesh, who desperately wanted his wife. There was no sin in that, of course, but it seemed ungentlemanly to want to bed her first and greet her in a more proper manner afterward.

The door to the countess's chamber was unlocked. Lad pushed it slightly open, peering into the darkness of the entryway and the greater room beyond. There were only a few embers glowing in the hearth to provide a shadowy light in the bedchamber and, shutting the door behind him, Lad moved toward it, slowly, soundlessly, until he stood in the midst of the chamber itself.

He looked about in the darkness, waiting for his eyes to adjust to the small measure of light. It was as large a place as Lad remembered, where he and Diana had spent their wedding night. The huge, comfortable bed standing against one wall was the single noteworthy piece of furniture in the room, save, perhaps, for what appeared to be an elegant grandfather clock. He'd not noticed it on his wedding night, but, then, he'd had little interest in anything save Diana.

Was she there now? Lying in the bed? He took one step toward it, then glanced back toward one of the two chairs set near the fire and stopped. A slender hand drooped over one of the armrests, small, white, and feminine.

Diana.

He drew in a deep breath, striving to steady the harsh beating of his heart, the strange tingling that possessed him all over. Her name whispered from his lips without thought or intention, and his body tensed even more hotly.

God, he'd been away from her for so long, he thought as he made his way slowly toward the chair. He stopped and said her name again, gently, his heart pounding so loudly now that he could scarce hear the sound of his own voice. She neither stirred nor turned, and he knew that she must be asleep. Silently, he stepped in front of the chair, at last gazing down upon her.

For a long time, he simply looked at her face, more beautiful than he'd remembered, so delicate and finely featured, caressed by flickering shadows and framed by her unbound black hair, which flowed in silken rivers down her shoulders and across her breasts. She looked like an angel, dressed in a pretty white gown and matching robe, so serene and lovely.

But she was flesh and blood, his beautiful wife. And he'd

had not a word from her in all the time they'd been parted, save for the solitary note that had been delivered by David Moulton's friend. The gown she wore had come from cloth that Eoghan Patterson had given her—or so David Moulton had told him. All of her new clothing had their source in Patterson. As did the fine wines in the cellar, and a portion of both the larder and pantry, and even such small, expensive items as wax candles and Danish lamp oil. Lad had tried to understand why Diana had accepted such gifts from a man she claimed to hate with such fervor but had found it difficult, save that perhaps as she had known so few fine things in her life, and as he himself hadn't yet been able to provide her with such luxuries, Diana had been unable to resist. His absence certainly couldn't have made it easier, especially if she'd had none of his letters.

Still, it stung hard that she had so little faith in him. If she could have only known what he'd gone through just to get back to her, to make everything right, even to rebuild her precious castle.

He cast his glance about the room, seeing now the open trunks, half-packed. Viscount Carden had made it clear to everyone at Kerlain that Diana would be moving to Lising Park—permanently—if the Earl of Kerlain didn't return by the end of three years. He'd been very sure of himself, and Diana clearly had been too, else she'd not have been readying herself to leave Kerlain.

Aye, it stung hard indeed.

"Diana."

He spoke softly, gently. She slumbered on.

He said her name again, a little louder.

"Diana."

With a murmuring sound her lips parted, and her head moved back and forth minutely. He began to grow impatient to have her awake, to speak to her and hear what manner of greeting she would give him, either gladness or damnation.

"Diana."

With what seemed to be a great effort, she opened her eyes and blinked into the darkness of the room. Her movements were slow, sluggish, almost as if she were drugged, though he knew she was merely exhausted. Parting her lips, she drew in a long, easing breath, exhaled it slowly, and let her eyelids drift shut once more.

"Sleeping Beauty, is it?" he murmured, thinking that the name was very apt. She was so very beautiful. He was unable to stop from closing the distance between them and stroking her warm, smooth cheek with his fingertips. "Then I suppose I must be your Prince Charming." He leaned nearer, catching her sweet, womanly scent. His body surged with outright lust, tempered only by the love he felt for her. "Shall I wake you with a kiss?" he murmured softly.

That seemed to get through her stupor. She turned her face from his touch and uttered, in a fearful voice, *"No."*

"No?" he repeated, disappointed but keeping the fact of it from his voice as he stood away from her. Diana lifted a hand to rub her eyes, groaning as if she were in pain. Several moments passed before she finally straightened in the chair and blinked into the darkness, looking around. Lad was standing only a few steps away from her, and yet when her gaze fell on him she straightened and blinked at him as if he were an apparition. Perhaps, he mused, that was what she thought him after three years of absence.

She stiffened, and her voice when she spoke was filled with fear.

"Who are you?" she demanded, lifting a shaking hand to push the hair back from her face. "How do you dare to come here, to my chamber?"

Lord! She didn't know who he was, he realized. She thought him an intruder. He began to grow angry. But how could she *not* know? He would have known her in a blank darkness, with his eyes blindfolded yet, so fully were his senses attuned to her.

"I dare very easily," he told her, his pride pricked. "Stay where you are."

The moment he moved away, Diana leapt out of her chair, clearly ready to scream or make a run for the door. She pulled her robe more tightly about herself and demanded, "How did you manage to get into the castle? What have you come here for?"

Lad cast a brief glance at her before turning away toward a small table and striking a flame on a tinderbox to light a candle. A soft glow of light filled the room, and he heard her murmur with disbelief, "Lad?"

He turned to face her. "Do you know me now, Diana?"

She stared at him for a long, still moment, then slowly began to shake her head.

"No," she whispered.

But she did know. He could see it in her eyes. She knew him but was clearly far from pleased to see him. Lad's heart ached painfully at the knowledge, but he'd been too well trained by Sir Geoffrey to show his emotions in any game now. He retreated into what had become his salvation— being the Earl of Kerlain.

"I've changed a great deal since last we met, Lady Kerlain," he said in the measured, cultured tones Sir Geoffrey had wrought in him, marveling at how easily such mannerisms came to him now, "but I believe this will be welcome to you. I have fully claimed that name and title that you so insistently pressed upon me. You do not deny that you know who I am?"

Her beautiful face filled with sorrow, and she looked at him so sadly, as if she might weep.

"Yes," she murmured at last, despair heavy in the single word. "I know who you are."

Chapter Twenty-two

She claimed to have received no letters from him. She accused him of having taken lovers in England. Lad, for his part, noted that he'd had nothing but silence from her, as well, and pointed out that she appeared ready to leave him for Viscount Carden. She denied any wrongdoing—or faithlessness, though she clearly believed him guilty of the same.

It was a fruitless conversation, and Lad was both too weary and too needy to continue it further. He had come home. He was the lord of Kerlain, and she was his lady, his wife. On the night he'd left, she'd made it clear that she'd have nothing to do with him until he brought her the money she required to regain the estate; then, and only then, would she be a wife to him. He had dreamed of her too long, wanted her too badly, to be denied another moment, regardless of what she thought of him, even if she hated him.

"I bring what you demanded of me," he told her, indicating the document that he'd set upon the table—a banknote for seventy thousand pounds, written out to Viscount Carden. "Three years of my life I gave for it. Now you will keep your part of our bargain, Diana."

"My part? . . ." She began to shake her head, clearly understanding what he meant but not believing it.

Lad reached up to untie the cravat about his neck.

"Three years is a long time for a man to go without his

wife, and I don't intend to go another night—another hour, I vow—without mine.''

She looked at him as if he were crazed.

''I'll not share a bed with you this night!'' she declared angrily. ''Not after all you've done . . . all your faithlessness!''

The accusation burned in him. She couldn't begin to know how he'd suffered for her sake, denied himself not only sexually but in every physical sense. And all the while she'd had Eoghan Patterson paying her court, bringing her gifts, waiting in the sidelines for Lad to fail.

Oh, no. He'd be damned if he'd let her turn him aside after all he'd gone through. He would have his wife beneath him this night—this very hour—and pour his love and lust and frustrations into her slender body until he was emptied of them at last.

Uttering a dark laugh, he shrugged out of his coat and tossed it aside.

''My faithlessness, or what you may perceive as such, has certainly been far less dire than your own, Lady Kerlain. I wouldn't allow your sensibilities to worry overmuch on what's in the past, for I assure you I'll not let myself think of your dalliance with Viscount Carden—which is now at an end.'' With slow, measured steps, he neared Diana. ''I shall make certain that you've no cause to turn to other men for your needs. *Any* of your needs.''

Stumbling back, Diana said, ''I've done nothing to be ashamed of, certainly not with Eoghan Patterson.''

''It matters not, just as I've said. It's all in the past. Come, Diana.'' He fell still and held out a hand to her. ''I mean to have you, one way or another, as is my right. Come to me of your own free will. I don't wish to force you to lie with me.''

''I should think not,'' she said tightly. ''Raping your own wife will be remarkably dull after all you've experienced in London. I'm amazed you returned to Kerlain at all, my lord.''

''I am the Earl of Kerlain,'' he replied simply. ''And your husband.''

She gazed at him with open disdain. ''You may be able to claim both titles, but you're not truly Lad Walker. You're nothing at all like the man who left here three years past.''

''No,'' he agreed, his hand yet held out. ''I'm not. I'm the man you wished me to become. The Earl of Kerlain.''

''A stranger,'' she whispered. ''I prayed for Lad to come back to me.''

''He's gone, Diana.'' He took a step nearer. ''Now you must make do with me. Come.''

Mute, she shook her head.

He sighed and dropped her hand.

''Then I will fetch you.''

Diana backed away, farther from the light of the candle and into the darkness, wondering fleetingly whether she might escape the chamber—and this frightening man—altogether. But it would be impossible. The door that joined their two chambers was on the other side of the room, and Lad stood between her and the only other door.

He seemed so much larger and more powerful than he had three years ago, though she knew he couldn't possibly have changed that much. It was his manner of dress, the knowing expression on his handsome face, the sureness of his movements—all of it made him seem far more ominous and threatening a man than the sweet, gentle Tennessean she'd married.

''Don't,'' she whispered, coming up against a wall. He moved toward her relentlessly, a merciless hunter stalking his prey.

Diana pressed up against the chilly brick as he neared, not stopping until she could feel the heat and hardness of his body but an inch apart from her own. One of his hands slid gently across her shoulder, moving the cloth of her robe aside until his fingers found the bare skin of her arm. His touch was no longer cold, but warm and caressing.

"Diana," he murmured, "take pity on me. It's been three years, and not a moment gone by that I haven't wanted you." His other hand moved to her neck, gliding upward to lift her face to his own. "Take pity," he said as he lowered his mouth.

His lips touched hers lightly, tasting, teasing. Gently, he sucked her bottom lip into his mouth and rubbed his tongue across the captured flesh. When Diana murmured a protest he covered her mouth completely, silencing the sound and pressing her lips wide as his body pushed her hard against the wall, imprisoning her with his size and strength. His tongue pressed inward, exploring, licking the moist flesh within, teasing her own tongue in a seductive manner that she remembered so well, inviting her to join him in such intimate love play.

His manhood pushed against the center of her, hard and big and demanding. Diana tried to push back from the sensation, so strange and frightening after so many years, but the wall—and Lad—gave no purchase. One of his hands went to the back of her neck to hold her still while his mouth continued to ravage; the other slid to her bottom, cupping her hard and pulling her up against himself. He moaned into her mouth and began to rhythmically rock against her, an imitation of the sex act.

Diana felt her will slipping away and desire, hot and needy, taking its place. It had been so long since she'd felt him inside her, part of her, loving her as she loved him. Her body filled with wanting and she pressed against him of her own will, joining the rhythm he'd set and feeling the floodgates of her own desire melting within. She slid her arms about his neck, holding him tightly and opening her mouth wider so that her tongue might duel more ardently with his.

She was possessed with a wildness now that she never could have explained, save that it was a kind of starvation, and she was desperate to sate herself with him.

Lad tore his mouth from hers. "Diana," he said her name harshly, his hot, rapid breath pelting her face. "I've got to be inside you *now*." His hands tore at her robe, ripping both it and her gown from her shoulders and off her body, until they lay in a heap at the floor. His hands and mouth found her naked flesh, touching, kissing, licking. The fingers of one hand made their way to the core of her body, parting the delicate folds with gentle desperation and sliding within. Diana's head fell back and she moaned aloud. Lad's arm about her waist lifted her higher, and while his fingers continued to delve into her wetness, his hot lips closed over one of her breasts, sucking the hard, tingling nipple into his mouth and rubbing his tongue brazenly over the tip of it until she cried out from a mixture of pain and pleasure. Gently, he closed his teeth over the crest, suckling again and pressing his fingers up inside her writhing body.

"Lad!" she cried out.

His fingers left her and she both heard and felt him tearing at his breeches.

"Please," she murmured, her hands raking over his shoulders. "Please."

His mouth was at her ear, his breathing harsh. "Tell me what you want, Diana. Is it this?" She felt his manhood at the entrance of her body, pressing. "This?"

"Yes," she said, moaning, her head thrown back. "Yes."

"Like this?" He slid all the way inside her, hard and deep, filling her completely.

"Oh, yes. *Please*."

He was violent in his need, thrusting her up against the cold wall and coming into her strongly and fully, again and again, his hands at her hips, holding her captive against his impassioned demands.

There was no speaking now, only that vital, intuitive communication of thoughtless, heedless pleasure. Diana's fingers bit into the linen shirt that covered his shoulders, striving desperately to bring him closer, faster, harder into her. Wordlessly, he obeyed, the hands that held her grasping her even more tightly as he plunged firmly and steadily into her body, bringing her at last to a shattering climax that made her cry aloud. He followed but seconds later, helplessly shuddering and groaning out his pleasure.

For long moments, Diana concentrated on breathing, clasping his shoulders for safety, though she hardly had need of such. His body, sweating, trembling, pressed her against the wall so tightly that she could never have slipped away. His breeches had fallen to his knees, and she felt his bare skin against her own, warm and damp, as they stayed where they were, striving to regain some semblance of normalcy.

In time, he murmured her name, close by her ear, and drew in a long, steadying breath. Then he drew back, hefting her in his arms as if she weighed nothing, and carefully carried her—still joined to his body—to the bed.

"Lad," she protested as he laid her down, following to lie heavily on top of her.

"Shhhh." He made the sound against her lips, then began to gently kiss her with far greater care than he'd earlier done.

Beneath him, her legs spread wide, she realized with dim, exhausted amazement that his manhood was growing hard again within her, filling her once more with his desire.

"Wait . . ." she murmured, not sure what she meant by it, save that she couldn't possibly repeat the shattering experience that had just taken place. It would kill her, she knew.

"Love," he said, already moving, this time slowly, pulling nearly all the way out of her body before sliding back fully, carefully, each motion measured and purposeful. "My love. My Diana." He kissed her deeply.

She closed her eyes and felt him inside her, felt the completeness, the rightness of their joining. Nay, this wasn't sin. He was her husband, and she his wife, and no other joining could be so perfect as this. Three years she'd longed for him in so many ways, but especially like this . . . oh, yes . . . *like this* . . .

His mouth left hers to travel along her cheek and chin with slow, sensuous kisses, down to her neck and across her shoulder, which he nipped gently with his teeth as he continued to stroke in and out of her, slowly, deeply. His tongue soothed over the places where his teeth had gone, and she writhed at the wet, smooth caress across her sensitive skin.

"Don't be a dream—not this time," he whispered, groaning as he began to move in her more quickly, thrusting more forcefully. "Diana . . ."

She held him tightly, murmuring, "I'm not a dream."

It was only afterward, as he lay upon her, his harsh breathing slowing moment by moment, that Diana realized he was yet clothed and wearing his boots. He seemed to realize it, too, when he at last came to himself.

Pushing up on his elbows, he gazed at her, his chest rising and falling with each deep breath that fell warm on her face. In the darkness, their eyes met and held, and they were silent, looking at each other searchingly. A minute or more passed, their bodies yet joined, and then he kissed her tenderly and lifted himself away from her.

Standing, he bent over Diana and slid his arms beneath her, lifting her. With one hand he pulled the covers back from the bed, then set her down upon the sheets with care. His hands, as he stood, slid caressingly along the length of her body, and then he stood full height again, gazing at her.

Beneath his searching scrutiny, Diana began to feel

ashamed, not only of her nakedness, but of the abandon with which she'd given in to him—a man who was a stranger to her. How could she have been so wanton? So foolish, to give way with but a few kisses and caresses? Dismay welled up, and Diana shut her eyes and turned away, curling on her side and grabbing whatever blankets she could reach to cover her nakedness.

"You've had your pleasure," she said coldly, "which is most likely all you came for. Now be so good as to leave me in peace."

He was silent for a long time, and at last Diana said, more angrily, "What? Do you mean to possess me again? Have you not had enough to compare with your London conquests? Did I not give in as readily as your other women? You've gained so much skill, my lord, that I cannot think you used to much resistance."

"Do you remember our wedding night, Diana?" he asked, his voice low and striking in the stillness of the room.

Remember it? She'd relived it in her mind hundreds of times in the past three years—that, and every time he'd made love to her.

"Yes," she whispered, taking a fistful of sheet and pressing it against her face, wishing she might press the memories away instead.

"I gave you a promise that night, just as you gave to me," he said softly. "You doubt now the truth of that promise, just as I have doubted you. Three years is a long time to worry and wonder, to imagine the worst. But I swear to you upon my honor, Diana, that I was not unfaithful to you while I was in London. No matter what lies you've read in the London papers or been told by Eoghan Patterson, I give you the truth now. I have kept the promise I made to you."

Hot tears stung at her eyes. "I don't believe you," she said, her voice shaking with pain. She couldn't believe him. She didn't even know who he was anymore.

"Damn you, Diana!" he said furiously. "I've never lied to you. Will you believe those made-up fairy tales in the London papers rather than me?" He sat on the bed and gripped her shoulder, angry now. "I'll *make* you believe me!"

"Go away!" she shouted, weeping, and violently thrust his hand off. "You've had enough of me this night. Please, Lad." Sobbing, she pressed her face into the pillows. "Leave me alone."

"Very well, my lady," he said in a heated tone. "I grant you a reprieve for now. I'm too weary to argue the matter further. But we *will* speak tomorrow," he promised as he stood, "and both do our share of the talking. I'm not the only one, madam wife, who has a great deal of explaining to do."

Chapter Twenty-three

Morning arrived far too early, along with the rude awakening of Lloyd's thoroughly amused voice.

"Went that well, did it?" he asked, gazing down at the huge, dusty bed where Lad had curled up and pulled the heavy silk counterpane over himself in an effort to stay warm. "Lady Kerlain must've been awful glad at your return to make you sleep in here."

Blearily Lad came awake, blinking up into the chamber's dim morning light to find Lloyd grinning at him.

"Go away," Lad muttered. He was still dressed in the clothes and boots he'd yet worn upon quitting Diana's chamber the night before and consequently felt uncomfortable and cranky. "I want to sleep."

"Can't," Lloyd said with unsympathetic energy. He reached down to pull the conterpane away. "Not unless you want that old gent to come barging in, which he's been ready to do every minute since the sun rose. And such a fuss he puts out when I tell him I'm your man now, and not him, and that he's not to be pawing about in your things."

Lad groaned and with an effort sat up in the bed, rubbing his head. "Swithin can be very determined," he said.

"The old woman's even worse," Lloyd went on, deftly folding the conterpane and setting it aside. "She's been outside Lady Kerlain's door, trying to get in. Had to pick the old girl up and carry her down the stairs. Twice."

"Poor Maudie," Lad said, yawning.

"Well, I thought you was in there with her ladyship, didn't I?" Lloyd said. "How was I to know she'd sent you away with a tick in your ear?"

"She did not send me away with a tick in my ear," Lad retorted grumpily. "I left of my own accord."

Lloyd rolled his eyes. "Oh, surely, you did."

"I did!" Lad insisted, swinging his legs over the side of the bed. "I simply decided that I didn't want to spend what remained of the night arguing with an aggravated—and aggravating—female. Not that I need to tell you anything about it," he said more haughtily. Lloyd merely laughed, as he always did when Lad played at being lordly with him.

"I'll let her ladyship's maid go in next time, then," he said.

"Please do," Lad said, standing and stretching and groaning, all at once.

"And what should I do with all the footmen belowstairs who want to get up here and grub through Lady Kerlain's things?"

Lad came fully awake all at once; his gaze riveted on Lloyd. "Footmen? From Lising Park?"

Lloyd gave a curt nod. "And carriages too. Come to fetch Lady Kerlain's things afore their lord and master arrives to take her away."

"You've let none of them leave?"

Lloyd, who'd begun stripping the musty sheets from the bed, gave him an offended look. "Think I'm a fool? No one's run off to tell your friend the viscount that you've returned, if that's what you mean."

"When's Carden to arrive?"

"An hour or so."

"Damn!" Lad started pulling his clothes off. "Get me some kind of bath ready, Lloyd. I don't care if it's hot. And my clothes—where're my bags?'' He cast his gaze frantically about the room.

''Unless you're blind,'' Lloyd said dryly, ''you can see that your bath's sitting there by the fire. Been ready for half an hour now, and gone cold, mostlike. Serve you right if it has. And your clothes are laid out on that chair.''

''You're worth your weight in gold, Lloyd,'' Lad murmured thankfully as he sat down by the fire to pull his boots off. ''Send a message to Swithin while I bathe,'' he said, tossing first one boot and then the other onto the carpeted floor. ''I want to see him—and Maudie and Stuart Farrell, as well, in my study at eleven. Then be so good as to come back and help me dress.''

Lloyd gave a sigh. ''Going to be a long day.''

Lad laughed and stepped into the tub. ''Quite long,'' he agreed. ''I hope you ate a good breakfast. You'll need all your strength to get through it.''

The first order of business, once Lad was bathed and clothed, was to get rid of Eoghan Patterson's restless footmen, all of whom were seated in the great hall, wondering if they could possibly escape Kerlain before their master came to collect the countess. He was due to arrive at any moment and would be furious to discover that none of the lady's things had yet been packed in the carriages he'd sent. But far worse would be his temper when he saw that the Earl of Kerlain had returned. The footmen—every man among them—knew that life as Lising Park was going to be miserable indeed for a very long time.

They all stood as Lad descended the long stairway, dressed to the teeth in fine, elegant clothes that bespoke his nobility, followed by his big brute of a manservant, who was rather less well attired.

''Who's in charge?'' Lad asked without preamble.

"Me, my lord." A tall fellow with powdered hair, dressed in the elegant and expensive blue and white livery of Lising Park, stepped forward.

"Very good." Lad gave the man a cool, assessing look before turning his attention to perfecting the fall of his lace cuffs. "I understand," he said in a rather bored tone, "that you've come to collect my wife's things and take them to Lising Park." He glanced up. "Is that right?"

The man's face reddened. "Aye, my . . . Lord Kerlain."

"Forgive me for being so disobliging, but you cannot take anything from Kerlain, certainly nothing belonging to my wife. I'm sure you understand."

"Of course, my lord," the man agreed quickly, bowing low. "We'll leave at once. Pray, Lord Kerlain, forgive our coming."

"Without doubt," Lad murmured. "And Lord Carden will be arriving shortly, I understand?"

"I do not know, my lord," the man answered nervously, casting glances at his fellow footmen, who were standing on either side of him. "Please, my lord, will you give us your leave to depart?"

"Certainly you may," Lad said, all affability. "By the long route."

"The long route?" the footman repeated. "But, my lord, that will take us many miles out of our way."

"Yes," Lad agreed with a pleasant smile, "but that is the way you'll go. I'll ask Lieutenant Moulton to lend you an escort of men, to make certain you come to no harm. And you needn't worry over what to tell Lord Carden," he added when the footman opened his mouth to lodge another protest. "I give you my word of honor that everything shall be explained to his lordship's perfect understanding."

And with that, Lad turned and walked away, murmuring

to Lloyd that he was exceedingly hungry and ready for his breakfast.

Eoghan Patterson proved to be the next order of business.

Lad had just finished his morning meal when Lloyd sauntered into the recently renovated breakfast parlor—this was, in fact, the first time that Lad had ever eaten in it, as three years earlier it had been missing half a wall—and said, "He's here, just now arrived in a grand carriage. Time's come. You going to remember all Sir Geoffrey taught you?"

Lad tossed his napkin aside and drew in a long, slow breath to steady himself. He wasn't particularly amazed at how nervous he felt for the coming confrontation, but he'd rather have been perfectly calm. An impossible wish, he supposed. He picked up his coffee cup and drained the remaining contents. Now, he told himself, setting the cup aside, he was ready.

"I shall strive not to embarrass you, Lloyd," he said as he stood.

"Never mind that," Lloyd told him. "Just don't murder the fellow and we'll all be fine."

Lad began to walk past him. Lloyd stepped in front of him, putting out a staying hand.

"You want to kill him, don't you? This man who tried to steal your woman?"

Lad could hardly deny it. He felt the hatred and power to do the deed surging hotly in his blood.

"Yes."

"You just remember what Sir Geoffrey said," Lloyd repeated. "Vengeance is best served up cold. Bear it in mind."

"God help me," Lad said fervently.

Lloyd stood aside to let him pass.

"Never worry about God," he said. "If you get to being foolish, it's my fist on your head that'll help you."

Which was, Lad knew, a reassuring thought in its own

way. He certainly didn't have to worry about making too many missteps with Lloyd about.

"Send a maid up to fetch Lady Kerlain at once, with the news of Viscount Carden's arrival, and ask her to join me in my study."

"I've already done that," Lloyd informed him. "And told her to bring the ready to pay that sodden bugger off."

"Lloyd!" Lad couldn't suppress a bark of laughter. "I pray you used a different form of address for his lordship when sending your message to my wife. God help me if Diana should ever hear you calling anyone—even Lord Carden—a name so foul."

"It's not half what I *wanted* to call him," Lloyd muttered. "I'd better go fetch the fellow before Swithin gets to him first."

Lad was grateful for a few minutes alone in his study to collect his thoughts. The room had undergone an amazing transformation since he'd left Kerlain. David Moulton and his men had changed the dark, cold room that had been his grandfather's favorite haunt into one that was both comfortable and far more inviting to Lad's own frame of mind. Somehow, the amazing young architect had even managed to knock out part of one wall and add a window, and Lad stood at it now, gazing out over the prospect of the long span of lawn that fell before the castle proper and beyond that the rolling hills where Kerlain's apple orchards resided. A beautiful view indeed. On another day, when matters were less clouded than they presently were, Lad knew he would be able to appreciate it far more.

It was a strange moment, awaiting this first meeting that he would have with Eoghan Patterson after that man had so ignobly cheated him out of his estate—and had meant to cheat Lad out of so much more. He had never been more grateful for Sir Geoffrey's excellent training than at this moment. When Lloyd's scratch came on the door, Lad put on the calm, pleasant expression that he'd mastered while gaming and turned to greet his visitor.

It was evident by the look on Eoghan Patterson's face as he walked through the door, hat and gloves in hand, that he hadn't fully comprehended the situation. The smile on his handsome countenance died away at once, and he stopped mid-stride, just inside the room. Lloyd closed the door quietly behind him.

"Hello, Eoghan," Lad said, staying in his place near the window, keeping his stance perfectly easy, though his body tensed with rage at the sight of the man before him. "You appear surprised to see me, my friend. Did you think, perhaps, that my wife was playing a jest, telling the servants to say that I had at last arrived? But you do not look very pleased to know that I've returned to Kerlain. I can but wonder at this manner of greeting, after three years parting between us."

Viscount Carden stood frozen for a long moment, then asked, "The seventy thousand? You were able to raise the sum?" The words ended in a tone of incredulity.

"Yes. Lady Kerlain will arrive shortly with a banknote for the amount." He took a step forward, folding his hands behind his back, and smiled. "It was good of you to give me such a generous length of time in which to regain what I had lost to you, Eoghan. I'm sure I can never express my gratitude quite fully, knowing that you had every right to keep your winnings. This, I think, is what marks the difference between British honor and the more American ideal of profits and gains."

The stunned look began to fade from Viscount Carden's face, and by degrees his countenance took on the more familiar, cunning expression that Lad so well remembered.

"Of course I . . . of a great certainty, Lad, I was determined to give you sufficient time to regain what you had lost to me during that foolish game. Indeed, if you had but come to me the day following, I would have gladly returned the deed to you and begged you to forget the entire event. You were so taken away in grief, after all, that I could hardly expect you to honor such a debt.''

"Truly?'' Lad's brow furrowed slightly. "Diana did not make it sound so when she returned from her visit with you that day after our drunken game.''

"I'm sure she misunderstood me,'' Eoghan said at once, giving a wave of the hand that held his hat. "You know what women are. And she was most distressed at what had passed. Too, she insisted that your honor, though you are an American, is as dear to you as that of any British nobleman. I had no wish to give you insult or make you feel any manner of indebtedness by putting such an offer before you. Truly, that is the way of it, Lad.''

"You are kind to have thought so well on my feelings,'' Lad replied. "And now, the happy outcome is complete. I have regained Kerlain with my honor intact and will suffer not the least sense of''—he paused, smiling at his guest—"indebtedness.'' He took another step forward, more thoughtful now. "There is one matter that confuses me, however, and for which I would appreciate some explanation from you, Eoghan.''

Viscount Carden appeared to remain easy. Lad could almost feel Sir Geoffrey's presence—silent and still, as he had so often been—telling him to be steady, to keep a steely grip on his emotions, to give his opponent no sign of either his thoughts or his feelings.

"Yes?''

"There were several of your footmen here earlier this morning. They seem to have arrived with the intention of removing my wife's belongings from Kerlain.''

"Oh,'' said Eoghan. His color grew very pale.

"Yes,'' said Lad. "I'd not have you worry for them, however. I sent them on their way back to Lising Park, where you will find them upon your own return. You may wonder at not meeting them during your own ride here, but that is because I sent them by the long route. I was possessed of such an eagerness to see you, my dear friend, that I could take no chance of them warning you off."

Viscount Carden was clearly flustered. "Lad, you misunderstand—"

"I'm sure I do," Lad said congenially. "But this, I think, may require greater explanation than that of striving to maintain my honor."

He took another step forward, perfectly measured, and let his hands fall forward from where they'd been clasped behind his back. It was an easy gesture but had the desired effect. With satisfaction he saw Viscount Carden step immediately back, complete alarm on his face.

The game was on.

Lad experienced the biting rush of sensation that came with the start of every game—and just as Sir Geoffrey had taught him, he savored it for a brief moment, then tamped it down as with a twelve-pound stone.

The door opened to admit Diana, who entered the room and came to a stop, her eyes finding Lad at once and fixing on him steadfastly but with a decided chill. Eoghan Patterson, on the other hand, gazed at her with such heat that Lad thought she must surely feel scorched by it.

She looked pale and tired, as if she'd found as little sleep as he'd done after they'd parted so angrily the night before. She was yet angry, he readily saw, but for both their sakes he prayed that she'd not show it too openly before their guest. Eoghan Patterson would realize just how successful his lies had been if he saw but a hint of the bitterness and lack of trust that presently existed between the Lord and Lady of Kerlain.

Lad forced a cheerful smile and held out his hand to Diana.

"Ah, but here is my good lady wife," he said in happy tones. "Have you brought the banknote to give to Lord Carden, my love? He is anxious to have it and be on his way."

Diana didn't so much as glance Eoghan Patterson's way. She looked at Lad's outstretched hand with a slight frown, then slowly, her eyes shadowed with doubt, moved forward to set her own in it. Her slender fingers, as Lad's closed over them, were like ice.

"Yes," she murmured. "Here it is." Still not looking at Viscount Carden, she handed Lad the folded document that he'd given her the night before.

He realized that she was trembling and slid an arm about her waist, feeling, in that moment, a fearsome need to commit murder upon Eoghan Patterson's person. Yet his expression remained pleasant, and his voice even more so, as he held the banknote out to the other man.

"Now we have repaid the debt in full. You'll be so good as to return my note as being discharged? The one that I wrote out to you three years ago?"

Viscount Carden stared in silence at Diana until she finally lifted her gaze to glare back at him defiantly.

"I don't want the money," he said.

"No, of course not," Lad replied with his continued calm, perfectly aware how maddening it was, "but you'll take it." *If I have to shove it down your throat,* he left unsaid, but his meaning was clear.

Viscount Carden snatched the document from Lad's hand, gave Diana one last, fulsome look, and strode from the room.

"Oh, God," Diana murmured. "Dear God." She was openly shaking now.

Lad tried to tighten his grip on her, but she pushed free and walked to the other side of the room. She stood there, turned away from him, and lowered her face into her hands.

Lad wanted to go to her, to hold and reassure her. But she didn't want such as that from him—not yet.

"He's gone, Diana," he said gently, "and will never have any power over you again."

Silent, she shook her head.

"You don't believe me," he said, "just as you believe nothing I've said to you since I've returned. I know you've little cause to do so," he admitted reluctantly, "but I promise you, Diana, that Eoghan Patterson will never again be able to demand anything of you."

"You don't know him," she murmured, lowering her hands. "He'll never give up until he has his way." She wiped her cheeks with the backs of her fingertips.

"That I believe well enough," Lad said, his heart aching to kiss her tears away instead. "Many men are the same—unable to leave the game until they've either won or lost all they have."

Sniffling, Diana turned and looked at him, her gaze icy.

"But this isn't a game of chance, my lord, as you're so fond of playing in London. He's crazed, and you're mad to toy with him." Her tone grew softer, but far more damning. "I should have thought that you, of all people, would have learned the truth of that. Not that I expect you to listen to me. You never did before."

Stung, Lad lowered his gaze and strove to compose himself. He sought refuge among the many masks Sir Geoffrey had schooled him in, choosing, perhaps unwisely, one vividly marked with sneering indifference.

"Perhaps you would have preferred to leave with Viscount Carden, madam, so strongly as you object to your own husband." She would have exclaimed at this, but Lad turned away, seemingly uninterested, and picked up the first piece of paper he could find, perusing it as if it were the most fascinating document he'd ever beheld. He was certain that she could see nothing from his behavior of the turmoil that possessed him within. "But that can't be helped now," he went on blandly. "We've but ten minutes before Swithin and Maudie and Stuart arrive."

"For what purpose?" she demanded angrily. "Your manservant was already inexcusably rude to both Maudie and Swithin this morning. And they've already been terribly overset by the many new servants you've sent to Kerlain."

He turned about, folded his arms across his chest, and regarded her steadily.

"You've no cause for fear, my lady. I mean only to give them their due. Nothing more, and nothing less."

Chapter Twenty-four

"My lord," Swithin said in his most daunting and superior tones, "I have been manservant to the Earl of Kerlain for over fifty years and have served in that most trusted capacity in which his lordship, the former earl, was pleased to place me. Not only as his butler, my lord, but more especially as his valet. I am sorry to speak so bold, but being an American, you perhaps may not be aware of the propriety of such matters as these. I will—under duress, I admit—allow your London manservant to assist me in caring for your lordship, but beyond that, he must take his proper place. Otherwise," Swithin said, drawing himself up proudly, "I must—and will—quit Kerlain altogether."

"Swithin, please don't distress yourself so," Diana said hurriedly. "Your place at Kerlain is perfectly safe, just as it has always been. His lordship hasn't any intention of—"

"My dear," Lad interrupted her gently. "I shall explain myself presently. Come and sit down, if you please."

He spoke in such a firm, though polite, tone that Diana had little choice but to obey. She took the seat he offered and began to feel anxious. He was not the Lad she'd once known, whose actions she could have readily foretold and swayed if she'd not liked what they were. With *this* man, she hadn't the least idea what would happen, but even if she had, she possessed little power to alter it. He was the Earl of Kerlain, and on his own estate, at least, that was as good as being God. The Lad she'd married hadn't embraced that realization; this man clearly did.

Maudie, who was standing beside Swithin, began nervously folding and unfolding her hands, and Diana's heart ached for her, though even more so for poor Stuart, who stood very near the study doors, looking purely panicked, as if he'd like nothing better than to escape.

Lad, for his part, leaning indolently against the large, highly polished desk that had once been Diana's godfather's, seemed perfectly at ease and in command.

"I am fully sensible, Swithin, of the invaluable service you have given this family for so many years," he said. "And also you, Maudie." He nodded and smiled at her. "Indeed, the indebtedness owed you by not only my grandfather but also by my father and myself—not to mention, of course, Lady Kerlain—is without estimation. I do not think I overstate the matter by saying that Kerlain would not have survived without your goodness in remaining here for so many years not only without pay but also under such circumstances as could only be termed dire and uncomfortable." He looked at Diana. "Is this not so, my dear?"

Diana blinked, almost unable to believe that such an elegantly crafted speech was coming out of Lad Walker's mouth. Not once had he slurred so much as a syllable with his American accent.

"Yes," she said, bringing herself into the moment. "Indeed, yes."

He smiled warmly, then looked back at the waiting servants.

"Now the time has come to reward in full such goodness, diligence, and excellence."

He turned to the desk and took up three sealed packets. With the first of these, he approached Swithin.

"Our first attempt to do so will be in making payment of all wages due and past due. I have taken the liberty of adding to each a retrospective rise in salary, which is proper in accordance with what you should have been earning had Kerlain proved more profitable in years past. These amounts," he said, giving Swithin, Maudie, and finally Stuart their packages, "will redeem, I pray, the past five years during which you have gone without your proper, well-deserved salaries."

"No, please, my lord," Stuart said miserably, trying to give the package back. "I don't deserve it . . . nor anything from you."

Lad clapped him on the shoulder and pressed the package into his hands. "Most certainly you do, Stuart Farrell. You have served us so honorably and with such a measure of trustworthiness that you truly deserve far more. A man will pay a great deal to claim so honest a fellow in his service, and more especially one such as you, who comes from a family possessed of a name and tradition that is justifiably proud."

At this, young Stuart Farrell burst into shockingly loud tears, threw the packet Lad had given him onto the carpet, and ran out of the room.

Diana stood and called out, "Stuart!" and would have run after him if Lad hadn't reached out a hand to stop her as she gained the door.

"Let him go," he murmured. "Time is what he needs now."

Lloyd, standing in the hallway, exchanged meaningful glances with Lad, then reached out to close the door again.

Lad tried to put his arm about her, but Diana moved away, not looking at him, until she sat in her chair again. Maudie and Swithin were still in their places, looking very pleased with the heavy packets that Lad had given them.

"Our second attempt to commend such service," Lad said, walking back toward his desk, "will be to recognize and promote it." He sat down in the lordly chair that was the Earl of Kerlain's. "Many servants have been added to Kerlain's staff in the past months, but many more are required to completely fill our needs, and these will be tended to very shortly. To this purpose, I must, I fear, make even greater and far more strenuous demands upon your loyalty to Kerlain.

"Swithin," he said, looking directly at that man, "you will no longer be a mere butler . . . but our maître d'hôtel, with a commensurate rise in salary, of course."

It was too grand a boon to expect. To be the butler for a noble house was one thing, but the maître d'hôtel! It was the highest position that a manservant might ever attain, one of great power and dignity. In all its history, Kerlain had never had a servant so honorably deigned. Wide-eyed with amazement, Diana nearly gaped at her husband, and Swithin, for once, left off his stoic countenance and smiled fully and completely.

"Every servant in the household, save my own man, Lloyd, will be beneath your direction. But we must have that understanding between us now, that Lloyd will answer only to me. If this is acceptable to you, the change in status will be made this very hour."

"My lord!" Swithin uttered, as clearly happy as a man who'd been given his heart's greatest desire. "Oh, sir, I cannot tell you . . . after fifty years . . . how greatly I've—" He broke off, unable to say more.

"I will hear none of this," Lad remarked sternly, frowning. "It is too well deserved to merit thanks, and I will not have it."

At this commanding tone, Swithin straightened and resumed his great manner of perfect propriety. "No, of course not, Lord Kerlain. Forgive me."

"This once," Lad permitted regally.

Diana stared at him with a mixture of amazement and disbelief. He had done it all so perfectly—so beautifully. As well or even better than her godfather might ever have done. He'd even smoothed over Swithin's attempts at gratitude with the perfect mixture of gruffness and impatience, thereby salvaging the older man's pride. It could not have been an easy thing for Lad to do; she knew very well that he didn't even particularly like Swithin. But to have done this—she almost could have kissed him for it, despite all her anger and misgivings. Oh, yes. She could have kissed him just for gratitude.

Lad seemed to feel her gaze upon him and looked at her with a slight, bewildered frown, which eased away during the few seconds that their gazes met and held. For just a moment, she thought she saw something flaring in his eyes—a glimpse of the old Lad, sweet and open and oh, so gentle.

Then, giving a shake of his head, he abruptly turned his attention to Maudie. "A promotion will also be made to your position, Maudie Farrell, to that of housekeeper. We ask much in requesting that you take on this duty," he added, when she tried to speak, "for it is a new staff and many of the maids not properly trained. I believe that you alone possess the necessary knowledge of Kerlain to teach these young women what is required of them here. Your salary, also, has been appropriately raised."

Maudie didn't seem particularly happy at this news. Instead, quite the opposite. She looked at her lord pleadingly.

"My lord, I haven't any proper training, as Swithin does. I started at Kerlain when I was but a girl and never rose above an upstairs maid. I couldn't run such a grand household, my lord," she said sadly. "No matter how I wish I might."

"Maudie, but you can," Diana told her.

"Nay, miss . . . my lady," Maudie said. "It's beyond old Maudie, I fear."

"You mustn't worry over the matter," Lad said. "Think

on it for a day or two, and discuss the matter in full with Lady Kerlain. If you have no wish to take on this new position, I'll write to an acquaintance of mine in London and ask him to suggest someone to fill the post. But perhaps you may be willing to take on another post, Maudie—when the time comes necessary to fill it," Lad said cryptically.

Both Maudie and Diana looked at him in confusion, until he clarified, "As nurse, to the children that Lady Kerlain and I hope soon to produce."

At this, Maudie beamed, Swithin coughed, and Diana, sitting in her chair, turned scarlet. Her heart, already beating at a painfully rapid rate, felt as if it turned over entirely in her chest.

"Oh, my lord," said Maudie, her hands ceasing their nervousness and folding together in delight, "I should indeed like that very much. Of all things."

Lad nodded. "It is decided, then. But until the arrival of that happy time, I shall appoint a maid to help you in your service to Lady Kerlain. This is indeed not meant as any insult to you, Maudie, but you must no longer be required to carry heavy trays and pails of water up to Lady Kerlain's chamber. You will have someone to do the carrying and the harder labor. I insist upon it."

Maudie appeared displeased by this but said nothing, for which Diana was glad. She had thought for many months now that Maudie should be relieved of the burdensome chores that she insisted upon shouldering but knew very well that the older woman wouldn't listen to a word of argument on the subject. At least not from Diana. There could be no point of registering a complaint with the new Earl of Kerlain. It was quite obvious that he'd brook no disagreements.

If Swithin and Maudie had entered the study yet viewing Lad Walker as a pretender to the earldom, they had surely changed those opinions by the time they walked back out again. Diana had seen Swithin treat only one other man with such clear deference and respect as he now suddenly showed Lad, and that had been her godfather.

The older man bowed before making his departure.

"I shall begin with a review of the staff this very afternoon, my lord. Several of the footmen require more proper training to be acceptable in their posts."

Diana had to hold back a laugh. Swithin was now truly in his element.

"Very good," Lad replied. "I should also like a list by the end of the week regarding uniforms for the entire household. Every servant will be properly outfitted, and cost is not to be considered. You must understand that our situation now is quite different from what it once was and that Kerlain will be run in the manner due its history and greatness. Don't hesitate to list fully what our needs are, Swithin. I shall place my complete trust regarding this matter in your capable hands."

Swithin's craggy features suffused with pride. "Of course, my lord," he said, making another bow. "You may be assured that it will be just as you wish."

When they had gone, Diana stood from her chair and walked slowly to stand in front of her husband.

"What was that all about?" she asked. "Most especially with Stuart?"

Lad held out a hand to her, and Diana, hesitating, set hers in it. His fingers, strong and warm, folded over her own in a light, reassuring grasp.

"The truth of the matter, Diana, is that I should have thrown Swithin, Maudie, and Stuart out of Kerlain and made certain that they never returned. Along with Eoghan Patterson, they have been our worst enemies these past three years."

Diana was so stunned by these words that she couldn't

speak, but with a furious movement she snatched her hand away.

"I know that you don't wish to hear the truth of this," Lad said gently, "but in time, you'll see what's been going on much more clearly. For now, I've taken the necessary steps to cut Eoghan Patterson's links to Kerlain. Rather than send his fellow conspirators away, I've given them reason to return their loyalties to us. It is no longer in either Maudie's or Swithin's interests to do Viscount Carden's bidding. I cannot speak for Stuart."

Diana slowly shook her head. "You're mad. *None* of them would ever betray Kerlain. I realize that Eoghan deceived them into believing that he was a great man, but they'd never knowingly side with him against Kerlain. Maudie and Swithin have devoted almost the entirety of their lives to this estate, and to the earldom itself. And to me," she added.

"Yes," Lad said softly. "Think on that, Diana, and you'll understand fully their motivation. It was not mere deception. They willingly and knowingly lent Eoghan Patterson their aid."

"No!" she said insistently, horrified to know that he should believe such lies about people she loved so dearly. "You're wrong!"

"Eoghan Patterson was allowed to visit at Kerlain almost as often as he pleased," Lad told her, "without your invitation. Swithin did nothing to keep him out. Indeed, from what David Moulton has told me, Swithin ever greeted the viscount almost as if he were the Earl of Kerlain—or perhaps simply as his true master. And all of Eoghan Patterson's gifts to you—were you not persuaded by some of Maudie Farrell's pleading to accept them?"

"Maudie was far more concerned with my comfort than her own," Diana argued. "And Swithin . . . he was . . ." But she had no defense for Swithin. His partiality toward Viscount Carden over the Earl of Kerlain had been painfully clear.

"Swithin," Lad said, folding his arms across his chest, "believed that he was doing the right thing in helping Eoghan to take over not only Kerlain but you as well. Far better that you should be married to a proper nobleman than to an American pretender. If you couldn't understand the truth of that, then others would understand it for you and make certain that you were saved from so dire a fate. Swithin, Maudie, and Stuart saw themselves as your protectors. Perhaps even as your saviors. Eoghan Patterson knew their feelings and used them accordingly."

Diana continued to shake her head, feeling sick to her very soul. "No," she said. "You've mistaken everything. You *must* have."

"I don't particularly blame them, Diana. After all, how could they know what manner of man Viscount Carden truly is? I never saw his true colors until it was too late. And I'm certainly unable to cast stones. I'm sure they believed that the viscount would be far better to you—and to them and all of the people of Kerlain—than I should ever be."

"Oh, God," Diana said faintly, suddenly remembering the conversation she'd had the night before with Maudie, while they'd been packing Diana's things. "Merciful God."

"Diana?" Lad's voice filled with concern as he moved toward her. "Are you unwell?"

"I've just remembered something that Maudie told me," she murmured, letting him lead her to the nearest chair. "Last night she said that when Eoghan came to collect me this morning, she and Swithin would be going with us back to Lising Park. But he'd made it very clear that he would allow no one from Kerlain to accompany me—most especially them. But when I tried to explain the matter to her, she insisted that he'd told them so himself—and that such a fine gentleman would not lie.''

Lad went down on his haunches before her, taking Diana's hands in his. ''In return for their services, this was to be their reward,'' he said, ''that they not be parted from you. They acted as they did out of love for you, Diana, and though it was wrong, their motive can yet be admired. The shame of it is that they made a bargain with the very devil. Eoghan Patterson cares nothing for harming those whom he's taken in with his wiles.''

''No, he does not,'' Diana agreed bitterly. ''Indeed, he delights in giving as much grief as possible to anyone who trusts him. I'm glad that Swithin and Maudie—and Stuart, too, though I don't know that he's ever done more than speak very occasionally with Eoghan—I'm glad that they were spared such pain as he would have given them.'' She squeezed his hands and said, more softly, ''Thank you.''

''Don't thank me yet, Diana,'' he said with all seriousness. ''I cannot please you in all things during the coming days, but I shall do my best to keep any harm from coming to the people of Kerlain. And to us as well.'' He stood and moved back toward the desk.

''I told you last night,'' he said, turned away from her, ''that I have kept the promise I made to you on our wedding night. It's important for me to know that you believe me— and to know that you've kept the vow you gave me as well.''

Diana stiffened. ''I've betrayed you with no one else, if that's what you mean,'' she replied indignantly. ''Not in any way, in either deed or thought.''

''I'm glad,'' he murmured, relief evident in his voice. ''Do you believe me, as I believe you?''

Diana hesitated, unnerved by all that had happened.

''I . . . don't know.''

He turned to look at her, leaning casually against the desk.

"Why?"

"Because . . ." She shook her head, tears of hurt and anger stinging her eyes. "I've seen proof of it with my own eyes—in the London papers. Every detail of your affairs for the world to see. The handsome, charming, *unmarried* Earl of Kerlain, admired by every woman and available to almost all of them!"

Lad was quiet for a long moment, while Diana struggled to regain her composure.

"I'm sorry you saw those papers," he said in a low voice. "You once tried to warn me about how devious Eoghan Patterson can be, which is a truth that you know far better than anyone else—I realize that now. This was more of his poison, Diana. I know that sounds like a remarkably easy place to lay the blame, but I can think of no other reason why he should bring you such as that, save to turn you from me and toward him. He's determined to have you as his wife at any cost."

"Eoghan is devious," she admitted, "But I doubt that even he could produce such papers for his own, sole use. They were certainly real, and what was written about you— week after week—couldn't have been made up, even if Eoghan had paid for it. Not for that many papers."

He sighed and moved closer to her again.

"In their own way, they were true enough. I wrote to you and tried to prepare you for the gossip that you might hear, but you never received my letters, did you?"

"There *weren't* any letters," she told him. "There was no word from you at all—save those few missives you entrusted to those whom you sent to Kerlain." Sniffling, she gazed up at him. "Did you have my letters? I wrote so often, but you never replied. Six months ago," she admitted with a measure of shame, "I stopped writing altogether."

He reached out a hand to run the tip of one finger lightly across her cheek. "I longed to hear from you, love, but none of your missives reached me either. More of Patterson's evil, I suppose, and certainly the worst hell he could have consigned me to. There came a certain night for me, several months after I'd left Kerlain, when I despaired for you so greatly that I began to believe that I couldn't go on. It was such a dark time, Diana, that I don't know what would have happened if I hadn't had the great fortune to meet Sir Geoffrey.''

Diana blinked up at him. "Sir Geoffrey?''

Lad smiled. His hand wandered up to push stray strands of hair from her forehead.

"You don't know who he is, though I spent hours writing to you of him. Later, perhaps, I'll spend hours telling you. Without him, we'd never have regained Kerlain.''

"What of Miss Christabella Howell?'' she asked, then bit her lip at once, wishing she'd said nothing of that particularly painful topic.

His smile softened. "She's a dear friend, Diana. Nothing more. I know that the London papers had us as good as wed several times over, but she always loved her fiancé, Viscount Severn, and they're married now. I know how damning every story you read of me sounded, especially as I never told anyone that I was already married, but it was important to our cause that it be so. I never could have won so much money with my gambling otherwise. A married man will be invited to a great many balls and parties, but an available man—especially a nobleman—will be eagerly sought after for *every* possible event, and I needed very much to be able to move openly in society. But you'd have to understand Sir Geoffrey's plan to understand the full of it.'' He softly stroked her hair. "One day, very soon, I promise you'll know everything. For now, I must ask you a question of my own.''

"What is it?''

"You were preparing last night to leave Kerlain and go away with Eoghan Patterson. Why?"

"I made a bargain with him," she said slowly, wearily, "on the night that you lost Kerlain. You already know that he gave us the chance to regain the estate within the space of three years, but what I did not tell you was that if we failed to raise the money he required—"

"If I failed, you mean."

She nodded. "Yes, if you failed, I would . . . go away with him." She closed her eyes and turned her face to the side, unable to look at Lad any longer. "Without protest."

"Why didn't you tell me this before you sent me away? Do you love him?" His voice was low, intent.

"God's mercy, *no!*" she replied with feeling. "I despise him far more than words can say. But I couldn't tell you of what had passed between us. I was afraid you might kill him and end up on the gallows. As to the bargain itself, he threatened harm to the people of Kerlain if I refused to make it." At the touch of his finger upon her cheek, she turned to gaze up at him. "I did refuse him at first, Lad. I told him I'd go away with you to America, to Fair Maiden, before ever bending to his will. But when he made such wild threats against the Farrells and the Colvaneys, I couldn't turn the matter aside. I had promised my godfather never to let Eoghan have Kerlain and to keep the people here always safe. I knew that you would probably never forgive me once you knew the truth," she said more softly, "but I didn't know what else to do. I made the pact and sent you away. It was the worst moment of my life, though I don't expect you to believe me. Now I deserve what I have sown, though I am so very glad—I cannot tell you how much—that you've come back, Lad. Hate me if you will."

"Never that, Diana," he whispered somberly.

"But I sent you away so coldly," she said, "and regretted it so deeply afterward. We were separated for three years, and perhaps nothing will ever be as it was, even though you've returned."

He bent, drawing her to her feet, and kissed her with great tenderness. "No, love. Nothing will ever again be as it was. But, though I despaired at being apart from you, I would not have traded those years away."

The words hurt. Diana could scarcely believe he'd spoken them.

"No," she replied bitterly, "I suppose you would not. You lived a far grander life in London than you will ever know here. Indeed," she added, trying to move away from him again, "you must be sorry to have had to leave it and all your fine friends there. Please let me go."

He held her fast. "Never," he whispered. "Every moment that we were apart was an unutterable misery for me, Diana, and that I swear by my own life. But there is a great deal about myself that I should never have learned if I'd not gone to London, and very dear friends I should never have known. I spoke as I did to give you peace, to let you know that I don't blame you for sending me away. A measure of good was done, despite what I suffered, longing for you, and what you suffered here alone at Kerlain. But perhaps, in its own way, it was the best possible fate that could have befallen us, Diana."

"No," she retorted angrily. "Nothing could have been more awful. Three years in hell could hardly have been worse." The words were petulant and foolish, and Diana felt hot with embarrassment for sounding so childish. Especially when he'd clearly enjoyed himself so fully in London and suffered very little.

"I know," he said gently. She felt his mouth feather along her cheek, the side of her neck. "I know, love. I'm sorry that you were so alone and had Patterson to deal with. That especially." His lips found her ear and began, with great care, to press small, light kisses there. Diana drew in a sharp breath. "Forgive me for putting you through such wretchedness. For losing Kerlain in the first place. Can you, Diana?"

"I want to," she whispered. "It's hard to think at all when you're doing that, Lad." She took hold of his face in her hands, pulling his lips from where they were kissing her shoulder, and made him look at her. "How do I know if I can believe you? You're a stranger to me. I'm as much as a stranger to you."

"Then let's strive to know each other again," he said. "I must go out riding, to see what changes have taken place at Kerlain and to make certain that all is well. Come with me, Diana. Please."

His tone was so gentle and pleading, as if he feared being rejected by her yet again. Diana was not proof against it, but she was so very afraid to give way. How could she live through anything like the past three years and not go mad? She'd have nothing left if he abandoned her again. Nothing of herself; nothing worth living for.

Pulling free, she turned and moved a few steps away. The silence that stretched between them was loud enough to deafen all else.

Still turned from him, Diana gathered all her courage and put forth the question she was most afraid of. Not accusing him of the sin now, but asking, so fearfully.

"Are you going to leave Kerlain again, Lad?"

He moved up behind her and set his hands lightly on Diana's shoulders.

"You ask the wrong question, Diana," he murmured, his mouth very close to her ear. "I will leave Kerlain again . . . but I will never again leave you. For the remainder of your days, whether you wish it or not, you will have me at your side. No day will dawn, or night fall, that you will be rid of me. I fear you must resign yourself to it. Even if you should try to send me away, I'll not go."

She reached up a hand to grasp one of his own, tightly, and closed her eyes.

"Swear it to me," she whispered, horrified at how desperate and pleading she sounded.

His grip upon her shoulder tightened, and he pressed nearer against her. "I swear it on my own soul. On the graves of my parents and brother and uncle. On the love I bear you, Diana. If you ask me to stand here the day long and make vows, I will gladly do it. The day long, through the night, and for as many days and nights as it may take to let you know that I speak the truth. Only tell me what you desire, love, and I will do it."

She opened her eyes, blinking tears, and gave a watery laugh.

"What I desire . . . is that you share a meal with me by the lake, once we've finished our ride about Kerlain."

He lowered his mouth to touch the bare skin beneath her ear. Diana drew in a breath at the soft pleasure of the caress. His lips moved sweetly, kissing, and he murmured, "A picnic?"

"Y-yes," she managed, tilting her head to allow his wandering mouth greater access. "I shall help the cook you sent from London to prepare it . . . to make certain it pleases you."

"I need no sustenance other than your sweet company, Diana. But a picnic would please me as well." She felt him smiling against her skin, and then he lifted his head, dropping a kiss on her hair. "With the greatest pleasure, my lady, I shall do your bidding. But let us go and ready ourselves. There is much to do before this day finds its end."

Chapter Twenty-five

"I'm ready for a rest, aren't you, my love?"

Diana set her hands on Lad's shoulders and let him lift her down from her saddle. She had been riding Maeva, a very great treat after so many years, but she agreed fully with her husband. She was weary and hungry and so astonished by all that happened since they'd ridden out from the castle that she very much needed a rest.

"Yes, thank you," she murmured as he set her on her feet. She smiled up at him and he smiled back, sliding his hands to her waist and drawing her near.

"I'm also very hungry," he said, lowering his mouth to her own. "But first I must sate my need for you. It is far more elemental."

"It is certainly far more demanding, sir," she whispered against his lips, though shyly, still trying to come to know this strange new man who had returned in the place of her dear, familiar Lad. But his kiss was very pleasant, and Diana did not turn him aside.

His hands moved over her restlessly, caressing, pulling her more tightly to himself. Her bonnet came undone and fell to the ground, and Diana put her arms about his shoulders, going up on her toes to be closer to him.

It was a long while before he brought the embrace to an end, doing so very slowly and gently. He pressed his forehead against hers, his breath falling rapidly on her cheek. A few moments passed as they both calmed.

"I don't want to stop, but if we don't"—he pulled back, touching his nose to hers—"we'll end up with a great deal of dirt on our clothes."

Diana almost didn't care but gave way, knowing that he was right. To return to the castle with heavily stained clothing would have caused quite a sensation among their very unusual staff. Many of the servants Lad had sent from London were so far from being of the usual, and properly trained, sort that they had no compunction at all in speaking their minds not only quite openly but also quite loudly. Apart from that, Lad had left instructions with Swithin to have their lunch delivered to them at the lake by no later than two of the clock. It was nearly that now, and Diana, though possessed of a stalwart nature, wasn't *that* adventuresome.

"You have a reprieve," she told him, moving away toward the lake with an elegant swaying of hips, glancing back to add, meaningfully, "for now."

His reaction pleased her no end. His eyes widened, his body stiffened, and he stared after her with a peculiar look that made her shiver with anticipation. *This* was much more like the Lad she knew and loved.

She sat on the grass beside the water in a pleasant, shady spot, while Lad tended to the horses. A few minutes later he joined her and promptly lay flat out, putting his head in her lap without an invitation and sighing wearily.

"I'm fagged," he said. "It's not yet half done, but this day has been exhausting."

Diana lifted one hand and began to lightly stroke her fingers through his gold-streaked hair. He closed his eyes and, like a great cat, stretched and murmured with great contentment.

"You certainly gave The Farrell and The Colvaney a start today."

Eyes still closed, he smiled. "Do you think so?"

"Oh, yes," she assured him. "I'm not quite certain who you are, my lord, but I believe it's your intention to be giving all of us many fits and starts. At least for a time, until you've brought to completion whatever scheme it is that you've set into motion."

"I can't think what you mean, my dear," Lad said innocently.

"Can't you? I think you must readily comprehend what I mean. This morning you set to work at once, dealing with Eoghan's footmen, then Eoghan himself, and then Maudie and Swithin and Stuart. And now you've felled the two mighty men of Kerlain—The Farrell and The Colvaney."

He chuckled. "The mighty men of Kerlain. Very biblical, Diana. But I had no thought of felling them, as you say. I only wanted to see how matters stand at Kerlain and how the changes that I requested be made during my absence have progressed. So far, I'm very pleased."

Yes, he had seemed to be so, Diana thought, but the same could not be said of The Farrell and The Colvaney.

She and Lad had ridden out from the castle to find the two men hard at work with a variety of sons, grandsons, and nephews in one of the fields, preparing it for planting. The assembled there had greeted the arrival of their lord after so long an absence in much the same manner as they'd greeted his original arrival more than three years earlier—with thinly veiled contempt.

But, just as he had done with Swithin and Maudie, Lad had deftly and quickly turned the matter about.

He was not the rough, uncertain American commoner who'd left Kerlain three years before. Now he was the Earl of Kerlain, in every sense of the word. Proud, in a way, but so polished in his dress, manner, and speech that it was impossible not to recognize his superiority. The Farrell and The Colvaney certainly took note after a few minutes of conversation. Lad made certain of it. When The Farrell began to complain about the herd of cows that had taken over a portion of what had always been planted fields, Lad, sitting atop his horse, gave the man a look of such grave surprise at being thus addressed by one of his tenants that The Farrell had fallen silent mid-sentence.

"Mister Fitzhurst has the charge of the cattle," Lad informed him. "If you have some complaint, you must take it up with him."

They were merely a few words, softly spoken, but the effect was immediate. The Farrell and The Colvaney exchanged startled glances, and The Farrell replied, almost respectfully, "Yes, m'lord."

"I'm pleased with the progress of the fields," Lad continued, casting a glance out over the area of land where two dozen men labored. "You have done well in my absence. I would inform you, however, that early next week Kerlain will have a steward."

"A steward!" The Colvaney exclaimed. "We've not had a steward fooling about in our business for more than fifteen years, and a good thing it's been too. We don't need some stranger to be coming here, by God, and trying to tell us what—"

"Your dwelling is your own," Lad interrupted him sternly, anger quite evident in his tone now. "No one will take it from you, Colvaney, or cause you to leave Kerlain for such boorish offenses as you choose to make. Indeed, there is no need for you to answer to any man while you are within the confines of your home and that small plot of land that you farm for your own needs. Every person on this estate will ever be assured of the same. But when you stand here upon *my* land, sir, and deign to work it, you *will* answer to my wishes as well as to those of the men I choose to oversee it. If you cannot do so, there are a multitude of others in this country who would be very glad to.''

He gave them no further chance to speak, but, gazing coldly down at them from the height of his steed, stated, ''David Moulton's brother, Edward, arrives on Friday. By Monday next he will be installed as steward of Kerlain. You are to present yourselves at the castle on Monday at ten o'clock to be introduced to him and have his instructions.'' He took up the reins of his steed. ''Good day to you.''

Diana had tried her best to meet the eyes of The Farrell and The Colvaney as she'd set Maeva into motion, following behind her husband, but they were far too stunned to take note of her. The Farrell's mouth was gaping wide as he stared after the departing Earl of Kerlain, and The Colvaney was deeply flushed and clearly most insulted. Diana didn't know whether to be angry at Lad for treating these men whom she had loved since childhood in such a mean and haughty manner—or secretly relieved that he had at last found the best way of managing them. She knew The Farrell and The Colvaney too well to doubt that they'd spend the rest of the day, and much of the evening, as they sat together with the men of their clans drinking beer, complaining heartily about the earl's unkind speech. But she also had no doubt that come Monday, they'd present themselves at the castle and behave in a far different manner. For a moment, Lad had sounded very much like his grandfather, the late earl, and this, despite all their objections, was what The Farrell and The Colvaney would think on most in the coming days.

Not that they would accept Lad so easily, after only one meeting, but it was a beginning in the right direction.

''So we are to have a steward,'' she said, running both hands through his thick, soft hair now.

He looked as if he was going to sleep but, eyes still closed, gave a sigh and said, ''Yes. Edward Moulton. David assures me he's fully suited to the task. They come from a good family, and all the children have been thoroughly educated. I asked David to take the position first, you know."

"No, did you?"

He turned onto his side, getting more comfortable before replying, "Yes. I don't want to lose his good services once the castle is done, but he doesn't wish to work as a steward, and I can only think of enough additions to the castle to keep him busy for another four or five years. After that, I imagine we'll have to show our gratitude by setting him up in his own office and allowing other fortunate estates to command his talents."

"It would be very good of you to set him up in his own business," Diana said. "He's been a great help to me since the day he arrived at Kerlain. And all of his men as well. There were many times when I almost felt as if they'd come to keep an eye on me, rather than simply rebuild the castle."

At this, Lad opened his eyes. "I have a confession to make," he said. "One of many, in truth."

She looked at him curiously. "Yes?"

"David and his men were sent here, in the main, to be my spies. To make certain that all was well and also to protect you from Eoghan Patterson. Rebuilding the castle was the convenient excuse I used to make them acceptable to you."

Diana nearly shoved him off her lap but did not. Instead, she gaped at him with incredulity and demanded, "You did what?" Her fingers unwittingly curled in his hair, nearly pulling several strands out.

Lad reached up to still her hands and then to draw them down to hold against his chest.

"It was meant only to keep you and Kerlain safe, Diana, never to give you insult. Although I admit that, not having had any letters from you despite the many I had written, I had begun to worry that you might be falling in love with your dear childhood friend—yes, despite everything he'd done to us both. He's a charming, handsome fellow, after all, and you were alone here.''

She was very little appeased by this.

''You didn't trust me,'' she stated baldly, feeling a complete fool now as she realized that David Moulton and his men had been watching her so closely.

Slowly, Lad sat up, still holding her hands.

''We had not known each other long before I left for London,'' he said. ''After so many months of envisioning my beautiful wife alone and very angry with me—or so I assumed by your silence—yes, I began to think I did not know you.'' He searched her eyes. ''Did you not begin to think the same of me? You say that you wrote but had none of my letters. And without having the explanations I'd written, all that foolish nonsense in the London papers surely must have seemed most damning. Indeed, I know it was. You will not look me full in the face and claim, then, Diana, that you trusted me?''

''No,'' she admitted, much of her heated indignation flown. ''I'll not. I will even admit—though not happily, mind you—that if I could have had a spy in London, I'd have set him upon you at once.'' She jerked her hands free and rose to her feet. ''I'm filled with fury every time I think of those horrid newspapers, and I would be glad never to be reminded of them again.'' She turned away and walked down to the water's edge.

Behind her, she heard Lad sighing and lumbering up to his feet. A few moments later he stood beside her.

''Then you understand why I sent David and his men. I think I must tell you the full of it, for you must have wondered at the business David had so often in Woebley.''

Diana glanced at him. ''I did. I suppose now you will tell me he was meeting there with you, to deliver his report.''

''Yes,'' he admitted. ''Just so.''

"I see." Diana was hurt by the knowledge that he'd so often been but miles apart from her and hadn't made any attempt to either see or even speak to her. But she had no right to be angered, she knew. She had told him, in the severest manner possible, that he wasn't to come to Kerlain until he had all the money to repay Eoghan with. He could not have come to her even if he'd wished it. "Well," she said, "I suppose I must console myself with the knowledge that you were able to tear yourself away from your life in London to make certain that all was well here. But look," she said, turning away again when he would have spoken, "here are the footmen, just arrived with our lunch. You did say that you were hungry, did you not, my lord?"

They said not another word to each other as the footmen laid out their meal, spread upon a blanket near the water. Lad dismissed the servants as soon as the chore was finished, asking them to return in two hours to collect the remains of the meal.

When they were alone, Diana sat down on the blanket and began to fill a plate for Lad. He spread himself out more indolently on the other side, propped up on one elbow, and accepted the plate with pleasure.

As he began to eat, he said, "I told you this morning that I'd relate my tale of Sir Geoffrey Vear, of how I came to know him and what he did for me in London. I think this may also help you to understand how the London papers came to write so many damning lies. Would you like to hear the tale?"

Diana, filling her own plate, was still suffering the effects of her pique at discovering Lad and David Moulton's deceit and replied in chilly tones, "If you wish to tell me." She didn't look at him as she began to eat but cast her glance out over the lake, determined not to appear as if she cared at all about what he said.

But this pretense did not last very long. Before he finished telling her of how Sir Geoffrey and Lloyd had rescued him from near death after he'd been robbed, Diana's gaze had riveted upon him and she scarcely knew what she ate. By the time he'd recounted his first experience at the gaming tables, she'd put her plate aside and scooted even nearer to listen. Indeed, so enrapt did his tale hold her that she made only one comment, when Lad revealed that Miss Christabella Howell was, in truth, Sir Geoffrey's daughter, and that this was the reason for his great attentiveness to her.

"Oh, Lad," she murmured. "I am greatly relieved."

He grinned and refilled her wineglass with the cold champagne they'd been drinking.

"I realize how different the London newspapers made the matter sound," he said, "but Sir Geoffrey begged that I not only allow the misunderstanding but even encourage it, for the sake of his daughter."

"Oh, of course, and you did right in doing so," Diana told him. "Though it was hellish for me, how much worse for Miss Howell if the truth of her parentage had been revealed and therefore the reason for your attentions. No, I understand perfectly now. Poor Sir Geoffrey. How difficult this must have been for him. But how very glad he must have been to have your help in seeing his daughter well settled."

Lad reached out to take her hand and drew it to his lips. He kissed her fingers, then smiled and tugged her forward, leaning to kiss her full on the mouth.

"More times than once, I wished that Sir Geoffrey might know you, Diana. He would have loved you very well. And you would have liked him a great deal, I think."

"He saved your life," she murmured, setting her fingers to his cheek and stroking lightly, "and he made it possible for you to earn the money we needed to regain our estate. For this alone, I think him a very fine man indeed. But tell me, what happened after you fought with Viscount Severn over his mistaken thoughts regarding you and Miss Howell? Did you truly come to blows in the very midst of White's? The newspapers would have it that you broke all the glasses!''

"Not quite all," Lad said, "but enough. And most of them shattered on my head. Wulf did a very thorough job of making his displeasure known. After we became friends, he spent whole hours at a time apologizing for it, until I had to beg him to be quiet."

He told her of the never-ending nights of gaming, which he'd come to detest with all his heart, and of the wagers Sir Geoffrey had tutored him in making. Sir Geoffrey's good instruction didn't end with merely making Lad into a proper gentleman and teaching him how to be a gamester; he also imparted a wealth of wisdom about English society in particular and life in general.

"I've known many fine, intelligent men," he said, stretching out on the blanket as he had earlier done, making himself comfortable. "My father and Uncle Hadley. My Uncle Philip. But Sir Geoffrey—to learn from him was an honor I can't put into words. He was as a second father to me, Diana. Just as my first father taught me to be who I was in the United States, Sir Geoffrey taught me how to be what I am now. In many ways, it was like being reborn."

He told of how Sir Geoffrey's consumption had grown worse until, at the end, he was coughing up blood with almost every breath. Lad and Lloyd began taking turns supporting Sir Geoffrey's shoulders as he lay in bed, holding him up so that he could breathe until the very end came. They were both with him, and as he recounted the moment, Diana's eyes filled with tears.

"If I could have done so," Lad said quietly, fingering his wineglass, "I would have had him buried with all the grandeur and honor that he deserved. But he had made us promise that there would be no funeral, no notice put in the papers, nothing that would draw attention to his passing. He had cut himself off entirely from the *ton* during his life, for Christabella's sake, and had no desire to embrace it again after his death. But it was very hard to keep that promise, Diana. So very hard. He deserved so much better.'' He shook his head at the memory.

''It was impossible for us to stay in Stratton Street afterward,'' he continued after a silent moment. ''Too many memories, and far too expensive. Sir Geoffrey had easily afforded the rooms, having put away quite a fortune during his years of gaming, but every penny that I earned was precious to me. Apart from that my needs, and Lloyd's, were far from being so fashionable save when it was absolutely necessary. We moved to a set of rooms that were somewhat less grand, though still respectable enough to be able to hold the occasional card party with a few gentlemen friends. Jack Sommerton was a frequent guest.'' He smiled at Diana. ''He hated the rooms but preferred them to spending his nights in gaming hells.''

''As you did,'' she murmured.

''Yes,'' he agreed with feeling. ''Very much so.''

He'd had some amazing adventures during his years in Town, especially once his beautiful but unbridled American cousin Gwendolyn Wells had arrived in London. Once he'd had to help rescue both her and Lad's friend, the Earl of Rexley, in the dark of night from one of the town's most evil and notorious rookeries.

He described how Lord Rexley had fallen in love with the flame-headed Gwendolyn and consequently married her. This, Diana told him, she already knew from the papers, and with hesitation she related the pain it had given her, knowing that she'd been so excluded from his life that his relatives hadn't even invited her to such an important family event.

"Oh, my love," he said tenderly, reaching up to kiss her. "You were not alone in your feelings. Gwennie rang a peal over my head, you may believe," he said, "but I had sworn both her and my uncle Philip to complete secrecy, even before they journeyed to England." He gently squeezed her hand. "You understand, don't you, love? Even after Sir Geoffrey had died, I couldn't expose Bella to any manner of speculation. Not until she was safely wed."

"Yes, of course I understand it now. But what will happen when it's discovered that you *are* wed? Once the London newspapers discover the truth, won't it cause a great sensation?"

"Nothing can touch Bella now. People will shake their heads and believe that she dallied with a married man before she took Wulf as a husband—and I shall be labeled a cad who left his wife alone in the countryside while he enjoyed himself in London. But this is so common amongst noblemen that even I shall escape any dire censure. The truth of it is, my love, that I have a much greater fear of being called a complete fool. When I take you to London, as I intend to do next season, your beauty will confound the *ton* so greatly that it will be wondered at how any sane man, let alone your own husband, could leave you for even a day."

"Take me . . . to London?" Diana repeated, much stunned.

He smiled in his singularly beguiling way. "Yes, Diana. To London. We shall go once each year, even if for a few weeks. You will have clothes made—all the newest fashions—and meet others of your station, and have a wonderful time at parties and balls. And, of course, I shall then understand what poor Wulf suffered when Bella was so greatly admired by so many men, for you will be far more admired and flirted with, and I shall probably have to call out a dozen of your suitors every week."

He was smiling and clearly meant this as a jest, but Diana could feel nothing but the deepest distress.

"I can't—Lad, I couldn't possibly go to London," she told him with utter conviction. "Please, don't speak of it further. I'm sorry if you wish it so much. Perhaps you might go once a year." The thought made her want to weep. She cast about desperately for some other compromise but could think of nothing.

"Diana," he murmured, trying to draw her nearer.

She resisted, shaking her head.

"I've never been out of Herefordshire," she said. "At least, not since I was very small. I don't know anything of grand society, save what Eoghan and my godfather told me of it—and Eoghan, I confess, was truly the only one who said much in detail." She shut her eyes and lowered her head. "My knowledge of fashion and proper manners is shameful. Once I thought myself so far above your own understanding of such things and tried to bring you up to it—you know the truth of this full well. But now you outshine me in every possible way. I could be nothing but an embarrassment to you."

"My love, this hardly matters," he said, sounding clearly amused. Diana felt his fingers on her chin but refused to lift her head even at his urging. "You will learn, just as I did, how easy it is to take on the outer form that is so acceptable to society. It's foolish in many ways—do you not think I wish to be wearing the manner of clothes that came with me from America? Gad, they were a thousand times more comfortable than these ridiculous garments I'm wearing now. But to please society is everything in England, or at least to give the *appearance* of pleasing, as Sir Geoffrey ever told me. Diana, please, love." He pulled her into his arms, though she still resisted. "Don't distress yourself. I'll be with you, and so will Gwennie and Bella and Lady Clara— and even Lady Anna, whose acquaintance will give you the greatest consequence among the ladies of the *ton*. Her husband, the Earl of Manning, is one of the most powerful men in the House of Lords.''

''No!'' This thought horrified Diana even more greatly. She covered her face with both hands. ''Oh, please, no, Lad. They'll only laugh at how utterly stupid I am. If your cousin Gwendolyn and her husband should come to visit us at Kerlain, I'd be most happy to receive them. At least I should have some idea of how to go on in my own home. But in London—oh, please don't make me go! I can't even dance.''

He had the nerve to laugh. Diana uncovered her face long enough to strike his rocklike shoulder with one hand, imparting little damage. Then she covered her face again, and he laughed all the harder.

''No, I'll not have it,'' he told her as he gently, but firmly, pulled her hands away. ''You could never be anything but my greatest delight, Diana Walker. Come here. No hiding, now or ever.''

She knew her face was full red as he pulled her straight onto his lap, holding her closely.

''I will teach you to dance,'' he said, ''as I had to learn myself from a tutor in London, in such a foolishly proper manner as the *ton* insists upon. And I'll teach you how to get on in society, just as Sir Geoffrey taught me. My love,'' he said consolingly when she groaned, ''it is not so hard as it seems. And it is your right and duty, as the Countess of Kerlain, to take your place among the *ton*.''

''I can be the countess here,'' she said woefully, ''but nowhere else. Not even at Fair Maiden, though I would strive very hard never to embarrass you, especially there.''

''You will be the countess everywhere you go,'' he told her, ''no matter where it may be. And in London, I'll be with you every moment, just as Sir Geoffrey was with me, until you feel comfortable enough to go about on your own—though in London, of course, it must be with a maid or an acquaintance. But until you're ready, I'll be beside you. I give you my promise.''

He kissed her, then pressed his cheek to hers and held her tightly. ''It's so good to feel you in my arms again, Diana. To hear your voice. Just to see you even at a distance.'' She felt him smile against her hair. ''I never thought I'd understand what you felt for Kerlain—perhaps I never truly will. But one thing I do know. It's a part of you, and because of that it's precious to me. It's my home because you're here, Diana. Our home, for the rest of our lives.''

''What of Fair Maiden?'' she asked. ''I know how greatly you love it, how you long to return there. I . . . I told you that I could never leave England, but that's not entirely true. If you want to return to the United States, even for a very long visit, I'll be happy to go with you.''

''Thank you,'' he said softly, and tilted her chin up to kiss her again. ''That means a great deal to me, love. I know it's not an easy offer for you to make. Even facing the terrors of London would be an easier thing than for you to leave Kerlain for long. But you need not fear having to leave it to journey to America. I've sold Fair Maiden.''

Diana pushed away and stared at him. *''Sold—''* Horrified, she shook her head. ''Oh, Lad. Not because of the wager? Oh, my God.'' She covered her lips with trembling fingers. ''Oh, God, *no.*''

''Darling, don't be so distressed!'' he said quickly. ''It doesn't matter now. I needed the money for a gambling stake. A man needs something to begin with, you know. Without it, we'd never have regained Kerlain. With it, we not only have the estate back but enough money to rebuild the castle and live here in a proper manner.''

''But it was your home,'' she said mournfully, ''and you

loved it so. Your father and mother and brother and uncle—all your memories of them are there.''

"No," he said, taking her hand and placing it against his heart. "My memories of them are in here, where they belong. And Fair Maiden is my past. I'm a British nobleman now and my future is only with you, Diana, wherever that may be. I have no regrets for the decision I made. No regrets at all, because, having you, I've gained so much more than I've lost.''

They returned to the castle an hour later, sated and weary in a contended, happy way. Stable hands appeared to take their horses, and not for the first time did Diana notice how gladly the servants who'd arrived from London greeted their master.

"Kerlain is so different now," she murmured as Lad set her hand upon his arm to lead her into the castle.

"Different in a good way, I hope?"

"Yes," she said. "I don't think I ever would have thought it possible for anything—or anyone—new to make Kerlain better, but each man and woman whom you sent from London has made Kerlain complete in a way that I only used to dream of. Not that everyone feels as I do," she added with a sigh. "Swithin and Maudie were furious about what they believe is an invasion of outsiders, and I hardly need tell you how the Farrell and Colvaney clans feel.''

"I hope," Lad said as they made their way up the castle stairs toward the doors, "that they feel rather intimidated. Perhaps even threatened. Kerlain has a long, noble history, but the old ways here had brought nothing but a stagnation that eventually would have ushered in the end of the estate altogether. Or that was Sir Geoffrey's theory, anyhow," he admitted with a sheepish smile. The castle doors were opened by a footman to admit them, a seamless performance worthy of the staff of any great London town house. "He said," Lad continued, handing his hat and gloves to another waiting footman as Diana allowed her cloak and bonnet to be removed by a maid, "that only an infusion of the new would bring life back to Kerlain. And I do believe he was right." He took her elbow and began to lead her toward the great hall. "By the way, the new cook is wonderful, don't you think? I've had only two meals prepared at her hands and am very pleased. I'm looking forward to seeing—"

Lloyd appeared from out of nowhere, as was his habit.

"About time you showed up. Eat enough to feed the whole bloody army, did you?"

"Lloyd," Lad muttered, but Diana laughed behind her hand.

"Well, never mind," the manservant continued. "Come and see what's arrived. Swithin's waiting."

He walked toward Lad's study, waving a hand for them to follow. Inside the study were a darkly unhappy Swithin, The Farrell, and his son, Stuart. On Lad's desk sat a large pile of letters, tied together with twine in messy packets. Lad and Diana wordlessly approached the desk together, staring at the sight. The letters were clearly unopened but were in a filthy condition, as if they'd been covered by dirt or even mud.

"He brought them to me but an hour past," The Farrell stated. "I knew nothing of it, or he'd not have gone on with it—no matter what I think of you, my lord. It's not much for a man to say, but it's the truth, and so it is."

"Aye, Farrell," Lad said, still staring at the letters, reaching out to touch one. "I know it is. Your word will not be questioned by me, now or ever."

"Oh, Stuart," Diana murmured with disbelief. "How could you have done such a thing?" She looked at him with wide, tear-filled eyes. "You knew how I longed for a letter from Lord Kerlain. I sent you to Walborough so often. . . . I *trusted* you.''

Stuart had been crying quietly, but now he began to weep out loud, sobbing wretchedly like a child. ''He told me I was saving you from a terrible thing,'' he cried, ''and Kerlain too, and made it sound so right and good. He told me Lord Kerlain was never coming back. That he'd abandoned all of us, Miss Diana.'' Wiping a dirty sleeve across his face, he sniffled and gave a sob. ''I'm so sorry, miss. So sorry.''

''Oh, Stuart,'' she whispered sorrowfully.

''Viscount Carden paid you to intercept these missives,'' Lad said, ''and must clearly have had his hand in paying the post rider to forget having seen those that I wrote to Lady Kerlain. He was able to stop all communication between Lady Kerlain and myself save those few missives that were more directly delivered. But Lord Carden must have also asked that you destroy these letters, Stuart. He's far too cunning a man to take a chance that you might not do so. Yet here they are. How do you explain this?''

''I did burn some, my lord,'' Stuart told him, sniffling and wiping his face. ''He came to see me do it. It looked a great pile of paper, but that was only from the top. Beneath it was only wood shavings, my lord. The rest of the letters were already safe. Buried.''

Diana moved to stand in front of him, reaching out to touch his arm. ''Why didn't you destroy them, Stuart? You must have known what Lord Carden would do to you if he discovered you'd kept any.''

Stuart nodded. ''Yes, miss. But they were *your* things, and I couldn't bring myself to burn them.''

''Stuart,'' Lad said more gently, ''I'm going to ask you about another matter, separate from the letters, and I want you to tell me the truth. You were helping Lord Carden even before I left for London. The afternoon that I received the letter telling of my uncle's death, you were in the room, and you later told Carden what you'd heard and about the quarrel between Lady Kerlain and myself. Am I right? He came after me that night knowing full well the kind of state I'd be in, ready to take advantage of it—because you'd told him something that he never would have discovered for himself otherwise.''

"Yes, my lord,'' Stuart admitted, his face filled with shame. ''He wanted to know everything, especially about all the letters you had from the States. It's . . . it's my fault you ever had to go away at all.'' He began to weep again.

"No, my lord,'' Swithin said, stepping forward, ''the fault is mine. I often spoke openly of my disdain for you and did whatever I could to encourage Lord Carden in his plans. I truly had no knowledge that he'd paid Stuart to steal Lady Kerlain's letters and to keep yours from her, but my feeling and behavior clearly influenced the young man. I pray, my lord, that you will let me take whatever punishment you deem worthy of giving Stuart. Even if it should be to . . . to quit Kerlain.''

Lloyd, who stood just inside the closed door, looked at Swithin with new respect.

"No,'' The Farrell said tautly, pulling himself up. ''Stuart is a Farrell and will take his punishment as a Farrell would do. Only in this way can he remove the shame he's brought on our family name. If he must leave Kerlain,'' The Farrell said with a determination that ill-hid the pain he felt at saying such words, ''then he will go, and not so much as turn his face back toward us.''

Lad appeared to consider this, setting his hands behind his back and frowning in thought for several long moments. At last, he nodded and looked at the assembled.

"If he goes, Farrell,'' he said, ''he'll not have the chance to redeem himself. And this is what I ask of him—to repay and redeem. He must make up for this grievous crime, and his debt is great. My lady and I suffered much because of this lack of communication." He looked at Stuart with measured anger. "It will be difficult, but if you do as I ask, you can redeem yourself."

"Anything, my lord," Stuart said eagerly, wiping his wet face once more. "Ask anything of me."

"I must say again that it will be no easy matter, for it requires continuing your deception with Lord Carden."

"*Continuing* it?" Diana repeated.

"Yes, certainly," Lad said easily. "Eoghan Patterson and I have joined in a game, and as any good player would do, I desire to be kept apprised of my opponent's every move. Only those whom he trusts will be aware of what his plans are, and so we will play this game deep. His spies will be my spies. And in this manner," Lad said with a smile, "Lord Carden and I will now be well matched."

Still, I think I must say that the cattle will continue to be Kerlain's most profitable product until then. Unless the apple orchards recover more quickly than we think they may, of course."

"The cattle have been a blessing indeed," Lad admitted, "but I think, if we want to keep the Farrell and Colvaney clans on Kerlain land, where they rightly belong and where we could not get on without them, then we'd best not crow too loudly over the fact."

He exchanged a knowing look with Edward, who nodded his agreement of this. Together, they turned back toward the road where their horses awaited.

Three months had passed since he'd returned to Kerlain, and Lad considered himself the most complete and contented man on God's earth. How different everything was from when he'd first lived here! The entire estate seemed reborn, revitalized, and the people of Kerlain as contented as Lad himself was. The newcomers had slowly but surely fitted themselves into the ways of those who'd been here for generations, and several marriages among the two groups had already taken place. Better yet, many more were planned. Half of the ex-soldiers who'd come to Kerlain with David Moulton had taken wives from among the Farrell and Colvaney clans, and many of the London maids had likewise found husbands. Braen Colvaney had only a week earlier been married to a pretty girl whom Sir Geoffrey had rescued from a life of prostitution on the London docks. Braen's father, The Colvaney, had fought the marriage tooth and nail, until the wedding day, when he suddenly declared the girl to be as his daughter and kissed and wept over her. Rumor had it that Braen had already gotten his bride with child, which endeared her immensely to his stoic father. The addition of more Colvaneys to the clan was always welcome to him, especially when no less than five young women in the Farrell clan were with child—a fact that The Farrell gloated over as often and as openly as he possibly could.

Before spring came next year, Kerlain would greet the arrival of several new additions. One of these, Lad thought, feeling that sense of deep joy that the knowledge ever produced, would be his own. Diana had been with child for nearly a month now, and nothing, Lad believed, could have been happier news to either of them.

Though perhaps Diana might have been even happier if she'd not been so ill of late. The child made her sick in the mornings—also in the afternoons, evenings, and all during the night. Lad stayed with her as much as Diana would allow, mainly for his own reassurance in seeing her as comfortable as possible. But Diana didn't always want him there. Once or twice, following a particularly unpleasant bout of nausea, she'd relieved her ire on Lad with great vehemence, astonishing him with her command of the more objectionable parts of the English language. She could have put Lloyd to the blush, and that was not easily done.

Lad bore such abuse as patiently as he could. After all, he reasoned, it was his fault that she was suffering so horribly, and there was little else he could do to relieve it.

As to Viscount Carden, they'd seen nothing more of him since the day of Lad's return, at least not formally. Lad kept a close eye on him in several different ways, mainly through Stuart Farrell. Eoghan seemed not to have yet realized that the young man had changed sides, but, then, Stuart was so continuously shy and bumbling, just as he'd always been, that Lad could hardly blame anyone for thinking him incapable of deception. Through him, Lad knew that Carden was planning some manner of revenge upon Kerlain, but as of yet no definite plans had been discussed. Viscount Carden, Stuart told Lad, spent a great deal of time saying that Lady Kerlain had been unfairly taken from him—most unfairly, and that such an insult could never be borne.

Lad knew that the day must soon come when the game they were joined in had its final conclusion. Until it was over and done with, neither of them would have any peace. To force matters, Lad made a habit of sending his neighbor short, friendly notes every few days, saying such things as, "Have you had any good hunting of late?" and, "We must go down to the lake again sometime soon," and, "I've a new deck of cards brought from London; when next we meet, we must indulge ourselves in a hand or two of *poque.*"

It was dangerous to taunt a man who was already so clearly overwrought, but such was the manner of playing any game. It took patience to win; to prod one's opponent into losing that patience and making a foolish move was often a necessary gambit. He had no intention of spending the rest of his life as a neighbor to Eoghan Patterson. Not only for his sake but for Diana's and that of their future children he must secure far greater peace than Viscount Carden's presence would allow.

"Look, my lord." Edward Moulton lifted one hand in the direction of Walborough. "Here come two riders."

Lad gazed at the approaching figures, frowning slightly. "Indeed, there are. I wonder who——" He fell silent as they neared the road and as the gentlemen on horseback drew nearer. Then his face broke into a smile, and he stepped forward to greet the newcomers. "God's mercy, this is a grand surprise! Jack! Lucky!"

The two gentlemen brought their horses to a stop and slid down from their saddles. Soon the three men were laughing and shaking hands and clapping each other on the back. Lad should have known who they were right away, he thought, so distinctively different was their coloring. Like salt and pepper, they were, Jack being so blond and fair and Lucky as dark and swarthy as a Mediterranean pirate—which was just what he behaved like, much of the time.

"So this is your grand estate, Lad," Lucky Bryland, Viscount Callan, said, casting his gaze about. "I can understand why you were so anxious to return to it. Very pleasant, indeed. I never could have imagined you being lord of so fine a place."

"By gad, yes," Jack Sommerton, the Earl of Rexley, agreed. "We're all amazement, seeing Kerlain at last. London's most accomplished gambler is, in fact, a true and landed nobleman. And what's this, Lucky? He's even out overseeing his crops. Why, it appears that the Earl of Kerlain is really a farmer at heart."

They laughed and Lad said, "What more do you expect from an American farmer? But what the devil are you two doing here? I hadn't any idea you were coming."

Jack shrugged. "We should have sent warning. It was unpardonable of us not to do so. But our decision to visit you came about rather suddenly, and we could only hope that we'd be welcomed."

"Of course, always," Lad assured them. "I only wish you'd brought Clara and Gwennie as well. Or was that the point of the whole journey?"

In response to this, Jack sighed and looked very happy; Lucky clearly strove to be patient.

"I received a letter from Lady Rexley," he explained, "begging me to relieve her of her husband for a few weeks. She was ready to kill him."

"She's expecting our first child," Jack announced in ecstatic tones. "It's the most wonderful thing."

"Indeed," Lucky agreed, "save that he's driving his poor wife insane with his meddling. He won't let her walk two steps but that he picks her up and carries her. When I arrived at Rexley Hall, Gwennie nearly wept with gratitude and begged me to take him away at once. Kerlain was the closest place I could think of."

Jack was instantly affronted. "I was *not* meddling. But

it's my child as well as hers. I have a say in how she cares for herself, do I not?''

"She can't lie about in bed all day," Lucky told him.

"Of course she can."

"*No one* wants to lie about in bed all day," Lucky argued. "Let alone a pregnant woman. I've been through this twice already with Clara. I don't know why you won't believe me when I say that a pregnant woman must *always* have her way if you have any hope of surviving the ordeal intact."

"Well, I don't care *what* Gwen wants," Jack retorted indignantly. "I'll not have her racing about hither and yon and juggling my baby every which way. It's indecent. And exhausting for the baby. No," he stated firmly. "I'll not have it. Gwen will simply stay in bed for the next seven months and rest, and that's that."

"Gad," Lucky muttered.

Lad laughed. "I can see why Gwennie wrote to you, Lucky, and can only wonder at how you wrestled Jack off his estate. But this is indeed wonderful news. My sincerest congratulations, Jack."

"I hope you don't mind us intruding upon you so suddenly and without warning, Lad," Lucky said. "I pray we've not come at an unfortunate time?"

"Never," Lad assured them. "I'm exceedingly glad to see the both of you. If I told you how much, it would swell up your already overlarge egos."

They laughed, and Lucky said, "We missed your company too, especially since you left London so quickly, with hardly a word to anyone."

"But more than that," Jack added, "we're curious about this wife you've kept secret for so long. Imagine how we felt when Gwen told us you've been married all these years, and us never knowing it."

"You will meet my wife very shortly," Lad promised,

"but first, you may wish me happy as well. It appears that Jack and I will each have a child of a similar age."

They looked at him with surprise.

"Lady Kerlain is expecting?" Lucky asked. "This is very sudden, when you've only been back to Kerlain for three months."

Jack chuckled. "You can hardly be surprised, Lucky. Lad's a very thorough fellow, as we know only too well from the wagers we suffered at his hands. Congratulations to you, Lad."

"And to your good lady wife," Lucky added.

They were introduced to Edward Moulton after this, who had been waiting off to one side in silence, and expressed such a delight at meeting so promising a young man that the young man in question turned bright red and could hardly murmur his thanks.

"Come and see Kerlain," Lad said, mounting Maeva and waiting for his friends to follow suit in mounting their own steeds. "And then I'll take you to the castle. Diana will be exceedingly glad to meet the two of you, though there's no doubt she'll wonder at Wulf having been left out of this happy reunion."

"Oh, we would've gone to fetch him," Jack assured him happily. "But Bella is expecting—"

"Good lord, it's an epidemic!" Lad said, laughing.

"—and Wulf's in such a state that she's taking him off to Italy before he worries himself into an asylum. She's feeling perfectly well for it," he added, "and has decided it's the only way that she and Wulf will survive the pregnancy."

Lad gave them a brief tour of Kerlain, over which they exclaimed with some amazement. Edward Moulton left them when they came to the acres where the cattle were, explaining that he wished to speak to Mr. Fitzhurst. Lad and the others stayed where they were for a time, looking out over the herds as they grazed in fields of green grass.

"Beautiful," Lucky said. "You've a fine land here, Lad. And seem content to be here."

"Yes," Lad replied, "more than I can tell you."

"You told me once that you'd been banished from paradise," Jack said. "Now I understand what you meant by it."

Lad grinned. "You're crazed if you think I meant a bunch of cows and some trees and hills and rocks," he said. "Oh, I'm fond of Kerlain, never doubt it. But once you've met my lady, Diana, you'll truly understand."

"Then you'd best take us to her, my friend," Jack said. "We're awash with all impatience."

Acquiescing, Lad led the way.

The reaction they had to their first sight of Castle Kerlain pleased Lad no end. Both men pulled their horses to a halt and stared for some time, and then proclaimed themselves amazed.

"Magnificent," Jack murmured.

"It must cost a fortune to maintain," Lucky said more practically. "But it would be a fortune well spent. I've seen many a fine example of Britain's noble history, but this is certainly among the finest."

"Thank you," Lad said. "The first I saw it, I thought it quite the greatest wreck I'd ever seen. If either of you had offered me a hundred pounds, I'd have given you the deed with a glad heart. It hasn't been until very recently that I've seen the castle—indeed, all of Kerlain—for what it is. And now I would not part with it for anything."

They had only reached the castle courtyard before they were met by Lloyd, who was on horseback, getting ready to ride out in search of his master.

"Why, it's the indubitable Lloyd," said Jack in greeting.

"I never thought I should be glad to see such a shady fellow again," added Lucky, "but there it is. Hello to you, Lloyd."

Lloyd gave them a look of pure exasperation in return, made no similar greeting, and set his attention on Lad.

"Have you seen her ladyship?" he demanded. "She left the castle with Maudie over an hour ago and hasn't yet returned."

"Left the castle?" Lad repeated, his eyes narrowing. "She was far too ill to go anywhere this morning. And I *told* you to keep an eye on her."

"I *know* that," Lloyd said impatiently. "And she wasn't feeling very grand when I saw her last either, but a message came from The Colvaney, asking her to hurry and help that gel that his son just married."

"Liddy, do you mean? Braen Colvaney's wife?"

"Aye, aye," Lloyd said, nodding. "Said she was bleeding and begged her ladyship to come right away to see what could be done to save the babe. I only just now read the note and saw that she was gone."

"Dammit, Lloyd!" Lad said furiously. "I told you *never* to let her leave the castle unless you went with her." Maeva moved restlessly at the tone of his voice, and he was obliged to settle her.

"Well I can't bloody well keep an eye on her when she bloody well tells me she's going to bed and then sneaks out of the bloody castle behind my back, can I?" Lloyd shouted back just as loudly. "I thought she was sleeping all this time, and who's to know with Maudie gone? If Swithin hadn't found the note and one of the maids admitted to seeing her go, we'd none of us know yet, would we?"

"I perceive," said Lucky in his usual languid manner, "that your wife is in some manner of difficulty, Lad?"

Lad shut his eyes, striving for calm, knowing he must be able to think clearly if he was to play this hand well. Eoghan Patterson had taken him by surprise—that was a move well played. But what Patterson couldn't have known by any means was that Lad now had surprises of his own to strengthen his play—in the form of Jack and Lucky.

He lifted his head and looked at his two waiting friends.

"Yes," he told them. "I haven't the time to explain the whole of it now, but I fear that she's in great danger."

"Well, then," said Jack. "It's a good thing we came when we did. Shall we set out to find Lady Kerlain at once?"

"It's not necessary that you help me," Lad said, "but I'd be grateful."

Lucky sighed. "My dear fellow, please don't speak of gratitude. I find it excessively tedious talk, especially among friends. Of *course* we're going to help you rescue your wife."

Lad smiled. "Thank you."

"Gad," Jack put in. "Let's be on our way already."

A clattering of horse hooves filled the air, and they turned to see Stuart Farrell riding full speed into the courtyard.

"My lord!" he cried out with relief. "Thank our merciful God you're here. He's taken Lady Kerlain—Lord Carden has—and you must come at once!"

Chapter Twenty-seven

"I realize that you have no care for such things," Diana said as the coach came to a dip in the road and lurched precariously, "but I will very likely soon be ill if we don't stop."

Eoghan, sitting on the seat opposite the one that Diana and Maudie occupied, looked at her with the usual smirk absent from his face.

"You'll feel much better soon."

"Here, my lady." Maudie pressed a cloth that she'd wet from a small flask of water gently onto Diana's brow. "Lean back and keep your eyes closed."

Diana leaned back but refused to close her eyes. Instead, she speared Eoghan with a frigid gaze.

"Where are we going?" she demanded, adding for the tenth time since they'd begun their journey, "You're a fool, Eoghan Patterson. Lad will tear you apart from head to toe when he finds us, and whatever's left of you will be tried and imprisoned for abduction."

"It won't matter," he said, his tone void of emotion. "He won't want you after today has ended. No man will—except me."

For once in her life, Diana hardly knew what to make of this man. When she'd walked into Braen and Liddy Colvaney's small cottage, expecting to find both of them there and Liddy in a desperate condition, she had instead discovered that the only occupants were Eoghan and a strange, rough-looking man. Almost before she could open her mouth to speak, the man had grabbed Maudie and held a knife to her throat, threatening to kill her if Diana made any attempt to scream or flee.

Eoghan had calmly assured Diana that the man was speaking the truth, and she had readily believed him. He'd given her no chance to speak but had taken her arm and forced her back out of doors to a small shed, where two horses had been hidden. Realizing that he meant to abduct her, Diana protested loudly, but none of her objections touched Eoghan; she could not even draw out any of his usual taunting or cruelty, which at least would have given her some kind of foothold toward managing him. There was only a stony mask, as if Eoghan weren't really there at all and had instead been overtaken by a cold, unknown spirit.

She'd demanded to know if Braen and Liddy were safe, and he'd looked at her oddly and replied, as if she should already know, "Of course they are. I only sent them away on a picnic—a very fine one, with all the best that my larder and cellar had to offer. They were most pleased to have a little holiday. It was a gift from me to celebrate their wedding. Late, certainly, but I had little choice in that, as I wasn't invited."

Diana had been made to ride with Eoghan, and Maudie with the stranger. They'd not taken the main road but went directly into the trees, riding for some time until they came out to a road again—far outside of Kerlain—where a coach, manned by yet another rough-looking stranger, awaited them.

Eoghan had directed her and Maudie to get into the coach, but the ride on horseback had undone Diana. She stumbled to the nearest bush and was violently ill. Eoghan waited only until she'd wiped her lips and caught her breath before picking her up and depositing her into the vehicle.

That had been half an hour ago, and Diana's nausea, only briefly relieved, had returned full force, mainly thanks to the poor quality of the road they had turned upon a distance ago as well as the driving abilities of the two strangers, who were certainly not skilled coachmen. And with her wretched queasiness had come an aggravation that was almost overwhelming in its intensity. Never mind letting Lad kill Eoghan; she'd do it herself, with her bare hands, at the very first opportunity.

"Try to sleep, Diana," Eoghan suggested.

She gave him a withering glare. "No. Lad will be coming after us soon, and I wouldn't want to miss the look on your face when first you see him."

He gave a faint smile. "He'll no doubt have gone in search of you, but I've taken care of making certain that he's sent in the wrong direction. Stuart Farrell will lead him in the wrong way—aye, your own Stuart. Lord Kerlain will not find you until it's too late, and by then you'll have decided to stay with me."

"Not in this lifetime," she told him, "or the next. Or, let me assure you, *ever.*"

The smile thinned. "We shall see, Diana, my love." The carriage began to slow and, with a rough, clumsy jerking, came to a halt. "Ah," he said. "We're here."

And just in time. The door opened and Diana hurriedly tumbled out, shoving away the hands that tried to help her and making for a nearby tree, losing what little contents remained in her stomach. In a moment Maudie was beside her, wiping her face and lips with the cool, wet cloth. Diana leaned against the tree, trembling and weak and striving mightily not to faint.

"Women," one of the strangers muttered. "Not worth the trouble they give."

"This one is," Eoghan said in the same toneless voice that had maddened Diana since they'd started their journey.

"And will be more so when she's no longer so ill from the brat she carries." He bent and lifted Diana in his arms, ignoring her weak efforts to resist him. "We'll have you better in a very short while, my love."

They had stopped near what appeared to be some kind of abandoned, ancient inn. The windows were empty of glass, and the roof was caved in on one side. Weeds, shrubs, and rampant ivy had overgrown most of the building, making it a thoroughly unpalatable prospect to enter. There were no other buildings in view, and the road they'd been on—more of a lane than a proper road—was empty of any other traffic. As Eoghan carried her past the tavern door, which had been forcibly torn from its hinges, Diana caught a glimpse of another vehicle to the side of the building—what appeared to be a small, dusty curricle.

Her senses swam with the movement of Eoghan's rapid strides, but the coolness and darkness of the building was a welcome relief. Somewhere in the distance she heard Maudie protesting—and then so suddenly silenced that Diana lifted her head and tried to look about.

"Where's Maudie? What have you done to her?"

"Nothing, my love," Eoghan said assuredly. "But she'll be upset with what's to come, and I'll need her to nurse you afterward. She's being kept outside in the carriage, that's all. Once it's all done, she'll be brought to you safely, I promise. Now, here we are."

"Once it's all done?" Diana repeated with growing dismay. He had walked into a small room—what must once have been a private parlor—where another man and a woman were waiting. The dim light of several candles cast the room—filthy with dust, cobwebs, and disuse—into eerie shadows.

"My lord, we had begun to think you'd never come," the man said nervously. "Please, we must be quick."

"Certainly," Eoghan said, kneeling down with such a

swift, swooping movement that Diana's senses reeled. Blackness descended heavily, and she struggled against it. There was a great deal of murmuring all around her, and she felt her clothing being loosened and her heavy skirts being raised.

"What . . ." she murmured, trying to lift her head.

"Shhh, love," Eoghan said, kneeling beside her. "Be still. It will be over within but a few moments." He stroked a hand over the top of her head.

"No," she said more strongly. "Leave me alone." She felt hands peeling off her half boots and pulling at her undergarments and with sudden clarity realized how much danger she was in.

Fear and desperation gave her strength, and she flung her arms out and kicked with her legs.

"Don't touch me!" she shouted furiously, managing to push Eoghan away enough to sit up. In the dim light, she saw the other man sitting down by her legs, blinking at her in some amazement. The woman was standing at a small nearby table, and Diana could see the glint of shining metal instruments in her hands as she laid them in some kind of order.

"Oh, God." The words fell out of Diana's mouth without thought, and the next moment she went mad, like a trapped animal, striking out blindly in every direction, scrambling to her feet with such clumsy, violent desperation that she fell twice, once right on top of Eoghan. His arms came about to hold her fast, but she took fistfuls of his hair in her hands and slammed his head upon the bare floor, evoking a shout of pain. It was enough. He released her and Diana gained her feet, running heedlessly for what she hoped was the door.

The other man was shouting, the woman was screaming, and the roar that came out of Eoghan was inhuman. The horrifying combination of sounds spurred Diana forward with such dread that she could scarce think. She only acted, wildly, made so much the worse by the weak, dizzy confusion of her mind.

Clawing at the handle, she managed to fling the door wide. The larger room beyond was much darker, lit only by whatever sunlight crept in past the growth-covered windows. Breathing harshly, she moved forward, stumbling, looking everywhere for the door or any way out.

"Maudie!" she cried out. *"Maudie!"*

She thought for a moment that she heard a faint noise coming from one direction of the tavern, but it was instantly gone.

"You'll not be able to escape, Diana."

She whirled about. Eoghan stood in the doorway to the smaller room, holding one hand against the back of his head.

She stepped away from him.

"The door is there," he said, nodding to one side of the room. "But my men are on the other side of it, guarding your precious Maudie. You've nowhere to go, my love, but back in here with me." He held out a hand. "Come. The doctor is waiting."

She pressed both hands over her belly, a reflexively protective gesture.

"Don't do this, Eoghan," she whispered. "You're not this evil. No one is this evil."

"Evil?" he repeated, as if she'd grievously insulted him. "This is none of my doing. The blame must be laid at the feet of your husband—and even, my love, at yours. I warned you that I'd not accept any child of his. I warned you, Diana, but you've been so stubborn. You leave me no other choice but to take matters into my own hands."

Diana's heart was pounding thunderously in her chest. He'd clearly gone mad. If he'd been dangerous before, he was tenfold that now. Beyond him, in the doorway, she saw the face of the doctor, peering at her half curiously, half impatiently.

"Eoghan, please, listen to me," she begged. "You're not thinking clearly. Please—let's go home to Lising Park and we'll discuss everything. I promise you that I'll . . . I'll find a way to divorce Lad, and then we'll—"

"He'll never let you go," Eoghan said dully. "At least, not while you carry his brat in your belly. But we'll be rid of it, and then the doctor will make certain that you can conceive no others. Lad Walker will never want you back after that. No man will want you, except me, because I love you so very much, you see, Diana."

"This isn't love!" she cried. "To destroy what's most precious to me?"

Eoghan began to walk slowly toward her.

"We all must make sacrifices, Diana. Mine was forced upon me, when Lad Walker stole you from me. Now I will steal you back and repay him for his unspeakable crime. He must live with the knowledge that he alone is at fault for the loss of his wife and child."

Diana backed away from him, shaking her head.

"I'll not let you harm my child, Eoghan Patterson. You'll kill me before you'll ever touch my child."

"You'll not even know what's happened," he said in a soothing tone, still approaching. "The doctor will make certain you're insensible. By the time you've come awake, we'll be safely out of Herefordshire, where your husband will never find us. But he'll not come looking once he's seen the evidence of his loss. Tomorrow he'll receive instructions leading him here and will discover all that's left of his future heir."

The words made Diana gag violently, and she nearly became ill again. But the determination to save her child gave her an as yet unrealized strength, and she forcibly pushed the nausea away.

"Come, Diana," he said, holding his hand out as he neared her. "Don't be unreasonable. We haven't much time, and I don't wish to harm you."

She let him come another step closer.

"Very well," she said as calmly as she could. "If you cannot be persuaded, Eoghan, then I must simply give—"

The moment he lowered his hand, she moved, ducking her head and lunging forward to ram straight into his stomach. It wasn't much, pitting her smaller size against his own much greater one, but it was enough. He gave a gasp of pain and surprise and toppled backward.

Diana didn't wait to see where he'd landed but raced for the door. Eoghan's loud shouts filled the room, and the door was flung open just as Diana reached it. With a cry she reached up to scratch the face of the man before her, but strong hands gripped her wrists and held her fast.

"My lady!"

She fell still and gaped up at him.

"Stuart!"

"My lady, are you unharmed?"

"Oh, Stuart," she cried with relief, flinging herself against him. "You've got to get me out of here—Maudie and me. Get us away from him!"

Stuart held her gently in his strong arms, patting her back. He looked over her head at Eoghan, who was stiffly rising from the floor. When he gained his feet, he reached into his coat and withdrew a small pistol. This he aimed at Stuart.

"What are you doing here?" he demanded. "You were to lead Lord Kerlain in the wrong direction. If you've played me for a fool, I'll—"

"No, no, I did just as you told me," Stuart said quickly. "The earl is on his way into Wales, like you wanted. But he sent me back to warn my father and The Colvaney, and I came to ask what you want me to say to them. If they knew the truth, they'd come for you themselves.''

Diana pushed away from him.

''Stuart,'' she murmured. ''But you—''

The look he gave her quelled her into silence.

''Good lad,'' Eoghan said with approval, though he didn't put the pistol away. ''Very good. I'm glad you've come. Bring Lady Kerlain here, into this room. You can help me to hold her down.''

Stuart gazed into Diana's face, and she prayed that she did not mistake what he was silently striving to tell her. Beyond the door, she saw the two strange men sitting beside the carriage, passing a flask from one to the other, both of them looking back at her with lewd smiles.

''I'll help hold her down,'' one of them offered lecherously, and the other laughed.

''You've no choice but to do what his lordship asks, my lady,'' Stuart told her. ''I know you don't wish to, but he only wants what's best for all of us.''

''No,'' she murmured. ''Stuart, you can't believe that.''

''Stuart knows what's right,'' Eoghan said behind her, his tone irate. ''He's remained loyal to Kerlain, if you've not. Bring her here, Stuart.'' With the pistol, he waved toward the small room. ''She'll lie still for you, won't you, Diana? You'd never wish to make a humiliating fuss before one of your own people.''

''Would you feel better if you had a chance to make your prayers first?'' Stuart suggested. He had already taken her arm in one hand to lead her to the farthest corner in the room. ''Pray for the soul of the child, and you'll be much easier.''

''Stuart,'' Eoghan said impatiently, ''there's no time for such nonsense.''

''Yes,'' Diana murmured pleadingly. ''I would be easier

if I could have a moment to reflect and pray. So very much easier.''

"Kneel here, then,'' Stuart said, pushing her down into the corner, facing toward the dirt-encrusted walls. ''And I'll pray with you.'' He knelt as well, very close beside Diana.

''Be quick about it,'' Eoghan demanded. ''We haven't time for a liturgy.''

Stuart put his mouth against Diana's ear and whispered, ''Cover your head with your hands and hunch down tight, as small as you can. Stay right where you are, no matter what.''

Then, in the same moment, he lifted his head up and shouted, ''Now!'' and with his own body covered her own, cocooning Diana between himself and the wall.

The tavern erupted into an explosion of noise. Shouting, cursing, breaking wood and glass—and pistol fire. The horses at the carriage gave a loud, whinnying protest, and the woman with the doctor screamed as if she were being murdered. In the midst of it all, Diana heard Lad's voice, shouting more loudly than the others, and Eoghan making an equally furious reply. More shots were fired, much closer this time. Stuart, still protecting her from the violence, fell forward suddenly, uttering a soft murmur. He lay with his full weight upon her, and Diana gasped for air, unable to push him away.

''Stuart,'' she murmured with distress, but he didn't seem to hear. His face had fallen against her neck, and Diana twisted as best she could to lift a hand. His breath, she felt as her fingers touched his mouth, was very faint. *''Stuart.''*

The commotion ended as suddenly as it had begun, and loud, booted footsteps approached.

''Oh, God.'' It was Lad's voice. ''Stuart.''

''Here,'' said another man, a voice Diana didn't recognize, ''let me help you. He's a big fellow.''

Slowly, Stuart's heavy body was lifted away, and then strong arms reached down to pluck Diana from the floor.

"Diana, are you all right?"

Lad held her tightly, but it wasn't enough. Diana slid her arms about him and hugged with all her might, at last giving herself permission to cry.

"I knew you'd come," she sobbed, pressing her face against his chest. Her limbs trembled so mightily that she couldn't stand, and Lad lifted her up and crushed her to him, kissing her head, the side of her face.

"Of course I came," he murmured fervently. "He hasn't harmed you, love? You're all right?"

She nodded and began to collect her wits. Striving to calm and breathe more slowly, she pushed away from him slightly, looking into that handsome, much loved face.

"I'm fine," she managed, sniffling. "He meant to kill our baby"—at this she nearly began to weep again—"but we're fine. Both of us. Is Stuart all right?" She looked about for him. Lad carefully set her on her feet, and they turned together to where the young man lay.

A finely dressed, fair-headed stranger was kneeling over him and looked up as they stepped nearer.

"The bullet has lodged in his back somewhere. I don't know how serious it is, but if we don't stop this bleeding, he'll never make it back to Kerlain."

"Can we bind it?" Lad asked.

"I think so," the man replied, but his expression was very grim.

"That man"—Diana turned to look into the tavern and found herself staring straight at Eoghan. The sight made her falter. His eyes bore into her with an intensity that would have felled her if they'd been weapons rather than something far less. He stood very still in the middle of the room, while another finely dressed stranger—this one dark-haired—held a pistol on him. Diana swallowed and spoke again. "Eoghan said he was a doctor. That man there, in the smaller room." The doctor and his assistant were cowering beyond the doorway to the parlor, clearly hoping to get out of the tavern both alive and as quickly as they could.

The dark-haired gentleman turned his languid gaze on the physician.

"Is that right, sir?" he demanded. "Then come and bind this man's wounds. If he dies because your skill is lacking—or grudgingly given—I'll gladly send you into the eternal to accompany him."

The doctor scrambled to collect his instruments, then hurried to Stuart's side. His assistant was more timid but followed with a pile of linens that Diana perceived they had planned to use for her.

"And this must be the fair Diana," the dark-haired gentleman said, his gaze moving over her from head to toe.

"Yes," Lad said, "though I had hoped to introduce you under happier circumstances. Diana, this is Lucien Bryland, Viscount Callan, whom you've also heard me call Lucky. And this fellow"—he nodded toward the handsome blond gentleman who had stood to give the doctor room and who was presently tucking a pistol inside his coat—"is Jack Sommerton, the Earl of Rexley. He's the one who married my cousin Gwennie."

"My lady," the Earl of Rexley said warmly, making her a low, elegant bow. "It's an honor to make your acquaintance at last, though, like your husband, I wish it had been on a happier occasion. You've taken no harm, pray?"

Diana was yet shaken, but managed to smile. "Thank you, cousin. I'm unharmed. Thank you for coming to my aid. And you also, Lord Callan."

That gentleman gifted her with one of his rare smiles, which transformed his somewhat sullen expression into one filled with great charm.

"May I say that you are aptly named, Lady Kerlain? As

fair, indeed, as the goddess Diana. But this, I fear, is not the right time for such gallantries. Is young Stuart to live?''

The doctor, tending the wound, nodded and murmured, ''He'll do, sir.''

''Then what shall we do with this scoundrel?'' Lord Callan asked, tipping the pistol he held more closely at Eoghan, who yet stood in his place, staring hard at Diana. ''Shall I shoot him for you, Lad, and we'll be done with the whole nasty business?''

''Aye, if we shoot the vermin now,'' the Earl of Rexley said agreeably, ''we can take my dear cousin home at once for a hot cup of tea, which I'm sure she would greatly welcome.''

''No,'' Lad said. ''I'll not shoot the bastard, well though he deserves it. Vengeance is a dish best served up cold, as a very wise man once told me. Jack, will you be so good as to take Diana out to the carriage?''

Diana clung to him, shaking her head. ''Lad, please . . . send someone to fetch Sir Anthony, and let him deal with Eoghan. Don't take this into your own hands.''

''I don't mean to kill him, love. We're only going to play a simple game of cards, just as we once did, so long ago. Viscount Carden is very fond of playing cards, as you know.''

''I'll engage in no such activity with you,'' Eoghan stated quietly. He was yet staring at Diana. ''You'd cheat, as I'm sure you did in London to regain your wealth. As you did when you stole the woman who was rightfully mine.''

''Jack,'' Lad said, and pushed Diana toward him. ''Take my wife outside and make certain of her comfort and Maudie's. Send Lloyd here to me, if he's finished tying up those two outside.'' He began to move toward Eoghan. ''This won't take long.''

''Lad!'' Diana protested, but Lord Rexley set an arm about her waist to hold her back.

"Come and we'll make you most comfortable, dear cousin," he said, lifting her off the ground when she wouldn't budge and carrying her toward the door. "You look terribly pale, as women with child are given to do, I understand, and a cup of water will do you good. My own wife is with child, did you know?" he continued pleasantly, deftly unlatching her fingers from where they'd stubbornly grabbed the sides of the door frame. He pulled her outside and called for Lloyd.

"We need a table, Lucky," Lad said, standing in front of Eoghan now. "Anything will do."

Hesitantly, and giving Eoghan a warning look, Lord Callan lowered the pistol he held and walked into the small room. He returned a moment later carrying the table upon which the doctor had earlier placed his tools.

"It's not much," he said, setting it between the two men. "But it's all there is in this hovel."

Behind them, Lloyd entered the tavern.

"All well here?" he asked in his blunt manner. "Got them two coves tied up right and tight out by the carriage, and the women settled inside. Lady Kerlain's not very happy."

"I'm sure she's not," Lad murmured. "But the end of her worries are coming fast. Be so good as to oversee Stuart's care, will you, Lloyd? Lucky, bear witness to the game between myself and Viscount Carden, to make certain that neither of us cheats or behaves without honor."

"Gladly," Lucky agreed with a nod. He leaned against the wall where he stood and folded his arms over his chest.

"I'll not engage in any sport with you," Eoghan repeated.

"Why?" Lad asked. "Because your victims must be half mad with grief and full drunk with spirits before you're brave enough to take them on? You're not much of a man, *my friend.* It can hardly be wondered that Diana chose me over you.''

Fire flashed in Eoghan's eyes. "You'll not goad me."

"Will I not?" Lad replied, his lip curling. "We shall see, Eoghan Patterson. Here. Does this seem familiar to you?" From a pocket within his coat, he produced a small silver card box and laid it on the table. "Since the hour I left Kerlain, I've carried this with me, a heavy weight indeed. It was the weight of all my guilt and sin, and I've longed for the day that I might return it to its rightful owner. Take it, Eoghan.''

Eoghan stared at the elegant box as if it were a horror.

"I don't want it," he whispered.

"I don't care," Lad said tightly. "Pick it up. Take out the cards. No? Are you too weak even for that? I'll do it then.''

With expert hands, he flipped open the lid and pulled the cards out. With well-honed skill he shuffled them, all the movement a blur until he was done.

"There," he said, deftly parting the cards into six separate piles. "We haven't the time for a proper game of *poque,* which I know you love so well, but a simple draw for the highest card will do. If you win, I'll grant you your life and allow you to live in Lising Park in peace. We'll forget that today ever happened.''

"You don't mean that, Lad," Lucky said in a low voice. "No man could ever forget the attempted murder of his own child.''

Eoghan was more direct. "You're lying."

"And if I win," Lad went on in the same even tone, "then you'll sign over the deed to Lising Park to me, forswear your title, and vow to leave England forever. Choose your card.''

Eoghan almost laughed. "You're a fool," he muttered. "You always were a fool. You don't love Diana, to take such a chance. And if I stay at Lising Park, I vow I'll *never* leave you in peace. Diana *will* be mine one day." He cocked his head to one side. "Still willing to make such a gamble, Lad Walker?"

"No," Lucky said, pushing upright from the wall. Lloyd, from the other side of the room, murmured, "Steady."

Lad held Eoghan's gaze.

"Choose."

The silence was complete; even the doctor and his assistant, who had finished binding Stuart's wound, watched, wide-eyed.

Eoghan lifted one hand slowly, then lowered his gaze to the piles of cards. He contemplated each one with care, considering the six choices. His fingertips, trembling, hovered with indecision.

"Lising Park," Lad said sharply, and Eoghan's head snapped up. "Make your vow to me in front of Lord Callan that you'll sign over the deed, also that you'll leave England."

"Yes," Eoghan said irately, tensely. "You have it. You have my vow. I make it before Lord Callan and God."

"Very well." Lad stood back from the table to let his opponent make his choice.

He decided very suddenly, taking the fourth card to the left and dropping it face up upon the table. It was a jack of diamonds. Eoghan let out a breath and smiled at Lad with triumph.

"Well done," Lad said. "Here is my choice."

Without even looking, he reached down to flip over a card. The queen of hearts.

A brief, stunned silence followed this, and then Lad said, calmly, "Of course I might have done better to choose this one." He flipped over the card from the pile on the far left. It was the ace of diamonds. "But the queen of hearts is much more sentimental, especially in such cases as these.

It's fortunate for me that it chanced to come up. As many a gambler would say, God must be on my side.''

"They . . . they're marked!" Eoghan declared. "They never were before!"

"They're not marked, you fool," Lad told him with contempt. "They're merely stained from use. I've spent so many hours with the damned things that I've memorized every one by rote. If you'd not cheated so openly in taking my wife and home from me, I'd never have deigned to use such a trick. But you were neither drunk nor sick with grief nor half blinded by darkness, and I'll not feel the least guilt for having turned your own evil back on you. Here," he shoved the cards together with both hands, making one disorganized pile, "I make you a gift. Take them with you as you leave England, but never let me set sight on either you or them again, or I swear by God that I *will* kill you. I'll expect the deed to Lising Park in my hand by tomorrow noon. Have one of your footmen bring it. I give you three days to make your arrangements and depart.''

Lad turned toward Lloyd. "Can we safely move Stuart now? I want to be on our way back to Kerlain as quickly as—"

"Hey!" Lloyd shouted, his gaze riveting beyond Lad to where Eoghan yet stood. "He's—"

The loud report of a pistol shook the room, followed by the sharp, horrified scream of the doctor's assistant.

Lad whirled about to find Eoghan Patterson lying on the ground, a fresh, gaping wound in his chest, and Lucky standing in his very relaxed manner near the wall, holding a smoking pistol.

"The trouble with you," Lucky told him, clearly undismayed, "is that you're too damned nice. You turned your back on that fellow just as if he could be trusted, and he, as easy as you please, pulled a gun out of his pocket to kill you.''

Lad walked to where Eoghan's supine body lay and found the small pistol yet clutched in his hand. He knelt and set his fingers to Viscount Carden's neck.

"He's dead," Lad murmured, standing slowly. "You killed him, Lucky."

Lucky had found a spare cloth from the doctor's pile of linens and was wiping his gun with it.

"Yes, I usually intend that as the outcome when I shoot someone. That man," he said carefully, nodding at the late Viscount Carden, "tried to murder your child, and in the doing might well have murdered your wife. You pity him now, but on the first day—nay, in the first minute—that you hold your son or daughter in your arms, you'll understand full well how just and right my action was. And now," he went on as calmly, "I think we might leave Lloyd to take care of this mess and get Stuart and your lady and her maid safely back to Kerlain. God knows I could use a drink and a proper dinner."

Having said so, he walked out of the tavern, stopping only as he looked out the door to say, "Dear me, Jack. Has Lady Kerlain gotten ill all over your new coat? Well, don't despair. When you've been through two of your wife's pregnancies, you'll learn how to step aside much more quickly. Never liked that color of blue on you, anyhow."

Lad stared after him, then looked down at the still body of Eoghan Patterson, lying at his feet. He heard the woman weeping somewhere across the room and the doctor rapidly packing up his tools, and Stuart moaning faintly. But none of it made any sense. His mind was numb with sensation. This wasn't what he'd intended. Not at all. The game had been taken out of his hands, and now he wasn't quite sure what to do.

"He's right," Lloyd said, close by Lad's shoulder. "And a good, proper fellow he is too, that Lord Callan. Like him right well, I do, for a lordling."

Lad turned to look at him, utterly confused.

"What?"

"I said he's right," Lloyd repeated. "Lord Callan is. There was no saving this bastard. He'd gone too bad even to make the attempt. And he warned you himself, didn't he? Said he'd never leave you in peace, and he meant that, my lord. The next time he set out to hurt one of your own, he'd make sure he did it, and no turning back. I say it's a good thing he's gone. You and Lady Kerlain will have a bit of peace, and that's as it should be. You've earned it, these many years," he said, clapping Lad comfortingly on the shoulder, "and now, if you're wise, you'll take it, m'lord, with no looking back."

Chapter Twenty-eight

May 1819

The christening of Charles Geoffrey Proof Walker, heir and firstborn son of the Earl and Countess of Kerlain, was joyously attended by all the people of Kerlain and a great many members of the *ton*, who had journeyed specially to Herefordshire to mark the occasion. No less personages than the Earl of Manning and his wife, Lady Anna, honored the event with their presence, as well as Lord Kerlain's more particular friends, Lord and Lady Rexley, Lord and Lady Callan, and, recently returned from Italy, Lord and Lady Severn. All of these couples had brought their numerous offspring, of which three were themselves but recently born, and the day took on a greater resemblance to a crowded, noisy nursery than a solemn and holy ceremony.

This, however, was just as Lord and Lady Kerlain wanted it, and nothing could have pleased them better.

Lad was never happier than when with his friends, and he was especially glad to see Wulf, whose bumbling good nature had been sorely missed during his absence abroad. His wife, Bella, had cleverly presented Viscount Severn with twins—a huge son, promising very much to be like his father, and a sweet, tiny daughter, who, thankfully, took after him not at all. Wulf could hold the both of them at once in his massive hands and was so doting that their mother usually got to have them only when they needed feeding or changing.

Fatherhood had left its permanent mark on all of them. Jack was transfixed by his newborn daughter, Sofia, who had her mother's beautiful red-gold hair, Lucky doted unashamedly on his two young children, and Lad was hard-pressed not to burst with pride and love every time he beheld his young son.

After the ceremony was over and the guests returned to the castle to celebrate the day, the four friends gathered on the long balcony that ran the length of the great hall and toasted one another's good fortune.

"The past four years have seen a great many changes in all our lives," Jack said. "Much for the better, and mainly due to our fortunate choice of wives." He lifted his glass. "Here is to our good ladies, then. May God bless and keep them."

"And give us the wisdom to make them forever happy and content, lest our own lives be made miserable," Lucky added dryly, lifting his own glass. "Here's to our lovely wives, each and every one."

"Lady Kerlain appears more beautiful than ever," Jack said after they'd finished the toast. "And very happy. Gwendolyn is beside herself with happiness to know that her new cousin has agreed to come to London next year. She's already making plans for a great deal of shopping."

"As is Clara," Lucky put in, turning to look at where the women were sitting together near one of the hearths in the great hall, admiring the various newborns, talking and laughing and obviously having a wonderful time. "And Bella too, if that smile on her face is anything to go by," he added, grinning at Wulf.

Wulf, who spent a great deal of time gazing at his wife with intense adoration no matter where she—or he—was, and who was presently doing so, sighed and said, very happily, "Aye."

"You've had no trouble with your new neighbor at Lising Park, I pray," Lucky asked Lad, turning to give his attention back to his friends.

"No," Lad said. "The late viscount's only living relative was so distant a cousin that they never even knew each other. The new viscount is a wonderful old fellow. A scholar, in fact, as are his three daughters. My architect, David Moulton, has only recently become engaged to the eldest girl, and a charming couple they'll make when wed. The viscount and viscountess are here, as well as their daughters. I shall make certain to introduce you before they depart."

"And there's been no trouble with the other matter?" Jack asked.

The "other matter" referred to the death of Eoghan Patterson. Lad was still amazed at how completely unrepentant Lucky had been over the killing, but equally astonishing had been Sir Anthony's reaction. Having heard the confessions of the doctor and his assistant and of the two brutes the late viscount had hired to help him abduct Diana, as well as the accounts of Lloyd, Jack, and Lad, Sir Anthony—in his capacity as the sheriff of Herefordshire—had given a shake of his head and declared it a very sad business but had otherwise let the matter go. And that was the end of it. There had been no inquiry, no trial, no interest at all. Eoghan Patterson possessed no family who knew him well enough to force the matter and no friends who cared enough. He'd been buried and forgotten, and a month later his successor arrived.

"None at all," Lad replied. "We've been very happy since . . . that day. There's been nothing to mar our contentment."

"You don't miss the States anymore?" Wulf asked, at last pulling his gaze from his wife. "And your farm there?"

Lad shook his head. "At times I miss it. I suppose it's more the friends and family still there who I think of most, and my memories. One day, Diana and our children and I will journey back to Tennessee, but only to visit, not to stay. Kerlain is my home now, and Diana and Charles my family. And all of you half-demented fellows," he added, smiling at the men who surrounded him, "are my friends, may God help me."

They laughed. Jack lifted his glass.

"To us, then, and to lasting friendships, more valuable than any treasure," he said, to which they all agreed heartily and drank.

Many hours later, after the guests had either departed or sought their beds, and after Maudie had taken young Charles to the nursery, Lad and Diana lay in her bed, warm and content in each other's arms.

"It was a wonderful day," Diana murmured, snuggling closer to her husband, sighing and closing her eyes. It would not be long before Maudie opened the chamber door and tinkled a small bell, calling Diana to rise and nurse her son. "I'm going to miss Gwendolyn and Clara and Bella when they've gone. And Lady Anna too. She's so very kind."

"Jack wants us all to come to Rexley Hall for Christmas. Would you like that?"

"Oh, yes," Diana said. "Charles will be old enough to make such a short journey, and it would be wonderful to have a Christmas with so many friends. But the following year everyone must come to Kerlain to spend the holidays. Would that not be grand?"

"Indeed. That would be a nice habit to get into—having Christmases together. It's a long time between seasons in Town."

"A season in Town," she murmured. "It still sounds like a terrible ordeal, but now that I've come to know Gwendolyn and the others, I'm not so frightened of it."

"I'm glad," he said, and settled his cheek against the top of her head. "I've asked Mr. Sibbley to approach the owner of the house in London that once belonged to the Earl of Kerlain, to discover if he might be willing to sell it to me."

Diana sat up, looking down at him. "Oh, Lad, do you think he might? How wonderful that would be."

Smiling, he reached up to cup her cheek.

"It would please you?"

"Very much," she said fervently. "It would be so good to make Kerlain whole for Charles and for any other children that God may gift us with."

"Then I'll make certain to have Sibbley press the matter and offer a ridiculously large sum."

"Thank you," she whispered.

He tugged her down to meet his lips. "There is no need," he murmured, then kissed her gently. He wished that he could make love to her—just as he'd been wishing it for well over two months now. But she had not yet fully recovered from birthing their child, and he contented himself with pulling her into his arms and holding her. Diana rested her head against his shoulder and sighed happily.

"We'll make Kerlain whole for Charles," he promised, stroking his fingers gently through her hair. "And will pray that he'll be able to keep it so for his son—or daughter. God willing, it will shelter as many future generations as it has done in the past, and perhaps many more."

Diana's arm slid about his waist, and in the darkness she tilted her head up to meet his gaze.

"There was a time when you'd never have said such a thing. But now—you understand."

"I understand that it isn't simply a castle or a piece of land, or even a title, Diana," he said. "Kerlain is far more than anything so simple. It's you and me and Charles, and all those who came before us—including my father and grandfather. And all those who'll come after."

"Yes," she murmured. "But Kerlain had lost its soul before you came, Lad. Its very heart. Now you've brought Kerlain back to itself, and to all of us."

"No, love, that's not so," he said softly, tracing her lips with his fingertip. "Kerlain is alive because of you, as am I."

"Me?" she whispered.

"Your love for it kept Kerlain's heart beating strongly, Diana. Perhaps you couldn't have seen it, but I assure you all those around you knew the truth. Even my grandfather, else he'd never have left Kerlain in your care. And when I came, so empty of everything save grief, your love made me whole again."

She began to make a denial, but Lad gently touched a finger to her lips to silence the words.

"I can't begin to think on what my life would have been if I'd never come to England—and to you. And through those endless years in London, without the hope of your love I'd have surely given up altogether. Nay, Diana, all that's happened has come from you, from your heart, and from the love we share. That," he murmured, leaning to kiss her, "I understand best of all."

Author Note

I've taken a great deal of liberty in arranging the facts of the War of 1812 to suit my story, mainly because my original research on the war, used for the first book in this trilogy, *Dark Wager,* was flawed. Therefore, to make the books all "fit" together, I felt compelled to let the war end much earlier than it actually did and to change the date of its most significant engagement, the Battle of New Orleans.

In truth, the War of 1812 was not formally declared at an end until the Treaty of Ghent was signed on December 24, 1814. News of the treaty didn't reach the United States until February 11, 1815, and was some weeks longer in reaching those ships engaged in naval battle. In the meantime some of the fiercest fighting occurred, especially the Battle of New Orleans, which took place on January 8 and did not, as my books would have it, begin in November of 1814 and continue on through December of that same year.